'A novel that is beautiful in its story and important in its message. *A Walk Across the Sun* deserves a wide audience'
John Grisham

'Addison's debut is an unforgettable read'   *Star Magazine*

'An astounding novel full of first-hand insight that could only come from true-life experience' *Irish Sunday Independent*

'A powerful story about a difficult subject'
Stellar Magazine

'Thrilling, fast-paced and gripping ... this is a novel that will change how you view the world'   *Awaaz News*

'An accomplished, compelling thriller, drawing people towards a difficult, heartrending subject'   Bookbag

'A pulse-revving novel with a serious message' *O Magazine*

'A compelling piece of storytelling launching the career of a major literary talent'
New Books Magazine

'Addison uncovers the labyrinthine underside of human trafficking in this dazzling transcontinental story about the power of conviction, the bonds of family, and the tenacity of love'   *Publishers Weekly*

Corban Addison began his career specializing in corporate law and litigation. He has an abiding interest in international human rights, and is a supporter of numerous causes, including the abolition of modern slavery. *A Walk Across the Sun* is his first novel. He lives with his wife and two children in Virginia, USA.

A Walk Across the Sun

CORBAN ADDISON

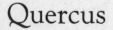

First published in Great Britain in 2012 by Quercus
This paperback edition published in 2012 by

Quercus
55 Baker Street
7th Floor, South Block
London W1U 8EW

A CIP catalogue record for this book is available
from the British Library

ISBN 978 0 85738 821 6

10 9 8 7

Printed and bound in Great Britain by Clays Ltd, St Ives plc
Typeset by Ellipsis Digital Limited, Glasgow

For the uncountable number of souls
held captive in the sex trade.

And for the heroic men and women across the globe
working tirelessly to win their freedom.

The dark places of the land are full of the habitations of violence.

—Asaph the psalmist

If we have no peace, it is because we have forgotten that we belong to one another.

—Mother Teresa of Calcutta

PART ONE

Chapter 1

Children have their play on the seashore of worlds.
—Rabindranath Tagore

Tamil Nadu, India

The sea was quiet at first light on the morning their world fell apart. They were sisters—Ahalya the older at seventeen and Sita two years her junior. Like their mother before them, they were children of the sea. When their father, a software executive, moved the family from the plains of Delhi to Chennai on the Coromandel Coast, it felt to Ahalya and Sita like a homecoming. The sea was their friend, its pelicans and pomfrets and crested waves their companions. They never believed the sea could turn against them. But they were young and understood little of suffering.

Ahalya felt it when the earth shook in the dawn twilight. She looked at Sita sleeping in the bed beside her and wondered why she didn't awaken. The tremors were violent but ceased quickly, and afterward she wondered if they had come in a dream. No one stirred in the house

below. It was the day after Christmas, a Sunday, and all
India was asleep.

Ahalya snuggled into her blanket, inhaled the sweet,
sandalwood scent of her sister's hair, and drifted off to visions
of the peacock-blue *salwar kameez* her father had given her
to wear to the conservatory in Mylapore that evening. It
was December and the Madras Music Season was in full
swing. Their father had bought them tickets to a violin
concerto at eight o'clock. She and Sita were both students
of the violin.

The household awoke in stages. At a quarter past seven,
Jaya, the family's longtime housekeeper, swaddled herself in
a *sari*, retrieved a small jar of limestone powder from the
bureau at the foot of her bed, and went to the front porch.
She swept the earth beyond the threshold with a stiff-bristled
broom and placed dots of the white powder on the ground.
She connected the dots with elegant lines and traced the star
shape of a jasmine flower. Satisfying herself, she placed her
hands together, palms flat, and whispered a prayer to Lakshmi,
the Hindu goddess of fortune, for an auspicious day. The
kolam ritual complete, she went to the kitchen to prepare the
morning meal.

Ahalya woke again when the sunlight streamed through
the curtains. Sita, always an early riser, was nearly dressed,
her sable hair shiny and damp from a shower. Ahalya watched
her sister apply her makeup in front of a small mirror and
smiled. Sita was a fine-boned girl blessed with the delicate
features and wide, expressive eyes of their mother, Ambini.

She was slight for her age, and the magic of puberty had yet to transform her body into the figure of a woman. As a result, she was self-conscious about her appearance, despite regular reassurances from Ahalya and Ambini that time would bring about the changes she so desired.

Partly to keep pace with Sita and partly to avoid being late for breakfast, Ahalya dressed hurriedly in a yellow pantsuit, or *churidaar*, and matching scarf. She slipped on bangles and anklets, and completed the ensemble by fastening a necklace around her neck and placing a delicate jeweled *bindi* on her forehead.

"Ready, dear?" Ahalya asked Sita in English. It was a rule in the Ghai household that the girls could speak Hindi or Tamil only if spoken to by an adult in that language. Like all Indians privileged to rise into the ranks of the upper middle class, their parents dreamed of sending them to university in England and firmly believed that a mastery of English was the likeliest ticket to Cambridge or Oxford. The convent school where the girls boarded taught Hindi—the national language—and Tamil—the indigenous tongue of Tamil Nadu—along with English, but the convent sisters preferred to speak English, and the girls never quibbled with the rule.

"Yes," Sita said wistfully, casting a fading glance toward the mirror. "I suppose."

"Oh, Sita," Ahalya chided her, "a frown will not endear you to Vikram Pillai."

The comment had the effect Ahalya intended. Sita's face

brightened at the mention of the family's plans for the evening. Pillai was her favorite violinist.

"Do you think we'll get to meet him?" Sita asked. "The line after the show is always so long."

"Ask Baba," Ahalya said, thinking of the surprise she and her father had planned for Sita—and had succeeded in keeping secret. "You never know, with his connections."

"I'll ask him at breakfast," Sita said and disappeared through the door and down the stairs.

Chuckling to herself, Ahalya followed Sita to the living room. Together, the girls performed their *puja*, or morning worship, before the family idols of Ganesh, the elephant god of luck, and Rama, avatar of Vishnu, who stood on an altar in a corner of the room. Like most members of the merchant caste, the Ghais were predominantly secular and visited a temple or shrine only on rare occasions when seeking a boon from the gods. However, when the girls' grandmother came to visit, the incense sticks were lit and the *puja* prepared, and everyone—small and great—participated in the ritual.

Entering the dining room, the sisters found their father, Naresh, their mother, and their grandmother assembled for breakfast. Before seating themselves, Ahalya and Sita touched their father's feet in a traditional sign of respect. Naresh smiled and gave them both a peck on the cheek.

"Good morning, Baba," they said.

"Good morning, my beauties."

"Baba, do you know anyone who knows Vikram Pillai?" Sita asked.

Naresh glanced at Ahalya and winked at Sita. "I will after tonight."

Sita raised her eyebrows. "What do you mean?"

Naresh reached into his pocket. "I was going to wait until later, but since you asked . . ." He pulled out a VIP pass and laid it on the table. "We'll meet him before the performance."

Sita looked at the pass and a smile blossomed on her face. She knelt down slowly and touched her father's foot a second time.

"Thank you, Baba. Does Ahalya get to come?"

"Why, of course," Naresh replied, placing three more VIP passes beside the first. "And your mother and grandmother as well."

"We can ask him anything we like," Ahalya chimed in.

Sita looked at her sister and her father, and her smile knew no bounds.

While the sisters took their seats at the table, Jaya darted around the room, placing bowls brimming with rice, coconut chutney, *masala dosa*—potato-stuffed crêpes—and flatbread, called *chapatti*, on the table. The food was eaten without utensils, and by the end of the meal, everyone's fingers were lathered with the remnants of rice and chutney.

For dessert, Jaya served freshly picked *chickoo*—a kiwi-like fruit—and *mysore pak*, a fudge-like delicacy. Cutting into a *chickoo*, Ahalya recalled the early morning temblor.

"Baba, did you feel the earthquake?" she asked.

"What earthquake?" her grandmother inquired.

Naresh chuckled. "You are fortunate to sleep so soundly,

Naani." He turned to his daughter with a reassuring smile. "The quake was strong, but it did no damage."

"Earthquakes are a bad omen," the old woman said, clutching her napkin.

"They are a scientific phenomenon," Naresh gently corrected. "And this one was harmless. We have no need to worry." Turning back to Ahalya, he changed the subject: "Tell us about Sister Naomi. She wasn't well when I saw her last."

The family finished their treats while Ahalya told her father about the headmistress at St. Mary's. A breeze blew through the open windows, cooling the air. In time, Sita grew fidgety and asked to be excused. After obtaining Naresh's permission, she pocketed a square of *mysore pak* and dashed out of the house in the direction of the beach. Ahalya could not help but smile at her sister's vivacity.

"May I go too?" she asked her father.

He nodded. "I think our little Christmas surprise was a good idea."

"I agree," she replied. Rising from the table, she donned her sandals and followed her sister into the sunlight.

By twenty minutes past eight everyone but Jaya and the girls' grandmother had left for the beach. The family's modest bungalow sat on a piece of waterfront property fifteen miles south of Chennai and a mile down the beach from one of coastal Tamil Nadu's many fishing communities. The location was rural by Indian standards, and Ambini, who grew up in the overcrowded neighborhoods of Mylapore, found it remote. But she had considered the sacrifice of distance from the city a small price to pay for the chance to raise her children so close to her ancestral home.

Ahalya walked along the beach while Sita raced along the waterline collecting conch shells. Naresh and Ambini strolled behind them in contented silence. The Ghais made their way north in the direction of the fishing village. They passed an older couple sitting quietly on the sand and two boys tossing rocks at the birds. Otherwise, the beach was deserted.

Shortly before nine o'clock, Ahalya noticed something strange about the sea. The wind-driven waves washing ashore didn't reach as far across the sand as they had only minutes before. She studied the waterline, and the sea seemed to retreat before her eyes. Soon fifty feet of sodden sand lay exposed. The two boys, shouting with delight, chased one another across the spongy surface toward the departing ocean. Ahalya watched the spectacle with foreboding, but Sita was more inquisitive than concerned.

"*Idhar kya ho raha hai?*" Sita asked, reverting to her native Hindi. "What is happening?"

"I'm not sure," Ahalya replied in English.

Ahalya saw the wave first. She pointed to a thin line of white stretched across the edge of the horizon. In less than ten seconds, the line expanded and became a roiling surge of water. The wave approached so rapidly that the Ghais had almost no time to react. Naresh began to shout and wave, but his words were drowned out by the hungry thunder of the wave.

Ahalya reached for Sita's hand and yanked her toward a stand of palm trees, straining against the resistance of the soft sand. Brackish water swirled around her legs, and then the wave was upon her, buoying her up and tumbling her over. Salt water filled her nostrils, clogged her ears, stung her eyes. She began to choke, to retch, even as she reached for the light. Breaking the surface, she gasped for air.

She saw a blur of movement, a flutter of color—Sita's turquoise *churidaar*. She clutched her sister's hand but lost it again in the violent suction of the wave. Her fingers brushed the smooth bark of a palm. She lunged toward it, desperately kicking against the current, but again her grip failed. As the sea swept her inland, she shouted blindly, imbuing her words with all her fading strength: *"Swim! Sita, grab a palm tree!"*

Swiveling around, she saw the trunk of the palm a split second before impact. As the pain exploded in her forehead, she wrapped her arms and legs around the tree and willed herself not to let go. Then she lost consciousness.

When she opened her eyes again, she saw blue sky peeking through wind-tossed fronds of palm. The silence around her was eerie. Her heart hammered in her chest and her head felt as if it had been cleaved in two. Seconds passed and then the sea began to retreat, yielding once again to the land. She saw Sita's face in the distance and heard a shout.

"Ahalya, help me!"

She tried to speak, but she had salt water in her mouth.

The word came out as a croak: "Wait." She spat once and tried again: "Wait! Sita! Wait until the water goes down."

And it did. At last.

Ahalya inched down the trunk of the banana palm until her feet met sodden ground. Her *churidaar* was in tatters, her face covered with blood. She waded across the distance to Sita and pried her arms free from the trunk that had saved her. Clutching her younger sister protectively, Ahalya looked through the palm forest toward the beach. The gruesome sight did not register at first. The thorn bushes that lined the sand were stripped of leaves. Around them, dark shapes floated on the surface of the muddy waters.

Ahalya stared at the shapes. Her chest heaved. At once she knew.

"*Idhar aawo!*" she commanded Sita in Hindi. "Come!"

Taking her sister's hand, Ahalya led her through the knee-deep water. The first body they discovered was Ambini's. She was covered in mud, and every inch of exposed skin was lacerated by thorns. Her eyes were open and her face was a mask of fright.

The grotesque transfiguration of their beloved mother turned Sita to stone. She clasped her sister's hand so powerfully that Ahalya cried out and yanked it away. Ahalya fell on her knees weeping, but Sita just stared. After a long moment, her mouth fell slack and she began to sob. Burying her face in her hands, she trembled so violently that she appeared to be in seizure.

Ahalya took her sister in her arms and held her close.

Then she took her hand and led her away from Ambini. Before long, they saw another body. It was one of the local boys. Sita went rigid. Ahalya all but carried her along the swampy ruins of the beach in the direction of the family's bungalow. She knew their only hope was to find their father.

Had Sita not stumbled, they would have passed by Naresh's remains. Stooping to help her sister up, Ahalya glanced inland and saw yet another dark mass floating upon the becalmed remains of a salt-water lagoon. The wave had swept Naresh through the palm forest and trapped him among some boulders at the edge of the lagoon.

Ahalya dragged her sister across the short distance to Naresh's body. For a long moment, she stared at her father uncomprehending. Then understanding dawned and she began to weep as the crushing weight of sorrow settled upon her shoulders. She was Naresh's favorite, as Sita was Ambini's. He could not be dead. He had promised to find her a respectable husband and to give her an enviable wedding. He had promised so many things.

"Look," Sita whispered, pointing to the south.

Wiping away her tears, Ahalya followed her sister's gaze across an alien world stripped bare by the wave. In the distance stood their bungalow. The familiar silhouette took Ahalya by surprise, as did her sister's sudden stillness. Sita had ceased her crying and was hugging herself in self-protection. The sight of her eyes so fraught with pain infused Ahalya with courage. Perhaps Jaya or her grandmother had survived. She couldn't bear the thought that she and Sita were entirely alone.

Ahalya took a deep breath and clutched her sister's hand. Wading across the submerged landscape, the girls made their way to the remains of the home they had known for nearly a decade. Before the arrival of the wave, the grounds around the bungalow had been a nature preserve of flowering gardens and fruit trees. Soon after moving the family from Delhi, Naresh had planted an ashoka tree near the house in honor of Sita. As a child, she had played beneath the evergreen sapling and imagined her namesake, the heroine of the Ramayana, rescued by Hanuman, the noble monkey god, from captivity on the island of Lanka. Now the ashoka and all of its verdant companions were matchsticks denuded of leaf, branch, and flower.

Sita paused beside the skeleton of her beloved tree, but Ahalya tugged at her hand and insisted she keep moving. The windows on the lower floor were washed out, and furnishings that once had graced the living area now floated in the yard. Still, the house seemed sound. As the girls approached the wide-open front doors, Ahalya listened for a human voice but heard none. The house was quiet as a crypt.

She stepped into the foyer and wrinkled her nose in the dank air. Looking into the living room, she saw her aged grandmother floating face down in the murk beside a mud-encrusted couch. Fresh tears sprang to her eyes, but she was too exhausted to weep. The discovery of the old woman's remains did not shock her. After finding her father, she had half-expected that her grandmother, too, had perished.

Summoning the last of her resolve, Ahalya waded through the living room to the kitchen, praying desperately that Jaya had survived. The housekeeper had been a fixture in the Ghai family for longer than Ahalya had been alive. She was like a member of the family, unique and indispensable.

When Ahalya entered the kitchen trailing a limp and pliant Sita, she found a wasteland of debris. Overturned baskets, containers of detergent, glass jars stuffed with sweets, and stray mangoes, papayas, and coconuts floated on the stagnant waters. Beneath the surface, pots, pans, bowls, and silverware littered the floor like sunken wrecks. But there was no sign of Jaya.

Ahalya was about to leave the kitchen and search the dining room when she noticed that the wooden door to the pantry was ajar. She saw the hand before her sister and wrenched open the door. Wedged into the cramped confines of the pantry was Jaya. Of all their departed family members, Jaya was the most peaceful in death. Her eyes were closed and she looked as if she were asleep. But her skin was cold and clammy to the touch.

The vertigo came without warning and Ahalya nearly fainted. Standing there in calf-deep water, the truth of their predicament hit her. She and Sita were orphans. Their only surviving relatives were aunts and cousins in distant Delhi, none of whom she had seen in many years.

Just as the thought crossed her mind that all hope was lost, Sita reached out and took her hand. The sudden sensation of touch stirred Ahalya to action. Shouldering again the responsibility of the firstborn, she led Sita up the stairs to their bedroom.

The wave had scaled the steps and mired the floor, but the second-story windows and furniture remained intact. A single thought occupied Ahalya's attention—finding her purse and mobile phone. If she could contact Sister Naomi and find a way to escort Sita to St. Mary's in Tiruvallur, they would be safe.

She recovered her purse from the bedside table and dialed Sister Naomi's number on her mobile. As the phone began to ring, she heard the sound of distant rumbling coming from the east. She moved to the window and looked out at the silt-stained surface of the Bay of Bengal. She couldn't believe her eyes. Another wall of water was hurtling toward the beach. In seconds, the noise of it escalated into a throaty roar and drowned out the voice on the other end of the line. "Hello? Hello? Ahalya? Sita?" Ahalya forgot about Sister Naomi. Her world narrowed to her sister and the second killer wave.

The churning mass of water reached the bungalow and flooded the lower floor. The house shuddered and groaned as the wave hurled itself against the foundations. Ahalya slammed the bedroom door and urged Sita onto the bed. Wrapping her trembling sister in her arms, she wondered whether Lord Shiva had chosen water over fire to bring about the end of the world.

The terror of the second wave seemed to last forever. Briny water poured in through the cracks around the bottom of the bedroom door and fanned out across the floor. The sisters huddled in a pile of blankets as the water level rose. At once the house shifted beneath them and the floor tilted at an angle. The bedroom door burst open and brown water rushed in. Ahalya shrieked and Sita buried her head in the damp fabric of Ahalya's soiled *churidaar*. Ahalya closed her eyes and mouthed a prayer to Lakshmi to absolve the sisters of their sins and assure them safe passage into the next life.

In that place of dissociation, she barely noticed when the noise diminished and then ceased. The house stood firm as the current reversed and the second wave retreated to the sea. The sisters sat unmoving on the bed. The ravaged world left behind by the waves seemed eerily bereft of sound.

"Ahalya?" Sita whispered at long last. "Where are we going to go?"

Ahalya blinked and her mind re-engaged. She let go of her sister and felt the weight of the phone in her hand. Numbly, she pressed the familiar numbers.

"We need to get to St. Mary's," she said. "Sister Naomi will know what to do."

"But how?" Sita asked, hugging herself. "There is no one to drive us."

Ahalya closed her eyes and listened to the ringing of the phone. Sister Naomi picked up. Her words were anxious. What had happened? Were they in danger? When Ahalya spoke, her voice seemed far away. A wave had come. Her family was dead. She and Sita had survived, but their home was destroyed. They had no money, only the phone.

The line crackled with static for long seconds until Sister Naomi found her voice. She instructed Ahalya to walk to the road and catch a ride into Chennai with a neighbor.

"Go only with someone you trust," she said. "We will be waiting for you."

Ahalya ended the call and turned to Sita, trying to look confident. "We must find someone with a car. Come now. We need dry clothes."

She led her sister across the room to a chest of drawers. She helped Sita peel off her wet, soiled garments and handed her a clean *churidaar*. Then she changed her own clothing. She tried the sink, hoping to wash her face, but found no water pressure. They would have to live with the grit coating their skin until they reached St. Mary's.

Sita moved toward the door, ready for the journey, but Ahalya stopped to collect a photograph from the bureau. The image showed the Ghai family at Christmas a year before. She removed the photo from its frame and slipped it into the waistline of her *churidaar*. She also retrieved a wooden box and placed it and her phone in a cloth satchel. The box contained gold jewelry the sisters had received as gifts over the years—the sum of their collective wealth. Ahalya took one last look at the room and nodded in farewell. The rest she would leave behind.

The sisters descended the stairs and waded through the foyer to the front yard. Outside, the sun was hot, and the standing water left by the second wave had begun to reek with the odor of dead fish. Ahalya led Sita around the back of the damaged bungalow and out onto the lane. The family's two vehicles, both parked in the driveway before the arrival of the waves, were nowhere to be seen. Ahalya thought to take a last look at the bungalow, but she resisted. The ruined world left by the waves was not the home they had known. The former world, and the family that inhabited it, lived now only in their memory.

When they reached the main road, they found it awash with debris from the palm forest. Ahalya felt a twinge of despair. Who would venture out on the roadway in such conditions? A thought came to her then: perhaps they could catch a ride with someone from the fishing village. She knew it was a long shot. Most of the villagers lived in seaside huts that probably had been leveled by the waves. But the survivors would need to obtain provisions and assistance from Chennai. Before long someone from the village would have to make the trek.

The sisters walked side by side without speaking. For nearly a mile they saw no sign of life. All ground-level vegetation had been swept away, leaving the earth on both sides of the tarmac naked and forlorn. By the time they reached the outskirts of the fishing village, they had begun to sweat heavily, and their throats were parched with thirst. Even in winter, the South Indian sun was merciless in its intensity.

Ahalya led the way down the road to the fishing

community. As they neared the shoreline, they saw a man wearing a muddy white skirt, or *lungi*, walking toward them with a child in his bare arms. Behind the man was a bedraggled line of fisherfolk, carrying palm baskets on their heads and colorful satchels on their shoulders.

The man stopped in front of Ahalya. "*Vanakkam*," she said in the customary greeting. "Where are you going?"

The man was so agitated that he didn't acknowledge her question. Pointing and gesturing wildly, he told her about the waves.

"I was in my boat," he said. "I felt nothing. When I returned, everything was gone. My wife, my children—I don't know what happened to them." He turned around and swept his hand across his ragtag band. "We are the only ones left."

Ahalya absorbed the man's grief and steeled herself against her own. She focused instead on practical things.

"Your chieftain has a van," she said. "Where is it?"

The man shook his head. "It is wrecked."

"And your drinking water? Surely you kept drums from the monsoon."

"They were washed away."

"Where are you going?" Ahalya asked again.

"Mahabalipuram," the man replied. "We have relatives there."

Ahalya tried to conceal her disappointment. Mahabalipuram was five miles in the wrong direction. "We must get to Chennai."

The man stared at her as if she had lost her mind. "You will never make it."

Ahalya took Sita's hand and spoke with defiance. "We will make it."

The sisters accompanied the villagers back to the main road, where they parted ways.

"We should go to Kovallam," Sita said softly, speaking for the first time in many minutes. "Maybe we could catch a bus."

Ahalya nodded. Kovallam was a larger fishing community two miles to the north. Even if they couldn't find a bus, she felt reasonably certain that they could get filtered water at the Kovallam market. Water was her first priority. Transportation would have to wait.

The miles passed slowly in the tropical sunlight. A breeze blowing in from the ocean brought occasional relief from the heat. Otherwise, the trek was monotonous and painful. Their sandals, soaked and sand-encrusted, made the soles of their feet raw with blisters.

By the time they reached Kovallam, Sita's face was locked in a perpetual grimace, and Ahalya was having difficulty maintaining her composure. From the angle of the sun, she judged that it was nearly eleven o'clock in the morning. Unless their luck turned, they stood little chance of reaching the convent by nightfall.

The village of Kovallam was a hive of activity. Oxcarts and wagons vied with cars and pedestrians on the narrow, waterlogged roads. Ahalya stopped an old woman wearing a mud-splattered *sari* and inquired about a bus to Chennai. The woman, however, was beside herself with grief.

"My son," she cried. "He was on the beach. Have you seen him?"

Ahalya shook her head sadly and turned away. She asked a man carrying a basket of ripe bananas for help, but he stared at her blankly. Another man trailing a cart loaded with grapes responded to her with a curt shake of the head.

"Don't you know what happened here?" he demanded, spitting a stream of *paan* juice on the street. "No one knows whether the buses are running."

Ahalya struggled against a sudden riptide of desperation. She knew if she didn't stay calm, she could make a rash decision and endanger them.

She led Sita into the Kovallam market. As she expected, only a few stalls were unshuttered. She asked a cane juice vendor whether he could spare a bottle of water. Mustering her best smile, she explained that the wave had taken her purse and that she had no money. The vendor gave her an unsympathetic look.

"Everyone pays," he said brusquely. "Nothing here is free."

Taking Sita by the hand, she approached a vendor of vegetables. She told him their circumstances and he responded with pity. He gave them bottles of water and a patch of shade beneath an umbrella.

"*Nandri*," Ahalya said, accepting the water and handing a bottle to Sita. "Thank you."

They took their leave of the sun and drank thirstily. After draining her bottle, Sita leaned her head on Ahalya's shoulder and dozed. Ahalya, however, resisted the urge to sleep and searched the market for a familiar face. Her father knew a number of men in Kovallam, but she couldn't recall their names.

As time passed and she recognized no one, she began to calculate the street value of the jewelry hidden in her satchel. How much would it cost to hire a driver to take them to Chennai? Her instinct cautioned her against securing a taxi, but she had seen no buses pass through the market, and she doubted any would make the trip that afternoon. She and Sita could not make it to Chennai by foot, at least not that afternoon, and she knew of no place outside the city where they could spend the night in safety.

The girls rested for over an hour in the shade of the umbrella. Sita didn't stir, and Ahalya finally drifted off to sleep. When she awoke, she saw that the sun had passed its zenith. She had to make a decision soon.

She turned toward the vendor to ask about a driver, but at that moment something triggered in her memory. A face in the crowd. A dinner reception in Mylapore earlier that year. The man had greeted her father warmly, and her father had responded in kind. Ahalya couldn't recall the man's name, but she never forgot a face.

She pinched Sita awake and told her not to move. She wove

her way through cows, automobiles, and rickshaws and approached the man.

"Sir," she said, speaking in English, "I am Ahalya Ghai. My father is Naresh Ghai. Do you remember me?"

The man looked at her and broke into a grin. "Of course," he replied with crisp English diction. "I am Ramesh Narayanan. We met last spring at the Tamil Historical Society." His look turned to puzzlement. "What are you doing here? Are you with your father?"

The question pierced Ahalya. She looked away from Ramesh while she collected herself. In halting speech, she told him the truth about her family.

The blood drained from Ramesh's face as she spoke. He struggled to find something appropriate to say. Finally he asked, "Where is your sister?"

Ahalya motioned toward the vegetable vendor's stall. "We are headed to our convent school in Tiruvallur. The sisters will take care of us."

Ramesh glanced back and forth between Ahalya and Sita. "To reach Tiruvallur, you will need a ride."

Ahalya nodded. "We walked this far, but Sita is very tired."

Ramesh pursed his lips. "We are in the same position then. The bus I was on is no longer running. I've been trying to find a driver to take me back to Chennai." He paused and gave her a small smile. "Don't worry. I will make sure you arrive in Tiruvallur by nightfall. It is the least I can do for the daughters of Naresh Ghai."

Ahalya was nearly overcome with relief.

"Wait with your sister," Ramesh said. "I will come for you as soon as I can."

Sometime later Ramesh returned with a wiry man dressed in a loose-fitting shirt, or *kurta*, and a pair of khaki pants. The man had gaunt cheeks, cold eyes, and a scar on his chin. He looked at the sisters and then nodded to Ramesh. Ahalya felt an instinctive distrust toward the scar-faced man, but she had no option but to accept Ramesh's help.

"Where are we going?" Sita asked, a slight tremor in her voice.

Ramesh answered her. "This man—Kanan is his name— has a truck with four-wheel drive. He is the only person in all of Kovallam willing to brave the road after the waves, and his price was remarkably fair. We were lucky to find him."

Ahalya took her sister's hand. "It's all right," she said.

Staying close to Ramesh, the sisters trailed Kanan through the marketplace toward an alleyway draped with brilliantly colored fabrics. The truck—a dust-coated blue Toyota—had seen better days. It stood battered and rusting beside an apothecary's shop. Ahalya, feigning claustrophobia, declined Ramesh's invitation to ride with Sita in the cab and motioned for her sister to climb onto the flatbed. The idea of sitting so close to the scar-faced man repulsed her.

Kanan started the engine and engaged the clutch. The truck shuddered and lurched forward. After navigating the streets of Kovallam, he took the highway toward Chennai.

The waves had turned the scenic coastal plain into a silt-infested swamp and the roadway into a mud flat. The truck made slow headway across the crust of sand. Although there was no traffic on the road, it took them an hour to reach Neelankarai, the southernmost suburb of Chennai, and another hour to reach Thiruvanmiyur, two miles shy of the Adyar River. The waves had destroyed many of the coastal dwellings, had flooded roads, overturned cars, and washed fleets of fishing boats ashore. The East Coast Road was overwhelmed with pedestrians, and traffic moved at a glacial pace.

Half a mile south of the river delta, traffic halted altogether. Horns blared and drivers shouted obscenities, but nothing dislodged the unseen logjam. After ten frustrating minutes, Kanan reversed course and took an inland road toward St. Thomas Mount. The sun was low in the sky when they crossed the river by way of the bridge at Saidapet. The thoroughfares north of the river showed no signs of damage.

The driver turned east toward Mylapore and the coast. Ahalya took a small measure of comfort in the chaotic dance of cars, trucks, buses, bicyclists, and auto-rickshaws. She squeezed Sita's hand to reassure her.

"We'll be there soon," she said, delivering a smile that found no reflection in her sister's eyes.

"What will we do?" Sita asked.

"I don't know," Ahalya admitted.

She fought against the grief tugging ceaselessly at her

heart, but this time the pressure was too great. Tears spilled down her cheeks, burning her eyes and tickling her chin. She took Sita into her arms and promised Lakshmi on her father's grave that she would allow no harm to come to her. She would be a mother to her. She would make the sacrifices necessary to ensure that Sita would find life on the other side of the horrors of this day. Her sister was her charge.

She could not fail.

A few minutes before six o'clock, the truck stopped beside an upscale complex of flats. The shadows were long upon the tree-shaded lane, and the sun was close to setting. Ramesh climbed out of the cab, smoothed his shirt, and gave the girls a sympathetic smile.

"I regret that I can't take you all the way to Tiruvallur," he said, "but I have an engagement in Chennai this evening. I have paid Kanan to take you the rest of the way."

He gave Ahalya a business card with his mobile number. "I can't express how sorry I am for your loss. Call if you should ever have a need." With a slight bow, he bid them farewell.

Kanan didn't speak to the sisters after Ramesh left them. He placed a brief call on his mobile phone and then turned the truck around and headed north-west toward the city center. They crossed the Kuvam River and took a left on a major thoroughfare. Kanan navigated through the traffic toward the western suburbs.

All was well until they passed through the intersection

at Jawaharlal Nehru Road. Without warning, Kanan took a left into an industrial park.

"*Neengal enna seigirirgal?*" Ahalya demanded of him, knocking on the cab window. "What are you doing?"

Kanan ignored her and drove faster down the dirt road. They entered a neighborhood of dilapidated flats. Dirty children and mangy dogs milled about; men smoked in the shadows of doorways; and elderly couples sat silently on cramped terraces. The neighborhood was unfamiliar to Ahalya, but there were countless others like it in the city. It was a place where generations had eked out a living on the margins of society, a place where people looked the other way and didn't ask questions. Ahalya knew that if she cried out, no one would come to her aid. Her instincts had been correct. Kanan was not trustworthy.

She reached for her phone in her satchel. Just then, Kanan slammed on the brakes and the truck slid to a stop. Grabbing the phone, Ahalya hid it in her *churidaar*. She took in her surroundings. The truck sat at the end of a row of dingy flats beneath a high stone wall. The area was poorly lit and deserted except for a group of three men standing in the gloom. The men surrounded the truck, and the youngest one climbed onto the flatbed.

Stooping in front of them, he said, "You have nothing to fear from us. If you do what we say, we will not hurt you." He noticed Ahalya's satchel. "What do we have here?" he asked, reaching for the bag.

Ahalya clutched the satchel tightly. Without hesitation,

the young man backhanded her across the face. Ahalya's cheek smarted from the blow and she tasted blood on her lip. Beside her, Sita began to whimper. The violence had been sudden and shocking. Ahalya handed over the bag.

The young man poured out its contents onto the flatbed and picked up the wooden box, unfastening its clasp. The jewelry sparkled in the light of a streetlamp.

"Kanan, you old bandicoot," he said exultantly, holding up one of Sita's necklaces, "look what you brought us! You must be blessed by Ganesha."

"Good," Kanan said, turning to a fat man with a pockmarked face, "then you can double my pay." The fat man scowled and Kanan immediately retreated. "Okay, okay. Double is too much. Make it fifty percent."

"Done," the fat man said and counted out the bills. "Now get out of here."

After the young man forced the girls out of the truck, Kanan hopped back in the cab, gunned the engine, and sped away in a cloud of dust.

The youth took Sita's arm, and the fat man flanked Ahalya. The third of their captors, a bespectacled man with a silver watch, trailed behind. Ahalya's heart pounded as the men led them into a dark hallway and up a flight of stairs. The door to a flat stood open. A *hamsa* charm was strung above the doorway as a talisman against the Evil Eye.

The men ushered the girls into the living room. An overweight woman in a *sari* sat on the couch watching television. She glanced up at the girls and then returned to her program. The youth and the fat man shook hands with the bespectacled man, whom they called Chako. The fat man spoke briefly to Chako in low tones. Ahalya heard nothing of the conversation except the fat man's promise to return in the morning.

Chako bid the others farewell and closed the door, locking two deadbolts. He turned to the girls with a neutral expression.

"Are you hungry?" he asked.

Ahalya's stomach rumbled. The thought of food had not entered her mind in hours. She traded a glance with Sita and nodded at Chako. Chako turned to the woman and spoke a terse command in Tamil. The woman rose from the couch, glared irritably at the girls, and made her way into the kitchen.

Minutes later, she emerged bearing two steaming plates of rice with chickpea and potato chutney and a pitcher of water. The sisters ate ravenously. The food was too spicy and the water lukewarm and unfiltered, but Ahalya had long since ceased to care. They needed to bide their time until they were alone and she could place a phone call to Sister Naomi.

After the meal, Chako told the girls to sit on the couch beside his wife. He took a seat on a nearby chair. Chako's wife was riveted by a talk show that the girls' mother had never let them watch. A Tamil movie star was the celebrity guest, and the topic of conversation was her most recent production, a saccharine drama set amid the civil war in Sri Lanka.

Ahalya sat next to her sister in a state of mute disbelief. In a single day her family had been ravaged by the sea and she and Sita had been kidnapped. What did Chako and his wife want with them? Had other girls been imprisoned here, or were they the first? Ahalya recalled that Kanan had received a commission from the fat man. That suggested they had done this before. But why? What was their motive?

The show lasted an hour and then Chako switched the channel to an international news station. Ahalya and Sita sat up in their seats, captivated by footage of devastation wreaked by giant waves along the coastline of the Indian Ocean. Orphaned babies squalled in the arms of aid workers, women wailed in grief before the camera, and whole villages lay in ruins, felled by a wall of water that appeared without warning.

According to the anchor, the tsunami had started its journey in the tumult of a colossal earthquake off the coast of Indonesia. A succession of waves generated by the quake had spread outward from the epicenter at the speed of a jetliner. In the span of less than three hours, the tsunami had left untold thousands dead along the shores of Indonesia, Thailand, Malaysia, Sri Lanka, India, and the Andaman and Nicobar Islands. The station showed projections of the death toll. Some said fifty thousand people had perished. Others estimated five times that number. The scope of the catastrophe was unimaginable.

They watched television until ten o'clock. When Chako finally switched off the set, he led Ahalya and Sita into a small room furnished with two beds and a bedside bureau. Chako told the sisters they would sleep on one bed and his wife would sleep on the other. The room had a window on the far wall, enclosed by rusting louvers and iron bars.

Chako's wife entered the room after a few minutes dressed in a nightgown and carrying a glass of water and two round pills. Chako told the girls that the pills would help them sleep. Thinking quickly, Ahalya trapped the pill beneath her tongue and swallowed only the water. Her phone was still hidden in the fabric at her waist; she intended to use it after everyone fell asleep. Chako's wife, however, probed her mouth with her finger and discovered the ruse.

"Stupid girl," the woman spat out, cuffing Ahalya on the back of the head. "You don't know what's good for you." She gave Ahalya the pill again and forced her to swallow it.

Chako took a look at his shiny watch and bid the sisters good night. Closing the bedroom door behind him, he turned the lock with an audible click. His wife sat down on the bed nearest to the window and fixed Ahalya with a nasty glare.

"There is no way out," she said. "Do not try to leave or Chako will bring a knife. Others have learned the hard way. And do not disturb my sleep."

Ahalya and Sita lay down beside each other on the bed. Sita cried silently into the sheets until she drifted off to sleep. Ahalya wrapped her arms around her sister like a protective shield, trying desperately to ward off the unseen forces that had turned their world into a nightmare. As the sedative took effect, Ahalya fought to stay awake, but the medication addled her mind and weighed down her eyelids.

With the last of her strength, she pushed her mobile phone deeper into her *churidaar*. Then her resistance gave way and she lost consciousness.

Chapter 2

Confess it freely—evil prowls about the land, its secret principles unknown to us.

—Voltaire

Kiawah Island, South Carolina

On the morning after Christmas, in the twilight before dawn, Thomas Clarke took a walk along the shoreline of Vanderhorst Plantation. He was the first of his friends at the beach house to greet the day. The holiday bash the night before had been wild, the wine and brandy had flowed, and most of his companions had drunk themselves into a stupor. Thomas had showed restraint, but only because his mind was on other things.

He regretted making the trip from D.C. It wasn't his idea. His best friend from law school had heard about Priya and invited him to spend Christmas on the island. Thomas appreciated Jeremy's desire to keep him company, but the diversion had had the opposite effect. It had been years since he had felt so lonely.

He crossed the dunes to the beach. The scene before him was picturesque—sky uncluttered and blushing pink, whitecaps on gunmetal surf kicked up by a blustery wind, and wide swaths of unbroken sand. Stuffing his hands in the pockets of his coat, he trudged toward the waterline and headed east, against the wind. At six foot two and a trim 180 pounds, he was built for exercise. In other circumstances, he would have gone for a long run. Today he was preoccupied. He set a steady pace and played mental games with himself, shuffling his thoughts like a deck of cards and searching for a safer subject. But eventually his mind rebelled and he saw his wife, standing beside the taxi, saying goodbye.

Her name was Priya, meaning "beloved". He remembered saying it to himself over and over again when they first met. The innocence of those days seemed surreal now. So much had happened. So much had changed. The blows when they came had been crushing, and the wreckage they left behind had been complete. The look in her eyes when she had left him said it all. Beyond bitterness, anger, and despair, beyond emotion itself, was a place of unfeeling. She hadn't looked at him as much as looked through him.

Their story had many parts, many stages. Some were comprehensible. The rest was a confused mess of fault and pain. There was tragedy and betrayal, divided loyalties and unspoken needs, and a cultural gulf never quite bridged. But that was how life so often went. Solid ground could turn into quicksand without warning. The rational world yielded to madness, and good people lost their minds.

Thomas reached the westernmost fairway of the Ocean Course and turned around. The empty beach on Vanderhorst Plantation was chilly in the winter air, but the rising sun shimmered on the water and gave the appearance of warmth. Heading back to the beach house, Thomas increased his pace. He had been raised by a championship athlete and ex-Marine who now served as chief judge of the U.S. District Court for the Eastern District of Virginia. The Honorable Randolph Truman Clarke, steely-eyed jurist and master of the Rocket Docket, was a glutton for early-morning punishment and raised Thomas and his younger brother, Ted, to crave the thrill of cool wind upon their faces and the sight of a distant sunrise.

When he reached the boardwalk that led across the dunes, Thomas paused for a moment and allowed the cadence of the ocean to steady his mind. He had a long day ahead of him. The thought of it made him cringe, but he couldn't put it off any longer.

For as long as he and Priya had lived in the city, they had spent Christmas Eve with his family in Alexandria. It was a tradition he had broken this year without explanation. His father had expressed his displeasure in few words, as was his way, but his mother had been crestfallen. She had asked about their plans, and he had given her no detail. He couldn't bring himself to tell her that Priya was gone.

In the end, however, they had boxed him in. His mother had insisted—*insisted*—that they come over for dinner—before or after the holiday, it didn't matter. He had pushed back, blaming his caseload at the firm, but the Judge had picked up the phone and intervened.

"The day after Christmas is a Sunday," he had said. "Nobody is going to be at the office that day. I'm sure you can take a break."

"The firm party is that night," Thomas had rejoined.

The gambit had worked until the Judge asked when the party started.

"Eight thirty," he had admitted.

"You can stop by beforehand," the Judge had said.

He returned to the beach house and packed his bag. Most of his companions were still asleep, and the house was a disaster. Dirty plates and shot glasses were strewn about, and the air still carried the faint scent of liquor. He didn't envy Jeremy the task of cleanup.

His friend met him in the foyer, dressed in a gray T-shirt and boxer shorts.

"Leaving so soon?" he asked. "I'm making pancakes later. Fuel for the road."

Thomas ran a hand through his dark hair. "It's tempting, but I have to get back. Clayton's party is tonight, and I have to stop by my parents' house for dinner."

"Sometimes it seems like the holidays never end," Jeremy replied with a grin.

"Thanks so much for thinking of me," Thomas said.

Jeremy clasped his shoulder. "I know this wasn't the same as sharing Christmas with Priya, but it was good to see you again. If there's anything I can do . . ."

"Thanks." Thomas gave his friend a thin smile, collected his bag, and took his leave.

He drove toward the gate in a daze. He was not looking forward to the ten-hour drive to the District. He left the resort property and headed in the direction of Charleston. Traffic was light, and he reached the city in forty minutes. He wasn't really in a hurry, but the absence of highway patrol officers encouraged his lead foot. He tried his best not to think about the empty brownstone waiting for him in Georgetown or the jasmine and lilac scent of Priya's perfume still clinging to the bedsheets.

Merging onto I-95, Thomas found a classical music station on the radio and ignored the speed limit. The Audi was as quiet at eighty-five miles an hour as it was at fifty-five. Around noon, he stopped for gas and remembered he hadn't eaten breakfast. At the recommendation of the station attendant, he bought a pulled pork sandwich from a local greasy spoon and drove half a mile to the Cape Fear Botanical Gardens. By midday, the air had warmed sufficiently to allow for alfresco dining.

He parked in the visitors' lot and entered the gardens on foot. The place was idyllic—lush with foliage. A few couples were out walking; an elderly man was throwing rice to a family of pigeons; and a blond woman in a hat was snapping pictures of a man in sunglasses beneath an oak tree. Not far away, a young mother and a girl about ten years old were heading down a path toward the Children's Garden. Thomas watched the girl run ahead of her mother and felt a familiar ache inside. When Priya was pregnant, he had a dream of Mohini taking her first steps at Rock Creek Park. It was one of so many hopes dashed by the little girl's death.

He walked to a gazebo in the middle of a grassy field and took a seat on the steps. He watched as mother and daughter disappeared into a stand of evergreen trees. Soon the woman with the camera lost interest in photographing her companion and turned her attention to the flora. Shutter clicking, lens tracing random arcs across the scene, she meandered toward the path to the Children's Garden, her male friend trailing after her.

Thomas took out his sandwich and began to eat. He watched the clouds drifting lazily in the jet stream and relished the tranquility of the place. After a while, he looked out across the grass and saw that the elderly man had taken a seat on a bench at the edge of the trees. Everyone else had disappeared. For a moment, all was serene. The air was still, the forest unperturbed, and the December sun hung like a lantern from the sky.

Then, in an instant, the silence was shattered by a scream.

Thomas put down his meal and stood up. The scream came again. It was a woman's voice, coming from the direction of the Children's Garden. His decision was instinctive. In seconds he was running down the path toward the trees. There was no doubt in his mind. The scream had something to do with the girl.

He entered the forest at top speed. The path was lonely

and dark beneath the evergreen boughs. He emerged from the trees to see the young mother doubled over in the midst of an empty meadow. She was clutching her stomach with one hand and her face with the other, repeating a name over and over again—Abby.

Thomas looked around.

The girl was gone.

He ran to the woman and knelt down. Her cheek was livid with the beginnings of a nasty bruise. She looked at him with wild eyes.

"*Please!*" she rasped. "They took her! They took my Abby! *Help me!*"

Thomas's heart lurched. "*Who* did?" he demanded, scanning the trees again.

"A woman with a camera," she gasped, trying to stand up. "And two men. One of them came up behind me." She motioned toward the trees separating them from the parking lot. "They went that way! *Do* something! *Please!*"

At that moment, an engine gunned and Thomas heard the sound of tires churning upon gravel. He hesitated only a second before leaping to his feet and running into the forest. Branches stung his face, and he stumbled on a fallen limb, but he didn't break his stride. He could think of only one thing—the girl.

Thomas emerged from the trees just in time to see a black sport utility vehicle tear out of the parking lot to the north. He pulled his mobile phone from his pocket and dialed 911. The dispatcher connected immediately.

"There's been a kidnapping," he said, breathless, finding his keys with his other hand. "It happened at the Botanical Gardens. They took a girl about ten years old. Her mother's still here and she's hurt. I saw a black SUV, but I didn't get the plate."

He hung up before the dispatcher could reply. He threw open the car door and slid into the driver's seat. Mashing the clutch, he made a tight turn onto the entrance road. He swerved onto Eastern Boulevard with a squeal of rubber, heading in the direction of the Middle River Loop. He drove a mile along the highway at twice the speed limit, hoping to catch a glimpse of the SUV before it turned onto a secondary road. Traffic was light, but he saw no sign of it.

He drove another mile toward I-95 without sighting the SUV. He pulled to the side of the highway, looking around in desperation. Every second that passed decreased his chances of success. The land north of the Middle River Loop was dominated by forest and rolling fields. He scoured the scenery on both sides of the road, looking for a flash of black against the background of green. A few cars passed on the highway, but he saw no sign of the SUV.

Thomas gripped the steering wheel. The brazenness of the crime enraged him. The SUV had at best a minute's head-start. Simple physics said it couldn't be far away. But he didn't know the area, and the kidnappers surely did.

After a while, he turned around and drove back the way he had come. During his absence, the entrance to the gardens had been besieged by four squad cars and an ambulance, all with lights ablaze. Two police officers stood behind the ambulance, watching an EMT nurse tend to the child's mother. Another officer was speaking into a radio and a fourth was taking photographs some distance away.

Thomas approached the officer on the radio and waited. The man was long-winded and seemed not to notice him. Before Thomas could introduce himself, a hand gripped his arm. He turned and saw the girl's mother. Her brown eyes were clear and imploring.

"Please tell me you saw them again," she pleaded, pushing away the nurse, who was trying to take her back to the ambulance. "Please tell me you know where they took her."

He shook his head, his failure weighing on him.

"Oh God!" the woman cried. "Oh dear God." The pain poured out of her in words. "She turned eleven today. I was taking her to a movie, but she wanted to stop at the gardens." Without warning, she thrust herself at Thomas and pounded on his chest. "*I should have said no!*" she shrieked, sobbing uncontrollably. "*How did this happen?*"

Thomas had no idea what to do. He traded a look with one of the police officers, who tried to intervene, but the officer's entreaties were half-hearted and ineffectual.

Eventually the woman collected herself enough to let go of him. "I'm sorry," she said, stepping back. "I just . . ." She hugged herself. "Abby's all I've got. I can't lose her. I don't know what I'd do."

Sensing an opportunity, the EMT nurse took the woman's

hand. "Come along, Ms. Davis. The police are doing everything they can. Let's get you fixed up."

This time the woman complied without objection.

Thomas stood stiffly, at once moved and disturbed by the exchange. The officer holding the radio began to ask him questions about the incident, and he answered, but his mind drifted to a different time and place—to a small hillock at Glenwood Cemetery, placing flowers on his daughter's grave.

It took him fifteen minutes to deliver his statement. Toward the end, an unmarked squad car pulled into the lot and a tall man in plainclothes emerged. After talking to one of the officers by the ambulance, the man approached Thomas.

"I'm Detective Morgan with the Fayetteville PD. I understand you made the 911 call."

"I did," Thomas confirmed.

"May I ask why you tried to follow the vehicle?"

Thomas shrugged. "I don't know. I wanted to help."

"Officer Velasquez here says you saw the perpetrators."

"Only at a distance. They looked like any couple you'd see at a shopping mall. I didn't think anything of them at the time."

"Could you pick them out of a lineup?"

"I doubt it. I might recognize the man, but not the woman."

The detective eyed him curiously. "What do you do for a living, if you don't mind me asking?"

"I'm an attorney in D.C. Why?"

The detective smiled wryly. "An altruistic lawyer. Not many of you in the world."

The comment was inane, and Thomas felt a stab of irritation. He glanced at the ambulance and saw the girl's mother being treated for lacerations on her wrists. There was something about the incident that nagged at him. Something didn't add up.

"What happened here?" he asked. "There were multiple kidnappers and they acted in broad daylight. The more I think about it, the more it seems premeditated."

The detective crossed his arms. "I can't answer that."

"You're telling me this was an ordinary crime? This is North Carolina, not Mexico City."

The detective's eyes darkened. "I'm not going to say it was, and I'm not going to say it wasn't." He softened his tone. "Listen, if it's any consolation, a lot of fine people will be working on this. The feds may get involved. We'll do everything we can."

"I don't doubt it. But will you find the girl?"

The detective looked toward the forest, and for a moment he let his guard down. "I won't lie to you. The statistics aren't good."

Thomas took a deep breath. He felt as if someone had buried a knife in his gut. He thanked the detective and shook his hand. The hand held a card.

"Call me if you think of anything else about the case. And make sure you keep your e-mail account open. We may have more questions for you."

Thomas nodded and walked back to his car, playing the words of the girl's mother over and over in his mind: "*Abby's all I've got. I can't lose her.*" He tried to shake off the woman's despair, but it wouldn't let him go.

He drove the rest of the way to Washington in a mental fog. The kidnapping replayed itself in his mind over and over again. If only he had seen the danger and told Abby's mother not to take her down the path. If only he had understood the intentions of the woman with the camera and her male companion. If only he had run faster and waited until he was driving before placing the 911 call. What did the kidnappers intend to do with the girl? Would they demand a ransom, or would they do something worse?

He reached the District a few minutes before six o'clock. He drove along the Potomac River before crossing the bridge into Georgetown. He found a parking spot in front of his home and took his duffel bag into the foyer. In the three weeks since Priya had left, he had never gotten used to the quiet of the place. He turned on a few lights, went upstairs to the bedroom, and changed clothes. After putting on slacks and a sweater, he stared at himself in the mirror and saw the dark circles under his eyes. His mother would tell him he wasn't taking care of himself. And she would be right.

The drive into old-town Alexandria was a blur of lights. He pulled into the driveway of his parents' modest Tudor-style home and sat in silence. Then he walked up the front steps and stopped at the door. The faint voice of Gene Autry drifted out to greet him. The old crooner was singing about Santa Claus. For a moment, he felt as if he were in a dream. One year ago, he and Priya had stood on this porch, holding hands. It wasn't bliss they had had, but she was pregnant and looking forward to motherhood, and he was satisfied with his life. He was a rising star at Clayton|Swift, defending Wharton Coal in a case that could make his career. They were doing well financially. How was it possible that everything had gone so wrong?

He knocked twice before opening the door. Elena Clarke met him in the foyer, wrapped in an apron, her face shiny with sweat from the stove. Her eyes narrowed when she saw he was alone. They stood for a moment in silence, neither willing to make the first move. Then Thomas mustered the nerve to speak.

"Priya isn't coming. She left three weeks ago." There it was, in the open at last.

His mother's eyes widened in shock, but she collected herself quickly. "You didn't tell us," she said softly.

"I didn't know what to say."

"Where did she go?"

He took a breath. "She went home."

Elena approached him, hesitantly at first, and then with greater confidence. He accepted her embrace without resistance.

"We knew it would be hard, but we hoped it wouldn't come to this." She backed off and looked at him again. "How are you feeling?"

He shrugged. "I've been better."

Elena nodded. "Your father is in the study," she said, rolling her eyes. "He's reading some impenetrable tome on the Peloponnesian wars."

Thomas mustered a smile. "What else is new?"

He made his way down the hallway, past framed school pictures from his childhood, and entered his father's sanctuary. The room was more a library than a study. The Judge sat on a leather chair, a pillow on his lap, and a fountain pen in his hand. The book before him was outsized, nearly as large as a dictionary. Thomas could see endless scribbles and marginalia on the pages. The Judge marked up everything he read. He was an arbiter of fates in his day job. Faceless authors were easy prey.

His father looked up at him. "Merry Christmas, Thomas."

"Merry Christmas, Dad." He stood awkwardly, unsure of what to say.

The Judge spoke for him. "I overheard what you told your mother about Priya. Was it Mohini, or did the Wharton case do her in?"

Thomas winced. His father was nothing if not blunt. "A little of both, I think," he replied, omitting that there were complications in the story, that they were as much to blame as their circumstances.

"She never did like that damned case," his father went on.

"It's hard to like a company that killed a schoolhouse full of kids."

The Judge nodded and stood. "The curse of the litigator," he said, leading the way toward the dining room, "is that you don't get to choose your clients."

"Priya would have disagreed."

"Yes," his father said. "She always was an idealist." He turned and put his hand on Thomas's shoulder. Not far away the clock sounded the hour. Seven chimes. "I'm sorry, Son. I really am. You've had a rough go of it in the past six months."

"Thanks, Dad," he said, moved by this rare display of emotion.

Elena met them in the dining room with a steaming basket of butter rolls. "Turkey, mashed potatoes, stuffing, cranberries, broccoli, the works," she said, trying to lighten the mood. "Ted and Amy ate all the stuffing on Christmas Eve, but I made a new batch."

The aroma was delectable, and Thomas allowed himself to smile. His younger brother worked at a finance firm in New York, and Ted's wife, Amy, was a model for a slew of fashion magazines. Despite their high-flying careers, they were actually quite down-to-earth people.

"I'm sure Ted had more to do with that than Amy," Thomas quipped.

His father chuckled. "The girl never seems to eat anything."

"Listen, I'm sorry I didn't come," Thomas said with a smile. He didn't expect to mean it, but he found that he really did.

"All is forgiven," his mother said. "Now dig in."

Over dinner, they tried to steer the conversation toward lighter topics. But the gravity of recent events caught up with them as they were finishing the main course. His mother asked Thomas if he had heard about the tsunami in the Indian Ocean.

"They were talking about it on the radio," Thomas replied.

"Your mother has been glued to the television all afternoon," the Judge said.

"It's unfathomable," Elena said, shaking her head. "All those people . . ." Her voice wavered with feeling. "How can something like that happen?"

"I don't know," Thomas said. It was the second time he had confronted that question in a single day. He thought of Abby's mother, crying in his arms. He turned toward his father.

"While we're talking about depressing topics, Dad, I'd like to get your impression of something that happened to me on the drive home."

He told the Judge about the kidnapping and his conversation with Detective Morgan. There was purpose in his disclosure. His father sat atop one of the most powerful judicial districts in the country. If anyone had a bird's-eye view of American crime, he did.

When Thomas finished speaking, his father rubbed his chin. "Hmm, Fort Bragg is in Fayetteville." After a pause, he went on: "It might not have been an ordinary kidnapping. We've seen a spike in trafficking cases in the past year."

Thomas frowned. "What does the fort have to do with it?"

"It's simple, really. The fort offers the pimps a steady client base."

Elena made the sign of the cross and stood up suddenly, starting to clear the dishes. Trading a glance with his father, Thomas stood to help her. Afterward, they retired to the living room. Thomas sipped a glass of eggnog while his father stoked the flames in the fireplace.

They congregated around the Christmas tree and Elena picked up an old leather Bible from an end table. She opened to the Gospel of Luke, as she always did at this season, but she just stared at the page. After a moment, she put the Bible down.

"I'm not sure I can read right now," she said.

"I'll read it," the Judge said and took the Bible from her.

He flipped to the Advent passage and read the time-worn words. Thomas listened as he had every year of his life, but the passage meant little to him any more. He had been confirmed into the Church like every other Catholic boy, but the ideas in the Catechism had frayed and faded during his years at Yale. In the real world, doubt was the only truth.

When the Judge finished the reading, Elena reached beneath the Christmas tree and handed Thomas a small package, wrapped in gold paper. Listening to the Scripture seemed to have calmed her nerves. She smiled at Thomas and glanced at the Judge.

"Your father picked them out," she said.

Thomas removed the paper and opened a jeweler's box containing a pair of silver cufflinks. The cufflinks bore his initials: TRC. The "R" was for Randolph.

"Priya was always trying to get you to wear those prissy French-cuff shirts," his father said with a little laugh. "I thought these would help."

"She was always trying to get me to do a lot of things," Thomas said.

Elena pulled out a second package. "I bought this for her," she said with a sigh. "I found it at a used bookstore. I suppose I could keep it, but I'd prefer you to take it with you."

Thomas shook his head. "She's not coming back, Mom. I don't see the point." He didn't mean to be harsh, but he didn't want there to be any doubt.

Elena took a deep breath. "Even so, take it with you. Please."

Thomas took the gift reluctantly. "Should I unwrap it?"

His mother nodded.

Beneath the paper he found a pocket-sized book of poetry by Sarojini Naidu.

"A good choice," he said. "She loved Naidu."

"Why don't you read something to us?"

His instinct was to decline, but he didn't want to disappoint her. He opened the book to a poem called "Transience" and read it out loud. The refrain had a haunting beauty, but it rang hollow in his heart.

Nay, do not weep; new hopes, new dreams, new faces,
The unspent joy of all the unborn years,
Will prove your heart a traitor to its sorrow,
And make your eyes unfaithful to their tears.

The room was silent after he finished. No one knew what to say. They were rescued by the sound of the grandfather clock. Eight chimes.

"I'm sorry to rush off," Thomas said, trying to hide his relief, "but I have to change before I head downtown."

"Of course," Elena said, though her eyes were filled with sorrow.

His parents walked him to the door. In contrast to the good cheer they had affected at the beginning of the meal, their expressions now were grave.

"Call us if you need anything," Elena said. "Day or night, we'll be here."

"I'll be fine," Thomas replied, giving her a kiss on the cheek and shaking his father's hand. "Don't worry about me."

But he knew they didn't believe him.

He drove back into the city and made a quick stop at home to change into his tuxedo. He felt profoundly weary. He had been a fool to drive all the way to South Carolina for Christmas. The holidays had their merits, but even in a good year all the socializing gave him a headache. He needed a drink. That was about the only benefit of Clayton's holiday party—bottomless booze.

He hailed a cab to the Mayflower Hotel. The taxi dropped him off at the entrance at nine o'clock. He knew from experience that the late arrival wouldn't be noticed. Clayton's parties went on all night.

He walked into the grand lobby of the old Beaux Arts establishment, and heard the din of conversation. Clayton's Washington office—one of twenty around the world—was home to two hundred attorneys and twice as many staff. When the whole group gathered and drinks were served, one had to shout to be heard over the clatter.

He entered the grand ballroom and greeted a group of friends. After trading a few jokes and a bit of office gossip, he excused himself to get a drink. At one of the bars, he ordered a Manhattan and watched the bartender mix the whiskey, vermouth, and bitters. He took the drink and sipped it, looking out across the sea of faces flushed with excitement and inebriation.

He always felt a rush in this crowd. Clayton was one of the most prestigious law firms in the world. In the last decade, especially, the skyrocketing housing market, the rise of international mergers and acquisitions, and the expansion of the global energy sector had turned the equity partners at the firm into multimillionaires and given associates like Thomas a taste of the good life yet to come.

Priya, on the other hand, had hated everything about the firm. She had lobbied hard against Clayton when Thomas put out his résumés. She had argued that a life spent in nonprofit practice was the only path to true satisfaction. He had listened to her. He always listened to her. But he had disagreed. Slaving away for breadcrumbs at a civil rights group might be emotionally gratifying, but as a career move, it was a dead end. He coveted what his father had—a seat on the federal bench. To get there, he had to play in the big leagues.

"Hey, stranger."

The voice startled him. He turned and looked into the aquamarine eyes of Tera Atwood.

"I called you all weekend," she said, "but you didn't answer." She sidled up to him and touched his arm. "Go anywhere fun?"

Tera was a graduate of Chicago Law and an associate one year his junior. She was smart, vivacious, and pretty. Tonight she was dressed in a silver-sequined gown that looked more cabaret star than big-firm litigator.

"I went to the beach with a few friends," he said, glancing around to see if anyone was looking at them. "I forgot my BlackBerry."

He tried to relax but couldn't. Tera's effect on him was overpowering. Her presence could be summed up in two words: desire and guilt.

She gave him a coquettish smile. "We could get out of here and go someplace private."

His guilt mushroomed. "I don't think that would be a good idea."

Tera looked confused and a little hurt. "My dear Thomas, you forget that Priya left you. What do you have to hide?"

He surveyed the crowd. "They don't know that."

"How long do you plan to keep it a secret?"

"I'm not sure," he replied, wishing this conversation were not happening.

"Are you ashamed of me, Thomas?" Tera's tone was light, but the question was barbed.

"Of course not," he replied quickly. Why was he so keen to placate her?

Tera put her hand on his arm again. "What about tomorrow?"

He saw one of the partners in the litigation division glance toward them, and he averted his eyes. "Tomorrow is better," he said, hoping she would take the cue and leave him alone.

"Can't wait," she replied and left him to greet a friend.

He watched her go and wished he could disappear. Tera was one of the incomprehensible parts of his story. He had always despised the culture of the firm—all the hanky-panky among colleagues, the mistresses on the side. He had been devoted to Priya. Tera had worked with him on the Wharton case for three years, but he had considered her a friend, nothing more. Then tragedy struck and the rules suddenly changed. She had reached out to him at just the wrong moment— when Priya's grief had transmuted from a suffering silence into hard-edged bitterness.

The affair had started innocently enough: a laugh here, a pat on the shoulder there. But somewhere in the maelstrom of preparing for the Wharton trial and Priya's caustic depression, he had crossed the line from attraction to infatuation. He stayed at the office later and later, dreading the diatribes he would endure at home for every little failure Priya perceived or invented. He couldn't talk to her about Mohini. She wouldn't even speak the little girl's name. He was profoundly vulnerable, and Tera was available. More than available: she was bewitching.

He had resisted her physical advances until Priya left, but in the last three weeks, he had been to her Capitol Hill apartment twice. He had never stayed overnight. His guilt was far too intense for that. But he had given in to the temptation to sleep with her because she was sensitive and beautiful, and his wife was gone.

He looked at his watch and saw that it was ten o'clock. He drew himself together and made the rounds, traded witticisms with a couple of senior partners, and then took his leave. He left the Mayflower on foot and walked south along 18th Street to K Street. The night was cold and clear. The brighter stars were visible through the haze of pollution. Thomas huddled into his topcoat. He considered hailing a cab but thought better of it. He would walk.

Twenty-five minutes later, he arrived home feeling mildly invigorated. He went straight to the kitchen and poured a glass of scotch. He brought the bottle with him to the couch and tried to empty his mind. But the guilt of his encounter with Tera lingered.

He thought again of the kidnapping in Fayetteville. Was his father right about the trafficking connection? Was Abby Davis really in the hands of a pimp? He imagined Mohini as she might have looked at the age of eleven and shuddered.

What would he have done if that had happened to his daughter?

He looked around for the book of poetry his mother had given him and saw it on the table by the telephone. He retrieved it and returned to the couch. He wasn't sure why he did it, but he read the poem "Transience" again. This time one of the stanzas spoke to him:

> *Nay, do not pine, tho' life be dark with trouble,*
> *Time will not pause or tarry on its way;*
> *Today that seems so long, so strange, so bitter,*
> *Will soon be some forgotten yesterday.*

He sat back and closed his eyes. He knew then the dimensions of the hole into which he had crawled. And he knew, with equal clarity, that there was only one way back into the light. Something needed to change. He needed a new horizon. He didn't know exactly what, but the status quo was no longer an option.

To do nothing would be to die one day at a time.

Chapter 3

Each being contains in itself the whole intelligible world.

—Plotinus

Chennai, India

Ahalya awoke to a haze of veiled impressions. She had a powerful hangover from the sleeping medication, and she didn't immediately know where she was. For a precious second, the thought crossed her mind that she and Sita were lying in their bed at home, their parents waiting downstairs to greet them with kisses and news of the day. The horror of her circumstances dawned on her slowly.

Sita was in her arms, their bodies spooned as so often they had been in their former life. But the bed was strange and lumpy, and the walls were bare of the tapestries they had hung in their bedroom with their mother's help. A woman came into view and Ahalya's heart lurched. The woman's face was obscured in shadow, but her shape was not Ambini's.

"Time to get up," Chako's wife said tersely. "The train is waiting."

Sita stirred in Ahalya's embrace, and both girls sat up on the bed. The digital clock on the nightstand read 5:40 a.m.

"What train?" Ahalya asked, taking her sister's hand.

"You'll find out soon enough."

Chako's wife went to the door and turned around. "By the way, I discovered your little ruse with the mobile phone. Don't ever hide anything from us again or your sister will suffer."

Instinctively, Ahalya touched her waist and felt the void. Her heart turned to lead. Her phone was gone.

"Where are you taking us?" she asked, trying to be brave.

"No more questions," the woman snapped. "Breakfast is on the table. You have fifteen minutes to eat. Prakash and Vetri will be here at six o'clock. They will take you to the train."

The sisters went to the table and found two sticky cakes of *idli* and two *dosa* crêpes on a plate beside cups of water. It was a poor excuse for breakfast. Taking her seat, Ahalya told Sita she wasn't hungry and encouraged her to eat everything. Sita eyed her closely and refused the second *idli* cake. Ahalya ate it gratefully.

Prakash and Vetri appeared promptly at six. A knock came at the door and Chako opened it. The youth—Vetri—strolled in and beckoned them with a curt wave. Neither Chako nor his wife spoke to them when they left the flat.

The colony lay dingy and quiet beneath a dark sky when

Ahalya and Sita emerged on the street. The area was deserted, except for a few stray dogs sleeping in the shadows of doorways. The fat man—Prakash—stood waiting for them beside a silver SUV that stood out in the dilapidated surroundings. His arms were crossed and he looked them over.

"*Caril utkarungal*," he said, opening the door to the back seat. "Get in."

Sita climbed into the cabin and Ahalya followed. The vehicle had a new-car smell and reminded Ahalya of her father's Land Rover. She shook off the memory and took Sita's hand.

"Are you all right?" she asked in English, hoping that the men didn't understand.

"Speak Tamil," Prakash barked, climbing into the front seat.

"I'm all right," Sita whispered, putting her head on Ahalya's shoulder.

Vetri jumped into the passenger seat and Prakash accelerated down the empty lane. They left the neighborhood and drove toward the ocean. The streets of the city were largely deserted at such an early hour. A few minutes later, Prakash pulled into the parking area at Chennai Central Station. Vetri leaped out and disappeared into the crowd of passengers waiting for the early departing trains. Prakash glanced at the girls in the rearview mirror and locked the doors.

"Where are we going?" Ahalya asked.

Prakash grunted. "No questions," he said.

Vetri soon returned, clutching a handful of papers. He gave them to Prakash, who scanned them and nodded. Turning around, he looked from Ahalya to Sita.

"The tickets are in order. Vetri will be traveling with you, as will Amar. You will meet him soon. Do what they say without question. Speak to no one or there will be consequences. And do not think of approaching the police. The deputy commissioner is a friend of mine."

The sisters left the vehicle and followed the two men through the crowd. Entering the terminal, they trailed Prakash up a flight of steps to a footbridge above the tracks. They crossed to Track 4 and went down to the platform. The train stretched out before them like a blue serpent, its carriages too numerous for Ahalya to make out in the gloom. She searched the cars for the name of the train. A sign read "Chennai Express". She had never heard of it.

Prakash told the girls to stand with Vetri in an alcove at the base of the stairs and left them briefly. When he returned, he was trailing another man. Short, with black hair and a large chin, the stranger had the pale complexion of a North Indian. He looked the girls up and down and turned to Prakash with a smile.

"Well done, my friend," he said in highly accented Tamil. His speech confirmed that he was not from Chennai.

"I thought you would like them."

The man handed Prakash a black bag. "Twelve thousand

rupees, six thousand each. That's two thousand more than normal."

Prakash pursed his lips. "I asked for fifteen."

"Thirteen thousand, no more," the man countered, reaching into his pants and removing two five-hundred-rupee notes.

Prakash nodded and took the money. He left without another word.

The man introduced himself to the sisters. "My name is Amar. Vetri is my assistant. He will be traveling with you. The ride is long and the train will be crowded. Behave normally, but do not encourage conversation. If one of you disobeys, the other will be punished."

"Where are you taking us?" Ahalya asked again, squeezing Sita's hand to reassure her. She thought of stories she had heard of men from the cities luring women away from their families to perform menial labor for little or no pay. The idea of slaving away night and day for a stranger in a distant city made her shudder.

Amar narrowed his eyes. "You will find out soon enough." He traded glances with Vetri and pointed down the platform. "Take them to their seats."

Vetri nodded and led the sisters to a sleeper carriage near the rear of the train. They climbed aboard and found most of the seats occupied. Vetri took them to a compartment near the center of the car. An old woman sat on the bench across from them. She delivered Ahalya a wrinkled smile but didn't speak. Next to her sat a large man of middle age, dozing. The bench was sagging beneath his weight, and a suitcase was wedged between his legs.

Though the morning was cool, the sleeper car was already warming with the heat of bodies, and the air was pungent with the smell of sweat. At the front of the car a baby was crying, and in the compartment behind theirs, two men were engaged in a loud dialogue about Tamil politics. Their conversation filled the cramped space. Ahalya could tell that this was going to be a very uncomfortable ride.

She gave Sita the window bench and sat down across from her. Sita looked back at her and whispered in English, "Where do you think we're going?"

Ahalya glanced at Vetri, but he was enraptured by a glossy film magazine and had no interest in their exchange.

She took a deep breath and replied, "I don't know. I've never heard of this train."

"I'm scared." Sita's words were barely discernible in the din.

"Be strong, Little Flower," Ahalya replied, using Sita's favorite nickname. "If Mother were here, she would say the same."

As the sun rose, the train left Chennai and plodded across the expanse of the countryside, passing villages and rice paddies and endless cultivated fields parched by the sun. To distract themselves and pass the time, Ahalya and Sita played language games, as they had done so often at St. Mary's.

"Name the poet," Ahalya said: " 'The light is shattered

into gold on every cloud, my darling, and it scatters gems in profusion.' "

"Tagore," Sita said, "that's easy."

"What about this? 'Love's way is life; without it humans are but bones skin-clad.' "

"Thiruvalluvar," Sita replied, solving the riddle with ease.

Ahalya thought of a more obscure verse: " 'The wind of dawn that sets closed blossoms free brings its warm airs to thee.' "

Sita pondered this for a long moment. "I don't know."

"Hafiz," Ahalya said.

"But he was Muslim, not Hindu," Sita objected.

"It doesn't matter to the poetry."

As the hours passed, the carriage became more and more crowded. The temperature inside the sleeper carriage was close to suffocating. Ahalya saw beads of sweat on her sister's brow, and her own *churidaar* was moist and sticky. To make matters worse, they were hungry. At every country station, hawkers plied the train platforms, offering food and drink, yet when Vetri purchased lunch and dinner for himself, he gave the girls only bananas.

The sun set at seven o'clock, and the cooling air brought welcome relief. Sita yawned and looked at her sister. Ahalya saw the question in her eyes. Surveying the tightly packed bodies, some clumped on benches, some seated on the floor, some standing, swaying with the train, she wondered how anyone would sleep.

But they did. In time, children stretched out beneath the benches, fitting their bodies among the luggage. The women wedged themselves together until they were protected and unafraid to close their eyes. And the men crammed into any remaining space, forcing their limbs into impossibly tight confines.

Ahalya took Sita into her arms and whispered a prayer that Ambini had taught them. It was a prayer to Lakshmi for luck, for health, and for courage. She knew they would need each of the three boons wherever it was they were going.

As the night wore on, bodies shuffled, babies cried, and children whimpered; yet even Ahalya and Sita managed to sleep. Sometime in the black morning hours, exhaustion finally overcame them.

When Ahalya opened her eyes again, she noticed that the train had begun to slow. The carriage was less crowded now. Many of the people she remembered were gone. The lights outside the window were scarce at first, but soon buildings appeared. The dread she had succeeded in repressing during the journey returned. Most of the remaining passengers were still asleep, but a few were stretching their arms and moving about. All the signs suggested that the train was close to its destination.

Ahalya turned again to the window and found Sita awake, watching the approaching cityscape. "It's bigger than Chennai," she said softly.

"Yes," Ahalya agreed, squeezing her sister tight.

The train decelerated and a platform appeared. Painted signs posted above pedestrian benches read "Dadar". Ahalya's breath caught in her throat. She had heard of Dadar Station.

It was in Bombay.

As the train drew to a halt, passengers shoved their way toward the rear door, lugging bags and children. Amar entered the car from the front and waded through the sea of bodies.

"Come with me," he said, without explanation.

Dadar Station was a madhouse in the twilight before sunrise. Fluorescent bulbs overhead cast a pallor of bluish-gray light upon the platform. A steady stream of *taxi-wallas* propositioned Amar in a foreign language. Ahalya glanced around, looking for a police officer, but she didn't see one. If she ran, she might lose herself in the crowd. But she had no way to signal to Sita or ensure her safety.

Amar reached into the breast pocket of his *kurta* and took out what looked like tickets.

"We need to hurry," he said, pointing to another platform. "The local train will arrive any minute."

They scaled a footbridge over the tracks and descended to another platform. Seconds later, a commuter train pulled into the station from the north. The car was bulging with people. Men were standing in open doorways and hanging out of the train. There didn't seem to be enough room in the carriages for the crowd on the platform.

Amar spoke to them rapidly. "Stay with Vetri. You must push to get on the train."

When the train stopped, the crowd surged toward the doors. Ahalya gripped Sita's hand and joined the rush. As the girls neared the entrance to a carriage, the pressure increased until they were nearly running. The prospect of climbing aboard seemed impossible, but a gap opened up and the sisters slipped through it. They followed Vetri to the center of the car and took hold of metal handles above their heads, as bodies sorted, sidestepped, and compressed around them.

The train traveled at a rapid pace, bypassing a number of stations. After ten minutes, Vetri shoved his way toward them and said they would be getting off at Mumbai Central.

The station arrived in a blaze of lights and motion. The girls followed Vetri onto the platform, and Amar met them there and led them out through double doors to a waiting taxi. He muttered a few unintelligible words to the *taxi-walla* and they were off.

The city was brightening beneath the rising sun. They were in a densely populated urban area. Black and yellow taxis swarmed the roads like bumblebees, and pedestrians darted across the traffic. The taxi followed the main road for a few blocks and then turned onto a dusty road intersected by smaller lanes. A few women were about, haggling with vendors, but the neighborhood was strangely quiet.

The taxi pulled up to the curb, and Ahalya saw a man

wearing a gray shirt and black jeans move toward them. He was about her father's age, but his hair was almost completely white. Amar climbed out of the cab and shook the man's hand. Vetri told the girls to get out. They stood on the sidewalk before the man with the white hair.

"Sealed pack?" the man asked.

"Yes," Amar replied.

"Forty thousand." The man spoke with authority.

"Seventy-five," Amar countered.

The man frowned. "Sixty thousand. No more."

"Good," agreed Amar. "You will recover it quickly."

The man looked at the girls and said, "Come."

Leaving Amar and Vetri on the street, they followed the man through a doorway and into a twisting stairwell. The steps were steep and the passageway narrow. A door was open at the top of the stairs. A young man in a dark shirt and jeans stood beside the door.

"Take them to the upper room," the man said.

The young man nodded. "This way," he said to the girls.

The space beyond the door was bare except for an L-shaped couch and a mirror along the opposite wall. The room was painted yellow and had a curtained window and a second door. The young man led the girls to the opposite door. They entered a hallway about twenty feet long and studded with doors, all of which were closed. Ahalya heard the sound of low voices and shuffling feet in the rooms beyond, but no one appeared to greet them.

They followed the young man to a large wooden bookcase

at the end of the hallway. The man felt along the left frame
of the bookcase and tugged. The bookcase moved quietly
on oiled hinges, revealing a hidden staircase. The young man
slid through the opening and beckoned to the girls to follow.
Ahalya clutched her sister's trembling arm but didn't move.

"I will not go any further until you tell me where we
are," she said in Hindi, giving her words what strength she
had left.

The young man frowned. "You are in no position to
make demands."

Ahalya's heart raced, but she delivered a stinging rebuke.
"You can't do whatever you want with us. We are your
guests. Where are your manners?"

The young man spat out a curse that shocked her. "*Kutti!*"
Bitch! He stepped into the hallway again and slapped her
across the face. The blow threw her against the wall and
blood trickled from her lip.

"If you rebel, there will be consequences," he hissed. "You
are ours now. Suchir paid sixty thousand rupees for you.
You will do what we say and you will repay your debt."

Sita looked imploringly at Ahalya. "Don't fight. Do what
they ask."

Ahalya touched her throbbing cheek. Taking Sita's hand,
she followed the man into the shadows of the stairwell. The
walls were nearly black with soot and mold stains. The man
led them into a small room furnished with a bed, a dresser,
a toilet, and a sink. He turned on an overhead bulb hanging
from wooden rafters.

"This is where you will live until Suchir decides otherwise. Food will be served on a regular schedule. If there is an emergency, you may pound on the floor. Someone will hear you."

"How will we repay the debt?" Ahalya asked softly.

The young man smirked. "*Bajaana*. You will sleep with men, of course." He laughed. "You didn't think this was a hotel, did you? This is Kamathipura."

With that, he turned and closed the door behind him.

Sita slumped to the floor and wept silently. Ahalya wrapped her arms around her sister, reeling from the man's words. After all they had suffered, it was simply unthinkable that the white-haired man, Suchir, intended to sell them for sex. Sita was a child. Neither of them had ever slept with a man. The horror of it was beyond imagining.

Ahalya heard a knock at the door. She looked up when a woman of middle age appeared. Her large frame was wrapped in a purple *sari*, and her black hair was tied in a bun. She was carrying a pot of water in one hand and garlands of delicate *malati* flowers in the other.

"Do you speak Hindi?" she began.

Ahalya nodded.

"Good. I am Sumeera, but the other girls call me *Badi ma*."

Sumeera sat before them and took a cloth from the water bowl. Wringing it out, she offered it to Ahalya. "You must be tired from the journey."

Ahalya took the cloth, her eyes clouded with mistrust.

She handed it to her sister and watched as Sita wiped her face and pressed it against her forehead.

"I brought you garlands for your hair," Sumeera said, looking at Ahalya. "May I?"

Ahalya didn't reply. A torrent of conflicting emotions raged within her. Every year on her birthday, her mother had garlanded her hair with jasmine and marigold. She had done the same for Sita. A garland was a symbol of festivity and well-wishing. This was a house of sin. How could this strange woman be asking to do the same?

Sumeera nodded and fixed Ahalya with a look of resignation. "I once was like you," she said. "I was taken from my home and brought here by strange men. Life in the *adda* is hard, but you must accept it. There is no use fighting your karma. Accept the discipline of God and perhaps you will be reborn in a better place."

Draping the garland over the edge of the pot of water, she stood heavily and disappeared down the stairs.

When they were alone again, Sita dipped the cloth in the water and handed it to Ahalya. "Is she right?" Sita asked in a whisper. "Is this our karma?"

Ahalya took the cloth and stared at the floor, tears forming in her eyes.

"I don't know," she said.

It was the truth.

Chapter 4

The highest moral law is that we should work
unremittingly for the good of mankind.
                                        —Mahatma Gandhi

Washington, D.C.

Thomas Clarke sat in the tenth-floor conference room at
Clayton|Swift, staring out the window at the law firm of
Marquise & LeClair across the street. The dark-wood
conference table in front of him had room to accommodate
twenty-four. There were eighteen people at the present
meeting—twelve lawyers, four paralegals, and two interns.
The Wharton Group, as it was called, was the largest
litigation team in the firm's history.

The topic of discussion today was the Wharton appeal.
Of the dozen lawyers present, five did most of the talking.
The rest, including Thomas, stayed silent, their BlackBerrys
keeping track of the seconds that passed on sophisticated
billing software that would be automatically synchronized
with their firm-issued laptops at day's end. The meeting was

critical. The coal company executives were outraged at the jury's verdict and were calling for blood.

No one wanted to believe it had come to this. Clayton's lawyers had played marionette with the judicial system for more than three years, searching for a way to kick the $1 billion wrongful death case out of court or to settle for pennies on the dollar. At all points, the evidence had been against the defense. The blowout at the coal company's mountaintop removal facility in West Virginia had been predicted by activists. The contractor who had pronounced the slurry safely contained in the mining tunnels was under review by the government. And then there was the problem of the kids. Ninety-one of them drowned at their lunch tables by fifty million gallons of blackwater that erupted from the mountainside upslope of their elementary school. The Wharton Group had only one strategy to defeat the families of the dead, and that was to prevent them from ever telling their story to a jury.

The strategy had almost worked. The pressure of litigating against a firm and a coal company with near-infinite resources had driven the plaintiffs to the brink of civil war, and they almost bought Wharton's last-minute offer of settlement. In the end, however, they had stayed the course, and the jury trial when it came was a fait accompli. The only question was how high the verdict would go.

After three grueling weeks, Judge Hirschel sent the jurors out to deliberate. They returned an hour later with a verdict that shocked even the thickest-skinned courtroom veterans:

$300 million in compensatory damages and $600 million in punitives. Nine-tenths of a billion dollars. It was not simply a message. It was a bombshell.

The fallout had been immediate and devastating. Overnight, Wharton's stock lost half its value. But Clayton's strategy was not yet complete. Standing on the courthouse steps, Wharton's chief executive proclaimed his company's innocence and vowed to fight the verdict all the way to the U.S. Supreme Court. In reality, he wanted nothing more than to kick the can down the road. Even if the verdict was ultimately affirmed, the plaintiffs would spend five years waiting for the money to come. By then, who knew how many of them would settle for a song?

Despite the meeting's importance, Thomas had struggled to keep his mind on the appeal. His thoughts had drifted from the kidnapping he'd witnessed in Fayetteville, to Tera Atwood sitting across the table from him, to the school pictures the plaintiffs' attorneys had showed the jury. What he had told his father last night was true: it was hard to like a company that had killed a schoolhouse full of children. On the other hand, liking Wharton was irrelevant to the representation. A lawyer's job was to fight for his client and let others decide what was right and what was wrong.

He tuned in to the conversation when Maximillian Junger stood from his seat at the head of the table. Junger was the managing partner of the litigation division and the leader of the Wharton Group. He was also a personal friend of Thomas's father.

"The appeals team will be led by Mark Blake," Junger said in the oracular voice that had charmed juries for more than thirty years. "He'll be assisted on the briefs by Hans Kristof and a core group of associates."

Junger used a remote control to access a flat-screen television mounted in the wall behind two retracting wood panels. He powered on the unit, and the names of those on the appeals team were displayed. Thomas's heart sank; he was not on the list. He glanced at Tera. Unlike him, she had been selected for the assignment. She smiled at him, but her eyes were sad. Their days of working closely together on the case were over.

Thomas looked back at Junger. "To the rest of you," he was saying, "allow me to extend the firm's thanks for your efforts over the past forty months. The verdict was a disappointment, but as we've discussed, there are many grounds for appeal. If you're not on the appeals team, talk to your supervising partner. We have a number of pending cases that need attention."

Junger glanced at the clock on the wall. The thirty minutes blocked out for the meeting were over. "Thanks for your attendance," he said. "This meeting is adjourned."

Thomas stood up quickly and headed for the door, hoping to escape before he had to face any of the other associates, especially Tera. Max Junger met him in the hallway and walked with him to the elevator. When they were inside, Junger pressed the button for the twelfth floor. Thomas reached for the seventh-floor button, but Junger stopped him.

"It's been a while since we visited," he said. "Why don't we chat in my office?"

Thomas nodded, but his mind raced with the implications of the invitation. A private meeting with Junger was not a propitious sign. Good news was always channeled through the chain of command.

"How is your father?" Junger asked, making conversation.

"He's well," Thomas said, trying to calm his nerves. "He talks about you all the time."

"And uses me as a point of humor, I'm sure," Junger said with a self-deprecating smile. "He's been doing that since law school."

Before he was elevated to the bench, the Judge had been one of Clayton's star litigators and a colleague of Junger's. Years before that, they were classmates at Virginia Law.

The elevator door opened, and Junger led the way through the ornate twelfth-floor lobby and into his office. The room had enough space to accommodate at least fifteen of the cubicles in which associates like Thomas had to work. The walls were cherry-paneled and studded with bookcases and original artwork. It was an intimidating setting in the best of times. In the worst of times, it was suffocating.

"Make yourself comfortable," Junger said, gesturing to a sitting area with an overstuffed couch and wingback chairs. Thomas sat in one of the chairs, and Junger took a seat on the sofa. He crossed his legs and tented his hands, looking at Thomas with his piercing hazel eyes.

"How are you?" he asked. "It was September, wasn't it, when you lost your little girl?"

Thomas took a deep breath and nodded. "I have good days and bad days. It's about what you would expect."

"Hmm." Junger paused reflectively. "When Margie and I lost Morgan, I felt like I was underwater. I had no idea where the surface was."

Thomas had heard the story from his father. Junger's sixteen-year-old daughter had been killed in a head-on collision with a logging truck a decade ago.

"An apt description," Thomas replied, wishing Junger would get on with it.

"Do you know what brought me back, what gave me a sense of purpose again?"

Thomas shook his head.

"It was Margie's idea. She told me I needed to take a break from the firm. I remember laughing at her. When you're a partner, you'll understand: there is never a good time to get away. In the end, though, she didn't leave me much choice. So I called up Bobby Patterson, who was then dean at Virgina, and asked if he could use an old warhorse in the classroom for a year. Teaching was the best decision I could have made. It gave me new life."

Junger fell silent, and Thomas waited for the axe to fall. A clock ticked nearby. It was the only sound in the office, other than the hammering of his heart.

"I spoke to Mark Blake," Junger said, confirming Thomas's suspicions. "He told me about the *Samuelson* case."

Thomas pursed his lips but made no pre-emptive defense.

"My sense is that Mark overreacted, but you have to understand the pressure he's been under, leading the effort in the courtroom. Wharton Coal has paid this firm over twenty million dollars in the course of our representation—a huge fee. Jack Barrows, Wharton's chief, desperately wanted us to keep the jury from seeing that morbid simulation of the blowout. All those computer-generated children running for their lives. The sludge catching up to them. The little markers where the bodies lay, red for boys, blue for girls. It was inflammatory, prejudicial, and predicated on any number of unprovable assumptions. You know the argument. You wrote the brief."

Thomas nodded.

"The *Samuelson* case was the linchpin of Mark's argument. Who can blame him? The judge who wrote the opinion was a friend of Judge Hirschel's. It had all that beautiful language about the dangers of unscientific evidence designed to exploit the jury's passions. As you can imagine, Mark was humiliated when Judge Hirschel told him the Third Circuit had overturned the decision. And Jack Barrows was apoplectic. I think Jack overreacted too. My guess is that the judge would have let the plaintiffs show the simulation to the jury anyway. But Barrows blamed Mark for the fact that the simulation came into evidence."

Junger eyed him closely. "None of this is surprising to you, I imagine."

Thomas shook his head.

"But there's more, and this is confidential. After the verdict was handed down, Barrows threatened to sue the firm for malpractice. The threat is still on the table. Only a few people know that at this stage. We're hopeful the appeal will sort things out."

Thomas blanched. He had no idea the coal company had taken the issue so far.

"In any event," Junger went on, "I'm sure your perspective of what happened is different from Mark's. But none of that matters. Mark has taken a beating, and the client needs to be reassured. There were some who suggested drastic measures, but I intervened. I told them it wasn't your fault. It was the fault of the firm. We made the mistake together." Junger held out his hands magnanimously. "And we have to bear the consequences together."

Junger paused and then changed direction. "Thomas, do you know why I love your father so much?"

"No, sir."

"He's brilliant, yes, and he's loyal and a damn good lawyer and judge. But more than that, he's relentless. He never stops until his work is perfect. I see that same quality in you. I know how much you've devoted to the Wharton case. I admire your tenacity and your skills. But I think it fair to say that your personal circumstances have had an effect on your work product. Wouldn't you agree?"

Thomas thought no such thing. He had told Mark Blake that the *Samuelson* case had been appealed. He told him that the Third Circuit was expected to hand down a decision soon. He strongly advised him to share that fact with Judge Hirschel. In the end, Blake humiliated himself because he was too stubborn to listen. But Thomas couldn't say that. Not to the managing partner. Not with a $900 million verdict and a malpractice suit hanging over their heads.

As much as it galled him, he submitted to Junger's assessment. "I imagine you're right."

Junger nodded. "I don't fault you for it. But the bottom line is that you need a break. So I'm offering you two options. The first is a vacation. I checked. You have over eight weeks saved up. Go to Bermuda or Bali. Sip *mai tais* on the beach. Spend time in the bedroom with Priya. Find your compass again."

Thomas was fuming, but he held his tongue. "And the second option?" he inquired, hoping for a penance he could serve without disappearing from the face of the earth.

Junger smiled. "The second option may suit you better. A parent never gets over the loss of a child. But there are ways to move on with your life. You have to put your mind on something worthwhile."

Junger paused and folded his hands on his knee. "As you know, every year Clayton gives a pro bono scholarship to one of our associates. An all-expenses-paid trip to any corner of the world. Pro bono associates interface with the United Nations, the European Union, and top-flight NGOs. The selection process for the coming year is over, but the partners have agreed to create an honorary scholarship for you. If you want it, that is."

Thomas was stunned. He could almost see Priya smirking at him. A year-long sabbatical with a nonprofit? He felt like a leper.

"I appreciate your sincerity, sir," he said, "but this feels a lot like being sent to Siberia."

Junger shrugged. "Call it whatever you want. The choice is yours."

Thomas took a deep breath and let it out. "Okay, let's say I take your advice and go somewhere for a while. How are you going to spin it in the firm? People will wonder."

Even as he asked the question, Thomas knew the answer.

"We'll tell them you took a leave of absence for personal reasons," Junger said. "Everyone knows about your daughter."

Junger's moves had been perfectly planned. Check and checkmate. "What will happen when I get back?" Thomas asked wearily.

Junger put out his hands. "I will see to it that you are placed on the best assignment the firm has to offer. It won't be long until no one remembers you were gone."

Thomas looked out the window and tried to piece together his shattered pride. "I'll think about it and let you know."

Junger's expression didn't change, but his shoulders relaxed. "That's all I ask."

At six o'clock that evening, Thomas left the offices of Clayton|Swift with no intention of returning for a long time. A freezing rain was falling, and the sidewalks were slick with ice. He avoided the clump of associates headed to happy hour at the Hudson Restaurant & Lounge and caught the Metro at McPherson Square. He got off at Foggy Bottom and hailed a cab into Georgetown. The first snowflakes began to fall as he reached his house.

He left his sodden shoes in the foyer and went upstairs to change. He was about to head back down to the kitchen to fix dinner when his BlackBerry chimed, indicating he had a new e-mail. The message was from Andrew Porter, an old law school classmate and a lawyer at the Justice Department.

Porter had written, *Hey, buddy, we still on for tennis tonight? Seven o'clock at EPTC?*

Thomas kicked himself. He'd scheduled the match a month ago. He toyed with the thought of canceling but quickly decided against it. Playing tennis was far more appealing than moping around.

After scarfing down a tuna sandwich and an apple, he locked the house and crossed the sidewalk to his Audi. The drive into East Potomac Park took longer than expected, thanks to the weather. Porter was waiting for him in the locker room. His friend was slightly shorter and stockier than Thomas, but he was a fitness junkie and his body looked like it was sculpted out of marble.

Porter shook his hand and issued a friendly challenge. "You ready to get slaughtered? Wait till you see my new serve."

"Nice to see you, too," Thomas replied. "Before you run me over, I have to work out a little rust. How long has it been? Two months?"

"Two months for you. A week for me. Clayton doesn't let you have a life, buddy."

"You don't know the half of it."

Thomas changed into his tennis clothes, and then he and Porter took their gear out to the court. The East Potomac Tennis Center was a vast facility with nineteen outdoor courts and five indoor courts enclosed in an inflatable tent affectionately called "the Bubble." Though it was snowing outside, the temperature inside the Bubble was a comfortable seventy degrees.

They made a few laps around the court to loosen their muscles and then went on to stretch.

"So how are the heirs of Larry Flynt?" Thomas asked.

Porter laughed. "Flynt's a choirboy compared to the lowlifes I'm dealing with."

Porter had started his career at the Justice Depatment prosecuting securities fraud cases. The work, however, had been colorless and mind-numbing, and his superiors had quickly learned that if they wished to keep him around, they needed to give him some real action. So they transferred him to the CEOC—the Child Exploitation and Obscenity Section—and gave him the grisly stuff, the child pornography cases. It was the sort of prosecutorial work that most civilized attorneys wouldn't touch. Porter, on the other hand, seemed energized by it.

"Game on," Porter said, retrieving his racket. He walked to the baseline and hit a few warm-up serves before powering a flat serve into the corner of the box.

Thomas whistled appreciatively. "Not bad." He warmed up with a few serves of his own and then walked to the baseline. "Show me what you've got," he said. Balancing on his feet, racket spinning in his hands, he could almost imagine that his life was normal again.

Almost.

They played two sets under the lights, and Porter managed to win only a handful of games. Thomas could tell that the whipping annoyed him, but Porter's good nature never faltered. At the end of the match, they met at the net.

"You're too good," Porter said, clasping Thomas's hand. "I've never seen you hit the ball so hard. You sure you're not taking steroids?"

Thomas laughed. "I just needed to get a little aggression out."

Porter's face turned serious. "How's Priya holding up?"

Thomas weighed his options and decided to trust his friend. He gave Porter a summary of his wife's departure and his conversation with Max Junger.

Porter shook his head. "I'm so sorry to hear about Priya. You guys always seemed to have something special. Any chance you'll get back together?"

"Not likely," Thomas replied.

"The Clayton thing makes me sick," Porter said, changing the subject. "I can't believe the firm sacked you like that. Wharton deserved that verdict. If anything, it wasn't tough enough. For them to threaten malpractice is a complete joke."

"Maybe so, but they've funded the salaries of half of the litigation division this year."

"So what are you going to do?"

Thomas shrugged. "I have no idea. Any advice?"

"If it was me, I'd get the heck out of the District. It's miserable this time of year. And I'd give thought to the sabbatical. Clayton's drained you. I can see it in your eyes."

Porter's assessment was surgical in its accuracy, and Thomas didn't have a ready reply. They sheathed their rackets and headed for the locker room.

"Have you ever heard of a group called CASE?" Thomas asked on the way. "I think they have a connection to the Justice Department."

Porter nodded. "The Coalition Against Sexual Exploitation. They work on trafficking and sexual violence issues in the developing world. The guy who founded the organization was a bigwig at the Civil Rights Division. Why?"

"They were listed on Clayton's pro bono page."

Porter raised an eyebrow. "You're thinking about an internship?"

Thomas shrugged. "Does that surprise you?"

Porter opened the door to the locker room. "Let's just say the brothels of Cambodia are a long way from K Street."

Thomas knew his friend was right. A week ago he wouldn't have given CASE much thought. The trade in human beings was a global tragedy, but like child labor and the AIDS epidemic it was irrelevant to his world. The incident in

Fayetteville had changed that. Abby Davis had made it personal.

Thomas took a seat on a bench. "Something happened to me yesterday," he said by way of explanation. "I witnessed a kidnapping."

Porter stopped unlacing his shoes and looked up. "You're not kidding, are you?"

Thomas shook his head. "The girl was eleven years old."

He gave Porter a summary of the incident and his conversation with the Judge over dinner the night before.

After he finished, Porter was silent for a while. "Your dad may be right about the trafficking angle. It's anyone's guess. But I'd say there's a real chance she'll be sold."

"The detective in Fayetteville mentioned that the feds may get involved." Thomas said.

Porter narrowed his eyes. "It's possible."

"Would your office get a piece of that?"

Porter looked uncomfortable. "Maybe. We've been working on a number of rings in the south-east." He paused. "That's confidential, by the way."

Thomas nodded, understanding his friend's position. "I don't want any details. Do me a favor, though. If you run across her, let me know."

Porter nodded. "Sure. But I wouldn't get your hopes up. I don't see many happy endings in my line of work."

Thomas left Porter in the tennis center parking lot and drove back to Georgetown. When he pulled up to the curb, he saw that his house was brightly lit. He had left in such a hurry that he'd forgotten to turn off the lights. The snow was falling in larger flakes now. Nearly an inch had accumulated while he was away.

He locked his car and walked up the flagstone steps. He didn't hear her until she was next to him, her hand on his arm.

"Hey," Tera said.

He was caught completely off-guard. He looked at her for a long moment, gathering his wits. She was wearing black leather boots, a black-and-white check city coat that reached to her knees, and a crimson scarf. Her ears were adorned with diamond pendants. She was the most fashion-conscious woman he had ever met.

"What are you doing here?" he asked.

"I tried calling, but you were out. I wanted to see you." She spoke softly, deliberately, her eyes never leaving his. She took his hand. "I've missed you."

Thomas stood stiffly for a moment before defaulting to hospitality. "Why don't you come in for a drink?"

They entered the foyer and Tera doffed her coat and scarf. Underneath, she wore a red turtleneck sweater, a gray skirt with dark stockings, and a string of large pearls.

She walked into the kitchen and looked around. She had never been inside before.

"I love these old brownstones," she said. "You did a nice job with the space."

Thomas went to the wine cabinet and selected a bottle

of burgundy. Retrieving the opener from the drawer, he drew out the cork. His motions were mechanical, his heart at war with itself. He couldn't help but be drawn to her.

He poured two glasses of wine and handed her one. They took seats in a nook by the living-room window and watched the snow fall.

"You seem withdrawn," she said. "Are you all right?"

He took a sip of the rich, earthy wine, relishing its calming effect. "I suppose."

"I'm sorry you didn't get assigned to the appeal."

He debated with whether to tell her about Junger, then decided against it. He shrugged.

"The partners do what they want. *C'est la vie.*"

She looked at him strangely. "Something happened. I can tell."

Something is an understatement, he thought.

"I'm okay," he said, preferring a bald-faced lie over the alternative.

"Do you want to talk about it?"

"Not really."

She seemed stymied and sipped at her wine, her earrings sparkling in the lamplight.

"Why are you doing this?" she asked.

"Doing what?"

"Why are you here with me?"

The answer seemed obvious: she had waited for him outside his home. But he sensed that the question had a deeper meaning.

"I don't know," he said. "I like your company."

Her eyes flashed, but he couldn't tell whether it was melancholy or anger.

"Do you want me to leave?" she asked quietly.

There it was, the question of the hour, a question that had no definitive answer. Yes, he wanted her to leave. No, he didn't want her to leave. He wanted his life back, but his life wasn't coming back. He wanted to be free of the haunting he felt in this house. He wanted to feel the warmth of skin on skin, to feel the unity of love transmuted to passion. But the face in his dream wasn't Tera's. It was Priya's, as she was before. The girl who had stolen his heart in the lecture hall at Cambridge while her father, the Professor, talked about quantum physics. The woman who had conceived and borne his child.

Tera put down her glass on a side table and moved toward him. She sat down in his lap, her face inches from his.

"I don't want to leave," she whispered.

She kissed him then and he didn't resist. He forgot about Junger's ultimatum. He forgot about the ghosts of his wife and child. His mind went blank, his heart tranquilized by desire and despair. Only his body was left to act.

But for a moment, his body was enough.

He lay in darkness, Tera asleep beside him. Above them, the ceiling fan swung in lazy arcs, barely stirring the air. He remembered accidentally bumping the switch when Tera had pushed him into the room. He remembered the rest, all of it, with extraordinary vividness, but he couldn't think about it. His conscience had returned, calling him names he deserved.

He slipped out from under the covers, threw on a sweatshirt and flannel pants, and went downstairs. The lights were still on in the kitchen and living room. He turned them off one by one. The only illumination came from a streetlamp that cast a pale glow on the polished wood floor. The snow had stopped, but the ground was white, and he guessed that three inches had fallen. He glanced at his watch. The luminescent hands showed that it was after midnight.

He stood perfectly still, listening to the street sounds. Then he went to the door to the basement and descended the steps. He knew where the box was. He had hidden it himself after she left. He returned to the living room and took a seat in the chair by the window. He could still smell Tera's perfume in the air. He set the box on his knees and lifted the lid. The photographs were in disarray. His objective had been to erase the memories, not curate them.

The first photograph showed Priya in her wedding gown. She was in a garden beside a bench surrounded with flowers. There was an ease in the way she stood, a comfort in her own skin that he had always found appealing. Her eyes were brown, her olive skin a contrast with the white of her dress. She was smiling at something in the distance. Children had been playing on the lawn nearby, he recalled. She had always adored children.

They had married at River Farm, a sprawling estate on

the Potomac south of Alexandria. The ceremony had been the sort of cross-cultural spectacle that had satisfied no one except the bride and groom. After the traditional Christian rites, they had completed their vows with the *saptapadi*, or Seven Steps, around a ceremonial flame. Priya had recited the blessings in Hindi and given herself over to her new life. She had married Thomas over her father's objections. He wondered now whether the decision had cursed them in some way.

He set the photograph aside and picked up the next one in the box. The grief returned as if it had never left. The photograph showed Priya holding a three-month-old Mohini at Rock Creek Park. The little girl and her mother were smiling at one another. It had been their favorite picture of the baby. Her soft skin, blotchy for the first two months, had cleared. Her chocolate-brown eyes were open and she was effervescent with life.

The tears began to flow, but he didn't wipe them away. He thought again of that dreadful morning in September when they had found her. He remembered the shrillness of Priya's scream, remembered running up the stairs and wrestling Mohini from her grasp. He remembered the clammy chill of the baby's face and the intensity of his fear when she didn't respond to CPR. He could still hear the wail of the ambulance pulling up to the curb; he could still smell the antiseptic odor of the emergency room; he could still feel his anger at the sterile efficiency of the doctors as they poked and prodded Mohini's tiny body, searching for the explanation they would never find. The coroner's report had called it SIDS—Sudden Infant Death Syndrome. Mohini had died while they were asleep. Cause unknown.

The resident physician had allowed them to spend fifteen minutes with their baby before sending her to the morgue. Alone in a bare room, Priya took the little girl into her arms and chanted to her in Hindi. Listening to his wife whisper-singing over their daughter's body only heightened Thomas's sense of loss. Eventually, Priya laid Mohini down on a white sheet and kissed her a final time. She turned away and did not look back.

Thomas closed the box of photographs. After a while, he climbed the stairs and opened the door to Mohini's room. The crib stood empty along the wall, the brightly colored mobile keeping watch over it in silence. Everything was as it had been when they put her down to sleep the evening before she died.

He walked over to the crib and rubbed the wooden railing with his fingers. He had built it himself. It wasn't money he had wanted to save, but Priya's opinion of him. He wanted to prove that he could do it—more, that he *wanted* to do it, that his long hours at the office didn't mean he wasn't interested in the baby. He remembered her smile when he had finished. They had made love that night for the first time in many weeks. Her swollen belly got in the way, but they managed. The release had been cleansing, an act of liberation. How different it was with Tera. Every time he touched her, he felt the noose tighten around his neck.

He knelt down before the crib and placed his forehead on the slats. In this posture of supplication, he sang the chorus from "You Are My Sunshine" as he had for Mohini every night of her life. He realized as he sang that the song was actually a prayer, a prayer to the God of children, a prayer for safety and peace. In Mohini's case, the prayer had gone unanswered. Tears came to his eyes again, and he whispered the words he never ceased to feel.

"I'm sorry, sweet girl. I'm sorry I didn't come for you. I didn't know."

He left Mohini's room and entered his office. He powered up his laptop and opened his Web browser. He thought about Junger's two options. He ran a Google search for a Bahamian island he had read about in a magazine. The photos were inspiring. Beaches lined with palms, iridescent water lapping at white sand. He imagined himself with a piña colada, watching the sun set. Then he tried to imagine the rest. He would be alone. He couldn't spend all day reading. He would quickly tire of the resort life. As much as he hated to admit it, Junger was right. A vacation would be a black hole. He needed a reason to get out of bed in the morning.

He closed the window and saw that he had two new messages in his e-mail account. The first message was from his mother. She had sent it a few hours before. The subject header was blank, but that wasn't surprising. Elena had never quite figured out her computer.

She had written:

Thomas, I had a thought today that you can take or leave. You said that Priya is not coming back, but you didn't mention divorce. If that was an oversight, then ignore this. If not, then consider: what if you followed her to India? What if you gave your marriage one last chance? I know it sounds crazy. She might reject you. You might come home a failure. But at least then you would have the closure I didn't hear in your voice. There is always time to build a career. Love is a much rarer thing. Your father probably wouldn't agree with me, but it doesn't matter. It was good to see you yesterday.

Thomas was astonished. The idea of following Priya had never occurred to him, and now that it did, he saw in it only potential for disaster. True, Priya hadn't mentioned divorce, but her exit had been so premeditated, so cold and devoid of feeling, that he had never questioned her intent. Indeed, it was that very sense of finality that had driven him into Tera's arms. And therein lay another problem. Even if by some chance Priya had meant to leave the door open to reconciliation, there was no way to undo what he had done since her departure. He had been unfaithful. Tera was asleep in their bed. His broken vows were an indictment against him.

He closed his mother's message and opened the next one. It was from Andrew Porter.

Hey buddy, I gotta say I'm still smarting from being so thrashed by you, but I deserve it. I always know I'm going to lose, but I keep coming back anyway. Listen, I hope you don't mind, but I called a friend of mine at CASE (she's the deputy director of operations), and I asked her whether they had any openings for legal interns right now. You'll never guess what she said. A slot just opened up in their Bombay office. Crazy, huh? Don't know if you'd be interested, what with Priya being there, but I thought I'd pass it along. Let me know if you want to explore this.

Thomas sat back in his chair and stared out the window at the night sky, aglow with light pollution. *Bombay!* The idea was absurd. Clayton's pro bono program was as wide as the world. Europe, South America, China, Africa—his options were unlimited. And even if he wanted to work with CASE, the organization had offices in fourteen countries. He might have to wait, but something would open up. *Bombay!* It was the last place on earth he should search for peace.

He left the laptop open and wandered through the house. He scoured the refrigerator for nothing in particular; he reorganized the wine rack by region; he watched a few minutes of a John Wayne rerun on television. After a while, he collapsed in the chair by the window and picked up the box of memories again.

He sifted through the photographs, finding the one he was looking for near the bottom. He had trimmed it to fit in his wallet. The photograph showed Priya at the entrance to Fellows Garden. They had met there many times during his summer at Cambridge, always in secret, away from her father. Priya smiled back at him across the years, her eyes sparkling with mischief and delight. Love had surprised them both. It had been such a weighty thing. Was there actually a chance that they could find it again?

Sometime during the wee hours of the morning, Thomas finally conceded. He stopped his pacing and walked slowly toward the stairs, compelled by a purpose he couldn't begin to understand. He returned to the computer and sent two e-mails.

To Porter he wrote: *Set up a meeting. I'm free any time.*

And to Max Junger: *I've decided to take your advice. I'm thinking about going to India to work with CASE. I hope Mark Blake and Wharton are satisfied.*

He entered the bedroom and looked at Tera asleep on Priya's side of the bed. Her back was to him, and her hair had fallen over her face. This was the last time, he decided. It wasn't her fault. She had been kind to him. But the charade had gone on long enough. He would tell her in the morning. She would be angry, but she would survive. He, on the other hand, was ready to commit himself. India? The fight against modern slavery? Facing his wife again?

How in the world was he going to explain this to his father?

Chapter 5

Darkness—black and painted—has come over me.
O Dawn, banish it like a debt.

—Rig Veda

Mumbai, India

After a few days in Suchir's brothel, Ahalya and Sita began
to lose touch with time. Each day took on the rhythm of
India's year, its two seasons defined by the presence and
absence of the sun. Day was benign and filled with all things
domestic—the chatter of the girls occupying the floor below,
the diverse sounds of commerce drifting up from the street.
Night, by contrast, was malignant, a soundscape of pounding
feet, drunken shouts, squeals of seduction and protestation,
and incessant moaning.

The girls had few visitors during those first days. Sumeera
came to check on them and brought their meals. Ahalya tried
to hate her, but the animosity was difficult to sustain. Sumeera
spoke softly, without any hint of command, and treated them
like daughters.

One morning she brought a doctor along to examine them. At first Ahalya resisted the gynecologist's probing, but Sumeera said the examination was routine. All young women in Bombay had it. Ahalya thought of Suchir and agreed so as not to invite his wrath. Sita, seeing her sister capitulate, was quick to follow, though the examination caused her obvious shame and pain.

After the girls had been poked and prodded, Sumeera spoke in low tones to the doctor.

"You are both healthy," she said, clasping her hands together. "We want you to stay that way. You will see the doctor once a month. Treat him well."

When Sumeera was not present, the sisters searched the attic room for a means of escape. The room was a rough square, fourteen feet by thirteen. It had no window, only two small exhaust vents. The only door locked from the outside. Beyond it lay a stairwell with no exit except through the concealed door behind the bookcase. Ahalya had no doubt that the secret door could only be activated from the other side.

After many fruitless attempts, she sat on the floor beside Sita and stroked her hair.

"There has to be a way out," she said.

"But where would we go?" Sita whispered. "We are strangers in Bombay."

Ahalya had no answer. Each night, she lay awake, listening to the sounds drifting up from below. Her imagination turned her into an insomniac. She thought of the girls and the men who visited them. She was a virgin, but she was not naive. She understood the mechanics of sex. She knew what women had that men wanted. What she couldn't comprehend was why a man would pay a prostitute, or *beshya*, for sex.

As the days dragged by, Ahalya began to wonder if Suchir would ever come for them. It was Friday, three days after their arrival, and no man had been brought to their room. Ahalya's only explanation was that the brothel owner was planning something for them. The thought of it terrified her. Sometimes when she heard Suchir's voice through the floorboards, a wave of vertigo came upon her. Her only remedy was to lie flat on her back. Sita worried over her, but Ahalya blamed the heat. Inside, however, her heart was consumed with fear.

The hour came when Ahalya least expected it. It was in the middle of the night on New Year's Eve, and she had been drifting in and out of sleep. The sounds of festivity were everywhere on the street, and the moans coming from downstairs struggled to keep pace. The doorknob turned without a sound, but the hinges creaked and startled her awake. The light came on suddenly and Sumeera stood at the foot of the bed holding a burlap sack.

"Wake up, children," she said nervously. "It's time to dress."

Ahalya's heart began to pound, but she knew better than to ask questions. She could still feel the sting of the young man's hand on her cheek the morning they arrived. Sumeera held out a beautiful crimson and gold *churidaar* and directed Ahalya to put it on. She gave Sita a *sari* the color of peacock feathers. Bangles came next and then anklets. Sumeera brushed the girls' hair and adorned it with garlands. Then she applied a light coat of foundation and thin black eyeliner. Standing back, she appraised them.

After a moment, Suchir appeared at the doorway and grunted his approval.

"Come," he said. "Shankar is waiting."

The sisters descended the steps behind Sumeera and Suchir and entered the hallway. There were perhaps twenty girls in the narrow space. Some were leaning against walls; others were sitting on the floor in open door frames. A few snickered when they appeared, but the rest were watchful. To Ahalya's surprise, most of the *beshyas* were plain looking. Only two or three could pass for pretty, and only one girl was truly beautiful.

Ahalya caught a few whispers as she walked past.

"Fifty thousand," a tall girl guessed.

"More," said her neighbor.

Suchir silenced them with a glare. He directed Sita to wait at the door and then ushered Sumeera and Ahalya into the brothel lobby. A man sat on one of the couches facing the mirror. He was forty-something, with a head of black curls and a gold watch on his wrist. He eyed Ahalya appraisingly while Suchir pulled the window shades. Sumeera, meanwhile, took her seat on the other couch and bowed her head.

Suchir flipped a switch, and a bank of recessed bulbs installed above the mirror flooded the room with light. In a gentle voice, he directed Ahalya to stand beneath the glare and to look at the man. Ahalya obeyed for a brief moment, and then her eyes fell to the floor.

"Shankar, my friend," said the brothel owner, "I have something delectable for you tonight. Two girls—both sealed pack. This is the older one."

Shankar murmured his delight. He stood up and walked toward Ahalya. He admired her skin, touched her hair, and grazed her left breast with the back of his hand.

"*Ravas*," he said with a sigh. "Magnificent. I do not need to see more. Save the other girl for another day. How much for this one? With no condom."

"Condoms are required," Suchir replied. "You know the rule."

Shankar shrugged. "Rules are worthless. How much do you want?"

Suchir seemed to hesitate, but then quickly conceded. "For a girl like this, sixty thousand, and only this time."

"Suchir, you drive a hard bargain," Shankar said. "I came only with fifty thousand in bills."

"You can visit the ATM," Suchir rejoined. "The girl is worth every rupee."

Shankar stepped back. "Sixty thousand. I will pay you the rest afterward." He handed a wad of thousand-rupee notes to Suchir.

Suchir looked at Sumeera. "Take them upstairs," he said.

"And keep the other girl in the stairwell. It will be a good lesson for her."

While the men negotiated, Ahalya stood in a state of near paralysis. In the harsh embrace of the stage lights, she felt transported. Her heart hammered in her chest, and she felt a prickly sensation begin at the base of her neck and wind its way downward. She didn't think of Shankar as a man. She imagined him as a ghost, a spirit from the underworld. A ghoul could not deflower her. Yet she knew the trick of her mind was foolish. He was a man like any other.

When she heard Suchir's directive about Sita, she looked up, horrified but unable to speak. Fear had absconded with the remains of her defiance. She would allow Shankar to have her so that Sita would learn not to resist. For resistance, she now understood, meant pain, and pain accentuated the misery of this beggar's existence. After tonight, she would be *awara*, a fallen one. The bridge into prostitution had only one direction.

"*Bolo na, tum tayor ho?*" Sumeera asked her. "Tell me now, are you ready?"

Ahalya nodded. She allowed Shankar to take her hand and lead her into the hallway. She couldn't bring herself to look at Sita. As Shankar drew her up the stairs, she thought of her father. He had taught her that she was strong, that the sky was the limit of her talents, and that she could be anything she wanted to be. It was a beautiful idea, but ill-fated. She thought of her mother as Sumeera fluffed the pillows and lit a candle. Ambini had been gentle and dignified, a role model to emulate. They were dead now, both of them, their bodies strewn like driftwood upon the ruin of a beautiful beach. All that remained was *jooth ki duniya*, a world of lies.

Sumeera left her with Shankar and closed the door. Ahalya stared at a spot on the floor, trembling. She could not bring herself to look at the man who had bought her. He approached her and lifted her chin until she met his eyes. He smiled at her as he unbuttoned his pants.

"Tonight is your wedding night," he said and pushed her back on the bed.

Sita sat in the darkness of the stairwell, weeping at the sounds of her sister's violation. In her fifteen years, she had acquired little knowledge of carnal desire, but she understood the meaning of rape. When the sounds of Shankar's pleasure finally ended, she heard her sister begin to cry. After a moment, Shankar appeared at the door and brushed past her. His eyes were glazed and his clothing was disheveled. He didn't speak; he simply disappeared.

Sita crept into the room. Her sister lay on the bed in a tangle of sheets, her *churidaar* in a heap on the floor. The candle flame cast dancing shadows on the walls. Ahalya's eyes were closed and her forehead was hot to the touch. Sita kissed her cheek and knelt at the bedside. Sumeera soon appeared and led Ahalya to the commode. She washed her and clothed her in a loose-fitting nightshirt. Then she returned her to the bed.

Sumeera spoke soothingly to Ahalya. "What you have experienced is difficult. The shame is natural. All feel it the first time. But you will survive. You will learn to accept it."

With that, she left them alone.

Sita undressed and slipped into bed, cradling Ahalya in her arms. Her sister had always been her fortress, her protector. In the loneliest nights at St. Mary's, Ahalya had never failed to comfort her. During the tsunami, she had positioned herself between Sita and the waves. Now it was Sita's turn to comfort and protect. She began to hum a song their mother used to sing to them. She knew the tune by heart, and she sang it with the passion of a prayer.

Ahalya woke on New Year's Day like a bird with a shattered wing. She spoke, but the joy was gone from her voice. She ate breakfast without a comment on the food. She received Sumeera's visits without a word. During the hours of day when the vendors on the street hawked their wares and the *beshyas* downstairs performed their chores, she lay on the bed, staring into space. She turned over on occasion, but she rarely sat up.

The *adda* lost texture in her mind; its sights and sounds became sensory impulses and vague impressions. Only Sita remained in focus. Ahalya was surprised at the extent of her younger sister's poise. It seemed that she matured years in the span of days. She wet a cloth and placed it on Ahalya's forehead. She sang songs that Ambini and Jaya had taught them and quoted verses from Ahalya's favorite poetry. When she recited a poem by Sarojini Naidu, Ahalya began to mouth the words along with her.

> *Here, O my heart, let us burn the dreams that are dead,*
> *Here in this wood let us fashion a funeral pyre,*
> *Of fallen white petals and leaves that are mellow and red,*
> *Here let us burn them in noon's flaming torches of fire.*

The rest of the weekend passed in relative solitude, and Suchir left them alone. Where Shankar had abraded Ahalya's skin, Sumeera applied ointment as a salve. Over and over again she repeated the refrain that Ahalya had to accept what had happened to her. There was no other way out of the tunnel of shame. Ahalya became more active with the rising of each new sun, but her eyes were wells of sorrow.

Early the following week, Suchir came for Ahalya again. Sumeera provided the same red and gold *churidaar* for her to wear, but she didn't ask Sita to dress. Ahalya closed her eyes and went through the motions in silence. The *beshyas* lined the walls to watch her, but this time they were not quiet. As she passed, two of them guessed the price Suchir would charge for her.

"Twenty thousand," one of them said.

"Ten," said another. "She is already used. The *dhoor* will see no blood."

Ahalya tried to ignore their words and kept her eyes locked

on the ground. She waited at the door until Suchir summoned her and then stood under the lights like a circus spectacle. Two customers sat on the cushions adjacent to Sumeera. One was middle-aged and the other was a boy no older than her. The man spoke excitedly to the youth, and she learned from his words that he was the man's son. It was the boy's birthday. Ahalya was his gift.

The boy stood hesitantly and approached her. He glanced at his father for reassurance, and the man urged him on. The boy touched Ahalya's lips with his fingertips and traced a line down to her chest. She shivered and wondered what the boy would do with her.

The man haggled with Suchir over the price and finally agreed upon fifteen thousand rupees. The boy took her hand and followed Suchir to the first sex room along the hall. An overweight older girl stepped aside and glared at her. The room was tiny, large enough only to accommodate a bed, a sink, and a toilet. Its purpose was entirely functional. This was the lot of all who were *awara*, Ahalya thought to herself. It was her destiny to live in perpetual shame.

When Suchir closed the door, the boy stood stiffly, unsure how to proceed. In his eyes, Ahalya saw a mixture of awe and apprehension. He moved closer and kissed her mouth. His excitement grew when she didn't resist. She lay back on the bed and submitted to his desires. He wasn't as rough as Shankar, but still he caused her pain.

Afterward, she lay on the thin mattress, staring at the ceiling and feeling profoundly unclean. She got up from the bed and washed herself at the sink. Sitting on the toilet, she realized the brute fact of her existence. A *beshya* could expect nothing more from life than air in her lungs, food and water in her stomach, a roof over her head, and the affections of her kind. To survive in such a world, she would have to sever her heart from her body. She had no other option. She thought of Sita, waiting for her in the upper room, fearful, wounded, yet somehow still inviolate after a week and a half in Suchir's brothel. Sita needed her to be a bulwark against the terrors that awaited her.

She couldn't allow herself to surrender to despair.

Chapter 6

The Battle of Bombay is the battle of the self
against the crowd.

—Suketu Mehta

Somewhere over South Asia

When Thomas awoke, he had no idea what time it was. He
looked at his watch and realized it was still displaying D.C.
time. The cabin of the Boeing 777 was dark, and most of
the passengers in business class were asleep. He needed to
use the restroom, but the passenger next to him was out
cold, his seat fully extended, blocking access to the aisle.

Thomas raised the window shade. The sun was setting
over snow-crusted mountains, painting them shades of ochre
and henna. *Afghanistan*, he thought. From thirty-five thousand
feet, the war-torn land reminded him of Colorado. Its beauty
was striking, at once severe and serene.

For the hundredth time, Thomas asked himself why he
was doing this. The obvious answer—that he had been
railroaded into it by guilt and circumstance—was no longer

adequate. He could have been on a flight to Bora Bora, Amsterdam, or Shanghai. As it was, he was two hours away from landing in Bombay, his briefcase stuffed with every government report, academic study, and news clipping on the worldwide crisis of forced prostitution he had been able to get his hands on.

He had planned his departure in a whirlwind; it wasn't in his nature to procrastinate. Lunch on the Hill with Ashley Taliaferro, CASE's director of field operations, between briefings she had scheduled with congressional supporters. An expedited visa appointment, courtesy of Max Junger. A trip to the mall to shop for travel gear. Updating his immunizations. Arranging with Clayton to deposit his pro bono stipend into his bank account to cover his bills. Exchanging e-mails with Dinesh—his roommate at Yale—and accepting his long-standing invitation to visit Bombay. And reading, reading, incessantly reading—on the Metro, waiting in the checkout line, and at home between research sessions on the Internet.

In the trafficking literature, he entered a world as astonishing as it was troubling, a subterranean realm inhabited by pimps and traffickers, corrupt officials, crusading lawyers, and a seemingly endless supply of women and children captured, brutalized, and transformed into slaves. He wondered how Porter was able to cope with it—the faces, the names, the stories of abuse as diverse as human cruelty. And now he was about to enter that world. Of the many cities known for the trade in human flesh, Bombay was among the worst.

"You're going to be doing *what*?" his mother had asked when Thomas had taken a break long enough to make the call. "But that's *dangerous*, Thomas. You could get hurt. I said you should follow *Priya*, not get yourself mixed up with the underworld."

At that point his father had taken the phone and asked what all the fuss was about. He listened only long enough to learn of Max Junger's ultimatum. "Why didn't you call me, Son?" he had asked. "I would have gotten this cleared up."

"Clayton needed a fall guy, Dad," Thomas said, feeling like the not-quite-grownup he had always been in his father's eyes. "Wharton demanded a sacrificial lamb, and Mark Blake wasn't about to put himself on the altar."

"Mark Blake is an egomaniac and a fool," the Judge replied angrily. "The man can't argue his way out of a paper bag." He ranted a while longer and then calmed down. "Did I hear your mother right? You're going to India to work with CASE?"

"That's right."

His father had been silent for a long moment. "When you get back, you're going to have a lot of catching up to do."

"I know," Thomas said. On such matters, the Judge was always right.

Turning his mind back to the present, Thomas watched a flight attendant walk down the aisle toward him. When she noticed he was awake, she asked him in a whisper whether he had any interest in a pre-arrival meal. He shook his head and asked for a bottle of water.

He looked out the window again. Darkness had fallen over the rugged land, but the crest of clouds was still tinged with light. Again, he pondered the unanswerable question: why?

Tera had been the first to ask it out loud. The morning after her surprise visit, he had awoken on the couch in the living room with a pounding headache and a powerful sense of remorse. After a hot shower, he'd met her in the kitchen, and she had offered to make him breakfast. He had looked at her strangely. She had never stayed overnight before. Yet here she was wielding a whisk, a carton of eggs beside the stove.

"I'm going away for a while," he said.

"What?" she asked, the whisk suspended in her hand. She blinked. "Where?"

"I'm not sure," he replied, preferring to lie than to elicit more questions.

She looked wounded. "What about Clayton?"

"I'm taking a leave of absence."

"For how long?"

"A while, I imagine."

"Did I do something wrong?" she asked, putting the whisk down on the countertop.

"Of course not," he responded and then realized how insensitive he sounded. "Look, I know it's abrupt, but it really isn't about you. I'm sorry."

It was at that point she had spoken the riddle. "Why are you doing this?"

He thought of any number of responses but decided on the simplest. "I don't know."

She had stared at him for a moment, blue eyes fraught with confusion and pain. Her mouth hung open, but she didn't speak. Instead, she gathered her things and left the house without another word.

"Ladies and gentlemen," said the disembodied voice, "we have begun our descent into Bombay. Please make sure your seatbacks and tray tables . . ."

The voice droned on, but Thomas didn't pay attention. Looking out the window, he saw the sprawling metropolis rise out of the void like a brilliant starburst. The sight reminded him of Los Angeles, but there the comparison ended. Bombay had three times the population in a landmass one-third the size.

Thomas's nerves were on edge as the plane made its final descent toward Chhatrapati Shivaji International Airport. Over the years, Priya had tutored him in the Indian mind and its sensibilities and had tried, with little success, to teach him Hindi. But that education had taken place on Western soil. The city beyond the tarmac was the real India, an alien world defined by a radically different set of cultural expectations. Colonialism and globalization had built bridges across the chasm, but the divide between East and West remained immense.

The aircraft touched down gently and taxied to the gate. The real India greeted him before he got off the plane. From his window, he could see a vast warren of slums, lit only by a network of bare bulbs strung doorway to doorway like Christmas lights. Children played in the streets and people were moving about in the shadows. Thomas watched the slum children with fascination. The West had its ghettos and barrios, but nothing like this.

After collecting his luggage, he met Dinesh at the taxi stand.

"Thomas!" his friend exclaimed in lightly accented English, wrapping him in a bear hug. "Welcome to Bombay!"

Dinesh took the second of Thomas's suitcases and led him through a dense crowd of *taxi-wallas* and placard-wielding hotel chauffeurs to a black coupe sitting in a dirt parking lot.

"I hope you don't mind being cramped."

"Not a problem," Thomas said, piling his luggage in the trunk and climbing in.

The night air was cool and dry, and Dinesh rolled down the windows. "We get two months with no air-conditioning," he said with a laugh. "The rest of the year we sweat."

Dinesh navigated the car out of the airport and into the chronic congestion of city traffic. For long minutes, they inched through the gridlock, crowded on all sides by vehicles large and small and choked by exhaust fumes. Eventually, Dinesh grew weary of the exercise and nosed his way toward the median. Flooring the accelerator and laying on the horn, he used the opposite lane to dodge around an auto-rickshaw, barely missing a collision with a bus. Thomas gripped the door handle, appalled by the maneuver.

Dinesh laughed. "You'll get used to it. In America, you drive with the steering wheel. In India, you drive with the horn."

He took a ramp onto an expressway where traffic moved more freely. "This is the Western Express Highway," he shouted above the wind. "The streets were so crazy the city decided to build the highway above them."

Ten minutes later they rounded a bend and paralleled a wide bay. The odor of urine and brine hit Thomas like a sledgehammer.

"Mahim Bay," Dinesh said. "The stink is another thing you'll get used to."

"Is it always like this?" Thomas asked, struggling to breathe.

"It's bad tonight. In the morning it will be better. The sewers run into the ocean. You don't want to swim anywhere in Bombay."

The highway did a 180-degree turn and dead-ended in an upscale residential neighborhood. Dinesh drove the car up a hill and took a stone-paved ramp that let them out onto a street lined with tall apartment buildings and lush vegetation.

"This is Mount Mary," he said. "The ocean is a block to the west."

Dinesh made a sudden turn into a parking lot at the base

of a ten-story stucco building. Two watchmen sat in chairs on either side of the gate, smoking cigarettes.

They parked in a garage and took an old accordion-door elevator to the top floor. From the grime coating the public spaces, the building looked as if it had been built forty years ago and never touched again.

Dinesh's apartment, by contrast, was a marvel of modern style. The fixtures were polished brass, the furnishings wood and leather, the floor was tiled and covered with rugs, and the walls were adorned with tapestries. The best part of the apartment, however, was the view. The windows along the western wall afforded a stunning perspective of the Arabian Sea, and French doors led onto a wrap-around balcony.

Dinesh showed Thomas his bedroom and invited him to share a beer on the terrace. They took seats on wooden deck chairs and looked out at the sea sparkling in the moonlight. The lights along the coastline extended far to the north and reached their terminus at a point that seemed to jut out into the sea.

"Santa Cruz West is first and then Juhu," Dinesh said, following the direction of his friend's gaze. "Many Indian celebrities live here." He paused. "So tell me, what brings you to Bombay? I heard from a friend that Priya is back, and then I received a message from you saying you need a place to stay for a while."

"It's a long story," Thomas said.

"All good stories are."

Thomas hesitated. He knew he owed his friend an explanation, but the thought of answering probing questions about his family made him weary.

"Priya's grandmother had a stroke," he began. "She came here to be with her."

"I hadn't heard that," Dinesh replied. "I saw her brother in Colaba a couple of months ago. He didn't say anything."

"It happened recently. No one expected it."

He thought back to the day Priya had delivered the news. He remembered how exhausted she looked, standing in the kitchen telling him about her brother's phone call. He was three days into the Wharton trial, and his stress level was at an all-time high. When she showed him the one-way Air India ticket, he reacted badly and accused her of abandoning him. He remembered the fury that had burned in her eyes. "How can you say that?" she had asked. "You're the one who abandoned me."

Dinesh took a sip of his beer. "So that explains Priya. What about you?"

Thomas took a breath. "I needed a break from work. The firm let me take a sabbatical." He saw his friend's eyes narrow and imagined him thinking: *Then why are you staying with me?* He decided to season the lie with a morsel of truth. "Things aren't great with Priya right now. That's why I got in touch with you."

Dinesh studied him for a long moment and then shrugged. "I'm sorry to hear that. You're welcome here as long as you like." He changed direction. "You mentioned in your e-mail a group called CASE. I've not heard of them before."

Thomas let out the breath he was holding. "They're a legal aid organization. They combat forced prostitution in the developing world."

Dinesh finished off the last of his beer. "I imagine Bombay keeps them busy."

They chatted for a while longer with the ease of old friends, reminiscing about their years at Yale, swapping stories about girlfriends past, and laughing at the pranks that they—usually Dinesh—had played on their classmates. Dinesh's wit and irresistible good humor lifted Thomas's spirits and left him with a sense of optimism about his presence in Bombay. If nothing else came of it, he would enjoy rooming with his friend again.

After a while, Dinesh yawned and stretched out his arms. "I think I'm going to turn in," he said, standing with his empty beer bottle. "It's great to have you here."

Thomas stood as well. "If you don't mind, I'm going to stay out here for a while. My body still thinks it's daytime."

Dinesh laughed. "Sure. I'll see you in the morning."

Thomas took out his BlackBerry and sent e-mails to his mother and Andrew Porter, informing them of his arrival. Then he walked to the railing and looked north toward Juhu Beach. His thoughts drifted to Priya. He wondered if she was asleep or if, like him, she was standing on a terrace somewhere looking at the sea.

He took a deep breath of the salt-laden air and tried to

imagine her childhood. The privilege of her upbringing had never seemed quite real to him. She had been born into a family of Gujarati real-estate magnates who had settled in the city when the British were still reclaiming land from the sea. Her grandfather owned something like a quarter of the apartments in South Bombay, along with diverse holdings around the world.

With any other parents, Priya might have turned snooty and pretentious. But her father had chosen a life of austerity at Cambridge over the luxuries to which his birth entitled him. Professor Patel had transplanted his family to England when Priya was a teenager, and she had spent the formative years of her adolescence among the ivy and stone of the Old Campus.

It was at Cambridge that she had matriculated as an undergraduate in art history. And it was there, a year from her tripos, that Thomas had met her on a summer exchange from Yale. He remembered the lecture her father had delivered at King's College and the umbrella she had left behind. Her absentmindedness had given him an excuse for an introduction, and the introduction had turned into a coffee-shop conversation that altered the course of their lives.

He took out the picture he had taken of her in Fellows Garden, which he had restored to his wallet before he left for the airport. He remembered the way she had kissed him in the shadow of the old gnarled oak. It had been a shy kiss, laden with the taboos of her culture and the memory of her father. But the fact that she did it at all had revealed the depth of her feelings for him.

He put away the photograph and drained the last of his beer. "*Namaste*, Bombay," he said, looking out over the city. Then he turned and went inside.

The next morning, he awoke to the alarm on his BlackBerry. It was seven thirty and the sky was yellow with smog. He checked his inbox and found two e-mails. The first was from Ashley at CASE informing him that he had passed his background check and introducing him to Jeff Greer, the director of the Mumbai field office. The second was from Greer himself, inviting him to meet him at Café Leopold for coffee at ten o'clock.

He found Dinesh in the kitchen brewing a pot of chai. They ate breakfast on the terrace overlooking the sea. Thomas told Dinesh about his appointment with Greer.

"Perfect," his friend said. "You can come with me to work and catch a cab from there. All the *taxi-wallas* know how to get to Leopold."

At eight o'clock, Dinesh hailed an auto-rickshaw to the Bandra railway station. The rick resembled a squat yellow beetle on wheels. The unmuffled engine sounded like a chainsaw. When the driver entered a swarm of identical ricks along Hill Road, Thomas fought the temptation to plug his ears.

The ride to the station was a riot of near collisions. The driver was either the boldest man on earth or a complete lunatic. He used the horn with fanatical persistence, as if the noise would shield them from the dangers of his driving.

"This man is insane," Thomas shouted to his friend over the wind and the engine.

Dinesh laughed. "By that standard, so is every other rick driver in Bombay."

At the train station, they bought first-class tickets and followed a steady stream of passengers to the platform. When the train came in, it was so packed with bodies that men were hanging from the cars by their fingertips, yet the crowd surged forward, undeterred.

Dinesh grabbed Thomas and pushed him forward. "Go, go, go," he said, the sound of his voice almost completely drowned out in the stampede.

Reaching the car in front of them was a miracle; finding room in the compartment a certain impossibility. Then, at once, he was inside and the car was moving beneath him. People ran along the platform, and unbelievably, a few more souls clambered aboard.

Dinesh took delight in Thomas's discomfort. "I bet you thought first class would be more civilized," he shouted.

Thomas thought to laugh, but his chest was so compressed that it came out like a grunt.

"The only difference between the classes," Dinesh explained, "is that in second class we abuse one another in Marathi. In first class, we abuse one another in English."

The train lumbered southward, its destination Churchgate Station at the end of the line. Fifteen minutes later, it entered the terminal in the heart of the city's commercial center. Before the train stopped, the crowd swept them out of the car and along the platform like leaves in a swift-moving stream. Thomas followed Dinesh to the exit and took a deep breath when they emerged on the street.

"How do you do that every day?" he asked.

His friend shrugged and waggled his head from side to side—a gesture Thomas soon realized meant just about anything an Indian wanted it to mean.

"There is only one rule in Bombay," Dinesh said. "You have to learn to adjust."

Dinesh worked as an investment analyst at the main branch of the Hongkong and Shanghai Banking Corporation, which was a short walk from the train station. He bought Thomas a guide to the city from a street vendor and waved down a taxi. He spoke a few words in rapid-fire Marathi and then grinned at Thomas.

"If you get lost, tell anyone that you need to get to Leopold. But you won't get lost."

Thomas climbed in, and the taxi pulled back into traffic. A few minutes later, the *taxi-walla* dropped him off in front of the red marquee of Café Leopold. Thomas fished in his pocket for some spare rupees. He checked the meter and paid the fare.

The café was airy and spacious. Its tables were half-full of patrons, most of whom looked to be Europeans. He took a seat by the street. Greer showed up a few minutes after ten. He wore khaki pants, a rumpled oxford shirt with the sleeves rolled up, and leather shoes that badly needed a shine. He moved without haste, his physique neither trim nor fat. His brown eyes were intelligent and he smiled easily.

"Thomas?" he said, extending his hand. "Jeff Greer. Great to meet you."

"Likewise."

Greer took a seat at the table and ordered a cup of coffee when the waiter appeared.

"What's good here?" Thomas asked, eyeing the drinks menu.

"Just about everything. But if you don't need the caffeine, I'd suggest a *lassi*."

Thomas took the recommendation and placed his order. Then they chatted for a while. Thomas learned that Jeff was thirty-five, unmarried, and a graduate of Harvard Business School and had been with CASE in Bombay for two years. He was a good listener and a winsome conversationalist, and Thomas warmed to him quickly.

"So Bombay," Jeff said. "How do you like it?"

"It seems less like a city than a thrill ride."

Greer laughed. "It takes a while to get used to."

The waiter arrived with their drinks. Thomas took a sip of the *lassi*. It tasted like light custard and lingered pleasantly on the tongue.

"Did you read the dossier Ashley gave you?" Greer asked.

"Twice," Thomas replied.

"So you understand your job description."

Thomas nodded. "The investigators get all the sexy work, and the lawyers push paper."

Greer laughed. "That about sums it up. Our attorneys aren't allowed to appear in court, but they can file briefs on behalf of the victims. That's what you'll be spending most of your time doing—reviewing, drafting, and filing briefs."

"Do we ever get to leave the office?" Thomas asked.

"What do you mean?"

"I mean, do we ever get to see what the investigators see?"

Greer thought about this. "What are your plans for the rest of the morning?"

"I was hoping you would give me some."

Greer smiled. "I think I can handle that."

After paying the check, Greer flagged down a cab and spoke a few unintelligible words in Marathi to the *taxi-walla*. The driver gave him a strange look. Greer repeated himself, this time more emphatically. Shaking his head, the driver pulled into traffic.

"So where are we going?" Thomas asked.

"I'm going to give you a glimpse of why you're here," Greer replied.

The taxi took them north out of Colaba and past the massive Victoria Terminus train station before merging onto Mohammed Ali Road. Thomas expected Greer to give him a briefing on their destination, but the field office director was content to ride in silence. Thomas rolled down his window, seeking relief from the heat. The city air was smog-choked and smelled of burning rubber, but the breeze compensated for the stench.

Twenty minutes later, the taxi left the highway and turned west along a crowded commercial boulevard. The driver spoke in rapid Marathi, trying to convince Greer of something. Greer held up his hands and spoke with calm deliberateness. He passed the *taxi-walla* a hundred-rupee bill and delivered concise instructions. The driver pocketed the money and didn't speak again.

They took a tributary road and made a series of turns, each road narrower than the last. The First World city of swarming sidewalks and flashy billboards had vanished. In its place, the Third World had emerged in a jungle of unpaved lanes and ramshackle buildings, bullock carts, cows, and street children.

Greer spoke a few words to the *taxi-walla* and passed him more money. The taxi slowed and turned onto a dirt road lined with dilapidated houses and multi-story *chawls* with rickety balconies. Except for a handful of bicyclists and cart-pushing vendors, there was almost no traffic on the road. The pedestrians and vehicles that thronged the nearby lanes seemed to avoid this street, giving it an eerie, abandoned look.

"This is Kamathipura," Greer said. "The largest red-light district in Bombay."

Greer's words gave Thomas new eyes. Suddenly, the old men lounging in the shade were not geriatrics but brothel owners. The young men smoking in shadowy doorways were not vagrants but pimps. The women wielding brooms in hallways and kitchens were not housewives but madams.

"Where are the girls?" Thomas asked, noticing the peculiar absence of young women.

"Some are sleeping. Others are doing chores. They aren't permitted to leave the brothel except in the company of a *gharwali*. That's what they call a madam."

Greer pointed toward the upper stories of the buildings they passed. "The underage girls are up there, hidden in attic rooms. They're invisible. If it weren't for our field agents who know these lanes by heart, we would never find them."

The taxi began to accelerate, but Greer touched the driver's shoulder and passed him yet more rupees.

"He's nervous because we're white," Greer explained. "The *taxi-wallas* get *baksheesh*—kickbacks—from the pimps to bring the customers, and the pimps know about CASE. If they see him with us, it will hurt his business."

Near the end of the lane, Thomas saw a young man with dark eyes talking with a white-haired man whose back was to them. The young man glanced at the taxi and his eyes narrowed when he saw its passengers. He gave the *taxi-walla* a stern look that spooked him.

In an instant, the driver lost all interest in guiding the tour. He touched the *hamsa* charm hanging from his rearview mirror and began to chatter fearfully. Greer tried to soothe him, but it didn't work. He left Kamathipura in a hurry and dropped them off on a street corner a few blocks away.

"We'll get another cab," Greer said, walking down the sidewalk between hawkers and street merchants.

Thomas felt intensely self-conscious. Theirs were the only white faces in a sea of brown. Three beggar children approached him, making a hunger sign with their hands. When Thomas didn't respond, they grabbed his arm and tried to reach into his pocket. He shrugged them off and nearly stepped on a blind man who sat beside a pile of burning trash.

Greer looked over his shoulder and noticed Thomas's distress.

"Just keep walking," he said.

At last, Greer hailed another taxi and directed the driver to take them to Mumbai Central Station. Climbing into the back seat, Thomas took a deep breath, his relief palpable.

"So now you've seen what the investigators see," Greer said. "By day, at least."

"It's hard to believe so many girls are hidden behind those walls," Thomas replied, thinking of the two men, presumably brothel owners or pimps, who had scared the *taxi-walla*.

"Thousands of them," Greer said, "some as young as twelve or thirteen."

At Mumbai Central, they hopped aboard a northbound train. The midday crowds were lighter than the morning madness. Thomas found a place by the door beside an elderly man and leaned out to catch the wind. The train headed inland toward Parel and the central suburbs. After stopping at Dadar, it skirted the fringes of Dharavi—Bombay's largest slum, according to Greer—and then crossed a mangrove swamp before pulling into Bandra Station.

Thomas followed Greer up a flight of stairs and across a walkway that overlooked a smaller slum. Beggars sat along the walkway, palms open, eyes pleading. Some were old; others were young, with children. A number were disfigured and displayed casts, crutches, and amputated limbs. No one in the multitude of commuters paid them any attention. Thomas took pity on a ten-year-old girl holding a baby and gave her a five-rupee coin. Then he followed Greer downstairs to the street.

A collection of rickshaws stood in a huddle, their drivers awaiting customers.

A young man approached them. "Where to? Bandra? Juhu? Santa Cruz?"

"Pali Hill," Greer replied.

Greer looked at Thomas. "The office closes at noon today, but I figured you could come by and meet the staff."

He climbed in the rick, and Thomas squeezed in beside him. The driver gunned the engine and entered the stream of traffic.

They were quiet for a while, enjoying the warmth of the wind. The midday sun blazed overhead, but the winter air held little moisture and the temperature was still comfortable. The sky was bluer than it had been earlier on. It looked as if some of the smog had cleared.

Fifteen minutes later, Greer tapped the rick driver on the shoulder and said, "*Bas. Bas.*"

The driver pulled to the side of the road, and Greer paid the fare less one rupee—a Bombay custom he disclosed to Thomas without explanation. They were in a mixed-use neighborhood a few blocks west of the shopping district on Linking Road. The CASE office was located in a nondescript building, and there were no signs advertising its presence.

Greer led Thomas up a flight of stairs to an unmarked door armed with a keypad. Beyond the door was a modern, air-conditioned office suite. Greer explained that CASE had twenty-nine employees in Bombay. Approximately a third were short-term interns from the United States, Australia, and Britain. Two of the full-time employees were Westerners; the rest were Indians from all over the subcontinent. Thomas was immediately impressed by the intensity of the CASE staff. The office was abuzz with activity even on New Year's Eve.

Greer took Thomas to meet the executive staff. The legal director, Samantha Penderhook, was a blond woman from Chicago. Petite and pretty, she was a vision of thoughtful efficiency. She shook hands with Thomas and motioned for him to take a seat.

"I'm sure Jeff painted an honest picture of what we do here," she began. "But I'm more blunt than he is. Bombay is not D.C. The court system here is backlogged to the breaking point and full of idiosyncrasies that will drive you nuts even after you learn them. To compensate, we offer you two perks—the chance to make a difference in the lives of some real girls and Sarah's homemade chai." Samantha paused and looked at the door. "What timing!"

A young Indian woman entered the office with a tray of steaming mugs. She smiled and handed around cups of chai.

Thomas looked at Samantha. "Well, I like chai. The rest I can handle."

Samantha delivered him a wry grin. "If you can say that in two months, I'll know you mean it."

Next, Jeff introduced Thomas to Nigel McPhee, the director of field operations and a garrulous bear of a man. Born in Lockerbie, Scotland, he had been a British special forces commando and a field agent with MI5 before he "saw the light", as he put it, and joined CASE.

"Bombay is a long way from Lockerbie," Thomas remarked.

"Might as well be on the moon," Nigel shot back. "This place is as pleasant as a malarial swamp most of the year. But I didn't come here to take a vacation. Bombay's full of bad guys—street thugs, traffickers, pimps, gangsters, drug dealers, brothel owners. The bad guys I like. They're predictable. The police are another story. About the most corrupt and incompetent lot I've seen. Except for a few. I'd give my life for those guys."

"Shouldn't this office be down in South Bombay somewhere?" Thomas asked. "It's a long way from the action."

"I took him down M. R. Road," Greer explained for Nigel's benefit.

Nigel chuckled. "My boy, Kamathipura is only the

beginning. There are poets who call this entire town Golpitha—the brothel district. Scratch the surface and you get a disease."

Thomas frowned. "My wife is from Malabar Hill. She never told me that."

"It's not something the well-heeled like to think about." Nigel checked his watch. "Sorry to be abrupt, but I have to finish up a report. Come and see me any time you want something to keep you awake at night. My stories are better than coffee."

Rachel Pandolkar, director of rehabilitation, was last on Jeff's list. She was a thin-boned Indian woman of about thirty-five with gentle features and wide eyes. She was on the phone when Jeff knocked. They stood outside her office for a minute, waiting for her to finish.

"Nice to see you, Jeff," she said after putting the phone down.

"And you, Rachel. This is Thomas Clarke, the new legal intern."

"Welcome," she said. "What can I tell you?"

"Give him an overview of pending cases," Jeff said.

Rachel folded her hands. "We have twenty-five girls right now, ten in government homes and fifteen in private homes. All are minors. Our people visit the girls on a weekly basis. We work closely with the Child Welfare Committee to ensure they get proper education, health care, supervision, and attention."

"I don't mean to be cynical," Thomas remarked, "but

there are thousands of underage prostitutes in this city. Two dozen doesn't seem like much of a dent."

Rachel's eyes flashed. "It's a fair point. Do you have a better idea?"

"I didn't mean it that way," Thomas said. "The problem just seems overwhelming."

Rachel nodded. "Someone once asked Mother Teresa how she dealt with world poverty. Do you know what she said? 'You do the thing that's in front of you.' That applies here, too. The academics talk about statistics. We tell stories. Which is more compelling?"

Rachel let the question hang in the air and looked at the clock on her desk. "It's noon, Jeff. We should probably wrap this up."

"Is it noon already?" Greer exclaimed, standing. "I lost track of time." Thanking Rachel, he led Thomas back to the common area.

"So that's our work," he said. "The glossy stuff they put on the brochures is a fragment of what we deal with." He gave Thomas an appraising look. "I know what you've signed on for. But I need to know one thing—that you're the sort of person I can trust. If there's a chance you're going to have second thoughts, then you should think about backing out now."

Thomas looked around at the staff tidying their workspaces for the holiday. He felt at once attracted and repulsed by what CASE offered him. The place was brimming with camaraderie and challenge but entirely bereft of the privileges he had come to expect from the law. Most of the Clayton attorneys he knew would find an excuse to walk away. But he was here and he had a year to kill. There was no going back.

"I'm in," he said in his best no-nonsense tone. "I'll be here on Monday."

Greer nodded. "Welcome to the team."

Chapter 7

Million-fueled, nature's bonfire burns on.
—Gerard Manley Hopkins

Mumbai, India

For Ahalya and Sita, the attic room in Suchir's brothel was a prison of boredom and fear in equal portions. In the long hours of monotony, the fear came almost as a relief, for it meant human interaction. But the relief was short-lived. Each time the stairs creaked and the door handle turned, the sisters traded a look that resolved many meanings into one: what do they want with us now?

During the long days, when the sun blazed overhead and the *beshyas* below slept and ate and chatted and quarreled, Ahalya struggled to keep her sister's hope alive. She told Sita stories from the past—stories of their parents and stories of ancient India written by the sages. Stories were Ahalya's only weapon against the despair that threatened them both. The cadence of her words spirited the sisters away from

Golpitha, at least until the stairs creaked and the doorknob turned again.

Sita's favorite stories were from the bungalow by the sea. She seemed never to tire of hearing Ahalya conjure the voice of their mother, correcting their grammar, nagging them to tidy their room, and calling them to help with dinner; or the voice of their father, teaching them about the sea, the tides and the coastal flora, and reading to them from the Ramayana.

Each morning, at Sita's request, Ahalya recreated one of Jaya's *kolam* designs at the foot of the bed using kernels of rice they had salvaged from the previous evening's meal. Jaya's drawings had been of flowers and Hindu charms, each with personal significance to her. Sita liked the flowers best, and Ahalya traced them out painstakingly with rice.

Each evening, Sumeera brought them a meal of *dal* and chutney. She saw the *kolam* designs, but she never reprimanded them for wasting their food, as Suchir or his young lieutenant—the girls now knew him as Prasad—might have done. Instead, she often lingered in the room and told them a story of her own.

When Sumeera left, the sisters ate their *dal* with their hands, saving only those morsels of rice needed for the next day's *kolam* design. Sumeera returned half an hour later to collect the dishes. By then darkness had fallen upon Kamathipura. The brothel's first customers usually arrived a few minutes after Sumeera bid them farewell. They knew the men by the sounds that erupted from the sex rooms.

In the hours between dinner and sleep, the sisters sat opposite one another on the floor, and Ahalya told Sita stories. Each night when her sister's eyelids grew heavy, Ahalya accompanied her sister to the sink and they washed their hands and faces together. After that, they slipped into bed and spooned as they had at home. Sita seemed to find it easy to sleep, despite the noise in the brothel. But insomnia kept Ahalya awake.

In the daylight, she found distraction in caring for Sita's needs. At night, despair returned and shame metastasized. She lay on the thin mattress, remembering Shankar and the birthday boy and contemplating the limits of her fortitude. She was strong, but she could resist for only so long. One day she would have no more stories to tell.

Something touched Ahalya in the night. She opened her eyes and tried to see through the gloom. She looked toward the door and her eyes began to adjust. A shape stood at her bedside. She suppressed the urge to cry out. Sita was asleep next to her, unaware of the intruder.

The shape changed and she felt hot breath on her neck. A male voice whispered in her ear in Hindi: "Do as I say and make no sound."

The man reached for her hand and drew her out of bed. She stumbled, but he caught her and kept her from falling. He led her down the stairs. Still half-awake, she barely registered the fact that the moaning had ceased and the *adda* was quiet. Even the street sounds were muted, distant things. It seemed that all of Bombay was asleep.

They left the stairwell through the hidden door, and the man pulled her into one of the sex rooms. His skin was rough, his grip viselike. She bumped into the bed and stubbed her toe, but she stifled her cry, for terror had seized her.

He pushed her down on the mattress and closed the door behind them. He struggled with his clothes and then he was on top of her, exploring her with his hands. She writhed beneath him, pushing him away, but he was powerful and restrained her long enough to do his business. When a small cry escaped her lips, he clamped his hand over her mouth. He made sounds like all the others, but she knew he wasn't a customer. No customer stayed the night or had access to the attic room. The man was short and young. It couldn't be Suchir.

It had to be Prasad.

When he had finished, he lay beside her, breathing heavily. She moved her *sari* back into place and cried silent tears. The act, in all its sudden and inexplicable violence, had left her feeling numb with shame.

He began to speak then, whispering words of devotion and love, words he had stolen from the poets. On his tongue, however, they were leprous. She resisted the urge to lash out at him, to drive her fingernails into his eyeballs and leave him blind. She knew it would solve nothing. She and Sita were entirely at the mercy of Suchir.

At last Prasad fell silent. He turned to Ahalya and kissed her on the cheek. Then he took her by the hand and led her back to the attic room. Prasad was smitten with her; that much was obvious. But his infatuation had been deformed by the lust of the brothel. In Golpitha, love was sex and sex was rape. It came to her that his affections knew no other outlet.

She walked to the foot of the bed and saw that her sister was still asleep. She knew that Sita's innocence was all too fragile. She had not yet been defiled, but it was only a matter of time.

Prasad leaned toward her and whispered, "This is our secret. Tell no one."

Ahalya nodded, as much to herself as to her rapist. She slipped under the covers and watched as Prasad glided silently out of the room, closing the door behind him. She listened to the noises drifting in from the street. They were louder now. She heard the horn of a rickshaw and the rumbling passage of a bus. The city was waking up. Dawn was coming.

And with it another day.

Prasad came for her again the next night and the night afterward while the rest of the *beshyas* slumbered. During the day, Ahalya kept up the routine she and Sita had established. She bled a little, but not too much, and she masked her injuries. Inside, however, she felt hollow. When she told Sita stories, her tone often fell flat, and she struggled to smile. She was listless when she drew Jaya's *kolam* designs. She didn't laugh when Sita told one of their mother's jokes.

Sumeera must have noticed Ahalya's sadness, for one evening after she delivered their meal, she sat down on the floor beside the girls and shared a lesson in religion she remembered from her childhood. She told them it had come from a traveling Brahmin, and it had become her lifeline in the *adda*.

"Desire is the enemy," she said. "Desire for the past, desire for the future, desire for love, desire for family. Everything. A *beshya* has to detach herself from all affections and accept her karma. You will never be happy here. But you don't need to be sad."

When Sita fell asleep that night, Ahalya watched her with a trace of envy. She resembled one of the angels stained in glass at the convent school, her peace unbroken. Ahalya lay back against her pillow and stared at the ceiling, certain in the knowledge of what the night would bring. She couldn't sleep. She knew he would always come again.

Night turned toward morning, and the sounds in the brothel diminished. Ahalya lay awake, watching the door. He came for her in time as she expected. They were the only people awake in the *adda*. He touched her arm, and she rose from the bed without a sound. There was no use in struggle, no purpose in resistance.

The room was waiting for them, the bed barely large enough to accommodate them both. She did what he asked. It was shameful and disgusting, but it proved Sumeera right. Detachment was the only escape.

When Prasad tired of lust, he rolled off her and started to talk. He surprised her by sharing about his family.

"Suchir is my father, did you know that? He has sired

many children, but I was the first. My mother was a *beshya* and died when I was a boy. I grew up in the *adda*."

As Prasad continued to share, Ahalya learned that Suchir had inducted him into manhood on his thirteenth birthday. The girl had been one of the *malik*'s youngest acquisitions. Her name was Manasi, and Prasad considered her his first love. He had come to her in the attic room many times. She had stayed in the *adda* until she was nineteen. That year she tested positive for some venereal disease or another.

"I don't remember what it was," he said, "but it wasn't HIV."

When Sumeera gave Suchir the news, he put Manasi on the street. She had haunted the *adda* for weeks, begging for food, until Suchir had paid a police officer to put her in jail. Prasad had never seen her again.

Ahalya listened to Prasad's confession with astonishment and revulsion. In her mind, he was a demon in a man's body. She found it profoundly disturbing that he could sound so human. Worse—*far* worse, in fact—she felt a twinge of pity when he told her the brothel was all he had known. It was a moment of weakness, and she drove the feeling away. The pain between her legs reminded her that his sins were unpardonable. His childhood didn't excuse them.

Nothing did.

After Prasad finished talking, he lay beside her in silence, making no move to take her back to the attic room. He reached for her hand and squeezed it. The intimacy of his touch nearly made her retch. She swallowed the bile in her throat and thought of her sister. *What if Sita wakes and finds me gone?* An idea came to her then. It was risky, but she needed to know, and Prasad could tell her. It was the first time she had addressed him directly.

"What does Suchir intend to do with my sister?" she asked.

"Sita is like you," he said. "She is special. But Suchir will break her in."

Ahalya controlled her rage. "When?"

"Soon," he said enigmatically, and then he took her back to her bed.

The next day was a Sunday, the only day of the week when Golpitha seemed to rest. At breakfast, Sumeera brought them a box of colorful beads and lengths of string, and the sisters spent the day making jewelry. Despite the heat, Sita was playful, engaged, almost happy. Ahalya practiced the art of detachment. The pain in her lower abdomen was part of her existence, like the walls around her and the floor beneath her feet. She could bewail her karma or she could see the pain as a sign that her life still had meaning. It was all a matter of the mind.

When it came time for her evening story, Ahalya began to recount a tale from the Mahabharata, the great epic of love and war. Sita, however, interrupted and made a request. She wanted to hear the story of her namesake. Ahalya took a deep breath. The tale was long, and she had slept little in three nights.

"Are you sure you don't want to hear about Arjuna's great victory?" she asked.

Sita shook her head. "You told me about him last night. I want to hear about the princess of Mithila."

Ahalya sighed. She had never been able to resist her sister's enthusiasm. "Sita of Mithila," she began, "was a woman of great virtues. Yet in her kindness she was unwise. Without knowing it, she gave her trust to Ravana, lord of the underworld, and he took her by force to the island of Lanka, where she remained in exile, awaiting rescue by Lord Rama and Hanuman."

"Tell me about Hanuman," her sister said, her large eyes brimming with interest.

"The noble monkey had received a blessing at birth," Ahalya went on. "He could assume any size he wished, large or small. When he learned that Ravana had carried Sita through the skies to Lanka, Hanuman grew so large that he stepped over the sea. He carried Rama's signet ring across the water and gave it to her—"

Ahalya stopped speaking when the stairs outside the attic room creaked. The sisters turned to watch the doorknob. Ahalya expected to see Sumeera on a housekeeping errand, but instead it was Suchir who appeared at the door. He stood on the threshold and studied Sita in silence. His wrinkled face was impassive, but his calculating eyes made Ahalya's skin crawl. Prasad's words came back to her. "*Sita is special. Suchir will break her in.*"

At last the brothel owner spoke. "Come," he said to Sita.

Ahalya stood desperately, hoping to intervene. "Take me. Leave her alone."

Suchir turned to Ahalya and frowned. "You stay here," he said, his voice harsh. He reached out and took Sita by the arm. Sita glanced fearfully at her sister and followed Suchir down the stairs.

The click of the door sounded like a gunshot to Ahalya. She buried her face in her hands and wept. Blood rushed to her head and the walls seemed to close in on her. The thought of her sister lying beneath a man in the throes of lust rendered absurd her novice attempts at detachment. She teetered on the edge of collapse, wondering how she would find the strength to comfort Sita in the aftermath.

Suchir led Sita past a group of chattering *beshyas* and into the brothel lobby. Business was slow on Sundays. Men were home with their families, watching soccer and cricket on television and sleeping with their wives.

Following Suchir's direction, Sita stood beneath the lights. She placed her hands together to keep them from trembling. She saw a man no older than thirty-five sitting on the couch. He was dressed in expensive clothes and wore a silver watch on his wrist. The man appraised her openly but kept his seat.

"Suchir says you are an orphan," he said in Hindi. "Is this true?"

Sita nodded, confused.

"He says you are healthy and that you aren't pregnant."

She nodded again.

The man turned to Suchir and they exchanged a few words in an indecipherable tongue. Eventually, the man nodded and shook Suchir's hand. He took a last look at Sita and left the brothel. During the entire exchange, he made no attempt to approach her.

Sita was relieved—overwhelmingly so—yet she was also troubled. Both the man's behavior and Suchir's were a mystery. She thought back to New Year's Eve when Shankar had purchased Ahalya's virginity. Sumeera had dressed them both in the finest *saris* and jewelry and garlanded them with flowers. The costumes had been an enticement to the buyer, a lure for his money. Tonight, Suchir had simply appeared and taken her as she was.

Sita followed Suchir up the dank wooden stairs to the attic room. In the doorway she looked at Ahalya and saw her tears. She ran to her sister and clutched the fabric of her *sari*. She wept even though she had not been violated. She wept over the death of her parents. She wept because her sister had wept.

In time Sita drew back and answered Ahalya's unspoken question. "Nothing happened," she whispered. "A man was there, but he didn't touch me."

"Did he say anything to you?"

"He wanted to know if I was an orphan and if I was pregnant."

"And Suchir, what did he say?"

"I couldn't understand him. They weren't speaking Hindi."

Suddenly, Ahalya's arms were around her again, hugging her to her breast. "Rama was watching over you, Little Flower," she said. "He kept you from harm."

"Not Rama," Sita corrected her, "Baba. He promised always to protect me."

Sita closed her eyes and pictured her father's face. The strong chin, the salt-and-pepper hair receding at the crown, the gold-flecked eyes full of wisdom and kindness. He had made the promise when she was five years old. And she had never doubted him.

"You're right," Ahalya agreed, stroking her hair. "It was Baba."

Chapter 8

If thou has not seen the devil, look at thine own self.
                                        —Jalal-uddin Rumi

Mumbai, India

Thomas's first week at CASE was a study in immersion learning. The days began at eight thirty with an office-wide meeting led by Jeff Greer. The three departmental directors reported in with news from the field—investigations ongoing, leads being pursued, cases up for trial, and rescued girls making progress or regressing. No punches were pulled, no rosy portraits painted. Whether delivering hard-boiled grit or a hopeful report, the CASE directors had no patience with sensationalism or spin.

Thomas realized on his first day in the office that working for CASE was light years away from the stereotypical nonprofit job—at least as he and his colleagues at Clayton had conceived of it. The hours were long, the professional standards high, and the cases intellectually demanding. In addition, there was danger in the work. CASE had few friends in Bombay and many powerful enemies. Most of the permanent staff members had been threatened or accosted by a pimp or trafficker, some more than once.

In many ways, life in the legal department at CASE was little different from life in the trenches at Clayton. The similarities ended, however, where the law itself began. The particulars of Indian jurisprudence were largely foreign to Thomas, and the vernacular of Indian law suffered from a profusion of strange phrases and archaic terminology left over from the days of the Raj. Thomas kept a pen handy and took copious notes, but they usually left him more bewildered than enlightened.

His education took a giant leap forward when Samantha Penderhook asked him to review a legal brief written by one of CASE's Indian lawyers. The case involved a pimp who had operated a makeshift brothel in the Jogeshwari slum. He had a friend who was in the business of trafficking girls from villages in the far north of India on the pretense that he would give them work as waitresses and nannies in Bombay. The pimp had five girls in his stable when the police, assisted by CASE, took down his operation. All five were minors. Two of the girls were barely thirteen. The evidence against the pimp was damning. Yet the case had been pending in court for four years, and the pimp was still on the street.

The Jogeshwari case highlighted the crisis in the Bombay judicial system. The pimp had admitted his crimes to the police, but the confession was not admissible into evidence because the police were presumed to be corrupt. The police also bungled the First Information Report they prepared at the scene. The FIR contradicted the statement prepared by the *pancha*—the third-party witness—giving the pimp's lawyer an opening to attack the credibility of the FIR and the police constables.

In addition, the trial process had been a model of inefficiency. The victims were called to testify six months after the raid, but the prosecutor had to wait more than two years to cross-examine the pimp. By then neither the judge nor the lawyers could quite remember what the victims had said. The only records of the victims' testimony were "depositions" typed in shorthand by the judge's clerk on her ancient computer. Unfortunately, the victims' "depositions" contradicted the notes taken by the CASE lawyer assisting the prosecution.

Finally, there was the problem of the language barrier. The girls were from a region of Uttar Pradesh near Nepal and spoke a dialect called Awadhi. It took CASE two months to locate an Awadhi translator. When at last the girls were placed under oath, the translator admitted he was hard of hearing. Although he stood directly beside the girls, he interrupted them incessantly, asking them to repeat themselves.

The Jogeshwari case was a complete disaster. After reading the brief, Thomas went to Samantha's office. She was on the phone, but she waved him in anyway.

When she hung up, he held up the brief. "Is this a joke?"

She smiled. "No joke. I told you Bombay legal work would drive you crazy."

He put his outrage into words. "Four years ago, this pimp was selling these itty-bitty girls to his friends in the slum, and today his lawyer is arguing he should be let off because the police couldn't write a coherent sentence in the FIR and the clerk couldn't hear the girls testify and the confession of the pimp was unduly influenced by the cops, even though there were five witnesses and two third-party *panchas* present at the scene who said the guy just spilled his guts. What kind of kangaroo court are these people running?"

"It's a circus," Samantha admitted. "That's why we get so few convictions. Even when the evidence is airtight, the perpetrator absconds or the victim refuses to testify or the lawyer pulls some stunt with the judge and delays the case so long that the file starts to grow mold."

"If the whole system is broken, then why are we doing this?"

Samantha gestured toward the chair in front of her desk. "Sit down."

When he did, she went on, "I'm sure you've heard the old Burkean maxim that evil prevails where good people do nothing. It's a nice hoary statement, the sort of thing politicians throw around on the stump and activists put on bumper stickers. But Burke was right. Bombay is a den of thieves because people sat on their hands and let it become that way. When CASE opened this office, everybody said we would close our doors in a year."

She paused and swept her arm around.

"Well, we're still here and, by God, we've made a difference.

The pimps are afraid of us. The police are starting to think twice about accepting bribes. Girls who were once being raped in the cages fifteen times a day are recovering in our private homes. It's small, but it's a start. The question you have to answer is simple: do you want to be a part of it?"

She leaned forward in her chair and placed her hands on the desk. "I imagine Jeff gave you the spiel about sticking around for the duration. He does that with everyone. But this is my department. If you reach a point where you want out, I'll run interference with headquarters. I don't need to remind you that you're not getting paid."

Samantha meant the statement as a joke, but Thomas winced. She had no way of knowing that, if not for that coward Mark Blake and the threat from Wharton Coal, he would be back in the District, billing $325 an hour for his time. CASE's work was commendable, but he hadn't signed up for moral reasons. He was different from the other volunteers. The world of human trafficking sickened him, but he was on a career path with a defined objective: the federal bench. He would stay the course here because it was the only way back into the arms of grace.

"Don't worry about me," he said, standing up again. "I'm on board."

"I thought so." Samantha grinned. "So here's your test. Make the Jogeshwari brief sing. Make it so compelling that the judge can't wait to send that bastard to the jail at Arthur Road."

★

On Saturday night, Dinesh invited Thomas out to dinner in Bandra with a couple of his friends. The friends were single, white-collar types who had studied in Britain. They ate on the porch at Soul Fry, a hip hangout serving traditional cuisine with a modernist flair.

Dinesh's friends demonstrated absolutely no interest in Thomas's work at CASE and spent most of the meal questioning him about American girls. Thomas avoided the subject of Priya, thinking that one of them might know her family. But they didn't ask about her, and Dinesh had the good sense not to bring her up.

After dinner, the foursome climbed into a pair of rickshaws and made the twenty-minute trip to Dinesh's favorite club—a place called White Orchid. The club was located on the third floor of a commercial building that housed a clothing boutique and a travel agency.

As the lift ascended, he heard the muffled sound of throbbing bass and tinny vocals. They were met in a lobby by three bouncers wearing white shirts and black pants. One of Dinesh's friends shook hands with a bouncer and whispered in his ear. The man nodded and gestured his assent. He waved the group through another set of doors.

As soon as Thomas entered White Orchid, he understood that the main attraction was neither alcohol nor fraternity. The club was circular, its perimeter lined with plush couches and square tables. Men of all ages sat on the couches, sipping drinks. At the center of the room was a wooden dance floor with two floor-to-ceiling brass poles. Between the poles stood eight young women adorned like princesses in gold, jewels, and elegant pantsuits. Unlike the performers in an American strip club, these girls were fully clothed. Yet there was an unmistakable sensuality in the way they stood, they way they looked at the men, and the way they danced.

The girls took turns at center stage, only one dancing at a time. The rest stood by, casing the room with their eyes. If a man liked a girl, he offered her a tip. The girl would saunter over to the man, take the bill with a smile, and then return to the bar line. Occasionally, a man would place a stack of rupees in his hand and wink at a girl. Drawn by the more generous tip, the girl would dance for him alone. At no time, however, did the girl and her admirer touch.

To enforce these rules, several muscle-bound waiters stood by, scanning the patrons for any hint of impropriety. The waiters collected orders and delivered drinks, but their primary duty was obvious. Thomas took a seat beside Dinesh and tried not to look as uncomfortable as he felt. The girls eyed him, searching for a sign of interest or the appearance of money in his hands. His options were limited. Either he could be rude to his friend and walk out of the club or he could stay and watch with the rest.

He glanced at Dinesh. His friend looked relaxed, unselfconscious. He and his buddies had ordered drinks and were munching on peanuts provided by the club. Thomas motioned to the waiter and asked for a Kingfisher. He wished that Dinesh had warned him about what to expect. Then again, if Dinesh had, he probably wouldn't have come.

Thomas watched as a girl dressed in an emerald-green *salwar kameez* danced alone. She was lovely, with lotus-shaped eyes and an almond complexion. She closed her eyes and moved with such open sensuality that Thomas felt a stirring within him. After a moment, he caught himself and turned away, awash in guilt. He searched his mind for a polite excuse to leave, but none came to him. He was frustrated with Dinesh and angry at himself.

Sometime around midnight, one of Dinesh's friends stood abruptly. He had spent the evening lavishing a bar girl with five-hundred-rupee notes. He looked at the girl and then nodded at a nearby waiter. He shook Dinesh's hand and headed toward the exit. The girl, meanwhile, left the dance floor, heading toward the back of the club.

"Where's he going?" Thomas shouted into Dinesh's ear.

His friend opened his palms as if he didn't know, but at once Thomas understood. He sat back and studied Dinesh. His friend was enamored of a tall girl with long eyelashes. He had offered her at least three thousand rupees over the course of the evening, and she had danced for him a number of times. She was in the bar line now, gyrating to a song that Thomas vaguely recognized. Dinesh reached into his wallet and took out eight five-hundred-rupee notes and held them out to her like a falconer calling down his prize bird.

The girl's eyes lit up and she glided across the room to stand before him. She looked at no one but Dinesh and then she began to move, first her hands, then her arms, then her shoulders. The movement spread inward from her extremities until it found fullest expression in her core. Thomas watched the spectacle unfold, seeing now what he hadn't seen before. He was watching a ritual as old as time.

His friend turned to him and shouted over the din, "You know how to get home?"

Thomas met his friend's gaze. He nodded.

"I'll see you tomorrow morning," Dinesh said and stood. The waiter led him to the door, and the bar girl retreated to the back of the club.

Watching them go, Thomas knew what would happen next. Dinesh and the girl would meet again on the street. They'd take a taxi to a hotel somewhere in the city. In the privacy of their room, Dinesh would pour his passion into her until he was spent. And then she would take his money and walk away. Another night, another john. She would use the money to feed her children, or she might buy herself a new outfit on Linking Road. Then she would dance again. Tomorrow, probably, and then the next day and the day after that. The ritual would continue, and Dinesh would be forgotten.

Until he decided to pay again.

Thomas finished his beer and left a hundred-rupee tip for the waiter. Bidding the last of Dinesh's friends farewell, he left the White Orchid, feeling disgusted with himself. He wondered what the people at CASE would think of him for patronizing such a place. He wondered what Priya would think or whether she would care.

He hailed a rick and told the driver to take him to the Bandstand. Tuning out the racket of the engine, he wrestled again with his mother's idea. Twice in the past week he had been on the verge of dialing Priya's number, but he had stopped short. How was it that the thought of looking into her eyes again could strike such terror in his heart?

Searching for a distraction, he pulled out his BlackBerry and checked his e-mails. That morning, he had written a missive to his mother to calm her fears—she had always been a worrier—and to reassure his father that one week in India hadn't altered his long-term goals.

Elena had replied to his e-mail:

Thomas, I'm delighted you are safe. Your father is off on another one of his obsessions. Ever since you left, he has been reading nonstop about the sex trade. The postman just dropped off a box of books he ordered. I'd prefer a more pedestrian topic to hear about at the dinner table, but I shouldn't complain. I'm glad he isn't dull. Please stay in touch and come home soon.

Her words brought a smile to Thomas's face. He continued to scroll through the list of unread e-mails. Among a host of spam solicitations, he saw a message from Andrew Porter.

Hey, Thomas, I thought you'd like to know that we heard from the Fayetteville police about the incident you mentioned. Nothing concrete as yet, but we're moving on it. It's nasty

here—lots of sleet and ice. Be happy you're in a warm place.
I envy you.

Thomas typed back:

Thanks for keeping me posted. Right now I'm breathing
exhaust fumes. Not quite paradise, but I guess it beats the
sleet.

After sending the message, he scrolled farther down in
his inbox and saw her name. He closed his eyes, wondering
why life had to be so complicated. He should have told her
directly that it was over. He considered deleting the e-mail,
but curiosity made him read it.

Tera had written:

Thomas, I'm a fool, but I can't help missing you. Where
are you? The partners won't say anything except that you
took a leave of absence. It's cold here. I miss your warmth.

He sat back and looked out at the lights of the city. She
was a decent, generous girl. He had encouraged her feelings
and then cut her off at the knees without explanation. She
was a fool, yes. But so was he.

Lost in thought, he didn't notice that the rick had come
to a stop outside Dinesh's apartment building. The driver
turned around and glared at him, pointing at the meter.
Thomas handed him the bills and wandered through the

gate. The elevator was waiting for him. When he reached his friend's apartment, he poured himself a glass of brandy and went out onto the veranda. He stood at the railing, inhaling the salt-laden air and trying to make sense of his life.

When at last he grew tired of the subject, he went to his room and undressed for bed, listening to the sounds of Bombay filtering in through the open window. He lay down on the mattress and closed his eyes. Sleep, when finally it came, was a blessed relief.

On Monday, Thomas went to see Nigel McPhee after the morning meeting. A thought had been nagging at him since he left the White Orchid and had intensified after Dinesh returned home on Sunday afternoon wearing an untroubled smile. By the time the weekend was over, Thomas needed an answer.

Nigel motioned for Thomas to take a seat. "What can I do for you?"

Thomas got to the point. "A friend of mine took me to the White Orchid on Saturday."

"Ah," Nigel said. "And you weren't prepared, I take it." Thomas shook his head.

"Like I said before, this whole town is a brothel."

"Which brings me to my question. The White Orchid didn't feel like a brothel. And the girls didn't look like slaves."

Nigel regarded him thoughtfully. "What does a slave look like to you?"

"I have no idea. But these girls seemed like they wanted to be there."

"Appearances can be deceiving."

"So you're saying they were trafficked?"

"It's more complicated than that. Most of them were born into it."

"What do you mean?"

"They're Bedia girls. Women from their caste have been prostitutes for centuries. You noticed, I take it, that all of them were gorgeous?"

Thomas nodded.

"Their blood is a mystery. But their stories are all the same. Their parents groom them for this. They bring them here when they're teenagers and put them on the bar line. They're not controlled like the girls in the brothels down south. They live on their own. They have spending money. But it's hard to say they're free. It's the only thing they know."

"Do the customers realize this?" Thomas thought of Dinesh.

Nigel laughed. "The customers don't care. A bar girl is a fantasy. The guys convince themselves that the girls are in love with them. They're not buying a prostitute. They're giving a gift to a girlfriend."

Thomas pondered this. The logic was twisted, but it made sense of Dinesh's behavior.

"What is CASE's position on the dance clubs?"

Nigel shook his head. "Places like the White Orchid are

untouchable. The police take bribes from the club owners and say the girls are dancing because they want to. And they might be right. The only bars we take down are the beer bars in the suburbs where the pimps keep the girls locked away."

"You know," Thomas said, "my wife once called Bombay the city of *maya*. I'm starting to understand what she meant."

Nigel nodded. "Everything is an illusion in this place."

Thomas thanked him and returned to his desk. Grabbing his laptop, he went to the CASE library and read every published decision he could find on trafficking prosecutions. He found a few quotes that he could use in the Jogeshwari brief, but the pickings were slim.

Around noon, he returned to his seat in the legal department, determined to restructure the brief in his mind. He sketched out the main points on his laptop and then bulleted ideas for the headers and subheaders. Half an hour later, the logical framework of the argument was in place. He glanced at the clock and wondered about lunch.

Suddenly, he heard the sound of excited voices in field operations across the room. Though the three departments—field operations, legal, and rehabilitation—shared one large common area, most conversations were muffled by a trio of massive air-conditioners that rattled and hissed from morning to evening.

He stood up and saw three Indian field agents and a case officer enter Nigel's office.

"What's going on?" he asked Eloise, an expat from the Bronx.

Eloise set down a volume of the *All India Reporter* and looked over the partition at the nearly empty field operations division. "What gives, John?"

The case officer looked up from his computer. "Rasheed got a tip. Two minor girls in Kamathipura. One of them is 'sealed pack'. Nigel wants to move quickly."

Thomas's heart quickened. "Who gets to go on a raid?"

Eloise smiled. "Ask Greer. He'll probably let you tag along."

Soon Nigel and his entourage emerged from his office, and Nigel went to consult with Samantha. Not long after that, she appeared and briefed the legal staff.

"Rasheed was down on M. R. Road last night. He engaged a girl who had given him information before. She said that the pimp who ran her brothel had brought in two minor girls before New Year's Eve. We're going in tonight. Deepak will be the bogus customer; it turns out he knows the brothel owner."

After the briefing, Thomas went to Greer's office and found him on the phone.

"Exciting times," Greer said when he hung up. "Rasheed's pounding the pavement to confirm the tip."

"Would you mind if I go along?" Thomas asked.

Greer took only a moment to think about it. "Now is as good a time as any," he said.

★

At five o'clock that afternoon, after a whirlwind of preparations, Greer and Nigel assembled the field team that would participate in the raid. There were six of them. Deepak, Rasheed, and Rohit were the field agents who had knowledge of the brothel. Ravi was a field agent who often doubled as the driver of CASE's Land Rover. Dev Ramachandra was the case officer handling the investigation. And Anita Chopra was the rehabilitation specialist assigned to provide support for the minor girls.

Nigel asked Rasheed for the most recent report. Rasheed leaned forward in his chair.

"The word on the street is that Suchir made the purchase about two weeks ago. Nobody knows where the girls came from, but my contacts say that he made sixty-thousand rupees on the first one. There is no word on whether the other girl has been broken in."

"Deepak," Nigel asked, "tell us about the layout."

"It's a typical welcome brothel," the field agent replied. "There is only one entrance I'm sure of, and that's at the front. I've heard rumors that there might be an escape route, but I've never seen it. The lobby is on the third floor of the building. The sex rooms are behind it. Suchir has fifteen or so girls. His son, Prasad, works with him. I know he has an attic room, but I don't know how to access it."

"What level of violence can we expect?" Nigel asked.

Rohit spoke up. "I've never known Suchir to carry a weapon. His madam is very submissive. Prasad is the wild card. He has a temper."

Nigel spoke to Greer. "Make sure the police know about that."

"Will do." Greer scribbled a note to himself on a notepad. "How much can we trust the Nagpada cops?" he asked Dev. "It's been a while since our last operation down there."

"Inspector Khan is incorruptible," Dev replied. "The rest of his squad will take the path of least resistance. All of the constables take *baksheesh* from the pimps, but they're afraid of Khan and will follow orders."

"How suspicious is Suchir?" Greer asked. "Will he check for a wire?"

Deepak shook his head. "He's never been raided. Word is he pays *hafta* to Chotta Rajan's gang. He thinks he's invincible."

The planning continued until six, at which time the team went out to dinner. They returned to the office at seven and piled into two vehicles for the forty-five-minute drive to the Nagpada police station. Nigel wished them success and stayed behind.

During the ride, Greer placed a call to Inspector Khan. He learned that Khan had selected a team of six constables, or *halvadars*, to accompany him on the raid. To prevent any of his men from tipping off Suchir, the inspector hadn't briefed them on the target. He would tell them on the way. Khan had also arranged for two *panchas* from another NGO to join them. The police would take three squad cars and two wagons. If they rounded up too many girls, they would have to shuttle them to the station.

"Everything is coming together," Greer told Thomas when he hung up. "Khan is living up to his reputation."

The drive from Khar to Nagpada took them through the heart of central and southern Bombay—through the Dharavi slum, bright with burning piles of trash and endless strands of bare bulbs, through the taxi-infested streets of Dadar West and Lower Parel, and into the crowded narrows of Nagpada.

They parked on the street a block from the station and walked the rest of the way. Inspector Khan met them in the lobby and ushered them into a cluttered room furnished with metal desks and wall-to-wall bookshelves. He asked to see Deepak's equipment, and the field agent opened a rucksack and took out a tiny video camera disguised as a ball-point pen and the audio wire that he would tape to his stomach. Khan nodded. He reached into his pocket and handed Deepak an envelope.

"Twenty thousand rupees," he said. "I entered the serial numbers in my notebook."

Deepak passed the envelope to Jeff, who took out his notepad and counted the bills.

"The *panchas* will be here soon," the inspector continued. "My constables still don't know anything. I will lock the door to this room. We will leave at a quarter to ten."

Thomas watched as Deepak put the pen camera and the wire in place. Both were so small they blended into his clothing.

The *panchas* arrived a little after nine. They were Indian natives who looked about thirty. In passable English, the man introduced himself as Kavi and the woman as Mira. Rasheed briefed them in rapid-fire Hindi.

Eventually, Greer checked his watch. "It's about time," he said. "I usually say a prayer before we go. Do you mind?"

"Feel free," Thomas replied. "I grew up Catholic."

Closing his eyes, Greer offered up a brief petition for safety and success. Then he looked toward the door, where Inspector Khan had appeared. Khan summoned them to the lobby and introduced them to his men. There were six constables in the raid group. All were armed with wooden clubs, called *lathis*, and two of them wielded antiquated carbine rifles.

The inspector raised his voice above the ceiling fans. "We will stay on Bellasis Road until Deepak sends the missed call. No one goes in before then. I will take the lead car. If anyone moves before I move, I will have his badge. Is that clear?"

There were grunts and murmurs all around. The khaki-clad *halvadars* were nervous and fidgety, and two of them glanced sideways at Jeff and Thomas, barely veiling their contempt.

Khan eyed each of his men personally. "It doesn't matter where you're from or what you feel about the *beshyas*. Think of the girls we're going to rescue as you think about your own children. Do your job. Any questions?"

No one spoke up.

"Let's go," he said.

Chapter 9

We have crossed to the far shore of this darkness;
Dawn spreads her radiance like a web.

—Rig Veda

Mumbai, India

It was ten o'clock in the evening when the doorknob to the attic room turned. This time only Sumeera came for Ahalya. She sat alone on the bed, her hair disheveled and her face a mess of tears. Sita had been gone for twenty minutes, but to Ahalya, it felt like forever.

As before, Suchir had appeared without warning and left with her sister. Ahalya hadn't been surprised. She had spent the day in dread, knowing the hour was coming. Baba's promises could not save Sita from the ways of the brothel.

"Come," Sumeera said, taking Ahalya's hand. "You are needed for a customer. You mustn't look so sad."

So I am going to be sold tonight, too, she thought. The horror of it left her numb.

She dressed in her outfit of seduction and followed

Sumeera down the stairs, bracing herself for the touch of a stranger's hands. Only one *beshya*, the oldest and least attractive girl, stood in the hallway watching her. Most of the sex rooms were occupied. Ahalya examined each door she passed, listening for Sita's voice amid the sounds of male pleasure. She clenched her fist. *How can they do this to her? She is just a child!*

The man sitting on the couch in the lobby was young and bearded. Suchir stood near the far wall and switched on the lights. As before, Ahalya was dazzled by the radiance.

"A true *rampchick*," the man said, standing and walking toward her. "Suchir, you are always so discriminating."

"I will give her to you for ten thousand."

"So expensive, my friend? How many times has she been with a man?"

"Only twice. She is very fresh."

So Prasad has kept the secret, Ahalya thought grimly. *Suchir has no idea that his son has had me every night for the better part of a week.*

The man circled Ahalya and then stood in front of her. She did not meet his eyes.

"I will take her," he said at last. "But I want to use the upper room. It is more comfortable."

"Of course," Suchir agreed. He glanced at Sumeera, and she left quietly.

The man gave the brothel owner a wad of rupees and took Ahalya by the hand. "Come, my princess," he whispered.

Ahalya shuddered and followed in his wake. All but one

of the doors in the hallway were closed, and she saw no sign of Sita.

When they entered the attic room, Sumeera was straightening the bedsheets. She fluffed the pillows and went to Suchir's side. The brothel owner wished the bearded man a pleasant adventure and closed the door from the outside.

The man motioned for Ahalya to go to the bed and took out his mobile phone.

"Just a moment," he said, pressing the keypad once. He held the phone to his ear and then cut off the call. "No one home."

Ahalya sat on the bed and looked down at the sheets. She expected the man to unbutton his pants and caress her face as Shankar had done. Afterward, he would ask her to undress. But he did none of these things.

"What is your name?" he asked gently.

The question pierced her. Her name. The gift of her father—its meaning "non-imperfection". Her namesake was a model of feminine beauty, the chaste wife of a noble Brahmin, seduced by the god Indra and cursed by her husband for her unfaithfulness. The parallels between her life and that of Ahalya of the Ramayana were striking, yet there was one profound difference—the Ahalya of old had been saved from the stone that bound her.

"I am Deepak," he went on when she failed to respond. "I'm not going to hurt you."

He sat quietly, making no move to touch her. She looked at him strangely, not understanding.

Seconds later, a commotion erupted on the floor below. Thuds were accompanied by squeals and the troubled voices of men. Ahalya heard Sumeera issue urgent commands. At once feet pounded on the stairs outside the attic room. Deepak went quickly to the door and braced it with his back. Someone turned the knob and tried to push the door open. When it held fast, a man—it sounded to Ahalya like Prasad—cursed and threw his weight against the wood.

Deepak grimaced but held firm.

Thomas stood beside Greer and watched from across the street while the Nagpada constables moved in. Inspector Khan handcuffed Suchir without a struggle and then led three members of his squad up the steps to the brothel. After securing Suchir in a police wagon, the rest of the Nagpada squad entered the brothel with the *panchas* to take names and statements.

Meanwhile, Greer and Dev had a brief exchange with the CASE field agents and gave Rasheed and Rohit the task of watching the nearby lanes for a backdoor escape attempt. They separated and disappeared into the crowd.

Traffic on M. R. Road had slowed to a standstill as *taxiwallas* and passersby fought for a glimpse of the action. Pimps and brothel owners stood on the periphery, gauging the seriousness of the threat. Murmurs of discontent began to ripple through the onlookers. Many regarded Thomas and Greer with suspicion, even outright hostility. The crowd began to press in, hungry for a confrontation.

Dev looked at Greer. "We need to get off the street before this gets ugly."

Greer nodded and beckoned for Thomas to follow them. Anita brought up the rear.

When the CASE contingent entered the brothel, the lobby was overflowing with people—police, girls, customers, *panchas*, and Prasad, who was hurling obscenities. When Prasad saw the Americans, he turned his abuse on them. He shoved his way through the bodies and planted himself in front of Greer. His clothing carried the smell of cigarettes and cheap cologne.

"*Bhenchod!*" he said, spitting betel juice on Greer's shirt.

Greer stepped back as one of the constables put Prasad in cuffs and forced him to take a seat in a corner of the room.

Thomas stared at the young brothel lieutenant. He shook his head.

"What?" Greer said, noticing the gesture.

"I recognize him. He was on the street when we drove by a couple of days ago."

"You're right," Greer replied. "Interesting coincidence."

They followed Dev across the lobby to the sex rooms. Dev spoke to Khan, who was taking the statement of a young *beshya* cowering in one of the doorways.

"Have you seen Deepak?" Dev asked.

Khan shook his head. "He's probably upstairs somewhere, but I haven't had time to look for the passageway."

"May we?" Dev asked.

"Be my guest," Khan replied and turned back to the frightened girl.

"I'll get one of the *panchas*," Greer said. Looking at Thomas, he explained, "This is the crucial step. Suchir will be open for business tomorrow if we don't do this by the book."

After Greer returned with Mira, Dev walked down the hallway and opened each of the doors. All were identical, and it seemed unlikely that any of them led to a hidden chamber. He moved to the end of the hallway and examined the bookcase. He tugged at it, but it didn't move. Greer circled him and ran his fingertips along the right side of the bookcase. He found nothing. Dev tried the left side and felt a weakness in the wood. He pressed down with his fingers and heard a latch disengage.

"Got it!" he said.

Khan joined them as Dev swung the bookcase outward. They peered beyond it into the murk of the stairwell. They heard the faint sound of a man's voice in the distance. Dev went up the stairs, with Mira, Greer and Thomas on his heels.

Dev knocked on the door at the top of the stairs. "Deepak?" he said.

Inside the attic room, Deepak released his hold on the door. He turned to Ahalya, who sat motionless on the bed.

"My friends have come," he said. "You will soon be free."

Ahalya stared uncomprehending as a group of strangers—some in uniform, others in plainclothes—entered the attic room. An Indian woman came to her side and introduced herself as Anita. She took a seat on the bed and promised to stay with Ahalya until she was safe. Ahalya looked intently at the policemen in uniform. For the first time since Suchir came for Sita, she felt a glimmer of hope.

One of the policemen approached Deepak and spoke words that Ahalya could not understand. Deepak shook his head. The policeman turned to Ahalya and spoke in the same unintelligible tongue. She stared at him blankly, and he switched to Hindi.

"I am Inspector Khan of the Nagpada police," he said. "We received information that there were two minor girls in this brothel, not one. Where is the other girl?"

Ahalya looked into Khan's eyes, thinking there must be some misunderstanding.

"My sister, Sita," she said. "She is downstairs."

Khan went to the door and barked an order. After a few seconds, another policeman appeared. They traded words, and then Khan turned back to Ahalya.

"There are fifteen girls downstairs, but none of them is named Sita."

Ahalya's hands began to tremble. She stared at Khan, trying to take in the implications of his statement. She stood from the bed and walked out of the attic room. Khan was so surprised that he made no attempt to stop her. She made her way downstairs, scouring the now-empty sex rooms for any sign of her sister.

When she reached the lobby, she pressed into the crowd, searching the sea of faces. The *beshyas* were together in the far corner, but Sita was not among them. Ahalya pushed her way to Sumeera, who stood watching the frenzy with tired eyes.

"Where is Sita?" Ahalya demanded. "What did you do with her?"

Sumeera glanced around the room and then looked back at Ahalya. "She is gone," she said simply.

Ahalya shook her head fiercely, trying to ward off the truth. "No, you are wrong. Suchir came for her an hour ago. She was to see a customer."

Sumeera looked at the ground, saying nothing.

A shapeless terror gripped Ahalya's mind. She fell to her knees and began to rock back and forth. Tears streamed from her eyes and collected on her chin. She reached out for Sumeera's *sari*.

"Where did she go?" she begged, sobbing, but the *gharwali* failed to respond. "How could you?" she cried. "Have you no soul?"

Sumeera gently prized Ahalya's fingers loose. She knelt down and spoke the words quietly, looking directly into Ahalya's eyes.

"It is the way of Golpitha," she said.

PART TWO

Chapter 10

In the dark of night live those for whom
the outside world alone is real.
                                    —Isha Upanishad

Mumbai, India

Forty minutes before the raid, Suchir had led Sita into the
brothel lobby and greeted a man sitting on the couch. When
Sita saw him, she remembered him. He was the same man
who had come the night before. He was wearing the same
expensive clothes, the same silver wristwatch. A duffel bag
was at his side. He stood and lifted the bag, nodding to Suchir.

"One lakh now," he said. "The rest after the girl does
her job, as usual." He paused. "You can count it if you like."

"That won't be necessary. You have earned my trust,
Navin."

Navin nodded again and took Sita's hand. "Time to go,
Sita." He pronounced her name in Hindi with the familiarity
of a cousin.

Sita stood uncomprehending and then pulled her hand

away. "I can't leave my sister," she said desperately. "Please don't take me away from her."

Navin looked at Suchir and then back at Sita. "Maybe I will bring your sister next time. But I have bought you today. If you submit, your life will be easy. No pimp, no madam, no sex with strangers. But if you fight, you will regret it."

He took her hand again and pulled her down the stairs to the dusty street, shrouded by night. A black sport utility vehicle was waiting at the curb. Navin opened the back door and gestured for Sita to get in. She shook her head, her eyes flashing with terror. With a sigh, he took hold of her shoulders and pushed her into the vehicle. She sat stiffly and cried silent tears.

There was a large man in the driver's seat, but he paid no attention to her. Navin slipped in beside the man and said, "New Bombay. George said ten o'clock. Do not be late."

The driver grunted and accelerated down the narrow lane. They drove for many minutes before crossing a long bridge over a bay and entering another part of the sprawling city. On an unremarkable street corner buried in a warren of lanes, the driver pulled over and Navin got out with a knapsack. Through the window, Sita saw a gangly black man standing in the shadows, his hand clutching a cloth-covered package. Navin approach the man and spoke briefly. He handed the man the knapsack and took the package. Then he returned to the car.

He glanced back at Sita. "Why are you crying?" he asked, sounding annoyed.

Sita closed her eyes, afraid to look at him. She felt the night closing in on her. Who was this man? Why had he taken her away from Ahalya? The words found their way to her tongue before she could restrain herself.

"Please let me go back to my sister," she pleaded. "Please."

Navin shook his head and muttered an expletive. "Take me home," he said to the driver. The large man grunted and pulled the SUV into the traffic.

Sita crossed her arms over her chest, suppressing the sobs that were so close to the surface. She watched the lights of the city, passing in a blur, and tried to ignore the package on Navin's lap. But curiosity got the better of her when he unwrapped it. Inside the cloth was a plastic bag, and in the bag was brown powder. He unzipped the bag and took a whiff.

"George must have been a Brahmin in another life," he exulted. "His powder is like the Soma juice of the gods."

Drugs, Sita thought, feeling the terror return.

They crossed the long bridge and returned to downtown Bombay. After they passed the international airport, they turned down a dirt road that led to a complex of flats. The driver parked the SUV, and Navin retrieved Sita from the back seat. She went with him without a word. The sight of the powder haunted her.

They took an elevator to the top floor of the building, and the driver opened the door to a modest flat. Sita followed Navin to a small bedroom furnished with nothing but a mattress on an iron frame. She sat down on the bed and stared at the wall. She heard Navin ask if she needed to use the restroom, but she didn't respond. He shook his head again, clearly displeased, and then left the room, locking the door behind him.

She held herself tightly, clenching her teeth against the fear and sorrow, but this time the pressure was too great. She doubled over and began to sob. Her family was gone. Ahalya was gone. She was alone in a flat in Bombay with a strange man who dealt in drugs.

Navin kept Sita locked in her room except to deliver her food and to allow her use of the bathroom. Sita never spoke to him when he appeared. She sat on the bed, her back against the wall, staring blankly out the window. The monotony was nearly insufferable. The only regular interruptions came from the planes taking off and landing at the airport. She found herself counting the minutes between departures and arrivals. Occasionally, she tried to picture the faces of the passengers and imagine where they were going or coming from.

After three days of this, Navin brought a chair into Sita's room and sat down, facing her. He was holding a bunch of large grapes and a jar of coconut oil.

"We travel tomorrow night," he began. "You must do everything exactly as I say. If you listen to me, I will take you to a better place. If you disobey, you could die."

Sita didn't process his words right away. The hours of her confinement had been so long she had almost ceased to feel. She stared at the grapes as his words hit home. Suddenly, the boredom turned into dread. *Travel?* she thought. *What does he mean that I could die?* She looked at him at last and saw that he was angry.

"Your sister is gone," he said irritably. "She is a *beshya*. You are one no longer. It is time to stop this ridiculous mourning."

She looked at the grapes again. "Where are we going?" she whispered.

Navin collected himself. "You will find out soon enough." He paused. "Have you ever swallowed a grape whole?"

Sita's eyes grew wide and she shook her head.

"Then you must practice. You must become proficient in twenty-four hours. I will use oil as lubrication. It will help."

She watched as he took a grape from the bunch and dipped it in the coconut oil until its skin was shiny. He offered it to her, but she didn't take it.

"Why do I have to do this?" she asked, staring at the grape in fear.

Ignoring her question, he reached out, prized open her fingers, and put the grape in her palm. "You will feel like you are choking, but you must overcome the urge to regurgitate. Swallowing the grape is a matter of the mind."

Sita felt the grape in her hands. It was slippery and felt strangely heavy. She thought of Ahalya and wondered how she would respond to this challenge. Ahalya would be strong, she decided. She would do what needed to be done. And she would survive. Sita placed the grape in her mouth, tasting the oil on her tongue.

"No, no," Navin interjected. "You must tilt your head back and look at the ceiling. That will open your throat."

Following his directions, she felt the grape slide deeper into her mouth. She choked violently and her throat burned. Navin waited until she had caught her breath and then dipped another grape in coconut oil.

"You will learn," he encouraged her. "The others did."

Hands trembling, Sita tried a second time and nearly succeeded before the choking reflex threw her body into spasms. She slid off the bed and fell on her hands and knees, retching.

"I can't," she moaned.

"You can."

She tried again, and this time the grape slid slowly down her throat and she managed not to gag. She breathed heavily and closed her eyes, relieved and yet horrified.

"Well done," Navin complimented her. "You learned quickly. I will return every three hours and you will swallow another grape until it is second nature."

Sita's stomach churned and her throat ached from the strain, but she acquired the skill Navin demanded of her. She didn't ask again about his reasons. She understood that he owned her and could do anything he wanted to her.

On Thursday, Navin delivered Sita her lunch and told her it would be her last meal for more than a day. "Don't worry," he told her. "I will make sure that you are well fed when we reach my uncle's restaurant."

That evening, about two hours after sunset, he allowed her to take a shower and gave her a fashionable blue *churidaar* and sandals to wear. When she was clean and dressed, he sat her down in front of a mirror and gave her a makeup kit.

"You must paint yourself like a film actress," he said. "I need you to look like you are eighteen. Can you do that?"

Sita thought for a moment and nodded. She applied foundation and blush, eyeliner and mascara, until her face looked like that of a young woman.

When she had finished with the makeup, Navin studied her reflection in the mirror.

"Excellent work," he said. "Now come with me."

Sita followed Navin into the living room. A cricket match between India and England was playing on the television. She obeyed when he told her to sit on the couch, and then he sat down beside her. On the coffee table in front of them was an array of objects—three boxes of condoms, the bag of brown powder he had bought on the street, a pair of scissors, a tiny spoon, a jar of coconut oil, a spool of thin string, and a rubber hand clamp.

Sita watched with a growing sense of unease as Navin took a condom and cut it off about three inches from the tip. He discarded the upper portion and picked up the small spoon. Scooping powder from the bag, he poured it carefully into the remnant of the condom. When the condom was half-full, he compressed it with his fingers and clamped the loose end just above the bulge. He cut two lengths of string and used the first to tie the loose end of the condom between the bulge and the clamp. Then he pulled the loose end back over itself and made a knot with the second length of string. He trimmed off the remaining latex with the scissors and set the packed condom on the table. It had the shape of a pellet about an inch long and three-quarters of an inch wide. In this manner, he created thirty pellets. When he was finished, only a trace of powder remained in the bag.

He left the room and returned holding a large glass of water and a round pill. The medicine, he said, was an anti-laxative and would slow Sita's digestion. He told her to take it and to drink all the water. Then he took the first pellet and dipped it in coconut oil.

"You will swallow all of these," he said, gesturing at the pellets. "They will fit in your stomach."

Sita shuddered at the thought of the drugs inside her. She took a sharp breath. "Is it *khas-khas*?" she asked, thinking of the poppy fields of Afghanistan.

"Not opium," he replied. "Heroin. The finest in India."

Sita's hands began to tremble. "What if they break in my stomach?"

Navin spoke with brutal honesty. "If a condom ruptures, the heroin will send your body into shock and you could die. To avoid this, you must remain as still as possible and not eat or drink anything until we reach our destination. Do not make any sudden moves. Do not compress your stomach. Do exactly as I say and everything will go well for you."

Sita struggled to breathe. She looked at the heroin-stuffed condoms, arranged neatly in a row, and thought of Ahalya trapped in Suchir's brothel somewhere in the city. She made her decision. She would survive this ordeal. Ahalya would wait for her. It might be years, but Sita would find her again.

She took the first pellet from Navin and swallowed it with effort. It hurt her throat, but she didn't allow herself to choke. She took the condoms one by one until she had swallowed the last. She felt leaden inside, as if she had feasted at a holiday meal and returned for seconds and thirds against all common sense.

The clock on the wall showed that it was eleven o'clock. Navin placed a brief call on his mobile and then took Sita's hand.

"It is time to go," he said. "I will explain more on the way."

Navin's driver met them in the garage. Sita walked slowly, feeling the mass in her stomach quivering with every step. She tried not to think about what would happen if one of the condoms burst. She said a silent prayer to Lakshmi for protection and climbed into the SUV.

On the drive to the airport, Navin turned around in his seat. "You've done well so far," he said. "I'm pleased. The next step is the most difficult. Our flight to Paris departs at two a.m. There are four obstacles we must overcome—the ticket agent, airport security, the flight attendants, and French customs. The ticket agent and airport security are easy. The X-ray machines can't look inside your stomach. The flight attendants will leave you alone as long as you appear to be asleep. French customs, however, can be a challenge."

Navin produced a folder with a set of documents. He showed Sita a forged marriage license and passports. "You are Sundari Rai. You are eighteen years old. We were married here in Bombay. I am in the insurance business. We are traveling to Paris on our honeymoon. The rest of your life is yours. If you are asked questions about your family, tell the truth. If anyone comments on how slowly you move, tell them you are pregnant. The most important thing to remember is that these people have no reason to suspect you. Our documents are first rate. We don't look like criminals. Therefore, we are not criminals."

Sita stared at Navin and tried to absorb all of this. Paris. Worlds apart from Bombay and thousands of miles from Ahalya. Fear twisted her heart into a knot. What would her life be like once the drugs were flushed from her system? She considered whether she should approach a police officer at the airport but rejected the idea. Would anyone believe her story?

In her mind she went over the particulars of her new identity. She would become Sundari Rai. She would accomplish this deception. It would take less effort than Navin imagined. All her life she had wanted to trade places with

Ahalya. As Sundari, she would become her sister. She would be bold, daring, and strong. She would leave behind the girl that she was and become a woman, a *married* woman. For Ahalya's sake, she couldn't afford to fail.

When the driver pulled up to the curb at the airport, Navin gave his final directions.

"Remember, don't drink anything until I tell you to. If the acids in your stomach become agitated, one of the condoms could rupture. Also, don't think of talking to the police. I will tell the authorities that you were helping me. Believe me when I say that you do not want to see the inside of a Bombay jail."

"I understand," Sita said, feeling more confident.

"Good. Time to go."

Although it was after midnight, the airport was brimming with activity. Navin gave Sita a black leather handbag and took the handle of his own rolling suitcase. He led her to the Air France ticket queue. There were fifteen people in front of them, but the line moved swiftly. The ticket agent was a pretty Indian girl of no more than twenty-five. She smiled at Sita and checked them in without suspicion.

They passed through airport security without incident, and then Navin led the way to their gate. Beyond the window Sita could see a wide-body aircraft painted in the red, white and blue colors of Air France. Navin took a seat and buried himself in a magazine. Sita struggled to find a comfortable position and alternated between sitting and standing.

When the flight was called for boarding, she followed Navin down the jetway and onto the plane. Their seats were in the last row near the restrooms. Navin gave Sita the window seat and asked a flight attendant for a pillow and a blanket. His wife was pregnant, he explained, and she was desperately tired.

Sita took the pillow and blanket gratefully. Navin had spoken a partial truth. She *was* desperately tired. It was half past one in the morning. She placed the pillow against the window shade and rested her head against it, closing her eyes.

She opened them again only briefly when the plane took off over Juhu Beach and the black Arabian Sea. Navin had told her that flight time to Paris was a little over nine hours. She meant to sleep through all of it.

Chapter 11

O thou lord of life, send my roots rain.
—Gerard Manley Hopkins

Mumbai, India

Ahalya looked up when Anita returned to the file room at
the Nagpada police station. Around her were the other *beshyas*
from Suchir's brothel and one constable keeping watch. The
CASE specialist sat down and took her hand. Ahalya didn't
react to Anita's touch. She looked down at the ground.
Sumeera's pronouncements rang in her head: "*She is gone
. . . It is the way of Golpitha.*" The words were worse than a
death blow. In death, at least, she would not have suffered.

She rested her head on Anita's shoulder when it was
offered, but she found it impossible to sleep. At last, another
constable appeared and summoned her to the office of
Inspector Khan. Anita accompanied her. The noise and
activity of the station were a blur in her mind. Out of the
corner of her eye, she saw Prasad staring at her. She ignored
him and didn't turn her head.

Khan directed her to sit on a chair opposite his desk and began to ask questions. Ahalya tried to listen to the inspector's words, but her answers were unfocused. At one point the inspector had to repeat himself. He grew impatient, but Anita intervened and took Ahalya's hand again. This time, the sensation of human touch helped stabilize her.

She shook her head. "I'm sorry. What was the question again?"

The interview lasted thirty minutes. Khan took her statement in painstaking detail, reopening her wounds and piecing together the story of her exploitation. When he had finished writing his report, he went over it again, line by line, making sure everything was accurate. Then he signed his name and summoned the female *panchas*.

Following Anita's lead, Ahalya took a seat outside Khan's office. Across the room, Suchir sat in handcuffs, a bored *halvadar* by his side. She flashed back to the morning he had bought them from Amar for sixty thousand rupees. Looking at him, this time with the tables turned, she made a vow to herself. She would make sure that justice was served. Even if she had to wait years, even if it took the last of her strength, she would see him put behind bars. She would do it for Sita's sake, and she would do it for herself.

The rest of the night passed uneventfully. Ahalya dozed fitfully, her sleep beset by nightmares. The roar of the tsunami blended with the clickety-clack of the Chennai Express and the repulsive sounds of Shankar's lust.

In the morning, she was transferred into the custody of a government home for orphaned girls in Sion. The *maushi*, or warden, treated her with disinterest. She showed Ahalya the large dormitory where the girls slept, assigned her a bunk, and explained the meal schedule. Then she left her alone.

Ahalya looked out the barred windows and wondered how long she would have to endure this new form of confinement. Anita had assured her that CASE would find her a place in a private home, but Ahalya had no idea what that meant or whether it would change her circumstances. Her only desire was to be reunited with Sita.

Life had lost all other meaning.

After three days, Anita returned with good news: the Child Welfare Committee had approved Ahalya's transfer to an ashram in Andheri operated by the Sisters of Mercy. Anita escorted her to the private home in a rickshaw.

During the ride, Ahalya asked about Sita. Anita told her the story Inspector Khan had passed along to Jeff Greer. Under interrogation, Suchir had confessed the name of the man who bought Sita—it was Navin. But the brothel owner had no idea where he had taken her. Suchir expected Navin to return to make an additional payment, but it could be a month or two. In the meantime, Khan would keep watch.

When they arrived at the ashram, Sister Ruth, the superintendent, met them at the gate. She was a heavyset woman with a moon face and wore the *sari* habit of an Indian nun. She welcomed Ahalya cheerfully, taking no offense when Ahalya failed to respond.

Ahalya followed her through the gate and onto the Sisters of Mercy property. The ashram was located on a sprawling estate with gardens, winding paths, and well-kept buildings. They followed one of the paths through a grove of tall trees, passing buildings on either side. As they walked, Sister Ruth gave Ahalya a verbal tour. She spoke with such enthusiasm that Ahalya found it impossible not to pay attention.

The sisters operated a day school, an orphanage, and an adoption center for infants, along with the recovery center for girls rescued from prostitution. The girls at the recovery center took classes at the school and helped with chores. All the girls were expected to complete the tenth standard, but those who excelled in their studies were educated through the twelfth standard. Once in a while, one of the brightest students was given a scholarship to attend the University of Mumbai. The sisters had two objectives for each rescued girl—healing of body and soul and reintegration into society. It was an ambitious project, Sister Ruth admitted, but the ashram had a sterling success rate. Only twenty-five percent of the girls who graduated from the program returned to prostitution.

Ahalya walked with Anita and Sister Ruth to the recovery center, which stood at the top of a tree-shaded knoll. A breeze blew from the north-west and offered relief from the heat of early afternoon. Large bushes of bougainvillea proliferated around the perimeter of the center. The wind rustled the branches and turned their colorful flowers into pinwheels.

Ahalya stood on the threshold of the stucco building and noticed that the noises of the city no longer crowded her ears. Gone were the horns of taxis and rickshaws, the cries of hawkers, and the chattering conversations of the street. In their place, she heard the laughter of children and the sound of wind playing in the leafy boughs of a banyan tree.

She walked up the steps and stood at the entrance to a trellis-covered walkway lined with flowers. There were violets, primrose, jacobinia, and marigold, all vibrant in the loamy soil.

"Each of the girls is given a plant of her choice to tend," Sister Ruth explained. "What would you like, Ahalya?"

"A blue lotus," she replied, recalling the cherished *kamala* flowers that her mother had cultivated in a pond beside her family's bungalow. They were Sita's flowers. As a small child, her sister had believed them magical.

Sister Ruth looked at Anita. "We have a pond near the orphanage," she said. "I think a lotus would grow well there."

The nun's words lifted Ahalya's spirits. She looked toward Sister Ruth and then at Anita.

"You would let me plant a lotus?" she asked, astonished. Blue lotus seeds were rare and expensive, and germinating them successfully was difficult even under ideal conditions.

"I have a pot that would be just right," Sister Ruth said. "What do you think, Anita?"

Anita took Ahalya's hand. "Give me a few days. I'll see what I can do about seeds."

Chapter 12

The heart will break, but broken live on.
—Lord Byron

Paris, France

Sita awoke when the plane landed at Charles de Gaulle International Airport. Her mouth was parched with thirst, but she knew she couldn't drink anything until Navin gave the word. She distracted herself by looking out the window. It was seven-thirty in the morning, Paris time, and the winter sky was still dark.

The plane taxied to the gate. Navin took his suitcase out of the overhead bin and handed Sita a down coat. "It's cold outside. Put this on."

Sita stood slowly and donned the coat, ignoring the sloshing of the pellets in her stomach. The garment felt awkward over her *churidaar*, but she was grateful for its warmth.

"We're almost there," he said. "Two more hours at most."

Sita trailed Navin up the jetway to the international terminal. With the other passengers, they were funneled through a series of hallways to a bank of glass-encased cubicles. In each cubicle sat an immigration official. Sita ran through the details of her new identity again. *I'm Sundari Rai. Navin sells insurance. We're in Paris on honeymoon. Don't act like a criminal because you aren't a criminal.*

The immigration agent eyed them wearily. He flipped open Sita's passport and barely glanced at her photograph before stamping her visa and setting it aside. Then he took Navin's passport and opened it. At once something registered in his face. He held the passport up to the light, peering at the photo. Then he looked hard at Navin, all sleepiness gone from his eyes. He punched a few keys on his computer. Frowning, he picked up a handheld radio and placed a terse call. Within seconds, two security officers approached them, looking at Navin.

The immigration agent stepped out of his booth. "You must come with us," he said. "We have some questions for you."

"What kind of questions?" Navin demanded. "What is the problem here?" When the agent didn't blink, he went on: "I'm a French citizen. You can't hold me without a reason."

The agent shook his head, unimpressed. "We will speak in private. I am sure we will be able to correct any . . . misunderstandings, no?"

"This is outrageous!" Navin said, but his protest met a blank stare.

Standing beside him, Sita felt a stab of gas in her intestines and tried not to wince. She looked at the immigration agent and wondered for an instant whether he knew the truth. The thought of being caught smuggling heroin terrified her.

The security officers escorted them from the checkpoint area to a concealed door in the far wall. Navin took Sita's hand as if to reassure her, but the pressure he applied sent an unmistakable message. Sita's heart began to race. The weight in her belly was as heavy as lead, and she felt the strong urge to relieve herself. She didn't know how much longer she could wait.

On the other side of the door was a corridor with security cameras. The immigration agent led them to another door not far down the hallway and gestured for Sita to enter. She glanced at Navin and fear blossomed in her. Instead of anxiety in his eyes, she saw only menace.

She stepped into the room, and one of the security officers followed. The room was featureless, furnished only with a table and two chairs. The officer pulled out a chair for her, and she took a seat. She wanted to speak, to ask what was happening, but she knew her voice would betray her. The security officer took up a post beside the door and stared into space. It was obvious he was waiting for someone.

The delay seemed interminable to Sita. In the vacuum of silence, her thoughts spun and tumbled. She pictured the inside of a French jail and imagined herself imprisoned behind bars of iron, a convict among hardened criminals. She folded her hands and looked down at the table, struggling to steady her breathing.

At last the door opened and a woman appeared, dressed in the uniform of an immigration agent. She was thin and her blond hair was cut short. She glanced at the security officer, and he disappeared without a word. The woman sat down at the table and placed Sita's passport and a pad of notepaper in front of her. She regarded Sita coolly, twisting her pen in her fingers.

"Your name is Sundari Rai?" Her English was crisp, with only a trace of a Gallic accent.

Sita nodded meekly, steeling herself against her raging heartbeat.

"You do not look like you are eighteen."

For a split second, Sita considered telling her the truth and letting karma take its course. Perhaps a judge would give her a lighter sentence for confessing. Perhaps he would believe she had acted under Navin's compulsion. But then the second passed and the terror returned. If she were deported, she would be delivered into the hands of the Bombay police. In all likelihood, she would be charged with drug smuggling under Indian law. She recalled Navin's words the night before: *Believe me when I say that you do not want to see the inside of a Bombay jail.*

"I am eighteen," she said, trying to give her voice the confidence of an older girl. "I have always been small for my age."

The woman tapped her pen on her pad. "Your family, where are they from?"

"Chennai," Sita said.

"Where is that, exactly?"

"It is on the Bay of Bengal in south-east India. It used to be called Madras."

The woman wrote something down. "The man you are traveling with, who is he?"

"He is my husband," Sita replied, clasping her hands together in her lap to keep them from trembling.

The woman looked nonplussed. "You are very young to get married."

Sita tried to imagine how Navin might respond if asked the same question. "It was arranged by our parents," she said at last.

The woman thought for a moment and then took the conversation in a different direction. "Have you ever been to Pakistan?"

The question took Sita by surprise. "No," she said simply.

The woman looked at her with sudden intensity. "Did your husband ever tell you about his frequent trips to Lahore?"

Sita narrowed her eyes and shook her head slowly, having no idea where this was going.

"Did he ever mention his connections to Lashkar-e-Taiba?"

Sita shook her head again. Her father had spoken about LeT. It was a radical Islamic organization responsible for numerous terrorist attacks on India. If the woman was right, Navin was far more dangerous than he seemed.

"No," Sita replied. "All I know is that my husband is in the insurance business."

The woman looked down at her pad. "You are in Paris for pleasure?"

Sita was about to nod when she felt a lancing pain in her gut. She grimaced involuntarily. The wave of intestinal gas persisted for a long moment before passing.

The woman noticed her discomfort. "Are you in some kind of distress?" she asked, leaning forward in her chair.

Blood rushed to Sita's face and her mind went blank. She had managed to avoid tripping over her words, but the churning mass in her colon had a life of its own.

"It's just . . ." she began, grasping at the bits of the story she was missing. What was it Navin had said? What was her excuse? It came to her: "I'm three months pregnant. I've been feeling a little nauseous."

The woman sat back and regarded her. After a long moment, her face seemed to soften. Suddenly, they heard a knock at the door.

"Just a moment," the woman said and left the room. When she returned, her face had transformed. In place of her interrogator's mistrust, she wore an apologetic smile.

"There has been a misunderstanding. Your husband resembled a man we are looking for, but the match was a mistake. You can go now."

Relief flooded Sita. She tried to stand too quickly and winced at the pain.

"Let me help you," the woman said, steadying Sita on her arm. "I remember the feeling. I have two children of my own."

The woman escorted her to the end of the corridor where Navin stood waiting. He smiled at Sita and gave the woman a look of profound annoyance.

"If anything happened to my wife or my child . . ." he said, dangling the threat in the air. It was an effective ploy. The woman actually looked afraid.

"Please accept our sincerest apologies for your inconvenience," she said, opening the door to the checkpoint area and handing back their passports. "I hope you enjoy your stay in Paris."

Navin took Sita's hand and led her across the floor to the ramp leading to the baggage carousel. He didn't speak until they entered the airport ticketing area.

"You were wise not to talk to them," he said. "They would never have believed you."

Sita blinked and looked away. Her emotions were a chaotic mess. She had escaped the clutches of French immigration, but her intestines were stuffed with pellets of heroin and the pain was increasing with each passing minute.

"We will take a taxi into the city," Navin said. "It is faster than the Metro."

Sita followed Navin out of the terminal to the taxi stand. The Parisian winter shocked the breath out of her. She began to shiver and huddled deeper into her coat. Navin hailed a taxi and gave instructions in French. The only words Sita understood were the last: Passage Brady. The driver nodded and accelerated into traffic.

Sita held her stomach and winced. She looked out the window and watched as the city of Paris appeared—first as a network of gray and white suburbs, then as a patchwork of industrial parks and train yards, and last as a city of wide boulevards and elegant buildings.

The taxi driver deposited them at the entrance to a pedestrian passage and took two twenty-euro notes from Navin. Navin led her through an archway to a set of heavy double doors painted blue. He placed a call on his mobile and spoke in Hindi to a man he called "Uncle-ji."

"We are here. Yes, she is with me." He grunted and hung up.

After a minute, the door swung wide and a man greeted them. He was short and balding, with round eyes. He shook Navin's hand and welcomed him with a fleeting smile. He turned to Sita and his gaze lingered.

"She will do," he said cryptically and gestured for them to follow.

Beyond the doors lay a private courtyard with entrances to a number of flats. The man led the way into a dark foyer.

"Use the washroom at the end of the hall," he said. "I will be in the restaurant."

Navin gestured toward a door at the end of a short hallway. He entered the bathroom and switched on an overhead bulb. The room was equipped with an ancient porcelain toilet, a grimy sink, and a stained bathtub.

"How are you feeling?" he asked.

"I'm thirsty," Sita replied, her mouth as dry as cotton.

"Take a seat on the toilet. I'll get you a glass of water."

She sat down slowly and took a deep breath. Navin returned with a mug brimming with water. She accepted it and gulped the water down. She looked at Navin, her eyes making a plea for more. Navin took the mug and replenished it. This time, however, before giving it to her, he handed her a round pill.

"It is a laxative," he said. "It will help you flush the drugs. Otherwise, you could wait for a day or two before the last condom leaves your system."

She took the pill and swallowed it and drank the water to its last drop. Navin turned on the faucet over the tub, and hot water poured out in a billow of steam.

"You will soak in the bathtub to loosen your bowels. When the drugs come, they will float. Place them gently in the sink. If the condoms rupture now, I will not be pleased."

Navin turned and left, closing the door behind him.

Sita looked at the floor, disgusted by the thought of what she must do. She allowed the water level to rise in the bathtub until it was three inches shy of the upper rim. She disrobed and slipped into the hot water. It gave her welcome relief from the pain in her belly. She closed her eyes and thought of Ahalya as she was before the madness, before the tsunami came. She listened for the sound of her sister's voice, singing sweet songs and reciting poetry. Would she ever see her again?

What did Navin and his uncle have in store?

*

The pellets began to emerge quickly. She didn't urge them along for fear they would burst. When they appeared in the water, she cleansed them of waste matter and placed them gingerly in the sink. The process was disgusting and extremely uncomfortable, but she persisted, her skin shriveling like a prune, until she had accounted for the thirtieth pellet. The latex and Navin's knots had held. She breathed a huge sigh of relief and felt the spring of tension in her body begin to uncoil.

She released the drain plug and allowed the filthy water to retreat. When it was gone, she turned on the faucet and rinsed the bath and her skin. Then she let the tub refill until the water covered her core and warmed her again. She soaked in the bath for many minutes and tried to relax.

In time a knock came at the door. Her heart lurched and she watched the doorknob, anxious that Navin would enter.

"Sita," he said through the doorjamb, "how many condoms have come?"

"All of them," she replied.

"Perfect. And they are in the sink?"

"Yes."

"There is a plate of food outside the door. Dress and eat quickly. I will introduce you to Aunti-ji."

Five minutes later, Sita left the bathroom wearing her *churidaar*. She collected the plate of food—chicken, rice and chutney—and ate hungrily. Soon Navin reappeared and led her through the living quarters to a door she had not noticed before. The door led to a hallway and the hallway to a cluttered kitchen. In the kitchen stood a matronly Indian woman dressed in a *sari* along with a boy about ten years old clad in jeans and a Western-style shirt. The woman was scolding the boy in a language Sita didn't understand.

They turned toward Navin, and the woman switched to Hindi.

"How was Bombay?" she asked.

"Hot, congested, and crawling with slums," he replied. "Each time I return I like it less."

"Don't say such things," she scolded him. "It will always be home."

Navin chatted with the woman briefly. The boy, meanwhile, ignored Navin and regarded Sita through guileless eyes. She looked back at him and felt a twinge of nostalgia. He resembled a boy at the convent school who had always doted on her. The pleasant thought disappeared almost as soon as it came.

"Does she cook?" the woman asked Navin.

Navin looked at Sita inquiringly, but she shook her head.

"A *ladki* who does not cook," said the woman harshly. "What good is she?"

"She can clean the restaurant," Navin's uncle said, walking through a doorway on the other side of the room. "Navin has done us a great favor."

The woman frowned at her husband and shook her head. "It is bad luck bringing her here. The priest says an ill omen is written in the stars."

"Silly woman," Navin's uncle said, "stop your ranting

and get to work." He turned to Navin and handed him an envelope. "Five thousand euros."

"Five thousand!" the woman exclaimed. "What a waste!"

Navin's uncle glared at his wife and she turned away, clucking.

Sita looked at the envelope, and despair spread through her. She knew that another deal had been made.

The woman handed Sita a mop. "Use the sink," she hissed. "Start with the kitchen. Then do the restaurant. Earn your keep."

Sita had never before wielded a mop. Jaya had done all the cleaning in the Ghai household, and Sita's chores at St. Mary's had been limited to gardening and laundry. She took the mop and awkwardly doused it with water.

"Stupid girl," the woman spat. "Fill the sink, soak the mop, wring it out, and then use it. Where on earth did Navin find a girl as dumb as you?"

Despite the barrage of insults, Sita did not allow herself to cry. She followed the woman's instructions and steeled herself against the pain. By some instinct, she understood that exhibiting weakness would only invite more abuse.

She spent the afternoon mopping and sweeping and scrubbing thick, oily grime off a multitude of surfaces in the kitchen. The woman was a cruel taskmaster; nothing Sita did was right. She rubbed so hard on the upper surface of the stove that her fingers began to lose sensation. Her nails chipped on exposed edges, and the rags and scalding water burned her hands. By the time the restaurant opened at six that evening, she was bone-tired and famished. The woman banished Sita to the flat and gave her a broom and a dustpan.

"I don't want to find a speck of dust on the floor, or you will have no dinner," she said.

The woman tended the stove with the help of an Indian girl. They served up *tandoori* cuisine to a handful of their neighbors. It was a Friday night, but business was slow. The low table count made the woman even more irritable. When Navin's uncle closed the restaurant, the woman fetched Sita from the flat and gave her the mop again.

"Make this floor shine," she said. She pointed at a plate of rice and chutney on the counter. "You may eat when you are finished."

She mopped until midnight and collapsed in a heap in the corner with her food. She ate the meager offering but still felt hungry when she put the plate back on the counter. She thought of sleeping on one of the benches in the restaurant but feared that if the woman found her there, she would beat her. She returned to her corner and sat down.

As she began to drift off, the young boy appeared on the other side of the kitchen. After a long moment, he made a hesitant approach.

"What is your name?" he asked in Hindi.

"Sita."

"I am Shyam," he said, kneeling down in front of her. "Can we be friends?"

Sita shrugged, but Shyam persisted. "I am ten. How old are you?"

Sita didn't respond. She could barely keep her eyes open.

"I brought you a gift," the boy said. He removed a small figurine from his pocket and placed it in her hand. "It is Hanuman. He will keep you company."

Suddenly, he turned his head and looked at the door in fear. His mother was yelling his name. "I have to go," he said.

He stood up and switched off the lights. A few seconds later, Sita heard the door close and the lock snap into place.

In the darkness, she traced the shape of the figurine with her fingertips. She could feel Hanuman's tall crown and scepter. She held him to her chest and remembered Ahalya's voice as she told the story of the great monkey on the night Navin first came. She wrapped her arms around herself and tried in vain to fall asleep.

At some point, she began to shiver. The kitchen was poorly heated and cooled quickly with the stove off. She struggled to her feet and searched a nearby closet for a way to cover herself. She found a sack of soiled tablecloths. Spreading one on the floor, she lay down in the closet beneath a rack of cleaning supplies. She pulled a second tablecloth over herself and buried her feet in the lightweight fabric. She still felt cold, but at least now the temperature was bearable.

She placed her head on the sack and clutched Hanuman beneath her chin, warding off the icy tentacles of isolation and fear.

At last, she slept.

Chapter 13

The soul, it is said, is enclosed in bones, that
human love may be.
　　　　　　　　　　　　　　—Thiruvalluvar

Mumbai, India

Thomas placed the call the day after the raid. The rescue had
affected him profoundly, and he could no longer justify
irresolution. Either he was going to contact her or he was going
to let her go. His heart quickened with the sound of the ring
and then her voicemail picked up.

"Hello, you've reached Priya. Leave your number and I'll
call you back soon. Ciao."

Thomas searched for words and spoke after the beep.
"Priya, I'm in Bombay. I know this is a surprise, but I'd like
to see you. Please call me back." He left his new mobile
number and hung up.

It was two in the afternoon, and he was on Linking Road
in Bandra. After the long night, Jeff Greer had given him
the day off. Thomas had spent a lazy morning at Dinesh's

flat, reading and watching the news. After lunch, he decided to explore the suburb.

He turned north and walked slowly along the commercial strip. The stores were as diverse as those in an American mall, and the sidewalks were a hive of activity. Vendors propositioned him from their stalls: "Sir, sir, we have jeans, just your size." Touts approached him aggressively, peddling packs of undershirts, *bhel puri* snacks, and colorful maps of the world.

"No, no," he said, waving them off.

"But, sir, these are the *finest* maps," one of them said.

He walked on. The tout, however, kept pace: "You look like a film star. What movie were you in?"

Thomas laughed. "I've never been in a movie and I don't want a map. Thanks."

At last the tout gave up and let him go.

He window-shopped for a while and then tried on a few pairs of shoes in an upscale haberdashery before returning to the street. He waited for his BlackBerry to ring.

Finally, fifty minutes later, it vibrated. He took out the phone and saw he had an e-mail. The address on the screen was Priya's. He angled away from the curb and found a quiet alcove beside a luggage shop. He took a breath and opened the message.

Thomas, this is a shock. I don't know what to think. But I can't ignore that you are here. There is a park on Malabar Hill. Take the train to Churchgate and tell the taxi-walla to drive to the Hanging Garden. I will meet you at the seaside overlook at 4:30.

Thomas immediately hailed a rick and instructed the driver to take him to Bandra Station. Following Priya's directions, he caught the fast train to Churchgate and a taxi to Malabar Hill. Inside he was tied in knots. He had no idea what to say to her. It was almost as if they weren't married, as if they were back in Cambridge, a boy and a girl from different worlds, tentatively exploring the intersection. Yet that was not true. They had a past, years of intimacy, of happiness and tragedy. None of it could be erased, but he didn't want to erase it. He wanted . . . what? To begin again? To woo her back to Washington? To win over her father? The complexities were confounding.

The taxi passed the wide sand of Chowpatty Beach and entered the posh neighborhoods of Malabar Hill. The steep terrain and towering apartment complexes reminded him of San Francisco. The driver took a right and followed a serpentine street up to the crown of the highest hill. Buildings gave way to leafy foliage and lush parkland.

The *taxi-walla* dropped him off at the entrance to the Hanging Garden. He walked up the steps and looked out across the carefully tended expanse. Shade trees rimmed meadows of grass, and flowers and sculpted bushes proliferated.

A boy approached him, carrying fans made of peacock feathers. "You like a fan, sir?"

Thomas shook his head.

"Very nice, sir, for your wife or girlfriend? Only fifty rupees, sir."

"I don't want a fan, but I will give you fifty rupees for directions to the seaside overlook."

The boy pointed back the way Thomas had come. "Cross the street and go into the park on the other side. The overlook is that way."

Thomas took out his wallet and gave the boy his money.

"Here is your fan, sir," the boy told him, placing it in his hand. "Directions are free." He smiled and walked away.

Thomas held the fan awkwardly, but then he started to laugh. He crossed the street and saw the shimmering blue of Back Bay in the distance through the trees. He followed a path through rock gardens and spotted the overlook in the distance. A few people sat on scattered benches, but he saw no sign of Priya. He glanced at his watch and realized he was ten minutes early. His wife would probably be late. She had always possessed a carefree sense of time.

He walked up to the railing and looked out across the bay toward Marine Drive and Nariman Point. His thoughts drifted to Suchir's brothel. He found it scarcely imaginable that the filth and abuse of the red-light district were only a few miles away from Malabar Hill.

Before long, Priya stepped quietly to the railing. "Thomas," she said simply.

He turned to her and found himself speechless, gripped

by the terror he had imagined since he stepped foot on Indian soil.

She rescued him by speaking first. "I see the *fan-walla* found you."

Thomas looked at the trinket in his hands, and it became a lifeline. "He was persistent," he said at last, the pressure in his head easing slightly.

"So you are here. I can't believe it." She spoke softly, testing the water.

"I'm here," he replied simply.

"Did you come to see me?" She had never liked small talk.

"No," he admitted. "I came to work for a public interest group."

Priya was astonished. "You left Clayton?"

Thomas nodded.

"I don't understand," she said, shaking her head.

When the silence became awkward, he spoke a half-truth. "I needed a change. Nothing was right about the way things were."

She shook her head again, visibly perplexed. "Four years and you never budged an inch. Now all of a sudden you take the leap? What about partnership? What about your obsession with the federal bench?"

He thought furiously, working out an excuse that would interrupt the interrogation. She was a natural at cross-examination, in some ways better than he was.

"You'll be gratified to know we lost the Wharton case," he said. "The verdict was $900 million and change."

Priya blinked but lost only a second of focus. "I'm happy to hear that. But this isn't about Wharton. It's about you. And you haven't answered my question."

"People change," he said. "You know that as much as I do."

Priya gave him an intense look. "Why does that sound like a cop-out?"

Backed into a corner, he held up his hands. "What do you want me to say? I'm sorry I had goals? You knew that when you married me. But I'll apologize for what I did. I wasn't there when you needed me."

His contrition, however qualified, seemed to soften the edge of Priya's skepticism.

"What did your father have to say?" she asked in time.

Thomas swallowed hard. "He didn't understand."

"But he accepted it?"

"What else was he supposed to do? It wasn't his decision. You put your father in much the same position, if you recall."

She pondered this. "What NGO did you join?"

He tried not to look relieved. "I'm working with CASE in the red-light areas." He gave her a summary of his work, emphasizing the points that would impress her most. It was self-serving, but it was the only advantage he had.

"A worthy cause," she replied. "I grant you that." Then she turned the tables on him again. "And Tera, what did she have to say about all this?"

Thomas controlled his breathing. He had dared to hope she wouldn't bring Tera up, but he had been foolish. He feigned a bit of righteous indignation and delivered another half-truth. When it came out, however, it tasted like a lie.

"Come on," he said, "leave Tera out of this. I told you before, nothing happened. I needed somebody to talk to. If I crossed any lines, it was because I needed a friend."

"And I wasn't good enough?"

"We've been over this before. We weren't in any condition to help each other. Frankly, we needed to see a shrink. We had at least five people tell us that. But we were too stubborn. So you talked to your mother and I talked to Tera."

Priya's hands began to tremble and she gripped the rail, looking at the sea. She took a deep breath and thought about his words.

"Suppose I decide to accept that," she said at last. "Suppose I believe you when you say you've changed. What makes you think that anything is different between us?"

"I'm here, am I not? That has to mean something." It was a gambit, he knew, but he was running out of clever answers.

"I'm not going back to the United States," she said quietly. "At least not soon. You should know that."

"Okay."

"Is that all you're going to say?"

He shrugged.

"You don't seem surprised."

"The only thing I'm surprised about is that you're standing here."

Priya stood silently, the breeze lifting her raven hair. He wanted to stretch out his hand and touch her face, but he restrained himself. When she spoke, she took the conversation in a different direction.

"My grandfather used to bring me to this overlook when I was a little girl. He showed me the skyline of the city and pointed out all the buildings he owned. My father hated it when he did that. He never wanted what my grandfather had. His only love was the life of the mind. When I was old enough, I took my father's side."

Thomas waited. He knew she had more to say.

"You'll never understand how hard it was for me to do what I did. To leave my family, to defy my father's wishes, to cross the ocean and marry you. I never fully realized it until I returned to Bombay. I'm not sure my father will ever forgive me."

Listening to her speak, Thomas marveled at the clarity of her thought and the evenness of her tone. When he last saw her, she had been a wreck—haunted, conflicted, occasionally delusional. Her time in India seemed to have restored her balance, though he could see the sorrow buried just beneath the surface.

"How is your grandmother?" Thomas asked, relieved to be on surer footing.

"She has the best nursing care that money can buy, but she is old. My father is struggling with regret for taking us to England. We lost so much time."

"I take it the Professor doesn't think much of me."

Priya shook her head. "He doesn't talk about you. I don't know what he thinks."

"I'll never be Indian," he said. "Nothing will change that."

"It doesn't matter. His opinion is his. Mine is mine."

"Would he have you divorce me?"

Priya stiffened. He could tell the question stung. "In Hinduism, when a girl marries a man, she marries him for seven lifetimes. My father is secular in many ways, but he is devout in that sense. I doubt he would suggest divorce."

"Does he think we were never properly married?"

"Perhaps. But we performed the *saptapadi* and took our vows. He can't deny those things, even if the ceremony wasn't traditional or complete."

"Was it complete to you?"

Priya took a moment to answer, and Thomas held his breath, kicking himself for putting so much on the line so quickly. It had always been this way between them. She drew him out without so much as an ounce of effort, and he said things he regretted.

"Yes," she said at last. "I've never doubted that."

Thomas let out the breath he was holding. "So where does that leave us?"

"In a complicated place."

He waited for her to elaborate, but she left it at that. "Can I see you again?" he asked.

She turned toward him and their eyes met. "I need to think about it."

He nodded. The answer was about the best he could hope for. "Can I walk you back to the road at least?"

"Sure," she said, giving him the faintest glimmer of a smile.

They turned away from the sea and strolled quietly through the light and shadows of the park. Thomas listened to the wind soughing through the leaves and thought of the many walks they had taken in Cambridge beneath the oaks and willows along the Cam and afterward through the forests of Virginia. Their love had always been an improbable venture. Considering the feat they had attempted—the unification of two races, cultures, and civilizations—he had been naive to think that the world would grant him happiness without tempering it with trial.

When they reached the road, Thomas flagged a taxi for Priya and another for himself.

"It was good to see you," he said, surprising himself with the depth of his feeling.

Her smile brightened, but she didn't reply.

"You'll think about it, right?" he asked as she climbed into the waiting taxi.

"I'll think about it," she said.

He watched the taxi pull away and waved once, hoping she would look back. She didn't. He stood in place until the vehicle disappeared around a bend. Then he turned to the waiting *taxi-walla*.

"Churchgate Station," he said.

*

On Wednesday morning, Jeff Greer greeted Thomas and the CASE staff with the news that Suchir's attorney had pulled strings at the Sessions Court and scheduled a bail hearing for eleven o'clock. The attorney had connections with the Rajan gang and had perfected the art of manipulating the judicial system. If he wanted a hearing for his client, he got one.

"The prosecutor told Adrian that she is going to recommend against bail," Greer said, "but she isn't hopeful. Chances are, Suchir and his people are going to walk."

"Will they skip town?" Thomas asked.

"Doubt it," Nigel answered. "They know nothing but the sex business. The girls will be given small fines and they'll open up the brothel again in no time."

"Even when they were prostituting minors a couple of days ago?"

Nigel laughed. "Hard to believe, isn't it?"

After the meeting, Thomas approached Samantha Penderhook, CASE's legal director, and asked if he could accompany Adrian to the bail hearing.

Samantha hesitated. "It's not that I don't want you to go. It's just that a white face in a Bombay courtroom can cause a stir. These people are very sensitive about anything that looks like foreign interference in their system."

"What if I sit in the back? I can be a fly on the wall."

Samantha drummed her fingers on her desk. "Okay. But do exactly what Adrian says. And if the lawyer for the other side tries to make an issue, have the good sense to step out into the hallway."

Thomas thanked her and went to find Adrian. The young advocate wasn't enthusiastic about Samantha's decision, but he nodded cooperatively.

"Are you ready?" he said. "We need to leave in ten minutes."

"I'm ready now," Thomas replied.

On the way there, Thomas peppered Adrian with questions about courtroom practice in Bombay. He learned that the public prosecutor assigned to handle the bail hearing was one of the best in the city but that her competence was irrelevant to the outcome. The jail at Arthur Road was beyond overcrowded, and some of the trial judges tended not to regard trafficking cases with much seriousness. If the defense lawyer presented a thoughtful argument for release, it was likely the judge would buy it.

"Will Suchir offer the judge a bribe?"

Adrian shrugged. "Probably not. The judges aren't as corrupt as the police. But the gangs still have a lot of power in this town. It might not take a bribe to sway the court's decision."

When the train arrived at the station, they made their way to the Sessions Court. Although built in the grand Gothic style of the Raj, the building was a model of urban neglect. Its decor was spare and its walls and stairwells were dingy with grime. Adrian and Thomas took the stairs to the third floor. Adrian checked the docket outside the courtroom and nodded.

"Sit in the back," he instructed Thomas. "Try not to be seen. The advocate is aware that CASE was involved in the raid. Any white face he will affiliate with us."

They entered the courtroom together, and Thomas found a seat in the corner. The courtroom had an elevated bench for the judge and clerk and a long table facing the bench, where members of the bar waited their turn at the podium. A middle-aged woman dressed in a black and white *sari*— Thomas guessed she was the public prosecutor—sat at the far left of the table near a group of police officers. Adrian took a seat beside her.

Like the rest of the Sessions Court, the courtroom was long past its glory days. The wood trim was scuffed and fading, the paint on the walls drab and worn. The windows were arched in the Gothic style and grated to keep out birds. Eight ceiling fans were spinning at high speed, creating a downdraft and an incessant whir.

The judge was a grizzled, expressionless man with reading glasses perched on the bridge of his nose. He looked either chronically bored or ready to fall asleep. An overweight advocate was examining a witness in the dock. Thomas wondered if the judge could hear any of the testimony over the muffled roar of the ceiling fans.

Eventually, the advocate and witness finished their exchange. The judge dismissed the advocate with a flick of his hand and turned to the next lawyer in line. After two more cases, Adrian glanced back at Thomas and nodded. He stood with the public prosecutor, while defense counsel took his place at the podium.

The prosecutor made an impassioned plea for the judge to deny bail for Suchir, Sumeera, and Prasad. She told the court that Ahalya was a minor and that three of the legal-aged girls in the brothel had requested care from the Child Welfare Committee. Adrian whispered a number of additional points to the prosecutor, and she conveyed them to the judge.

At the end of her argument, the judge turned to defense counsel. The man was short, with a thick crop of black hair. He spoke at some length about the unfairness of the raid, the involvement of "imperialist interests from the United States", and the incompetence of the Nagpada police. He pointed out that none of the girls had been age-verified and that the evidence that Ahalya was under eighteen was merely anecdotal. He also contended that Suchir's confession about Sita's disappearance had been extracted from the brothel owner under duress. The man had a golden tongue and spun such a suggestive web of doubts and veiled accusations that the judge glanced at the prosecutor with visible irritation.

Thomas's heart sank. He knew at once that Suchir would walk.

Sure enough, the judge set bail at ten thousand rupees for Suchir and five thousand each for Sumeera and Prasad.

Adrian shook his head and motioned for Thomas to join him in the crowded hallway. They stood close together beside an open window.

"They'll pay the money this afternoon," Adrian said with a scowl. "This judge is contemptible. He never listens to the public prosecutor."

"What happens next?" Thomas asked.

Adrian looked out the window just as a flock of pigeons took flight. "We'll push for an early hearing and try to get Ahalya's testimony into evidence."

"How long will that take?"

Adrian shrugged. "With this defense lawyer, it could be months."

On Saturday morning, Thomas ate breakfast with Dinesh on the terrace, overlooking the gray-blue ocean. After his meeting with Priya at the Hanging Garden, he had told his friend the truth about Mohini's death and Priya's departure for Bombay. Dinesh listened with his typical sangfroid and gave Thomas a hug, waving off his apology.

"Now I understand why you didn't e-mail me during the fall," he said.

"I was in a fog," Thomas replied, and with that they put the matter to rest.

Thomas reached out and took a bunch of grapes from a bowl on the table. He broke off a grape and chewed it thoughtfully, wondering when he would hear from Priya. Three and a half days had passed without word, and he had begun to worry. Her assessment of their situation had been accurate. They were in a tangled mess. The past was immutable; the pain of it was indelible; and Priya wanted her father's forgiveness. Beyond that, there was the problem of his lies. He had no intention of staying in India more than a year or of giving up his dream of the bench, but he had led her to believe otherwise. And then there was Tera.

"What do you want to do today?" Dinesh asked, leaning back in his chair.

"I'll probably read for a while on the Bandstand," he said. "After that, I don't know."

Dinesh studied his face. "You still haven't heard from her."

Thomas shook his head.

"Well, cheer up. She said she'd think about it. I'm sure she's busy."

Thomas was about to reply when he heard his BlackBerry ring. It was inside on the kitchen counter. He stood up quickly and collected the phone. Warmth spread through him when he saw her number on the screen.

"It's Priya," he said, and Dinesh gave a thumbs-up.

Thomas placed the phone to his ear. "Hello?"

"Thomas," she replied. She let his name linger in the air for a few seconds and then put her words together in an uncharacteristic rush. "I've been thinking, as I promised to do, and I want to see you again."

He began to smile. In all the years he had known her, she had been nervous only when something significant was at stake.

"Okay," he said. "How do you want to do this?"

She took an audible breath. "My second cousin is getting

married tomorrow. The *mendhi ki rasam* will be held this afternoon at my grandfather's bungalow. My father should be in a festive mood. And there will be many witnesses so he will have to be kind to you."

Thomas closed his eyes. "Are you sure this is a good idea?" he asked. He was elated that she wanted to see him, but the notion of confronting her father at a gathering of her entire family terrified him.

"Are you having second thoughts?"

"No, no. I just . . . never mind. Tell me how to get there."

"Meet me at the entrance to Priyadarshini Park at five thirty. The *taxi-wallas* at Churchgate know the way."

"What should I wear?"

"Did you bring a suit?"

"Just one."

"One is enough. And Thomas?"

"Yes?"

"Don't forget to bring your sense of humor. You're going to need it."

He arrived at Priyadarshini Park five minutes ahead of schedule. The sun was low on the horizon and the sky was tinged with blush. He called Priya and she picked up on the first ring. She sounded nervous again.

"Stay where you are," she said. "I'll find you."

He stood at the side of the road, watching for her. After a minute, she emerged from a rickshaw and walked toward him. She was dressed in a *salwar kameez* the color of a tropical sea. The neckline of the dress was low-cut but tasteful, complementing her almond skin. She wore minimal makeup. She didn't need it.

She stopped five feet from him and smiled shyly like a schoolgirl. She had given him the same look the first time they met in Fellows Garden.

"Do you like my outfit?" she asked. "I can't wear this in the West."

"It's our loss," he said.

"You look nice."

"I feel like a stiff in a suit."

Her laughter was spontaneous. "You'll be right at home, then. My family is full of them."

"I have something for you," he said, reaching into his jacket pocket and pulling out the book of poetry his mother had given him. "My mom bought it for you for Christmas."

Priya looked at him with surprise. She took the book and admired it. "How did she know I love Naidu?"

"She must have guessed."

"Please tell her thank you," she said, clutching the book tightly. "It is a precious gift." She paused. "Did you . . . ?"

He nodded. "I told them."

"I'm sorry. It must have hurt."

Thomas shrugged. "They're grownups."

She looked away and recovered her composure.

"So where in the world is this party of yours?" he asked.

She led him to the rickshaw and gave the driver directions.

After a short trip, they arrived at a wooden gate flanked by plane trees. Two uniformed watchmen let them into the property. Beyond the gate lay a garden of breathtaking beauty. The soft light of dusk framed the trees in silhouette. A circular lawn lay in the midst of the garden, and upon the lawn was a candle-lit pavilion. At the center of the pavilion sat a young woman—the bride—in a yellow *sari* and a matching headscarf. An older woman wielding a tube of henna paste busied herself painting the bride's hands and feet with *mendhi* designs. Off to the side, a quartet of musicians serenaded them with Hindustani music.

Thomas stood inside the gate for a long moment. He saw the bungalow in the distance, situated in a grove of acacia trees. Its roof was tiled in terracotta, and its window shutters were open, inviting the breeze. Beside the house was a terrace dotted with guests.

"We called it Vrindavan when we were children," Priya said, making reference to the enchanted forests in which Krishna had been raised.

He nodded. "I have a hard time imagining you growing up in this world."

"Now you see why we left. My father would never have made his own name."

"Are all these people part of your family?"

"No. Some are friends. But don't worry, I won't introduce you to all of them."

Thomas smiled. "I'm okay so long as I can call all the guys Rohan and the girls Pooja."

Priya laughed again. "Behave yourself tonight. First impressions are everything."

He regarded her thoughtfully. "You know, it's been ages since we flirted."

She looked away and grew quiet.

"I'm sorry," he said, worrying that he had pushed too far, too fast.

"No," she responded. "Don't apologize."

Sensing her discomfort, he changed the subject. "Is your brother here?"

She gave a little laugh and the mood seemed to lighten again. "Abishek is on the guest list, but I doubt you'll see him. He's no doubt found some secluded spot to romance his new girlfriend. They've been inseparable for at least a month. All of us keep wondering when the novelty will wear off."

"And your father?"

She pointed toward the terrace. "He's up there, holding court with the intellectuals."

"In other circumstances, I would join him."

She took a deep breath and tried to sound optimistic. "You'll enjoy talking to him once he warms up to you. You have a lot in common."

"Too much, I think."

She didn't respond. "Come along. My mother wants to see you."

"Wait," he said. "You told her about me?"

"She asked me about it when I came home on Wednesday. I couldn't lie to her."

"And?"

"She has never objected to you, Thomas. She only wants me to be happy."

"So it's your father alone I have to convince."

She shook her head and looked into his eyes. "No. You only have to convince me."

He spoke carefully. "Then why are we here?"

Pain flashed through her eyes, and he knew that he had miscalculated. He held up his hands, entreating her forbearance, but she spoke before he could.

"These people are a part of me. Things can't be different between us unless they are involved from the beginning."

"You're right, of course. I didn't mean it like it sounded."

She studied him for a long moment, and he wondered whether she was going to escort him back to the gate. Then she smiled again and the moment passed.

He followed her down the twisting path through the garden. They crossed onto the lawn and walked toward the pavilion. Surekha Patel sat on a cushion, chatting with her neighbors. She was dressed in a purple sari, and her hair was tied in an elegant bun. Seeing them coming, she excused herself.

"Priya, dear," she said in accented English, taking her daughter's hand and strolling toward a tamarind tree on the edge of the grass, "isn't the music beautiful?"

"It is, Mama," Priya replied, her expression subdued. "As is Lila."

"She does make a lovely bride." Surekha turned to

Thomas, her expression inscrutable. "Welcome to Bombay. How do you find the city?"

"Fascinating in all respects," he said, trying not to appear nervous.

"I suppose that is a compliment." Surekha looked at her daughter and then back at him. "I do not blame you for taking Priya away from me. It was her decision, and I have always tried to understand it. Still, we are delighted to have her with us again."

Thomas plunged in, feeling like a man and a coward at the same time. "I understand, Mrs. Patel. Six years ago, I traveled to England to ask for Priya's hand. Your husband was gracious, but he didn't give me his blessing. I should have persisted until he did."

"You would have failed," Surekha said. "You were not what he wanted for his daughter. You couldn't have changed his mind then."

"And now?"

She looked away. "His mother is close to death. Perhaps he is different."

"If he gives me a chance, I will earn his respect."

Surekha nodded. "It is a worthy goal. But you must understand how difficult it will be. He has always been idealistic. When Priya was young, he told me that the man who married her would have to possess the character of Lord Rama. In Hinduism, Rama is a guiltless man."

"Yes," Thomas replied, "but even Rama questioned Sita's fidelity without cause."

"It is true." Surekha looked impressed. "Priya told me that you know our stories."

"Not as well as I would like."

"It is a beginning." Surekha looked at him again. "Come along. I will introduce you."

Thomas traded a glance with Priya as they walked toward the terrace. They climbed the steps to the veranda and turned toward a cluster of men ranging in age from twenty to seventy. A few were dressed in traditional *sherwanis*—long embroidered coats with matching pants—but the rest wore Western suits. Surya stood at the center, his distinguished face and silvered hair glowing in the firelight. His audience was silent, captive to his every word.

Surekha stood on the periphery, waiting for her husband to see her. At last he did.

"Pardon me, friends," he said and slipped out of the circle.

He glanced toward Priya and stiffened when his eyes fell on Thomas. He walked to the stone railing, looking out toward the *mendhi* tent, where Lila was receiving her adornment. After a moment, he turned around.

"Surya," Surekha began, "your daughter has a guest."

"I remember him," Surya replied.

Surekha frowned. "Try to be nice, dear. They have made vows."

"And neither of us was there to witness them," he retorted.

Thomas bore the brunt of Surya's anger without surprise.

Priya, however, was far less sanguine. Her eyes filled with tears and she began to tremble.

"Why have you come to Bombay?" Surya asked.

A cascade of thoughts passed through Thomas's mind, but only one answer seemed right. "I gave your daughter a ring," he replied.

Surya bristled. "Against my wishes."

"She gave me her hand." Thomas felt the heat rising under his collar.

"Your morals confuse me," the Professor replied. "You betray my trust and take my daughter from her family, and you attempt to justify it. This is the way of things in the West. The young have no respect for their elders."

"I tried to honor your family," Thomas replied. "I asked your permission. And you denied me. What was I supposed to do?"

Surya's eyes flashed and he balled his hand into a fist. "What were you supposed to do? What an infantile question! You were supposed to return to your life in the United States and leave her alone."

"Baba," Priya whispered. "*Please.* Don't *do* this."

Surya turned to his daughter. His fist unclenched when he saw her pain. He looked back at Thomas, searching for a target.

"You can never know what it means to me, to Surekha, that Priya didn't have a proper wedding. You can never know what it was like for us when she had a child and we were not there to see her born." Surya's voice broke. "Or to hold her before she died."

For the first time, Thomas felt the true weight of Surya's pain. Two thoughts came to mind in opposition to one another. First: *the fact that he wasn't there is his own fault*. Then: *he's just trying to figure out how to deal with the pain*. Thomas stayed silent.

The Professor turned around and leaned back against the railing, crossing his arms. "Are you here to take her back to America?"

Thomas shook his head. "I'm here to work in Bombay."

Surya stared at him. "Doing what, exactly?"

"I'm working with an NGO in the red-light areas."

"Ah," he exclaimed, "yet another Westerner who thinks he can fix all that is broken in India. My friend, you are neither the first nor the last to carry the white man's burden."

Thomas simmered. He could handle the accusation of stealing Priya, but to be called a racist was infuriating. He considered walking out, but he knew it would be a defeat.

"What is broken here is broken everywhere," he countered.

Surya was quiet, regarding Thomas through veiled eyes.

"And you feel you are contributing something with this work of yours?"

"We helped the Nagpada police take down a brothel on Monday night."

Surya shook his head. "There will always be brothels."

Thomas persisted. "We rescued a minor girl."

Surya paused. "Well, good for you." He looked across the terrace at the group of men he had left. "Pardon me, but I have friends to rejoin." He kissed his daughter's forehead and purposely avoided his wife's eyes.

Thomas watched the Professor walk away and then turned to Priya, masking his anger. She was hugging herself protectively, her eyes on the ground. Surekha touched her cheek and gave Thomas a look that said, "I told you it wouldn't be easy." She left them to attend to the other guests.

"I should go," Thomas said when they were alone.

Priya nodded, not meeting his eyes. "This was a mistake," she murmured.

Her words cut him, but he held his tongue. "I'll see you later," he said and left the terrace for the lawn. He walked quickly through the gardens and out to the street. After five minutes, a taxi appeared and he climbed in.

"Take me to Churchgate Station," he said.

It was then that he saw her standing at the gate between the watchmen. He held her gaze until the taxi pulled away from the curb and he lost sight of her. If she had come sooner, he would have said goodbye.

But the apology in her eyes was enough for him.

Chapter 14

The sky is overcast with clouds and the rain is ceaseless.
I know not what this is that stirs in me—I know not its
meaning.

—Rabindranath Tagore

Paris, France

For Sita, Paris was a dungeon of suffocation and toil. The
walls of the world closed in until nothing existed outside
the restaurant and adjoining flat. Her work was endless and
she was afforded no break. Navin's aunt, who insisted Sita
use the term of respect "Aunti-ji" for her, reminded Sita
constantly of her debt and showed no sympathy when the
girl exhibited signs of exhaustion. Aunti-ji's commands were
dictatorial: "Mop!" "Sweep!" "Scrub the floor!" "Scrub
the stove!" "Clean the bathroom!" The quality of Sita's
work was never satisfactory, nor did she ever finish fast
enough.

   She slept each night on the floor of the kitchen closet
beneath used tablecloths. For reasons she couldn't understand,

the heat that warmed the restaurant and the flat never seemed to reach the vent in the kitchen, and she was always cold. On occasion, she thought about escaping. But she was never left alone during the day, and at night Aunti-ji locked both doors to the kitchen using a key she kept on her necklace. Apart from the doors, the only exits from the kitchen were the heating vent and an exhaust vent over the stove, neither of which was large enough to accommodate her body.

One night the air in the closet grew so cold that Sita found it impossible to sleep. She shivered more violently by the hour and clenched her teeth against their incessant chattering. She kissed the little statue of Hanuman and bundled herself in tablecloths, praying for warmth, but by early morning she began to lose sensation in her toes. Reluctantly, she emerged from her cocoon to soak her feet in the sink.

The kitchen was as dark as the bottom of a well. She tripped over the mop she had left leaning against the refrigerator, and it fell clattering to the floor. She stood still, listening for the sound of footsteps. Aunti-ji had only slapped her once—when she spilled a bucket of cleaning solution in the bathroom—but she had threatened to beat Sita on countless occasions. Her heart raced when she heard a creak, but it came from upstairs.

She climbed softly onto the countertop and placed her feet in the sink. Feeling for the faucet, she twisted the knob slowly until water trickled from the tap. She turned it farther until the stream was steady and warming. The sound of the water flowing through the pipes petrified her. She was sure that Aunti-ji would appear, brandishing a broomstick.

Placing her feet in the water, she rubbed her toes to restore circulation. She wore the same *churidaar* that Navin had bought her in Bombay. Her undergarments had not been washed since she left India. Navin's uncle, who she was forced to call "Uncle-ji," allowed her to use the restroom in the restaurant, but only in early morning and late evening. Once, when she had the audacity to request a bath, Aunti-ji laughed cruelly and spat in Hindi, "You are not worth the price of the water."

After warming her feet and hands in the sink, Sita left her perch on the countertop and returned to the darkness of the closet. She fell asleep only an hour before sunrise and didn't stir until prodded with the handle of the fallen mop. She blinked her eyes and saw a fuzzy image of Aunti-ji standing over her. Her mind was a fog and her skin felt feverish. She tried to stand, but vertigo overcame her and she nearly collapsed.

"What do you think you're doing?" Aunti-ji demanded. "We use these tablecloths for our customers. How dare you sleep in them!"

"But I'm cold at night," Sita whispered.

Aunti-ji stared at her angrily. "You ungrateful girl. We feed you and provide you shelter, yet you complain." Aunti-ji started sniffing the air. "What is that stench?" She leaned closer to Sita and wrinkled her nose. "You smell like an unwashed pig. Come with me."

Sita followed her into the warmth of the flat. Her body felt prickly and unnatural. Her joints hurt and her throat was scratchy like sandpaper. She knew that she was getting sick. Aunti-ji threw open the door to the bathroom and gestured at the tub.

"Undress!"

Sita obeyed without thinking. Aunti-ji grabbed her *churidaar* and wadded it into a ball.

"Wash yourself! You have ten minutes. No more. I will clean this filthy rag of yours."

Sita climbed into the bathtub and scrubbed her skin until it was nearly raw. She ran her fingers through her tangled hair and began to cry, the tears flowing like a river of lava down her cheeks. She had left Bombay, thinking that she would be strong like her sister. But she had never expected such loneliness, such privation. When her ten minutes were up, she tried to collect herself, but the tears would not stop.

Aunti-ji barged into the bathroom and threw a towel and faded purple *sari* on the floor.

"Dry off and dress yourself. You have work to do."

For reasons Sita didn't understand, Aunti-ji allowed her to prepare for the day in privacy. She sneezed once, then twice, and felt her illness gestating. When she could wait no longer, she left the bathroom and walked to the restaurant. The boy, Shyam, was in the kitchen holding a broom and dustpan. He looked at her and smiled shyly.

"My mother went to the market," he said. "I am supposed to give you these."

Sita stared at him, unsure whether she should take the broom and sweep the restaurant. It was one of her morning duties, but Aunti-ji had always supervised her.

At once Shyam placed the cleaning supplies on the floor. "Do you like cricket?" he asked, extracting a handful of dog-eared sports cards from his pocket. He held them out to Sita eagerly. "I have Ricky Ponting and Sandeep Patil. But I do not have Sachin Tendulkar. Do you know Sachin Tendulkar?"

Sita nodded.

"Here." He thrust the cards toward her. "You may look at them."

She took the cards out of his hand. With the exception of a high-gloss Ricky Ponting card, their design was spare—just a photograph of the player's face rimmed by a white border.

"They're nice," she said, handing them back and managing a smile.

Shyam beamed with pride. "I will show you when I get Sachin Tendulkar."

Soon they heard the bell above the door to the restaurant jingle. Shyam stuffed the cards in his pocket, and Sita scooped up the broom and dustpan from the floor. She entered the restaurant and saw Aunti-ji holding a paper bag from the market. The warmth she felt on account of Shyam's kindness was short-lived. The woman glared at her and demanded to know why the floor hadn't been swept.

"You worthless creature," she said. "I let you bathe and you grow lazy. Get to work!"

*

The hours of toil turned into a millstone, grinding away at the last of her strength. She tried to stifle her sneezes, to stand upright and bear the burden of her illness invisibly. But her body failed her and sometime after noon she blacked out. She didn't know who found her, but she awoke on the couch in the flat, a pillow beneath her head. One of the girls who helped in the kitchen sat in the chair beside her. She held out a glass of water.

"Here," she said in Hindi. "You need to drink something."

Sita took the glass and gulped down the water. She felt as if she were floating in a cloud.

"I'm Kareena," the girl said. "I work in the restaurant."

"I'm Sita," she replied, beginning to shiver again.

Kareena covered her with a wool blanket. "Where are you from?"

"Chennai," Sita responded, trying to sit up.

"Easy now. You're not going anywhere today."

Sita grimaced and fell back against the pillow. Chills raced through her body and her skin was hot to the touch.

"You need to rest," Kareena said. "Uncle asked me to look after you."

Sita closed her eyes and fell asleep again.

When she awoke, the window to the courtyard was dark and Kareena was gone. A glass of water sat on the floor beside the couch. She drank it thirstily and listened to the sounds of activity in the kitchen beyond the wall.

She thought about Kareena. It was obvious that the girl

had nothing to do with her imprisonment. What story had Aunti-ji concocted to explain her presence in the household? Sita wondered if there were other girls like her in this city of endless winter—girls held against their will and forced to work until they collapsed from exhaustion or sickness. Navin had said there had been others before her. Where had they gone? And what had he done with the drugs she had carried from Bombay?

After a while, she lapsed into a dreamy state. She stirred only briefly when the family closed up the restaurant and retired for the night. Aunti-ji didn't bother her, and Shyam kept his distance. To Sita's surprise, it was Uncle-ji who replenished her water glass and asked if she was hungry. When she shook her head, he placed another blanket over her.

"Sleep well," he said. "When you recover, we will take better care of your health."

Winter deepened after Sita's fever broke. In keeping with his promise, Uncle-ji reduced her workload and allowed her to sleep on the couch in the flat. She kept a grueling schedule during the day, but she was allowed a ten-minute bath before breakfast and she ate freely from the restaurant's leftovers. Uncle-ji ordered his wife to buy Sita two *saris*, and Aunti-ji grudgingly allowed her to launder them with the family's clothing.

Each morning when Aunti-ji went to the market, Shyam met Sita in the kitchen and showed her his possessions. Once he brought a handheld video game and introduced her to Tetris. Another time, he brought a Bollywood magazine with a full-page photograph of Amitabh Bachchan and launched into a long-winded narrative about the famous actor.

The next day, he brought Sita a yellow marigold. He sat down on the floor and explained that he had secretly picked the flower from a neighbor's flowerpot. On impulse, she took a seat beside him and told him about her family's gardens on the Coromandel Coast and Jaya's *kolam* designs. Shyam listened carefully and then asked a question that took her aback.

"If you had such a nice home in India, why are you here?"

She looked at him for a long moment, realizing he had no idea of her predicament.

"Why do you think?" she asked.

Shyam furrowed his brows in puzzlement. "My mother said you needed work. She said you didn't have a family."

Sita took a sharp breath and folded her hands. "It is true about my family," she admitted, her voice little more than a whisper. "Only my sister is still alive."

"Where is she?" Shyam asked.

She thought of Ahayla in Suchir's brothel. "In Bombay," she said simply.

Shyam blinked. "I was born in Bombay," he said brightly. Then his eyes turned sad. "I don't like Paris. I miss India."

They talked for a quarter of an hour until they heard the ringing of the bell and Aunti-ji's footsteps. Sita scampered to her feet and hid the flower in her *sari*. Shyam, meanwhile, disappeared into the flat. Sita met Aunti-ji in the restaurant and endured her chastisement with a resurgence of poise.

Shyam was only a child, but for her his friendship was a ray of light.

Chapter 15

As a person acts in life, so he becomes.
—Brihadaranyaka Upanishad

Mumbai, India

CASE arranged for the delivery of blue lotus seeds to the Sisters of Mercy home. When they arrived, Sister Ruth gave Ahalya a clay pot to cultivate the plant. The lotus was a finicky flower and there was no guarantee that it would grow. But Ahalya was determined to try. She wanted to have a gift to offer Sita when they found one another again, something that would keep alive the spirit of their family. She planted the lotus seeds carefully in mineral-rich soil and filled the pot with water. She placed it in the pond near the entrance to the grounds.

Life at the home was highly structured, and all hours of the day were accounted for by some activity. Ahalya quickly learned to appreciate the schedule. Healing, she found, required motion, intention, purpose—the reassurance that life was still worth living.

She attended twelfth-standard classes at the day school, but the lessons were rudimentary in comparison with the rigor of St. Mary's in Chennai. Sister Ruth soon realized that Ahalya needed something more advanced to engage her intellect, and she spoke with Anita about the matter. Not long afterward, CASE arranged for a tutor to visit Ahalya twice a week and start her on university-level course work. She had always taken pleasure in learning, and the familiar rhythm of reading, discussion, and recitation gave her spirit new buoyancy and her future a renewed sense of meaning.

She met with Anita once a week, and they talked about many things. She always greeted the CASE specialist with a question about Sita. Each time, Anita assured her that CASE was working with the police to track down her sister. Anita told her that Inspector Khan had contacted the Bombay office of the Central Bureau of Investigation and the CBI had opened an investigation into Sita's disappearance. Ahalya walked with a lighter step for a day or two, but soon the silence began to weigh upon her again.

Where had her sister gone?

One morning when Anita was scheduled to make her weekly visit, Thomas asked Rachel Pandolkar, CASE's director of rehabilitation, if he could go along. Rachel gave him permission on the condition that he refrain from asking Ahalya any questions about Suchir's brothel. Thomas accepted the condition without hesitation.

Three weeks after the raid, he caught a rick to Andheri with Anita. The ride from Khar took the better part of an hour, and they arrived just before four in the afternoon. The gate to the ashram was unlocked, and Anita led the way into the grounds. They walked toward the fishpond situated in a stand of pink acacias.

"This place must feel like paradise after what the girls have been through," Thomas said, looking around in appreciation.

"You'd be surprised," Anita replied. "Most of them want nothing more than to go home. One girl tried to escape last week."

"Really?"

"The sisters caught her and brought her back. She was trafficked by her uncle from Haryana in the north. Her parents probably consented to it. For obvious reasons, we don't believe her home is safe, and the Child Welfare Committee agrees with us. It's hard to explain that to her, though."

Anita stopped at the pond and gestured for Thomas to take a seat on a stone bench.

"Ahalya will be along as soon as her tutoring lesson ends. This is where she comes during free time."

"Why?"

Anita pointed to a clay pot visible beneath the surface of the water. "In that pot are lotus seeds she planted. The lotus is the most prized flower in India. It is for her sister."

"She's still holding out hope that we'll find Sita?"

"Of course. Wouldn't you?"

Thomas thought for a moment. "I suppose the question was cynical."

"Cynicism is the curse of the West. In India, we still have faith." Anita turned around with a warm smile. "There she is."

Ahalya walked along the path toward the pond, her arms full of books. She glanced at Anita and focused on Thomas. She took a seat and continued to stare at him. The intensity of her gaze made him uncomfortable. He looked at the pond, hoping Anita would intervene.

Ahalya spoke first. "Have you found out where they took Sita?"

"Still no news," Anita replied. "The police are doing their best."

Ahalya turned to Thomas, and he saw the sadness in her eyes. "You were on the raid," she said quietly. "What is your name?"

"Thomas."

"You are British?"

"American."

She thought about this. "Why are you in India?"

"I'm a lawyer. And my wife is from Bombay."

"You practice law here?" Ahalya seemed confused.

"In a way. I'm interning at CASE."

"Your wife is Indian?"

He nodded.

"Do you have children?"

The question took Thomas by surprise and triggered a cascade of emotions.

"No," he said after a pause.

"Why not? Do you not like children?"

Thomas was unprepared for the girl's directness. He tried to think of a proper response.

"It's not that," he said finally. "We had a child, but she died."

Ahalya fidgeted with her schoolbooks. "I'm sorry," she said, her voice trailing off. Then she thought of something. "Do you know anyone at the American FBI?"

He smiled. "No. But I have a friend at the Justice Department. Why?"

"Maybe your friend could help find my sister."

He shook his head. "I don't see how he could. The Justice Department has no jurisdiction in India."

"But America and India are friends," she countered. "My father always said so."

"It's true. But the American government doesn't track girls who go missing in India unless they end up in the U.S."

At once a thought came to him. The United States was a member state of Interpol. In his research on trafficking, he had run across an article that mentioned Interpol's Child Abuse Image Database. The database collected pictures of missing children from around the world. If Ahalya had a photograph of her sister, perhaps Interpol would post it on ICAID.

"Do you have a picture of Sita?" he asked.

Ahalya's eyes brightened. "Wait here," she said. She dropped her books on the ground and walked briskly up the path to the recovery center.

"I bet you didn't expect to get interrogated," Anita said.

"No, but she has a right to her questions. I'm a strange sight in this place."

Anita didn't have time to reply. Ahalya returned to the pond holding a dog-eared four-by-six-inch photograph. She placed it in Thomas's hands and stood back, watching his expression. Thomas couldn't believe his eyes. It was a Christmas portrait of an Indian family. Ahalya was clearly recognizable in the foreground.

"Is that your sister?" he asked, pointing at the younger girl beside Ahalya.

"That is Sita," she confirmed.

"Where did you get that?" Anita asked, sounding astonished.

"I saved it from our house after the waves came," Ahalya replied.

"You carried it all this way?" Thomas asked.

"I hid it in my clothing," she said simply.

Thomas studied the image. Ahalya's father had a countenance that easily balanced affability and intelligence and her mother was doe-eyed and lovely. Their affection for one another was obvious in the way they leaned toward one another and drew their daughters into the center of the frame. The sisters held one another's hands and looked as if they had been laughing.

"Do you mind if I take this with me?" Thomas said.

Ahalya nodded. "If you promise to return it."

"Of course."

"Will it help you find Sita?"

Thomas waggled his head, then laughed at himself.

"You're picking up our mannerisms," Anita said.

"I'll be Indian before long." He looked at Ahalya. "I'm going to e-mail the photograph to my friend in Washington. There is an international database for missing children. I'm going to ask that he submit the photograph with Sita's name."

"You will do that?" Ahalya asked in mild disbelief.

"It's nothing," he said.

Ahalya studied him for a long moment. Then she did something that Thomas could never have predicted. On her wrist was a bracelet woven of rainbow-colored thread. She untied the band and knelt before him.

"Sita made this for me," she said, wrapping the bracelet around his arm. "Please give it to her when you find her."

Thomas was stunned. He wanted to shake his head and refuse the responsibility the bracelet implied. Girls who went missing in the underworld were almost never found, and when they were, they were usually too damaged to lead a normal life. Yet the band was on his wrist. He hadn't chosen it, but he saw no path of retreat.

"I'll do what I can," he said. "But I can't make any promises."

"Promise only that you will try," Ahalya said.

He took a deep breath and exhaled it. "I will try," he replied.

For the first time that afternoon, Ahalya smiled.

*

After work, Thomas took a rick back to Dinesh's place. His friend wasn't home yet. He set his laptop on the kitchen table and retrieved a compact digital camera from his suitcase. He placed Ahalya's photograph on the table, took a picture of it, and uploaded the digital file to his computer. Opening Photoshop, he cropped the image until only Sita was captured in the frame. Then he typed a message to Andrew Porter and attached the cropped photograph. When he sent the message into cyberspace, he felt a tangible sense of relief. The ball was now in the hands of the professionals. There was nothing more he could do.

He checked his inbox, hoping that Priya had replied to one of the three e-mails he had sent her since the debacle at her cousin's *mendhi* ceremony. It had been two weeks and still he hadn't heard from her. He scrolled through the list of messages and didn't see her name. He felt anger and impotence in equal doses. The Professor's dismissal had been rampantly unjust.

He perused a few messages from friends in the District. He had disappeared suddenly, and people were starting to wonder. He typed cursory replies and divulged almost nothing about his whereabouts. There would come a time for a more thorough accounting, but that time wasn't now.

He was about to shut down his computer when a new message appeared at the top of the screen. He couldn't believe his eyes. She simply would not give up. He clicked on the message. Tera had written:

Thomas, it's been over a month and no one at the firm has heard from you. I'm starting to worry. I keep telling myself that I should just let you go and lump you in with all the bastards who take a girl for a spin in bed and then cut them loose. But you're not like that. Something happened. Please don't leave me in suspense.

He walked onto the terrace, looking north toward Juhu Beach. Why was it that the woman he wanted seemed paralyzed by ambivalence, but the woman he had rejected wouldn't let him go? He hadn't wanted to use Tera. He hadn't seduced her. If anything, the opposite had happened. He considered sending her a terse reply but decided against it. He had no desire to reopen the connection between them.

Instead, he took matters with Priya into his own hands. He dialed her mobile number on his BlackBerry. He had no idea what he was doing, but it felt better than waiting around for her to figure out that her father had no intention of changing his mind. He listened as the phone rang. He expected the voicemail to pick up, but then he heard her voice.

"Thomas?" she said.

He heard indistinct noises in the background, like she was in a public place.

He took a deep breath. "Priya, I'm sorry to do this, but I couldn't wait any longer."

"I got your e-mails," she replied, her tone hesitant. "I've been meaning to call you."

"Can I see you?"

"Right now?"

"Any time. Now or later."

She thought for a moment. "There's a place called Toto's in Pali Hill. Meet me there at nine o'clock. Ask Dinesh if you need directions." He heard voices on the other end of the line.

"Gotta run," she said. "Nine o'clock. Toto's."

"I'll be there," he replied, but she had already hung up.

At five minutes after nine, Thomas sat at the bar at Toto's, sipping a beer. The place was incongruous. It was in the heart of Bombay's swankiest suburb, yet it had the look and feel of a Boston pub. The decor was urban retro—chain links and old automobile parts adorned the walls, and the shell of a VW Beetle hung from the ceiling. Every seat was taken when he arrived, almost all by young Indians dressed in Western clothing.

Priya arrived a few minutes later and shoved her way to the bar. She was wearing jeans, ballet flats, and a form-fitting oxford shirt. She looked every inch the *desi* girl.

"Remind you of home?" she asked, sitting down next to him. Her face was impassive, but she gave him the searching look she used when she was uncomfortable.

"Bizarrely so," Thomas replied. "They're even playing Bon Jovi."

Priya mustered a smile. "I never understood your fascination with rock music."

"I could say the same thing about the sitar. Who wants to play twenty-three strings?"

She laughed and signaled the bartender to bring her a beer.

"How's your grandmother?" he asked, making conversation.

Priya shrugged. "She's hanging on, but the doctors say it could be any day."

"I'm sorry."

An awkward silence followed. He could tell that she wanted to say something but couldn't figure out how to put it into words. The bartender set a bottle of Kingfisher in front of her, and she took a drink.

"How's your father?" he asked, pre-empting her.

She took a sharp breath. "Do you really care?"

He took a swig of his beer. "I care about you. I'm not sure if I care about him."

"At least you're honest."

He shrugged his shoulders. "Nothing else would work right now."

"He's not happy," she said, answering his question. "You upset him."

"*I* upset him? I think he upset himself. Life didn't turn out the way he wanted, and he's got to find someone to blame."

She shook her head. "You misunderstand him. He has a right to care about my decisions."

"Does that mean he has the right to control your life?"

Priya's eyes flashed and she pushed herself away from him. "How can you say that? I chose you, remember? I went against his wishes. I gave up four years for you."

He took a deep breath and calmed down. "Is that how you think of it?" he asked, quieter now. "That marrying me was a sacrifice?"

Her eyes moistened. "It was the hardest decision of my life."

"But do you regret it? If you do, I'll leave right now."

She looked away and sipped her beer. She was beautiful in profile, her black hair a striking contrast to her brown skin and eyes.

"What's that?" she asked, pointing at his wrist.

He saw the edge of Ahalya's bracelet peeking out beneath the cuff of his shirt. "You didn't answer my question," he said.

Her eyes spoke a challenge. "I'll answer yours if you answer mine first."

He showed her the bracelet. "The girl we rescued from the brothel gave it to me."

"Tell me about it," she said, suddenly intrigued.

He tried to keep the story short, but Priya would have none of it. So he delivered her the long version, complete with details of the raid, Ahalya's confrontation with Sumeera in the brothel lobby, his visit to the ashram, the photo of Sita, and the binding of the band.

When he finished, she gave him a piercing look. "Do you know what this means?"

"What?" he asked, mildly exasperated. "I told her I'd send the picture to Andrew Porter at Justice, and I did that this evening. I can't do any more. I wouldn't know where to start."

"You've never heard of a *rakhi* bracelet?"

"Oh no. Why does that sound ominous?"

"Could you drop the wisecracks? This is serious."

"Sorry." He held up his hands in apology. "Bad habit."

She collected her thoughts. "It's a tradition in India that goes back thousands of years. A woman delivers a bracelet to a man to wear around his wrist. The bracelet means that the man is her brother. He is duty-bound to act in her defense."

"You're joking, right?"

"Not in the least," Priya responded, enjoying his discomfort. "Legend has it that the wife of Alexander the Great saved her husband's life with a *rakhi* bracelet. She gave one to King Porus during Alexander's misadventures in the Punjab. Porus had a chance to kill Alexander in battle, but he restrained himself because of the promise implicit in the gift."

Thomas touched the many-colored band. "So, what am I supposed to do about it? I'm not James Bond. I'm just a lawyer working for an NGO. The police and the CBI can't find her. What are the chances that I can do what they can't?"

"A bit remote," Priya conceded.

"More like inconceivable."

"Don't be so gloomy. Maybe you'll catch a break."

Thomas shrugged. "That happens in the movies. Not in real life."

Priya looked at him with sudden gravity. "It happened to me."

It dawned on him that she had answered his question. "Does that mean I can see you again?" he asked.

She smiled. "Does that mean you're going to honor your promise to Ahalya?"

"A quid pro quo. I can handle that."

She raised her beer. "A toast."

"To what?"

"To miracles."

Thomas touched her mug with his. "To miracles. May a miracle find Sita Ghai."

Chapter 16

The most dangerous thing is illusion.
—Ralph Waldo Emerson

Paris, France

One evening at the end of January, Sita was in the kitchen closet organizing cleaning supplies when a well-dressed couple entered the restaurant. The evening had been slow, and there were few customers in the dining room. Sita watched through a crack in the door as Uncle-ji met the couple and escorted them to a seat in the corner. The man was stocky with a square, rugged face and close-cropped hair, and the woman was an attractive blond with pale skin. Sita thought nothing of them and returned to work.

Sometime later, after most of the guests had left, Aunti-ji shut down the stove and placed a plate of leftovers on the countertop.

"Mop the floor, scrub the stove, and then you may eat," she said, heading to the flat.

Sita filled up a bucket with soapy water and began to

mop. When she reached the entrance to the dining room, she saw Uncle-ji talking with the couple in the corner. Uncle-ji beckoned to Kareena's sister, Varuni, and pointed at the kitchen. Sita ducked out of view, hoping he hadn't seen her.

After a moment, Varuni entered the kitchen and retrieved a half-empty bottle of Smirnoff from a shelf. Sita thought to warn her about the wet floor, but she was too late. Varuni's foot slipped, and she fell in a heap.

Sita ran to her aid. "I'm so sorry," she whispered.

Varuni winced when she tried to stand. She rubbed her ankle. "Take this to Uncle," she said, handing the bottle to Sita. "The customer wants a refill."

Sita shook her head. "Aunti-ji told me to stay out of the restaurant."

Varuni gave her a reassuring smile. "She's not here. You'll do fine."

Sita took the bottle and walked hesitantly into the dining room. Uncle-ji and the man with the square face were conversing in French. The restaurant owner frowned when he saw her. He took the bottle of Smirnoff and waved her away. The man with the square face looked at her unblinking, and the woman beside him fingered her necklace.

She was about to turn around when the man said something to her in French. Seeing her blank stare, he tried again in English. "What is your name?"

The question took her by surprise. "Sita," she said after a moment.

"You are new here."

She traded glances with Uncle-ji, not knowing what to say.

The restaurant owner stepped in, sounding nervous. "She came from India. She is helping out in the restaurant."

The man seemed to ponder this. Then he looked at Uncle-ji and held up his glass. Sita retreated to the kitchen, feeling profoundly self-conscious. Varuni was still on the floor, massaging her foot.

"See, it wasn't hard," Varuni said.

"Who are they?" Sita asked.

"They are Russians, I think. Uncle calls the man Vasily. They live near my grandmother."

Sita looked at the clock and saw that it was after eleven. "Why are they still here?"

"Uncle and Vasily speak sometimes. I don't know what they say."

Varuni stood slowly and put weight on her ankle. "I need to finish up with the tables," she said, limping toward the dining room. She stopped on the threshold and tilted her head, listening. She narrowed her eyes and looked at Sita in puzzlement.

"What?" Sita asked.

"I think they're talking about you," Varuni replied.

"What are they saying?"

Varuni listened a moment longer. "Something about an arrangement." She shook her head. "I don't know."

Sita spent the night in a state of anxiety. She was desperate to find out what Uncle-ji and the man called Vasily had been saying, but Varuni had left for home before she could talk to her again. The next morning, Uncle-ji woke her early and told her to dress. He pointed at a coat folded neatly on a nearby chair. It was the coat Navin had given her on her first day in Paris.

"Put that on," he said, "and wait for me at the front of the restaurant."

Sita donned the coat and took a seat at one of the tables near the window, her apprehension mounting. Uncle-ji stood beside the door, looking out at the passage. Around seven thirty, a young man appeared and Uncle-ji greeted him in French. The man wore jeans and loafers and a leather jacket and carried himself with an air of authority.

The man nodded at Uncle-ji and looked at Sita without expression.

"*Viens,*" he ordered and held the door for her.

Sita didn't know the word, but she understood the man's intent. She glanced at Uncle-ji and began to tremble.

"Go," Uncle-ji said in Hindi. "Dmitri has work for you. He will bring you back later."

Sita hesitated a moment longer and then followed Dmitri out the door and down the cobbled lane to the nearby boulevard. The sky was clotted with gray clouds and the chilly air stung her cheeks. It was the first time she had been outside in nearly a month, but she was too afraid to appreciate it.

A black Mercedes was waiting at the curb, its hazard lights

flashing. Dmitri opened the back door, and Sita climbed into the plush interior. Dmitri slipped into the driver's seat and accelerated quickly up the street. After a minute or two, they stopped in front of a set of heavy double doors. The street was narrow and buildings crowded the lane, leaving it in shadow.

Dmitri got out of the car and approached a keypad beside the door. He punched in a code and the doors opened automatically. He drove the car through an arched passageway and into a cobbled courtyard. A silver Audi coupe and a white Volkswagen van were parked at the foot of steps leading up to a stone porch. Dmitri parked the car and let Sita out. Sita followed him up the steps to a red door.

She watched as Dmitri keyed another set of numbers into a security pad beside the door. The lock disengaged, and they entered a foyer lined with gilt-framed artwork. To the left was a sitting room furnished with thick rugs and antiques. To the right was a dining room with a polished table and high-backed chairs. A hallway extended straight ahead to an alcove and kitchen. Beside it was a staircase that led to the second floor.

A woman came down the stairs. Sita recognized her from the restaurant. Dmitri spoke to her in a harsh-sounding language that Sita didn't understand. The woman glanced at Sita unsmilingly and motioned for her to follow. They climbed the stairs and crossed the landing to a paneled library. The woman handed her a dust rag.

"I am Tatiana," she said. "Clean bookshelves."

Sita obeyed. The library was large with many shelves. All the books were coated in dust and looked as if they had not been touched in years. She removed each volume from its shelf and gently dusted its edges and spine. The library reminded her of her father. He had kept a study in the bungalow by the sea, and he had curated his book collection with care. Most evenings after dinner, he had retreated to his desk and pored over some monograph or another in the lamplight. Sita had often asked him what he was reading, just to see his eyes light up. His answers had been long-winded, but almost always she had learned something.

The chore of dusting took many hours. Tatiana brought her a sandwich for lunch. She appraised the shelves Sita had cleaned and smiled thinly.

"Job is good," she said. "Keep doing."

Sita finished the last book just before Tatiana reappeared. "Done?" she asked, and Sita nodded. "Good. Dmitri take you home now."

She followed Tatiana down the stairs to the foyer. Dmitri and Vasily were talking in the sitting room. A blond girl dressed in a halter top and black pants sat beside Dmitri, staring at the floor. Tatiana called to her son, and the blond girl glanced at Sita across the distance. Her eyes widened perceptibly, and the look struck Sita like a blow.

The girl was scared.

Sita averted her gaze and followed Dmitri out the door. Whatever had happened to the girl was none of her business. Working with Tatiana was far preferable to suffering the abuse of Aunti-ji. As far as she was concerned, the reassignment was a boon.

At long last, Lakshmi had smiled on her again.

Sita returned to the flat the next day and the day after, escorted by Dmitri. Each morning, Tatiana met her in the foyer and gave her a task. She dusted the furniture in the sitting room and polished the dining room table and chairs. She cleaned the bathrooms and brought order to the linen closet upstairs. She worked for eight hours with a fifteen-minute break for lunch. Tatiana was a perfectionist, but Sita was exacting and met her expectations.

On her fourth day at the flat, Sita's morning routine changed without explanation. After parking the Mercedes, Dmitri led her back across the courtyard toward the street. He stopped beneath the covered archway and punched in a code on a keypad beside a glass door Sita hadn't notice before. She heard a lock disengage. She followed him into a musty vestibule at the base of a spiral stairwell.

Dmitri delivered her a stern look. "You do not speak of what you see," he said in surprisingly fluent English. "You do what I ask and you keep the rest to yourself. If not, there will be consequences. Understand?"

Sita's breath caught in her throat. She recalled the blond girl on the couch that first day and wondered whether she was about to discover the source of the girl's fear.

She nodded and followed Dmitri up a flight of steps to a wooden landing. Two doors bracketed the landing.

Dmitri opened the door to the right, and Sita trailed him into a corridor lit by a single bare bulb. Taking a set of keys out of his jacket, Dmitri walked down the hall and unlocked six doors. He barked a few words in his strange language and retrieved a basket from a closet at the end of the corridor.

One by one, six young women emerged from the rooms. They were dressed in T-shirts and gym shorts. The last was the girl Sita had seen on the couch. Sita thought of the sex rooms in Suchir's brothel. She had no idea what Dmitri did with the girls, but the locks made it clear that they were not free to leave.

Dmitri handed her the basket and spoke in English. "Take the sheets and pillowcases off the beds and gather the dirty clothes."

Sita entered the first bedroom. The room was small and dimly lit, with space only for a single bed and a chest of drawers. The window on the far wall was covered with a shade, its edges fastened to the trim with staples. Sita stripped the bed of its linens and scooped up a pile of lacy underwear in the corner. She repeated the same motions in the remaining rooms. All had the same dreary austerity, the same sealed windows, the same invisible menace.

The girls used the bathroom and returned to the hallway while Sita busied herself with her task. When she had finished stripping the last bed, she took the basket back to Dmitri. She couldn't bring herself to look at the girls. The loneliness of their captivity reminded her of Ahalya. Dmitri spoke a few more unintelligible words and the girls returned to their rooms. In fifteen minutes, none of them had made a sound.

Dmitri locked the doors and escorted Sita to Vasily's flat. Tatiana met her in the foyer and led her to the basement laundry room. She showed her how to operate the washing machine and left her alone. Sorting the sheets and clothing into piles, Sita tried not to think about what she had seen. She didn't want to hate these people, but she couldn't abide the thought that six girls were barricaded in a makeshift prison not more than fifty feet away. Could Dmitri be a pimp like Suchir?

A few minutes before three o'clock, Sita heard the sound of heavy footsteps on the basement stairs. The door to the laundry room wasn't quite closed, and she could see a sliver of hallway through the door frame. Sita glanced toward the crack just as Dmitri came into view. A second later she saw a flash of blond hair and the profile of a young woman's face. She was almost certain it was the girl she had seen on the couch.

Dmitri dragged the girl down the hall and opened the door at the end, slamming it shut behind him. After a brief pause, Sita heard the sound of a woman speaking. The words were garbled and distorted by a peculiar echo. At first she thought the sound was coming through the wall, but then she realized its source was an air vent near the ceiling.

Sita heard a slap of flesh and a shriek of pain. She listened to the sounds of a scuffle and the gruff voice of a man making demands. A few seconds later, the young woman cried out and the man began to moan. Sita clutched the pillowcase she was folding and held her breath. She knew what she was hearing, and the thought of it enraged and terrified her.

Dmitri finished his business and returned upstairs. Sita heard the girl whimpering through the air vent, and her heart went out to her. She wrestled with her conscience. She was at Dmitri's mercy, and he was clearly ruthless. Yet her father had taught her that failing to act in the face of suffering is inhuman. She thought of Ahalya after the incident with Shankar, and the memory galvanized her.

She opened the door to the laundry room. Glancing at the clock on the wall, she saw that she had less than twenty minutes before Tatiana would return for her. She moved down the hall to the door at the end. She turned the knob soundlessly and entered the room.

The young woman was curled up on a bed, her body wrapped in sheets. At the foot of the bed was a pile of clothing and underwear like the garments Sita had washed. She saw three video cameras on tripods and an array of lights. She stood in confusion, wondering at the bizarre scene. Then she understood.

The cameras almost certainly had recorded the girl's rape.

She walked to the bedside and knelt down, her stomach churning. She touched the girl's shoulder, and the girl moaned and rolled over. She walked around the bed and knelt again. Reaching out, she cupped the girl's fingers in her hand. The girl grew still and her eyes focused on Sita's face. She lifted herself into a sitting position.

"Do you speak English?" Sita asked, fearing that she didn't understand.

"A little," the girl replied in a thick accent. "Who are you?"

"I'm Sita," she said, speaking slowly. "I do house chores."

The girl began to cry silently. "I am Natalia. Where you from?"

"India."

"I am from Ukraine."

"What are you doing here?" Sita asked.

"I come for work. I apply at agency. Men take passport and bring here."

Sita thought of how different their paths had been, yet how frighteningly similar. She heard a creak on the floor above and grew scared.

"I must go," she whispered urgently. "I will pray for you."

Natalia gave Sita a half-smile. "*Spasibo bolshoi*," she said and then repeated herself in English. "Thank you."

Chapter 17

Hope may vanish, but can die not.
—Percy Bysshe Shelley

Mumbai, India

Weeks passed and the police found no trace of Sita or Navin. Porter responded to Thomas's e-mail and promised to submit Sita's photograph to Interpol. He explained, however, that ICAID was useful only if a missing girl showed up on the Internet or happened to come into the custody of law enforcement in an Interpol member state. If she stayed below the radar, it was unlikely they would find her.

At the end of his message, Porter offered a piece of good news:

By the way, the Fayetteville cops have made some progress on Abby Davis's case. We know she's still in the city, and we're doing our best to pin down her location. Unfortunately, it looks like your father may have been right about the trafficking connection. I'll keep you posted.

Sitting on Dinesh's balcony, beer in hand, Thomas thought of Abby's mother and wondered how she was handling the excruciating wait. Her travail continued to stir him. Looking back, he wondered how much of his present situation had been influenced by their chance encounter. If not for Abby, would he have been interested in CASE? Would he have talked to Porter and learned about the opening in Bombay? Would he have come to India and sought reconciliation with Priya?

The weeks were eventful at the office. CASE conducted two more raids and rescued a total of fourteen minor girls. The second raid, which targeted a beer bar in a north-eastern suburb, was nearly blown by a tip-off that almost certainly came from the police. A field agent on the street saw the girls being moved an hour before the operation, and Greer obtained a last-minute modification of the search warrant that included the new location.

Thomas was impressed with the novelty of the sting. The CASE field agents had contacted the pimps to arrange a private sex party for three men. Enticed by the offer of a premium if the girls were under-age, the pimps turned out their stable. The police arrested the perpetrators in a *chawl* beside the bar and placed ten minor girls in protective custody. The rescue was the most dramatic in the history of CASE's Bombay office and made waves at headquarters in D.C.

Thomas spent his days working on closing arguments in cases set for decision in the spring. On the side, he continued to polish the Jogeshwari brief. The judge had continued the case at the request of the defense, which both outraged and gratified him. It meant the judge was sympathetic to the pimp, but it also gave him more time to weave his logical noose. When he finally turned in the brief, Samantha was effusive with praise.

"It's the best I've seen in five years here," she said. "You made it sing."

"I know it's bad form to get invested in a case," he said, "but I'd really like to wipe the floor with this bastard."

Samantha's eyes sparkled. "You never know. You just might get your wish."

Thomas didn't return to the Sisters of Mercy home. His excuse was that he was too busy, but in truth he didn't know what to say to Ahalya. Anita told him that the girl always made a point to ask about him when she came to visit.

"She's taken a liking to you," Anita told him one afternoon.

"She doesn't know me," he replied.

"She knows enough. Besides, there aren't too many other people around who have friends at the Justice Department."

He sighed. "I take it you told her I passed along Sita's photograph?"

Anita nodded. "I did."

"What more does she expect?"

"I don't know. You were the one who promised to try."

★

He spent two evenings a week with Priya. Often she would meet him for dinner with the CASE staff at Sheesha, a rooftop Irani place on Linking Road, or at Out of the Blue, an upscale restaurant in Pali Hill. Thomas wasn't surprised when she took a liking to the expats. Their good-natured restiveness and fascination with the world were a refreshing contrast to the cynicism and ennui that plagued so many of his friends back home.

As February wore on, the weather grew warmer by the day. Despite himself, Thomas thought often of Ahalya and the *rakhi* bracelet. He got permission from Greer to contact the CBI office, but the news he received was always disheartening. At one point, the officer assigned to the case put Thomas through to the superintendent, who assured him that there was nothing more they could do.

Thomas hung up and looked at the band on his wrist. There were many moments when he wished he could return it. It was a burden he wasn't qualified to bear. Yet he had made Ahalya a promise. And he had made Priya a deal.

He had to try.

The break came when no one expected it. In the third week of February, Thomas was eating lunch at the CASE office with Nigel McPhee and a few of the expats when Nigel's mobile phone rang. He fished the phone out of his pocket, and looked at the screen.

"Talk to me," he said, putting the phone to his ear. He listened for a few seconds, and his eyes widened. "Tonight? I'll let Greer know."

"What's going on?" Thomas asked when Nigel hung up the phone. The field operations director ignored him and walked immediately to Greer's office. Thomas set aside his lunch and followed on his heels, wondering whether it had something to do with Sita.

Greer looked up from a report he was reading.

"Navin is back in Bombay," Nigel said. "Rohit called in the tip."

"Has he confirmed it?" Greer asked, his expression turning serious.

Nigel shook his head. "But the pimp is a trusted source. He got the information directly from Sumeera."

"Navin is a common name. How does he know it's our man?"

"This Navin has a thing for minor girls."

"That isn't good enough," Greer objected. "If we're going to move on this, we have to be absolutely sure."

Nigel smiled. "Navin doesn't come for sex. He takes the girls away."

Greer's skepticism seemed to abate. "Did he say where?"

"The pimp said Europe."

Greer picked up the phone. "Send the rest of the guys down there. I'll call the CBI."

Nigel nodded and left the office, but Thomas stayed put. "I want in on this," he said.

Greer seemed nonplussed. "We don't know what kind of character Navin is. I can't guarantee your safety."

Thomas touched the *rakhi* bracelet. The band had begun

to itch in the heat, and the rash it left reminded him constantly of his promise.

"It doesn't matter," he replied. "I want to be there when you take him down."

Greer thought about this for a long moment. "Okay, you're in. But do me a favor and stay the hell out of the way."

Thomas kept close to Greer while CASE prepared for the raid. On Greer's order, Nigel sent the entire division of field agents into Kamathipura to squeeze the locals for information. In the meantime, the field office director contacted the CBI about leading the operation. The CBI chief agreed but only after Greer assured him that Nigel's team would verify the tip.

Two hours later, however, the field agents had uncovered no new information. They had approached the usual suspects—the *beshyas*, madams, and pimps who were their unofficial informants—but no one had heard of Navin. Nigel paced the floor and made increasingly terse calls on his mobile phone. Greer looked at the clock and clenched his fists as the minutes ticked away. Thomas had never seen him so unnerved.

Late in the afternoon, Greer called the CBI superintendent with the news that the tip still had not been confirmed. The conversation was tense, and Thomas could see the strain on Greer's face. He placated, cajoled, flattered, and ultimately begged the CBI chief not to give up on the operation. At last, the man acquiesced, but he cut his squad by a third and swore that they were wasting their time.

The CASE field agents were in position by six o'clock. Thomas rode with Greer to the Nagpada police station, where they met the CBI team and Inspector Khan. Greer explained that though the CBI had national jurisdiction, Kamathipura was the inspector's turf. The CBI chief had involved Khan to prevent interdepartmental squabbling later on.

The CBI agents drove to M. R. Road in three unmarked vans as darkness was falling. Khan followed in a separate vehicle with Greer and Thomas. To avoid being noticed by the pimps working the street, Khan was dressed in plainclothes, and the Americans both wore baseball caps and had darkened the stubble on their cheeks.

"Assuming this works," Thomas asked in the dim cabin of the car, "who gets jurisdiction over Navin?"

"We do," the inspector replied.

"Not the CBI?"

Khan shook his head. "The CBI doesn't have the stomach for dirty work. We will find out what he did with the girl."

"And if he doesn't talk?"

Khan smiled thinly. "We have our ways, Mr. Clarke."

The inspector turned down M. R. Road and pulled his car over to the curb in sight of Suchir's brothel. It was a Tuesday, and the streets were crawling with men looking for a "short-time", or quickie, before heading home after work. Looking down the street, Thomas saw Rohit and two other CASE field agents watching the brothel entrance. Suchir stood by the door, smoking a *chillum*, or hashish pipe.

When seven o'clock came and went, one of the field agents approached Suchir to light his cigarette. They chatted for a while before the agent sauntered away. Greer's mobile rang a few seconds later. He listened briefly and then hung up.

"Suchir said he's expecting a good customer in the next hour," Greer told Khan.

The inspector picked up his radio and relayed the information to the CBI.

The minutes passed sluggishly in the unairconditioned car. The moist air filtering through half-open windows was thick with the stench of garbage and cigarette smoke. Men walked along the street in clumps, fending off propositions from pimps. Brothel owners like Suchir stood idly, observing the marketing ritual but not participating in it. Thomas kept his head down, but his eyes were alert, observing everything.

At ten minutes past eight, a taxi pulled up to the brothel and Suchir put away his pipe.

A voice came over the radio. "We have a suspect. Mid-thirties, dark hair, fashionably dressed."

Thomas watched as a man in a pink shirt climbed out of the taxi and greeted Suchir on the street. The man handed Suchir a duffel bag, and the *malik* took it and opened it. Thomas felt his body tense. He was certain it was Navin.

The radio crackled again. "All units, move in."

At once field agents converged on the brothel. Suchir

clutched the duffel bag and fled up the stairs. At the same time, the man in the pink shirt moved toward an alleyway. Rohit stepped out of a doorway and blocked the man's path, but the man put his shoulder down and crashed into the field agent, bowling him over. Rohit landed hard and lost hold of the man's shirt. Scrambling to his feet, the man ran headlong into the maze.

In that instant, something snapped inside of Thomas. Before he could think, before his mind could calculate the risk or comprehend the instinct that had overtaken him, he threw open the car door and stepped into the street. Ignoring the shouts of Greer and Khan, he took off toward the spot where the man had disappeared. The man had a ten-second head-start, but Thomas was fast. He was confident that he could catch him.

Dancing around Rohit, who had lurched to his feet looking dazed, he ran down the lane, dodging bullock carts, customers, and clotheslines hung so close together they obscured the sky. All around him people stared, but Thomas paid no attention to them. As long as he could hear the man's feet pounding the dirt, his only interest was speed.

Time stretched out as he raced down the gully. As he moved, he scanned the path in front of him for a glimpse of his target. He heard a crash and moments later came upon an overturned vendor cart. He jumped it without breaking stride and ducked under a line of *saris* hanging out to dry. Rounding a bend in the lane, he caught sight of the man about fifteen paces away. He was moving quickly, but he appeared to be favoring his right leg. Thomas increased his speed, ignoring the pimps and brothel owners glaring at him from the shadows.

The man changed direction and darted into a brothel. Thomas hesitated only a moment before following him. The man disappeared through a door at the far end of the hall and Thomas ran after him, barely glancing at the lineup of girls loitering along the wall. He charged through the door, scaled a flight of steps, and entered a second hallway lined with girls. They laughed and blew him kisses, but he shrugged them off, concentrating on gaining ground.

The second hallway led to a third and then a fourth. All around were girls and sex rooms. The fourth hallway emptied into a larger space cluttered with mattresses and partitioned by sheets hanging from the ceiling. A number of the beds were occupied. He heard squeals and an angry shout and saw a girl and her customer scrambling to cover themselves. The man jumped over their bed, angling for a door in the far wall.

Thomas followed the man into another spiderweb of hallways. He ran down a set of stairs and felt a draft of cooler air. At last, he saw a doorway at the end of the tunnel. A brothel owner stepped in front of the exit, trying to impede his passage, but Thomas shoved him aside and ran into the street.

The man was only a few steps ahead of him and limping more obviously now.

"*Navin!*" he shouted. The man looked back.

Thomas poured all his remaining strength into half a dozen strides. When Navin came within reach, he launched himself through the air and hit him with an open-field tackle. They tumbled into the dirt and rolled into a cluster of pimps who were sharing a hash joint. In the melee, Navin tried to slither out of Thomas's grasp, but Thomas wrapped his arms around Navin's mid-section and held fast. In the rush of adrenaline, he was overcome with anger.

"What did you do with her, you bastard? Where did you take her?"

Instead of answering, Navin lashed out with his elbow and connected with Thomas's head. Thomas thought he was going to black out, but the moment passed and he tightened his grip. He heard shouts in the distance and, after that, footsteps. Rohit was the first to reach them. The field officer dragged Navin to his feet and threw him against a wall. A CBI agent stepped forward and put him in handcuffs.

Another CBI agent helped Thomas to his feet. "Okay?" he asked.

Thomas nodded, heaving in air and feeling sore all over. He wiped dirt from his face and watched CBI men lead Navin down the lane. Rohit approached Thomas, wearing a look that was part congratulatory and part embarrassed.

"Fine work," he said.

Thomas grinned. "It felt good to do that again."

Rohit frowned. "Again?"

"I was an all-state cornerback in high school."

When Rohit gave him a blank look, Thomas shook his head. "Never mind."

The CBI team escorted Navin to M. R. Road and locked him in one of their vans. After a brief turf scuffle with Inspector Khan, the CBI superintendent gave the order for Navin to be driven to the Nagpada police station. Greer, meanwhile, released the CASE field agents. He and Thomas drove to the station with Inspector Khan.

Greer rounded on Thomas. "Look, I understand why you did it. But do you know how dangerous it was? The lanes are completely unpoliced."

Thomas shrugged. "I take it you don't object to the outcome."

"Of course not," Greer replied. "It's just that if something had happened to you, it would be my head on a platter."

Thomas saw no point in responding to this. "So what happened to Suchir?"

"He got away," Greer said. "All of them did. Sumeera, Prasad, the customers, the girls. Apparently the attic room had a hidden door that led to the roof. They were gone by the time the CBI guys found it."

"Do you think he'll run this time?"

"That depends on how afraid he is of Navin. He'll probably stay away for a while. But I doubt he'll give it up. The money's too easy."

"What are the chances he'll stand trial?" Thomas asked. "I saw his lawyer. The judge was eating out of his hand."

Greer met his eyes. "Ahalya will get her day in court. We'll make sure of that."

When the caravan arrived at the station, Inspector Khan led Navin into a room at the back. Greer and Thomas found seats in the inspector's office and waited. Half an hour later, Thomas heard the first scream. He gripped the arm of the chair. The second scream came a moment later. After that, they came periodically. Thomas pursed his lips, struggling with the implications of what he was hearing.

He looked at Greer. "How long will this go on?"

Greer waggled his head. "Until Khan is satisfied."

"It doesn't bother you?"

"My opinion doesn't matter. This is Bombay. The police do what they want."

Thomas thought about this. "Will Navin talk?"

Greer nodded. "He'll talk. The better question is will Khan get him to tell the truth?"

Down the hall, Khan stood in front of Navin, catching his breath. He had shackled him to a metal chair and beat him until the trafficker's ribs began to crack, asking questions between punches. Navin, however, was surprisingly tough. He gave Khan his name and admitted to buying Sita. He claimed, however, that he had sold her to another pimp. Khan asked him where this man lived, and Navin told him Kalina. Khan said he didn't believe him.

"Tell me where you took her!" he shouted, cracking his knuckles.

Navin stared back at him defiantly.

"You can prolong this if you like," Khan said, hooking his fingers up to a hand-powered dynamo. "Or you can tell me the truth. What's it going to be?"

Navin screamed when the current flowed, but he didn't change his story.

Khan asked him about Europe. "You like *sambhoga* with European women?"

Navin nodded, his voice slurring. "Why not? You like *sambhoga* with your wife?"

The come-uppance infuriated the inspector. He moved the electrical leads to Navin's genitals and worked the crank. Navin shrieked and began to drool. He began to show signs of cracking.

"Tell me where you took the girl!" the inspector demanded. "You took her out of Bombay, I know you did."

Navin's head lolled back and forth, and then, almost imperceptibly, he nodded.

"Good," Khan said. "Is she still in India?"

Navin looked at Khan and spit a wad of saliva. Khan turned the crank again, and Navin screamed. "No, no, no," he said, chanting desperately. "Not in India."

"Where did you take her, then? Britain? Germany? Where?"

"France," Navin finally whispered.

Khan took a deep breath. "Why France?"

Navin sat silently and Khan waited. After a minute, the inspector got impatient and picked up the dynamo again. The prospect of further suffering compelled Navin to speak.

"I have an uncle in Paris."

Khan put the dynamo back on the floor. "Is your uncle a *malik* like Suchir?"

Navin shook his head. "The girl is not there for sex. She is working at his restaurant."

Khan heard a knock at the door. He turned around irritably. He had left strict orders that he was not to be disturbed.

"What?" he barked.

The door opened and into the room walked the deputy commissioner of police. He looked at Navin and then at Khan.

"Inspector Khan," the DCP said, "this man was arrested by mistake."

Khan could not believe his ears. "The suspect has already confessed to buying a minor girl from a brothel and transporting her to France. He has violated Indian and international law. What mistake is there in his arrest?"

"Inspector, I am ordering you to release him," the DCP said.

Khan stared at his boss, his spine tingling with rage and shame. He reached in his pocket for the key to Navin's cuffs. He had no choice. If he disobeyed, he would lose his job, and his family would be put out on the street.

As soon as he was free, Navin struggled to his feet and spat in the inspector's face.

"*Muth mar, bhenchod,*" he said under his breath. "You will never find the girl."

Khan walked back to his office. "We have a problem," he said, looking between Greer and Thomas. "The DCP released Navin."

"What do you mean the DCP released him?" Greer demanded.

"I mean just what I said. Navin is gone."

Thomas was aghast. "How could you let that happen?"

Khan frowned. "You don't understand. I had no choice."

"This whole place is a circus," Thomas said angrily, standing up and heading toward the door. "We have to do something."

Khan blocked his way. "Do you want to go to jail?" he asked. "Because the DCP will lock you up and throw the key in Mahim Bay. You will never win fighting the corruption. There is only one way to find the girl, and that is to talk to the French police."

Thomas took a deep breath and tried to calm down. "Navin took Sita to France?"

"She is working in his uncle's restaurant in Paris."

Thomas shook his head. "Of all places, Sita is in Paris."

"Why is that remarkable?" Greer asked.

"Because I know Paris. I spent a semester at the Sorbonne."

"So?" Greer stared at him. "You're not thinking of going after her? The French police are far better equipped to track her down."

"Of course," Thomas conceded. The idea was absurd, but for some reason it took flight in his mind and ran like a kite in the wind.

"I'll contact the CBI tomorrow," Khan said. "They will help with the French."

Thomas accompanied Greer into the sticky Bombay night. Greer flagged a taxi and told the driver to take them to Mumbai Central Station.

Thomas didn't speak on the ride. The easiest of his options—deferring to the authorities—was also the most reasonable. The thing that now mattered most to him— Priya—was in Bombay. It was possible that she might encourage a trip to Paris. But her opinion wasn't the only one in play. However persistently they had tried to ignore him, her father still had influence. Priya wouldn't leave India without his blessing. If Thomas stood any chance of wooing her back to the United States, he had to win over the Professor.

He and Greer bought tickets to Bandra and descended to the platform. Ten minutes later, the slow train lumbered up the tracks. They boarded a second-class car, and Thomas stood by the door, looking out into the night. The train started off toward the suburbs at an unhurried gait. The lights of the city were like a glowing river, endlessly in motion. The warm wind tussled his hair and smelled of *paan* and heavy cologne.

As the miles passed, he made his decision. Perhaps it was the rhythm of the wheels, the feeling of salt-laden air on his skin, and the cadence of foreign speech on the tongues of strangers. Or perhaps it was the euphoria of finding Navin after giving up hope. But as soon as he made it, the decision seemed inevitable, as if the path had chosen him. He would go to Paris.

He owed that much to Ahalya.

He owed that much to himself.

Chapter 18

Where is the extinguished lamp that made night day?
Where is the sun?

—Hafiz

Paris, France

As time passed, Sita continued to clean Vasily's flat. Every other day, at Dmitri's bidding, she gathered the linen and underwear from the adjoining apartments. The girls always appeared in the hallway dressed in T-shirts and gym shorts. Sita saw no evidence of men in the girls' quarters—no condoms or cigarettes or overnight bags. Their only possessions appeared to be lacy underwear and a few paperback books.

One morning, Tatiana led her to the third floor of the flat and asked her to dust a room filled with clutter and computer equipment.

"Vasily out of town," she explained. "Look at filth."

She lifted a glass of stale beer off a filing cabinet and

turned up her nose at the sight of a packet of cigarettes and a half-full ashtray.

"Disgusting," she said. She turned to Sita with a conspiratorial expression. "No tell Vasily you here. He not like." She shrugged. "But place needs clean."

Tatiana left her with a rag and a dusting brush and returned to the second floor. Sita knew a little about computers, but Vasily's array of electronics was far more sophisticated than anything she had seen. On a desk in the center of the room were two flat-screen monitors on standby, a keyboard and mouse, and a white tablet of some kind with a plastic stylus.

The room reeked of smoke and cheap alcohol. She started her cleaning with the frame and sill of a small circular window—the only window in the room. Then she moved to the desk and dusted the monitors. When she swept the surface of the keyboard, she brushed a key inadvertently. At once both screens came alive. She took an instinctive step back. The images depicted a masked man and a woman performing a sex act.

She looked away quickly, and her cheeks burned. She turned her back to the monitors, searching for a distraction. Taking the rag in her hand, she cleaned and polished the handles of the the filing cabinet until they shone. The rhythmic motions were soothing, and at last the monitors turned black. She glanced at them again. Where had the images come from? And who was the man in the mask?

When she reached the bottom drawer of the filing cabinet, she found that it wasn't properly closed. Her first instinct was to shut it and move on, but she was seized by a dreadful curiosity. Perhaps the filing cabinet could explain the images and the girls across the courtyard.

Her heartbeat quickened as she slid the drawer open. Inside, she found folders hand-labeled in foreign script. She removed the top file and found a dozen Polaroid pictures. Each picture showed a Caucasian girl dressed in underwear standing in an empty room. The walls were bare and crumbling with age. The girls regarded the camera with glazed eyes. No one else was present in the room with them, but the angle of the lens was identical in all of the frames. Also in the file was a sheet of paper printed in strange characters. Sita wondered if the words were names.

Placing the file carefully back in the drawer, she skimmed the folders behind it, all of which contained Polaroid photographs accompanied by an indecipherable list. She pulled the drawer all the way to its stop and found a stack of pornographic magazines in the well behind the folders. Recoiling in disgust, she shut the drawer and picked up the rag from the floor.

When Tatiana returned for her, she felt such relief that she nearly hugged the woman. Tatiana gave her another chore, and Sita applied herself to trifles for the rest of the day, trying to forget the things she had seen.

That evening at the restaurant, Uncle-ji told Sita that Varuni was ill and that she would be waiting tables. Sita donned a patterned *sari* supplied by Aunti-ji and wiped the tables in preparation for opening. Afterward, she hastily memorized the menu. It was written in Hindi and translated into French and English.

Aunti-ji scurried around arranging tablecloths and place settings. She gave Sita the job of lighting a candle at each table. In her haste, Aunti-ji had little time for criticism. For the first time since Sita's arrival, she treated her with a modicum of respect.

The customers began to arrive at seven o'clock. Uncle-ji greeted them and Sita ushered them to their tables. If the patrons were Indian, she spoke to them in Hindi. If they were Caucasian, she used English. Uncle-ji stood nearby to intervene in case she needed to communicate in French. She tried to mimic Varuni's delivery, but the effect was awkward and her inexperience showed. When all else failed, she smiled and recommended the chicken *tikka masala*.

Business was slow, but enough regulars showed up to keep Sita busy. What she lacked in skill, she made up for in intelligence. She had always been proud of her memory for detail. She took orders and delivered dishes to customers without using a notebook.

"Your new waitress is quite pleasant," one of the regular patrons said to Uncle-ji. "Where did you find her?"

"She is the daughter of my cousin in Bombay," he said. "We are privileged to have her with us."

Sita couldn't tell whether the praise was sincere or feigned, but she received it as a positive sign. Perhaps Uncle-ji would allow her to wait tables with Varuni when the weather warmed. It was preferable to scrubbing the bathroom with a toothbrush.

The last two customers—an elderly Indian couple—left a few minutes before closing. After wiping down their table, Sita retrieved a broom from the closet and swept the floor. A few minutes later, Uncle-ji took a call on his cell phone that left him visibly agitated. He paced in front of the door to the restaurant until a shadowy figure appeared.

The restaurant owner let the man in and welcomed him with a handshake. Sita looked at him and something jogged in her mind. His back was to her, but his hair and jacket seemed familiar. She continued her sweeping, watching the man out of the corner of her eye. At last the man turned around.

The stranger was Navin.

When he saw her, she blinked, astonished by the condition of his face. His cheeks were covered with red welts and one of his eyes was black.

He regarded her without emotion. "It seems she worked out well," he said.

"Yes," Uncle-ji replied, motioning Navin toward the corner booth near the window. He looked at Sita. "Bring our guest a bottle of brandy and a glass."

She retrieved the alcohol and returned to the table quickly. Placing the brandy and tumbler in front of Navin, she noticed that Uncle-ji's hands were trembling. The restaurant owner barely glanced at her. She moved away and continued to sweep the floor, listening intently.

Navin spoke quietly, but she picked up two words: "arrested" and "police".

Uncle-ji replied in a louder voice: "You didn't tell them anything, did you?"

Navin's response was inaudible, but Uncle-ji's reaction was not.

"What does this mean?"

Navin didn't respond. Instead, he eyed Sita and tilted his head ever so slightly in her direction. She turned away quickly, focusing on her sweeping. The room was silent for a moment before Uncle-ji barked: "*Wait in the kitchen!*"

She stiffened and scampered away, her mind abuzz with questions. Had the police been searching for her? Did Navin tell them where she was? She lurked in the doorway to the kitchen, straining to pick up more of the conversation. She heard only murmuring until Uncle-ji raised his voice.

"You have to help us!" he blurted out. "You brought her to us!"

Navin frowned. He glanced toward her and stood up abruptly, letting himself out of the restaurant. She watched through the window as he disappeared into the night.

She looked at Uncle-ji, wondering what he would do. He sat in the booth with his back to her, muttering to himself. The bottle of brandy sat unopened before him. He lifted the tumbler and stared into it for a long moment. Then he turned around and walked quickly toward her, his eyes wide and full of fear.

"You must come with me now," he said, taking her by the arm.

He led her through the kitchen and into the flat. Aunti-ji looked at him strangely, but he ignored her. He took her to a closet in the bedroom and turned on the light. The closet was stuffed with clothing.

"You must stay here," he said.

"Why?" she asked, thoroughly frightened.

"No questions," he said, pushing her inside.

When he closed the door, Sita sat down on a pile of shoes and struggled against claustrophobia and terror. Even after her eyes adjusted, she could see only the faintest glimmer of gray at the foot of the door. She forced herself to take deep breaths and clutched the little Hanuman figurine that she had secreted in the folds of her *sari*.

She thought of the Coromandel Coast before the horror of the waves. The sea sparkled. Ahalya was there, playing at the edge of the surf. Her mother and father watched from the gardens. Jaya busied herself at the clothesline. When the vision faded, tears came to her eyes and she began to cry. She carved a space for herself in the clutter and rested her head against something soft that felt like a wool hat. This was the second closet she had inhabited during her stay in Paris.

But at least this closet was warm.

Sita was startled when the closet door opened the following morning. She was famished and desperate to relieve herself. She blinked at the light from the bedroom and looked up at Uncle-ji, hoping he would offer her a plate of food and a visit to the bathroom. Instead, he summoned her with a wave.

She stood in the rubble of shoes and walked with him to the entrance of the flat. Dmitri was waiting for her in the alcove. She breathed a sigh of relief. She wouldn't have to endure the day in the loneliness of the closet. Tatiana would feed her a good lunch, and she would return to the restaurant to wait tables in the evening. Despite Navin's visit and Uncle-ji's fear, things were not going to change after all.

After donning her coat, she trailed Dmitri out of the courtyard and down Passage Brady to the black Mercedes. Tatiana met her in the foyer of the flat and assigned her the task of cleaning the rooms on the second floor.

At four o'clock in the afternoon, Sita was in the master bedroom, dusting a shelf of books. She glanced at the clock on the wall and watched the door for Tatiana. The woman didn't come. Four turned to four-thirty and then five o'clock. At last Tatiana appeared and led her to the kitchen. She saw one of Dmitri's girls standing before the stove, dressed in jeans and an apron. She was stirring a pot of soup and tending a skillet of sausage.

"Ivanna," Tatiana said to the girl, "this is Sita. She help you this evening."

The girl nodded obediently.

Sita's mind raced with confusion and apprehension. She was not afraid of Tatiana, but she was terrified of Dmitri and Vasily. The flat was haunted by terrible secrets that daylight seemed to hide. She did not want to be there when darkness fell.

Ivanna spoke little English, but she pointed and gestured, and Sita offered her whatever assistance she could. The food was very different from Indian cuisine—it was meat rich, savory with herbs, and accented by vegetables. Ivanna pointed at a pot and said, "*Borscht.*"

Sometime after six, Ivanna served Vasily, Tatiana, and Dmitri in the dining room and Sita and herself in the kitchen. Sita ate the food hungrily. After dinner, she helped Ivanna clear the dining-room table and clean the kitchen.

At seven o'clock, Dmitri appeared and Ivanna tensed visibly. She put down her dish rag and followed him. Sita heard their footsteps in the hallway, and then a door opened and closed. The sound was different, lighter than the thump made by the front door of the residence. Sita's heart raced and she wondered whether Dmitri had taken Ivanna to the basement.

Tatiana came for her a few minutes later. The woman took her up the stairs to the second floor and showed her to one of the bedrooms she had cleaned earlier in the day.

"You stay here," Tatiana said, showing her the bathroom and fluffing the pillows. "I come in morning. *Bonne nuit.* Have nice dreams."

She closed the door behind her, and Sita heard a lock click in place. The room had a queen-sized bed, a pair of reading chairs, and a broad window overlooking the courtyard. It felt like a palace in comparison to Suchir's attic room and Uncle-ji's closets.

She walked to the window and looked down at the white van and the silver Audi. The black Mercedes was absent. She browsed the shelves and found an English-language novel. Taking a seat in one of the chairs, she passed the evening reading. She heard occasional voices beyond the door, but the words were muffled and distant.

Sometime after ten o'clock, she heard sounds coming from the courtyard. She stood in the shadows and watched as Dmitri led Natalia, Ivanna, and the other girls to the white van. All of them were dressed provocatively in short skirts, high heels, and revealing tops. Although it was still winter, only Natalia wore a coat. None of them spoke or looked at the others.

Dmitri opened the rear doors of the van, and everyone but Natalia climbed in. Dmitri motioned for Natalia to get into the Audi. He spoke briefly to someone in the van, and then the van disappeared through the archway. Dmitri placed a call on his cell phone and took control of the Audi. He whipped the car around and left the courtyard.

Retreating from the window, Sita prepared herself for bed. The bath she took was luxurious, and the pillows and bedsheets were softer than anything she could remember. But she couldn't shake the persistent feeling of dread. For all their wealth and good taste, there was something diabolical about Vasily's family.

Where had Dmitri taken the girls?

*

The following morning, Tatiana fetched Sita for breakfast. Before leaving her room, Sita glanced out the window and saw that the van and the Audi had returned. The riddle of the girls' destination deepened when she met Ivanna in the kitchen, preparing the meal. The girl looked no different from the night before. Sita helped her serve the food and watched her for any sign of distress. The girl's blue eyes were vacant, but she didn't miss a step.

Sita spent the next few days in the same manner, performing the duties of a household maid, laundering the girls' sheets and underwear, and helping Ivanna in the kitchen. Each evening the van left the courtyard at ten o'clock and returned before dawn. On Sita's second night—a Sunday—Ivanna and another girl accompanied Dmitri in the Audi. On Monday and Tuesday, only Natalia went with Dmitri. Sita watched the nightly muster from her window and tried not to think about where the girls were taken or what they were forced to do.

On Wednesday after breakfast, Sita was summoned to the sitting room where Vasily was waiting. Soon thereafter, Uncle-ji and Aunti-ji came in with Dmitri. The Indian couple took their seats without looking at Sita. She stared at them in confusion. She had been told nothing about the purpose of the meeting.

"Here are the documents," Vasily said, opening a folder on the coffee table.

In the folder, Sita saw passports and airline tickets. Her heart lurched. Had Uncle-ji and Aunti-ji decided to leave France? What did they intend to do with her?

"How much will this cost us?" Uncle-ji asked in a quiet voice.

Vasily shook his head. "I told you before. It will cost you nothing. We are helping you, and you are helping us. It is an even exchange."

"And when we get there?"

Vasily shrugged. "That is up to you."

"*Merci beaucoup*," said Uncle-ji. "You have done us a great favor."

He glanced at Sita and she saw guilt in his eyes. She inhaled sharply. Suddenly, she was certain the meeting had to do with her.

Vasily handed the documents to Uncle-ji, and the men shook hands.

"Thank me tomorrow," Vasily said. "Until then, watch your step."

PART THREE

Chapter 19

The heart has its reasons which reason does not know.
—Blaise Pascal

Mumbai, India

Thomas sat in the Air France lounge at Chhatrapati Shivaji International Airport sipping a glass of red wine. It was just after midnight on Wednesday, one week after the deputy commissioner of police had released Navin. His flight wasn't scheduled to depart for another hour and a half. He considered reading a newspaper, but he knew the articles wouldn't hold his attention. He was a bundle of nervous energy. He closed his eyes instead, breathing steadily, remembering.

It had been an eventful week. He'd talked to Greer the day after the raid, expecting the field office director to tell him he was crazy and that CASE couldn't spare him while he gallivanted around Paris in search of Sita. Greer, however, had surprised him. Beneath his world-wise exterior, Greer, it seemed, was an idealist. He grilled Thomas only long enough to see that he was serious. Then he imparted his blessing, asking only that Thomas keep in touch.

Priya had been a different story. After the meeting with Greer, Thomas had called her mobile number, thinking she wouldn't answer. It was a Thursday and she was at the hospice facility in Breach Candy spending time with her grandmother. When she picked up on the first ring, he knew something was wrong. Her tone confirmed it.

"Thomas," she said, "my grandmother just passed away."

He took a deep breath and let it out. "I'm so sorry."

She took a while to speak again. "She was chatting two days ago. The nurses said she started slipping during the night. By the time I got here, she couldn't talk. She looked at me like she wanted to say something, but she couldn't. I was holding her hand when she died."

Priya broke down and began to cry.

Thomas left the office and climbed into a rickshaw. "Does your family know?"

"I was about to call my father."

He raised his voice above the throb of the rickshaw's two-cylinder engine. "It'll take me an hour to get to you."

"Come to my grandfather's house. They're taking her there for preparation."

It took him eighty dizzying minutes to reach Malabar Hill. He paid the fare at the gate and entered the grounds. The garden was cool and filled with the scent of jasmine and the chirping of birds. He stood for a moment and surveyed the sanctuary of Vrindavan. Three cars were parked on the stone drive. Priya's convertible was among them.

He braced himself for the inevitable confrontation with Surya. He hadn't spoken to the Professor since the *mendhi* event. He had no idea whether Priya had informed her father of the time they had spent together. The whole thing felt like *déjà vu*. It was as if he and Priya had been sneaking around in Fellows Garden again. Except that now they were married.

No one was on the veranda, but he saw movement beyond the windows. He knocked cautiously at the front door, hoping that Priya would greet him. He was not so fortunate.

The Professor opened the door and frowned. "Priya is with her grandmother," he said.

"She asked me to come," Thomas replied.

When Surya didn't respond, he thought the man was going to force him to wait outside. Then Surekha appeared and extended an olive branch.

"Thomas," she said, rebuking her husband with her eyes, "Priya will be out in a moment. Why don't you wait in the sitting room?"

Surya glared at him but stood aside. Thomas took a seat on a couch, listening to the sound of distant female voices speaking Hindi. After a few minutes, Priya appeared and beckoned him to follow her onto the terrace.

"How are you?" Thomas asked.

"I don't know," Priya replied. Her eyes were red-rimmed and teary. "I didn't expect it to come so soon."

"What can I do?"

"Nothing," she said, shaking her head.

"What happens next?"

"Her body will be adorned and laid in state. There will be an open house tomorrow for people to pay their respects, and then she will be cremated by the sea at Priyadarshini Park. After that, my father and his brothers will fly her ashes to Varanasi. We will mourn her here."

Thomas was silent for a long time. "I'm sorry. I know you loved her."

"I loved her as a child. I barely knew her as an adult."

"I am much to blame for that."

Priya looked across the grass toward the fountain. "We're both at fault. But blame is useless now. All we have is the future."

Thomas took a breath and let it out. "I keep wondering how this is going to work."

Priya shook her head. "You can't think your way through it."

"Then what am I supposed to do?"

Priya looked at him. "Why do men persist in asking that question? You're not supposed to *do* anything. You're supposed to be yourself. We'll figure it out together."

"Why do women persist in speaking in riddles?"

"Because love is a riddle," she replied. "As is life itself."

The Hindu funeral rites that followed were elaborate, and the public wake drew a crowd of nearly five hundred. The family garlanded Sonam's body with flowers and placed her on a bier with her feet facing southward, toward the abode of the dead.

On the evening of the second day, Surya and his brothers carried the bier to a hearse and drove their mother to Priyadarshini Park, where a pyre was lit and her body was cremated. A group of Brahmins chanted mantras to the percussion of the sea, and both the elite and commoners of Bombay paid their last respects.

After the cremation, the crowd dispersed and the family returned to the bungalow. While Priya tended to her grandfather, Thomas drifted along on the periphery of things, wondering when he would get a chance to talk to her about Paris. He felt guilty thinking so much about Sita. But as the hours passed, he grew more certain she was within reach and more afraid that time was against him.

At last, three days after Sonam's death, he took Priya aside after supper and led her onto the terrace beneath a darkening sky.

"You look troubled," she said. "Is something wrong?"

Thomas told her about the capture and release of Navin.

Priya was scandalized. "The commissioner is a family friend! He and his wife were at the open house. If one of his deputies is working for the *goondas*, he should know about it."

"I'm not sure it would help," he responded. "Anyway, I'm less concerned about the deputy commissioner."

"You're worried about Sita."

He nodded.

She looked thoughtful. "Do you know why Navin took her to France?"

"His uncle owns a restaurant in Paris. She's working for him."

"Are the French looking into it?"

"The CBI hasn't told us anything. What the French will do is anyone's guess."

She eyed him closely. "That isn't the end. You have something more to say."

"The CIA should hire you. You're better than a polygraph."

She smiled. "It's only *your* mind I can read."

"I need to go to France," he said. "I think I can find Sita."

She stared at him, her dark eyes shimmering in the torch light. "You mean that."

"Yes."

"My father won't understand."

"Of course he won't."

"It's too bad. He was just starting to like you."

Thomas's eyes widened. "What?"

"His exact words were, 'You picked yourself a smart one.' "

"Ah, but respect is not affection."

"Neither is it loathing."

He laughed. "I think it was I who picked a smart one."

She reached out and touched his arm. "Go to Paris," she said. "I'll deal with my father."

Thomas checked his watch and saw that he still had thirty

minutes before the plane boarded. He took out his BlackBerry and placed a call to Andrew Porter at the Justice Department. Porter picked up on the first ring. The ten-and-a-half-hour time difference meant that it was early afternoon in Washington.

Thomas briefed him on the situation and asked if he knew anyone in the French government who could offer assistance.

"Our relations with the French are always a bit sensitive," Porter said. "But a friend of mine works at the legal attaché's office in Paris. The legats know the diplomatic ropes and have the respect of the government. I could give Julia a call if you'd like."

"How good a friend is she?" Thomas asked. "What I'm doing isn't exactly orthodox."

"Julia and I were at Columbia together. She's one of my favorite people. Anybody else at the FBI wouldn't give you the time of day. But she'll do me a favor. Besides, she'll be intrigued. Her sister was abducted when she was a child."

"Okay," Thomas said. "Give her a call."

"Good. Wait twenty minutes and then dial this number."

Porter recited an eight-digit number with a Paris exchange. Thomas wrote it on the palm of his hand. After signing off, he read a copy of the *Times of India* and watched the clock.

When twenty minutes elapsed, he placed the call. Julia answered the phone in French. Although Thomas spoke the language passably, he identified himself in English.

She changed languages easily. "I'll do anything I can to help. Where do we start?"

"I want to know if the French police have heard from the CBI in Bombay."

"We have contacts at the BRP here in Paris. I'll ring them tomorrow morning. How familiar are you with Paris?"

"I spent a semester at the Sorbonne in college. Why?"

"I'm guessing you're going to want to do a bit of gumshoe investigating. It's better if you know your way around." She paused. "When do you get into Charles de Gaulle?"

"Seven thirty tomorrow morning."

"Take the RER Line B to Châtelet–Les Halles. I'll meet you outside the Église Saint Eustache at nine o'clock."

"How will I know you?"

"I'll be wearing a red coat," she said.

The plane took off on time and Thomas slept through most of the flight. At Charles de Gaulle, he passed through customs without delay and followed the signs to the RER suburban rail station, where he bought a five-day pass. It had been nearly a decade since his last trip to Paris, but it felt like yesterday.

The ride into the city was a bouquet of memories. He recalled the smell of espresso at the little café in the Fifth, where he had often eaten breakfast. He remembered the silence of the great lecture hall at the Sorbonne and the Beaux Arts reading room at the Bibliothèque Sainte-Geneviève, where he went to study when it became too cold to read in the gardens at Pont Neuf, overlooking the Seine.

The train made quick progress toward the city center. He

disembarked at Châtelet–Les Halles and followed the signs to the Forum Les Halles, a flashy underground shopping mall in the First Arrondissement. He walked by a multiplex cinema and scaled a long flight of steps before emerging on Rue Rambuteau.

The day was bright and cold. The edge of winter persisted, but the sun had reclaimed some of its natural brilliance, forecasting the arrival of spring. The Eglise Saint Eustache, one of Paris's many historic Gothic churches, dominated the skyline. He walked through the gardens and around the spiral plaza, looking for Julia. She was standing at the tourist entrance, hands pressed into the pockets of her crimson town coat. She was tall and attractive and wore her chestnut brown hair at shoulder length. He introduced himself and she greeted him with an airy kiss on both cheeks.

"*Faire la bise*," Thomas said, returning the gesture. "It's been ages since I did that."

"I've been here only a year, and I don't think about it any more," she told him.

He laughed. "You stay here long enough, you'll forget about everywhere else."

"Ah, a Francophile," she said, leading him back the way he came.

"I was infected long ago. It's an incurable condition."

Julia smiled. "Andrew told me I'd like you."

"He's not much of an authority," Thomas said. "He likes everyone, even the criminals."

"*Touché*," she said with a laugh. Then she changed

direction. "I placed a call to our contact at the Paris prefecture. He hadn't heard anything about Navin or Sita, but he's going to look into it. I sent along her picture from Interpol. I should hear from him this afternoon."

"So what's the plan for the morning?" Thomas asked.

"There's a man you need to meet," she replied. "Jean-Pierre Léon. He knows everything there is to know about trafficking in this city. And he's one of the most interesting conversationalists I've met in Paris. You won't regret it."

Julia led him down an alleyway along Rue Mondétour. They stopped at a nondescript door beneath a green awning. She pushed the button beside a sign that read *Le Projet de Justice*. The door opened with a buzz and she led him up two flights of steps to a windowless lobby. She greeted the receptionist in French and the woman waved her through.

"You're a known quantity here."

"Not really," Julia said. "I just called ahead."

They met Léon in an office so crowded with books that the furniture was nearly invisible. Thomas appraised the man and decided he would like him. The Frenchman was in his forties and had sharp eyes and a lean build. He was dressed foppishly in a sport coat and wool tie and had a pipe dangling from his lips.

He stood to greet them and gestured for them to take a seat. Thomas looked questioningly at a chair covered with a mound of hard-bound tomes.

"Sit, sit," Léon said in lightly accented English, waving his arms. "Move aside the books. I will find them later."

Thomas sat awkwardly in the cramped space and waited for Julia to initiate the conversation. Léon, however, had been briefed and he took the reins.

"Julia tells me you come to Paris looking for a girl. An Indian girl."

Thomas nodded.

"There aren't many Indians in Paris."

"I remember an Indian enclave in the Tenth."

"The Tenth is a global village. Most countries are represented. But you are right. There are Indians around Rue du Faubourg-Saint-Denis."

"Is that where I should look?"

Léon scratched his chin thoughtfully. "Perhaps." He glanced at Julia. "But Paris is a large city. She could be anywhere."

"Or nowhere," Thomas added. "She was trafficked in early January."

Léon shook his head. "If she came to work in a restaurant, I doubt she has gone. Good workers are hard to replace."

"So how do I find her?"

Léon shrugged. "Julia says the trafficker—Navin, was it?— had a family connection, an uncle. The police might be able to trace him if he is here legally. But if he purchased his documents on the black market, they won't find him. You know, I am sure, that France has a certain problem with illegal immigration."

"We have the same problem in the United States," Thomas said, trying to be polite. In truth, he wasn't satisfied with Léon's evasive answer. "Julia told me on the way over that you're the resident expert on trafficking in Paris," he went on. "Is that true?"

Léon held up his hands. "Some have said that. But there are others."

"I'm satisfied with you. So here's the deal. Sita was in the city in the past two months, and as you say, she's probably still here. She must have left a trace. I need you to give me a lead. Tell me where to go, who to talk to. If she's out there, there has to be a way to find her."

The Frenchman thought for a moment and asked a question: "Are you a religious man, Mr. Clarke?"

Thomas raised his eyebrows. "Not particularly."

"Too bad. I might have suggested prayer."

Thomas waited for something more. Eventually the silence became awkward.

"That's your answer?" he said, growing frustrated.

The Frenchman scrunched his face and sighed. "Forgive me. Julia will tell you that I have a visceral aversion to dispensing advice. It's a personal peccadillo, a fear of being wrong, I suppose. Do you have a picture of this girl?"

Thomas nodded and showed the photograph of Sita to Léon.

The Frenchman pursed his lips. "That will do. I have only one thought. If I wanted to find her, I would take the picture to the streets. I'd start in the Tenth and move into the Eighteenth. I'd ask women and children, especially South Asians. But I would be realistic. It will take a miracle to find her."

Thomas looked at Julia and she nodded. "Jean-Pierre's idea is as good as any."

"Occasionally we eggheads prove useful," Léon said. He stood and gave Thomas his business card. "Best of luck to you. Let me know if you find her."

"I will," Thomas replied and followed Julia to the street. He checked his watch as they walked back toward Forum Les Halles. It was nearly eleven o'clock.

"I forgot to ask where you're staying," she said.

"A hotel by the Luxembourg Gardens."

Julia smiled. "Your old haunts."

"I figured a flight of nostalgia couldn't hurt."

"Why don't you go check in? I'll give you a call later if I hear anything. You can start pounding the pavement this afternoon if you like. I might be able to help you tomorrow."

They entered the shopping complex and wound their way through the labyrinth to the Metro station. Julia stopped before the turnstiles and placed her hand on Thomas's arm.

"I think what you're doing is very noble," she said. "Andrew told you about my sister."

Thomas nodded.

"We still don't know whether she's dead or alive in some awful place." She gave him an imploring look. "I know your chances are slim. But promise me you'll do everything in your power to find this girl."

"Sita has a sister too," he said, showing her the *rakhi* bracelet. "She made me promise the same thing."

★

The boutique hotel he had selected was tucked away in a cul-de-sac off Rue Gay Lussac, a short walk from the Luxembourg Metro stop. The establishment's claim to fame was a long-ago visit by Sigmund Freud. After checking in and taking a shower, Thomas returned to the street and bought a map from a nearby bookshop. He took a seat at a café across from the eastern entrance to the Luxembourg Gardens and studied the map while sipping an espresso. The layout of Paris came back to him and he began to formulate a plan.

Returning to the Metro station, he took the train to Châtelet–Les Halles and traversed the endless tunnels and stairwells to the No. 4 line, which serviced the Tenth and Eighteenth Arrondissements. He boarded the train along with a cluster of Africans, Asians, and Eastern Europeans.

He got off at Château d'Eau and emerged from the underground tunnels onto Boulevard de Strasbourg. He checked his map and set off in the direction of Gare du Nord. Stopping at a bus stand, he fished in his coat pocket for Sita's picture. He surveyed the boulevard of shops and flats. The air was warming up, and pedestrians were out in force.

He veered left along Boulevard de Magenta and walked to the northernmost corner of Rue du Faubourg-Saint-Denis. He approached a shop with South Asian lettering overhead. The proprietor was standing outside, speaking to a customer. Thomas waited his turn, the photograph of Sita in his hand.

When the proprietor looked at him, Thomas nodded. "*Bonjour, Monsieur.*"

"*Bonjour*," the man replied. He didn't smile.

"I have a friend who lives in this neighborhood," Thomas began, spinning what he hoped was a plausible story. "I wish to surprise her. I have an old picture. I was wondering if you've seen her."

He held out the picture and pointed at Sita.

"*Non*," the man said with a wave. "Not here." He turned away and walked into his shop.

Thomas returned to the street and ambled south. A young African woman pushing a baby carriage smiled at him.

"*Excusez-moi*," he said, stopping in front of her. "I'm terribly sorry to bother you, but I'm looking for an old friend. She lives in the neighborhood."

The woman barely glanced at the photograph in his hand before shaking her head. "*Non, je suis désolée*," she said and continued her stroll.

Thomas asked the same question of three more women and two men, all of diverse ages. Each denied having seen her and none had any interest in follow-up questions. Thomas decided to change his strategy. He began looking for Indian restaurants, hoping to find one serving lunch. He saw a *tandoori* place a block away. The restaurant had a red awning bearing script in French and Hindi. He approached the door and saw that the establishment served dinner only.

He continued south along Rue du Faubourg-Saint-Denis. It was three o'clock in the afternoon and his stomach began to rumble. He realized he hadn't eaten since the pre-arrival meal on the plane. He stopped at a café and ordered a sandwich. Taking a seat at a table by the window, he watched people pass by on the sidewalk. At some point, he looked across the street and saw a narrow pedestrian walkway that led to the east toward Boulevard de Strasbourg. Inside the arcade, he saw what appeared to be an Indian restaurant.

He left the café and angled toward the passage. To his surprise, it turned out to be an Indo-Pakistani oasis dominated by South Asian restaurants. The first restaurant he saw was closed. The lights in the dining room were off and chairs were stacked on tables. He was about to turn away when he saw a light flicker on in the back. After a moment, a large Indian woman appeared, holding a hand broom and a trash bag. She was wearing a purple *sari* embellished with blue lotus flowers. She scurried about, sweeping up dust and straightening things.

He knocked on the glass and got her attention. She looked at him with an annoyed expression. She shook her head and said something he couldn't hear. He held up Sita's photograph to the windowpane, and she came closer, her face a mask of irritation. She spoke loudly enough to carry her words through the window.

"*Le restaurant est fermé*," she said, waving her broom in the air. "*Fermé!*" she repeated. Then she continued her sweeping.

Thomas turned away and approached an Indian man tending to a row of outdoor plants beside the entrance to another restaurant. He showed him Sita's picture.

The man glanced at the photograph and gave Thomas

the sort of beaming smile that Indians wore more naturally in Bombay. "How do you know this girl?" he asked.

"She is a friend from the university," Thomas replied, thinking quickly.

"The University of Paris?" the man inquired. "Are you a student there?"

"I studied at the Sorbonne." He held up the photo again. "Might you have seen her somewhere? Please think. It's very important."

The man shook his head. "I have not seen this girl. But I have a friend who might know her. You follow me, sir?"

Thomas trailed the man down the arcade. "Where are we going?"

"It's not far, sir," the man replied.

They left the passage and crossed Boulevard de Strasbourg. The man stopped on the sidewalk and pointed down a second passage, covered with a canopy of glass.

"My friend is this way," he said. "He comes to my restaurant all the time." He stuck out his hand. "I am Ajit."

Thomas shook the man's hand. "Thomas Clarke."

Ajit led the way into the second arcade. They entered a shop advertising hand-woven rugs from Persia and Afghanistan. Ajit made his way to the back and peeked through a door that led to a storage area. He spoke a loud greeting in Hindi.

"He is hard of hearing," Ajit said. "But he will come."

"Who is he?" Thomas asked.

"He is Prabodhan-dada. He has lived here a long time."

After a minute, an elderly man appeared, holding a calculator. He had salt-and-pepper hair and wore thick glasses. He greeted Ajit kindly and delivered Thomas a look that was at once open and quizzical.

"Prabodhan-dada," Ajit said, using French so that Thomas could understand, "Mister Thomas is looking for a girl."

The rug dealer tilted his head and blinked. When he didn't speak, Thomas took out Ahalya's photograph and handed it to him.

"She looks like this," he said, pointing at Sita. "Though she is older now."

The rug dealer ignored the photograph and focused on Thomas. He spoke in a quiet voice, but his words carried unmistakably authority.

"As you can see," he said, "I am a tradesman. I sell rugs. Why do you think I would know her?"

"They are friends from the Sorbonne," Ajit explained before Thomas could speak. "Mister Thomas hasn't seen her in some time."

"Do you not have a telephone?" the rug dealer replied. "Or the Internet? Surely, a man educated at the Sorbonne would know how to contact a friend."

"We lost touch," Thomas said. "All I know is that she is in Paris."

The rug dealer narrowed his eyes and thought about this. At last he seemed to relent. He drew the photograph close to his face and squinted at it through his glasses. He blinked a couple of times and then looked at Thomas again, less skeptical than curious.

"What if she does not want to see you?"

"Does that mean you know where she is?" Thomas asked.

The rug dealer stared at him for a long moment before nodding. "I have seen a girl who looks like this."

As soon as the old man spoke the words, Thomas's hope took flight. "Is she nearby?" he inquired, trying to control his enthusiasm.

The rug dealer took another look at the photograph and waggled his head. He exchanged a few words with Ajit in Hindi and then vanished into the storage room.

Ajit spoke: "Prabodhan-dada says this girl is working at a restaurant in the Eighteenth. He asks that you not mention him."

"Of course," Thomas agreed. "How do I get there?"

Ajit gave him a beaming smile. "I will take you, Mister Thomas."

Thomas followed Ajit to the Metro station at Château d'Eau. They bought tickets and hopped aboard the northbound train. At Barbès Rochechouart, Ajit stepped onto the platform and led Thomas through the disorienting swirl of the crowd. Exiting the station, Ajit walked east on Boulevard de la Chapelle and took a left up a narrow cobblestoned lane. He headed for the glass facade of an Indian restaurant. The restaurant was closed, but Thomas could see a dark-skinned man sitting at a table at one of the booths.

Ajit asked Thomas for the photograph and knocked on the window. The man turned around, clearly irritated by the interruption. He stood and came to the door.

"*Bonjour,*" Ajit said, pre-empting the man's question. He showed the man Sita's photograph, and the two of them held an animated conversation in Hindi. Eventually the man shook his head and closed the door.

"What did he say?" Thomas asked.

"He would not answer many questions," Ajit said. "He was not friendly."

"Did he say anything about the photograph?"

"He said the girl worked here once, but she is gone."

Thomas took a sharp breath, feeling certain he was close. He studied the restaurant and then walked back down the cobbled lane to Boulevard de la Chapelle. Ajit followed without a word. On the corner was a tourist shop empty of customers. Thomas stepped inside and made his way to the cashier—a young woman with spiked hair and a spider tattoo on her neck. Thomas showed her Sita's picture and gestured toward the restaurant down the lane, explaining the situation in French.

The cashier shook her head, looking bored. "It is not the same girl."

Thomas felt a surge of frustration. "How do you know?"

"I just know."

"A man told me he saw her there," Thomas argued. "He was pretty certain about it."

The cashier put her hands on the counter and leaned

toward him. "I don't care who told you what; it's not the same girl." She paused and her face softened slightly. "Look, I'm an artist, okay? I sketch people in the park. This girl," she said, pointing toward the picture, "has lighter skin than the girl who works at the restaurant. And the girl in the restaurant has a cleft chin, a wider forehead, and a mole beside her nose. I ate there not long ago. The food was awful, but I remember her well."

The cashier's certainty struck at the heart of Thomas's confidence. "The man at the restaurant says she doesn't work there any more," he said. "He didn't want to talk about her. Any idea why that would be?"

The cashier smirked. "Oh, she still works there. I saw her this morning. She's probably illegal, like half the immigrants in this city."

Thomas left the tourist shop, feeling depressed. The rug dealer's lead had seemed so promising. Then he remembered the old man's eyeglasses. *He didn't see her*, he thought to himself. *He saw a distortion of her*.

He stood on the corner and faced Ajit. "I appreciate all your help."

Ajit saw his dejection and tried to cheer him up. "Do you like Indian cuisine, Mister Thomas?"

"Yes," Thomas replied, trying to be gracious.

"My wife makes the best *tandoori* chicken in France. If you come to my restaurant, I will ask if she has seen your friend."

"I'll think about it," Thomas said, having no intention

of doing so. He put out his hand to end the conversation, and Ajit shook it, looking crestfallen.

"Come to my restaurant," Ajit said. "I promise you will not regret it."

Thomas took the Metro back to the Fifth and strolled south along the wide promenade of Boulevard Saint-Michel. He entered the east gate of the Luxembourg Gardens just as the sun was descending toward the trees to the south-west. He walked across the plaza to the Luxembourg palace and took a seat near the fountain. Unless Julia's contact at the BRP came up with something, he was out of live options. He could pound the pavement for weeks, casing different neighborhoods in the city and accosting every Parisian with a pulse, but he would almost certainly come up empty. The odds of success were overwhelmingly against him.

When the sunlight faded into afterglow, he left the gardens by the side gate, heading for his hotel. His BlackBerry vibrated in his pocket.

"Hey, Julia," he answered when he saw the number on the screen.

"Sorry for the delay," she said. "Our friend at the BRP just spoke with an envoy at the French embassy in Mumbai. The envoy promised to contact the CBI tomorrow."

Thomas took this in. "The wheels of justice grind slowly."

"Apparently. Did you have any luck this afternoon?"

"None whatsoever," he replied. He gave her a brief

summary of meeting Ajit and chasing down the rug dealer's erroneous tip.

Julia sighed. "I keep thinking what a shame it is that the Bombay police let Navin go. If we had his uncle's name, I could do wonders on our computer system."

"I don't doubt it," Thomas replied.

After a moment, she asked, "Do you have any plans for the evening? I know a fabulous Moroccan place on Isle St. Louis."

Thomas was about to accept when he was struck by an idea. He recalled the advice of Jean-Pierre Léon: "*I'd ask women and children, especially South Asians.*" And Ajit's invitation: "*My wife makes the best tandoori chicken in France . . . I will ask if she has seen your friend.*" He knew it was a shot in the dark, but it was better than waiting around for the BRP to produce a lead that might never come.

"I'd love to," he said, "but right now I'm craving a little Indian food."

Julia pondered this. "Does that mean you have a hunch?"

"I'd call it a wild guess. Don't get your hopes up."

"All right, I'm game. Tell me where to meet you and when."

Thomas smiled. "Eight o'clock at Porte St. Denis. We can walk from there."

Chapter 20

Yield not to calamity, but face it boldly.
—Virgil

Paris, France

After Uncle-ji and Aunti-ji left the flat with the travel documents, Tatiana returned to the sitting room. "Come," she said to Sita. "Work to do."

Sita followed her up the stairs to the library. Tatiana gave her the dust rag, and she spent two hours dusting books, her mind consumed by the morning meeting. Nothing made sense. When Navin had sold her to Uncle-ji, she had expected that she would work in the restaurant for a long time, perhaps years. But then Navin had showed up again and everything had changed. Uncle-ji had hidden her in the closet and handed her over to Vasily and Tatiana, and he and Vasily had made some sort of travel arrangement. She wished she had looked more closely at the airline tickets.

At midday Tatiana brought her a baguette sandwich. After she ate, Tatiana led her to Vasily's office on the third floor of the flat. Sita had cleaned the office twice in the past weeks, and each time it had made her skin crawl.

"Clean fast," Tatiana said. "He come home in one hour."

When Sita was alone, she took out her dust rag and went over the desk. She stared for a long moment at the flat-screen monitors, worrying that any vibration might jar them awake. She moved on to the circular window and the filing cabinet. She made quick work of these and looked around for something else to clean. She noticed that the closet door at the back of the room wasn't closed completely. She could see a pile of boxes through the crack along the doorframe. She hesitated, but her curiosity got the better of her.

She opened the door and stared at the boxes. They were banker's boxes, at least a dozen of them. She opened the top box and saw that it was full of paper. She extracted the top page. It was a bank statement for an account in Geneva, Switzerland. Vasily's name was not listed anywhere on the document. The statement was in French, but the figures didn't require translation. The balance in the account was over five million euros. Sita took a deep breath and pictured Natalia and Ivanna and the other girls. Whatever Vasily and Dmitri were up to, their business had made them very wealthy.

She replaced the account statement exactly as it had been and backed out of the closet. Just then, out of the corner of her eye, she noticed a small hook lodged in the wall beside the door jamb. On the hook was a ring with three keys. Sita looked around the room for a lock that would fit the keys, but she didn't see anything. Apart from the computer system and the desk and filing cabinet, the room was bare.

She thought about the layout of the house. The front door could be opened only by using a numerical keypad. She knew the six-digit code to the door because she had seen Dmitri enter it twice a day. The double doors to the street also had a keypad. The code was different, but she knew it, too. At first she had thought she might use the codes to escape, but the more she had considered it, the less attractive the idea had seemed. To slip out undetected would take sheer luck, and if she failed, she was certain the reprisals would be swift and severe.

She thought next of the internal doors. The door to the basement room where she had found Natalia had a bolt that could be locked by hand from the hallway. The door to the laundry room had no lock. Her bedroom door had a lock, but she realized that she hadn't given much thought to it in the past few days. Her sudden and inexplicable move from the restaurant to Vasily's flat had left her disoriented, and the night traffic of Dmitri and the girls had turned that disorientation into fear.

She closed her eyes and tried to recall as much about the bedroom door as she could. Tatiana always locked the door from the outside, and she remembered hearing a sliding sound when Tatiana said goodnight. It might have been the insertion of a key. Still, a keyhole on the outside of the door wouldn't do her any good unless it was mirrored on the inside. She thought harder, but the area around the knob remained blurry.

She looked at the keys and made up her mind. She took the ring off the hook just as she heard Tatiana coming up the stairs. Secreting the keys in her *sari*, she closed the closet door just so. When Tatiana appeared, she was dusting the desk again. The keys were cold against her skin, but she took comfort in them. Whatever Vasily and Uncle-ji had planned for her tomorrow, she had at least one more night in the flat.

And with the night came possibilities.

That evening, Sita helped Ivanna serve the family dinner. When the dishes were cleared and the kitchen clean, Tatiana escorted Sita to her room and wished her goodnight. She closed the door and locked it from the outside. Sita held her breath and looked toward the doorknob.

There *was* a keyhole!

She waited until Tatiana's footsteps receded down the hallway before withdrawing the keys from the folds of her *sari*. She placed her ear against the door and listened for a full minute to make sure no one was within earshot.

When all was quiet, she took the first key and slid it into the deadbolt. The key didn't turn. She tried the second key. It, too, met resistance. Her heartbeat increased. She held the third key and twisted it in the lock, praying it would turn.

It did!

The key swiveled softly from the vertical to the horizontal position, and she heard the bolt disengage. It was hard to believe it could be so easy. She twisted the key in the opposite direction and reset the bolt. She knew now that she could escape from her room, and if she could escape from her room, she could escape from the flat using the codes she had memorized.

She sat down on the bed and worked each move out in her mind. When she was satisfied, she took a long bath in the tub and then dressed again in her *sari*. She wished she had better shoes. She was still wearing the sandals Navin had bought her in Bombay. She rummaged through some drawers and discovered an old sweater and a pair of wool socks. She put the socks on her feet and slipped on her sandals. The fit was tight, but the sandals would have to do.

At ten o'clock, she stood by the window and watched Dmitri shepherd the girls across the courtyard to the vehicles. Again, only Natalia accompanied Dmitri, this time in the black Mercedes. The others climbed into the back of the van. The van left the courtyard first and the Mercedes followed. Sita didn't know how long they would be gone, but she guessed they wouldn't return until at least three in the morning. It was enough time for her to disappear.

She sat down on the chair by the window and picked up the novel she had been reading. She pulled a blanket over herself to conserve her body heat and read until midnight. Then she went to the door of the room and listened carefully. She had heard footsteps in the hallway half an hour before. Now there was no sound. It was a good sign, but the risk of detection was still high. She resolved to wait another hour or two.

She returned to the novel. As she read, her eyelids grew heavy, but she fought off sleep. Her mind began to drift. She saw Ahalya dancing on the beach. She shook her head and focused on the bookcase across the room.

Ahalya isn't here, she thought. *Stay awake!*

Before long, however, she drifted again. There was Ahalya, meeting her after class at St. Mary's. And Naresh, asking Ambini about her grades. There were mangy dogs barking and the ocean lapping at sand . . . and Ahalya swimming, diving with her into the depths . . . the blue sea turning to shade . . . turning to gray . . . turning to black.

When she opened her eyes, she sat upright. She glanced at the clock on the wall and fear lanced through her. It was 3:15 in the morning. She couldn't believe she had fallen asleep. She looked out the window and saw with relief that the courtyard was still empty. She walked to the door and pressed her ear against it, listening. She heard nothing. She slid the key into the lock and retracted the bolt. She stepped out into the hallway. The flat was dark, except for the glow of a night light in the foyer.

She crept down the hall, taking care to step on the balls of her feet. She looked at the stairway. The steps were wooden, and she couldn't recall if any of them creaked. She held the banister and stepped as lightly as possible on the first step. It sank beneath her weight, but it didn't make a sound. She took one step after another until she reached the foyer floor.

The alarm system was activated. She felt another twinge of fear. Would the system beep when she entered the code? She couldn't remember hearing a beep when Dmitri used it.

Crossing the floor to the entry closet, she put on the warmest coat she could find. The garment was made of black wool and had a fur collar and hood. She buttoned the coat and took two steps to the keypad. The red light glared at her. She took a deep breath and punched the six digits she had memorized, praying to Lakshmi that no alarm would sound.

The light turned green without a beep and the latch disengaged. She turned the handle and opened the door. The blast of wintry air took her breath away. She stepped quietly onto the porch. The courtyard was dark and the sounds of the city were muted. A light snow was falling. She moved across the cobblestones to the doors beneath the arch. She punched in the second code and heard a bolt retract. She pushed open one of the doors and slipped out into the night.

Looking both ways, she decided to go left. Her objective was to find a hotel with a night clerk who would agree to contact the police. She had no idea whether she could trust the French authorities, but she had no other option.

She walked quickly, her footfalls echoing in the still air. She reached an intersection with a major boulevard and peered into the distance, searching the street for a hotel sign. The boulevard was lined with storefronts, all of them closed. A couple of taxis passed her, and then silence descended again.

Pressing her hands into her coat, she started up the

boulevard. She passed two hotels, but the lobby doors were locked and she could see no one inside. The cold encircled her and needled her face. Her breath came out in clouds of vapor, and snow dusted her nose.

She felt the first signs of desperation. The sunrise was still hours away, and she was freezing. She almost didn't see the black Mercedes until it passed her going in the opposite direction. Something jogged in her mind and she turned around just as the driver slammed on the brakes. Adrenaline poured into her arteries and she began to run. She was hampered by the heavy coat and the lack of grip on her sandals.

The Mercedes turned around and raced back down the road. She heard the car pass her and slam on its brakes again. Dmitri jumped out of the car.

They saw the bakery truck at the same moment. It was coming toward them slowly. Dmitri stood still, watching her, a mere twenty feet away. She stopped in her tracks and began to wave her arms furiously at the truck.

"Help!" she shouted in English. "Help me, please!"

The truck decelerated, the driver interrogating her with his eyes. In the light of a nearby streetlamp, she could see that he was heavyset, with a round face and curly hair.

"Help!" she shouted again. She ran up to the side of the truck as it pulled to a stop.

The driver reached across the passenger seat and rolled down the window. "*Je peux vous aider?*" he asked warily.

"I don't speak French," she wheezed, trying to catch her

breath. She could see the black Mercedes through the windows of the truck, but Dmitri was not in sight. "Please," she begged him. "Please let me in."

"*Français! Français!*" the driver said, growing impatient.

"*No français!*" she exclaimed. "Please! Call the police!"

The driver looked scared. "*La police?*" he asked, looking around. "*Non. Je ne veux pas des problèmes,*" he said and rolled up his window quickly. He stomped on the gas and drove off.

Sita watched the truck depart with terror and despair. She turned around and bolted down the boulevard, her lungs burning in the cold. Dmitri caught up with her easily and lifted her off her feet. She lashed out at him, kicking and clawing at his eyes, but he held her tightly and piled her into the back seat of the Mercedes. He slipped into the driver's seat and floored the accelerator.

Sita buried her face in her hands and sobbed. She had been so close! If only she hadn't fallen asleep! If only she'd taken another street! If only she'd left at midnight when she first had the thought! She cried until the car stopped outside the flat. Dmitri jumped out and keyed the code into the system. The doors swung wide and he drove the Mercedes into the courtyard.

When the car stopped again, Sita looked up and realized she was not alone. Natalia sat beside her. Beneath an open black trenchcoat, she wore a low-cut halter top and a skintight skirt that showed all of her legs. Her face was a mess. Her makeup had run and her hair was disheveled. Her blue eyes were red, as if she had been crying.

She reached out and touched Sita's face, wiping away her tears. Their eyes met and held, drawn by understanding. Then the moment passed and Dmitri was at the door, reaching into the seat and dragging Sita out by her hair.

Chapter 21

Human nature is made of faith. As a person believes, so he is.

—Bhagavad Gita

Paris, France

Thomas arrived at the grand archway of Porte St. Denis a few minutes before eight. The streets of the Tenth looked different at night. The lamplight cast a warm glow upon the urban scene, but the shadows reminded him of all the things that remained hidden from view.

Julia showed up on time and greeted him with a double kiss. Thomas led her up Rue du Faubourg-Saint-Denis and pointed toward the entrance to the arcade. It was then that he noticed a sign above the wrought-iron gate. He'd missed it that afternoon. The sign read, Passage Brady.

"Have you ever been here?" he asked.

She shook her head. "I haven't spent much time in the Tenth."

Although it was a Monday, the restaurants along the arcade

were gaily lit and bustling with business. The only exception was the first restaurant on the passage—the one in which the rotund Indian woman had been cleaning. A curtain had been drawn across its windows, and a placard hanging in the door read, "*Fermé jusqu'à nouvel ordre.*" Closed until further notice.

Thomas saw Ajit standing at the entrance to his establishment. He brightened when he saw Thomas. He greeted him effusively and showered Julia with compliments. Then he showed them to a candlelit table beside the window and commented on the view. Handing them menus, he promised to make them the best meal in Paris.

When Ajit scurried away to greet another customer, Julia laughed. "You obviously made an impression on him."

After perusing the menus, they delivered their orders to a young Indian waitress. She returned a moment later with two glasses of red wine.

"Tell me about the District," Julia said, tasting the wine. "I grew up in Reston, but I haven't been back since college. My parents are in Boston now."

Thomas spent the next twenty minutes regaling her with tales of scandal and political malfeasance from the Metro section of the *Washington Post*. Once she asked a question about his family, but he was deft in deflecting her interest. He didn't mention Priya, and she had the decency not to probe. She seemed content to sip her wine and listen to him talk.

When the food came, they got down to the business of

eating. Julia told him about her years at Columbia, including a few humorous memories of Andrew Porter, and about law school at Cornell. She was gregarious and funny, and the meal passed swiftly.

They lingered over drinks until half past ten. After most of the patrons had left, Ajit approached their table and inquired about the fare. Thomas was full of praise, for the food was quite good. Then he took out Sita's picture.

Ajit nodded and took the photograph. "I will be right back."

He approached a portly woman across the room who was organizing receipts. They spoke briefly and he showed her the photograph. Ajit returned to their table, looking disappointed. He handed the photo back to Thomas.

"I'm sorry," he said. "My wife hasn't seen your friend."

"What about the waitress?" Thomas asked. "She might know something."

"Of course." He summoned the girl.

Thinking they wanted to pay, the waitress brought them their check. Thomas handed his credit card to Ajit. "Do you mind if I speak to her alone?"

Ajit gave him a strange look but took the card and left. For reasons he could not quite understand, Thomas decided to dispense with his cover story.

"I have a friend in Bombay," he said, meeting the waitress's eyes. "She's looking for her sister. I'm wondering if you've seen her."

He held up the picture. The waitress looked worried

for an instant but quickly recovered her composure. She walked across the room and met Ajit at the register. They had a brief exchange, and then he handed her a black folder with Thomas's receipt. When she returned to their table, she used the pen to write something on the back of the receipt.

"If I were you," she said, "I would call Information."

Thomas nodded and stood. After thanking Ajit for dinner, he led Julia out of the restaurant. When they reached Boulevard de Strasbourg, he took the receipt out of his pocket and read the inscription on the reverse. The girl had written in scrawling French: "Meet me here at nine o'clock tomorrow morning."

Thomas felt chills. His hunch had paid off. The girl knew something. He handed the check to Julia. Her eyes widened with astonishment.

"Can I come with you?" she asked.

Thomas grinned. "You'll probably put her at ease. I usually have the opposite effect."

Julia laughed. "It's something about you lawyer types. Andrew was the same way."

The walked briskly toward the Metro station, seeking shelter from the cold. After they passed through the turnstiles, Julia kissed his cheek, this time only once.

"You want company on the ride?" he asked.

She laughed again. "You're sweet, but I bet you don't have a black belt in judo."

"You've got me there."

"*À demain*," she said and walked away, leaving him to ponder how it was possible that she was unattached.

On Thursday morning they met at the base of the great arch beneath gunmetal skies. The air was cold and the ground was covered with light snow. In contrast to her merriment the night before, Julia's face was all business. She gave Thomas a brief smile and walked beside him toward Passage Brady.

The waitress was standing on the sidewalk beside the wrought-iron gate. When she saw them, she turned without a word and strolled north along Rue du Faubourg-Saint-Denis. Thomas traded a glance with Julia and trailed the girl, keeping a healthy distance between them.

The waitress made a right turn on Rue du Château d'Eau and walked for a number of blocks before turning down a side street. She stopped beside an alleyway and faced them, drawing the collar of her coat around her neck. She spoke quietly, looking at Julia.

"I am Varuni. The girl you are looking for is Sita. She worked at a restaurant on Passage Brady until a few days ago. The owners told me she was a relative, but I didn't believe them. Sita also worked during the day for some Russian people. Their flat is there." She pointed toward a set of double doors. "The man is named Vasily. I don't know the woman's name."

"Do you know where Sita went?" Julia asked gently.

"They didn't talk to me," the girl said. "She was there and then she was gone."

"Do you know what she did for these Russian people?" Thomas asked.

Varuni looked afraid. "I know nothing more than I told you."

Julia touched Varuni's arm. "It's all right. You're very brave to help us."

The girl looked at Julia. "I liked Sita very much. I hope nothing happened to her." She paused. "Please don't tell anyone I brought you here. It would make trouble for me."

"Don't worry," Julia replied. "We'll keep your secret."

Varuni nodded and disappeared around the corner.

Thomas approached the double doors and saw the keypad. The doors had no handle and didn't budge when he pushed on them. Julia took out her mobile phone and called the office. She recited the address of the flat and asked for information on the occupants.

When the answer came, she hung up. "Vasily and Tatiana Petrovich," she said. "Ukrainian. Possible connections to organized crime groups in Eastern Europe. Nothing confirmed. We know the BRP has been watching them for a while, but it isn't clear why. It isn't our case, and they don't share unless they have to."

They stepped away from the door and walked across the street.

"What do we do now?" Thomas asked.

"I'll give Varuni's story to the BRP and ask for a warrant."

"Will you get one?"

Julia shrugged. "Maybe. But if these people are high-profile targets, we may find ourselves waiting in line."

Thomas was about to reply when the double doors to the Petrovich flat began to open. Moments later, a black Mercedes nosed out of the courtyard. A blond-haired young man was at the wheel and beside him in the passenger seat was a middle-aged woman with dark skin, gesturing animatedly with her hands. Thomas couldn't see her clearly, but she looked vaguely familiar. The blond driver looked at them intently before accelerating down the street. The rear windows were tinted black, obscuring the back seat.

The connection dawned on him as the car approached the intersection with Rue du Château d'Eau. He took off running. Julia called after him, but he had no time to explain. The woman in the passenger seat wasn't wearing Western clothing. She was wearing an Indian *sari*. The woman cleaning the restaurant on Passage Brady—the restaurant that was now closed—had been wearing a *sari*. When the Mercedes passed, he had seen a flash of purple and blue. It was the same woman. It had to be.

Thomas was fifty feet away when the car disappeared around the bend. He ran as if he was in a race for his life, but on the street he was no match for the Mercedes. When he reached the intersection and looked down Rue du Château d'Eau, the car was gone.

He stared into the sky and struggled to catch his breath. He was still wheezing when Julia caught up with him.

"What in the world was that about?"

"The woman in the front seat," he said, taking a deep breath, "I've seen her before."

"Where?"

"Yesterday afternoon when I was showing Sita's picture around. She was cleaning up one of the restaurants on Passage Brady. Last night the restaurant was closed."

"Did you see the license plate?"

He shook his head. "It was too fast."

"I'll get you your warrant," she said, taking out her phone. "There's no way the BRP is going to sit on this one."

Chapter 22

The time that my journey takes is long and the way of it is long.

—Rabindranath Tagore

Paris, France

Minutes before, Sita had stood in the courtyard beside the black Mercedes, shivering and afraid. While she watched, Dmitri slipped into the driver's seat and keyed the ignition, bringing the car to life with a quiet rumble. Shyam climbed into the middle of the back seat, Uncle-ji sat on the far side of the bench, and Aunti-ji joined Dmitri in the front. Sita was the last to climb into the car. She took a deep breath and recalled the airline tickets. She felt sure now that they weren't just for Uncle-ji and Aunti-ji. One of them was for her.

Taking a seat beside Shyam, she looked out the window and tried to ignore the raging wound on her scalp. She remembered every step she had taken across the courtyard the night before. Natalia ahead of them, looking back, terrified. Dmitri yanking her hair. Entering the lobby of the apartment where the girls were kept. Being dragged up the stairs and thrown against the wall in Natalia's room. Natalia pleading with Dmitri to have mercy. Dmitri's face inches from hers, his breath hot and heavy with the stench of alcohol. He whispered to her then. She would never forget the words.

"I know you have seen the basement. If you were staying, I would teach you to enjoy it. But my father has made more profitable arrangements with Dietrich."

Natalia left with Dmitri and reappeared minutes later wearing a T-shirt and boxer shorts. She staunched the bleeding on Sita's scalp with tissues from a box on the dresser and offered her the bed. Sita shook her head and moved over, making a place for the Ukrainian girl. Natalia lay down beside her and held Sita close.

"I'm sorry," she said. "Dmitri is horrible man."

In the morning, Dmitri came for Sita and threw a brown wool coat on the bed.

"From my mother," he said with disgust. "If it were up to me, you would freeze." Then he took her to the car.

Sita watched through tinted glass as the double doors to the courtyard opened and Dmitri pulled the Mercedes out onto the street. She saw a couple standing on the far sidewalk, staring at them. The man was tall with dark hair, and the woman was wearing a crimson coat. As the car pulled away, she turned and observed the couple through the rear window. Something about the man arrested her.

She was sure he couldn't see her, but she felt as if he was looking directly into her eyes.

Suddenly, the man began to run. She clutched the handle of the armrest, riveted and bewildered by the spectacle. She felt the car accelerate and realized that Dmitri had noticed him, too. They reached the end of the street and turned the corner in a hurry. The rapid movement threw her against the door, and she lost sight of the man.

When she looked back, he was gone.

A moment later, she caught Dmitri glaring at her in the rearview mirror. He placed a call on his mobile phone and spoke a few inscrutable words. Remembering Navin's visit to the restaurant, Sita was struck by an exhilarating thought: had the man been looking for her? She searched her memory for his face but found no match. *He didn't look like someone from the police*, she thought. *But if he wasn't, then why did he run?*

In the front seat, Aunti-ji was prattling away about the *élégance* and *cosmopolitisme* of Dmitri's family, and Uncle-ji was staring out the window in the seat behind her, oblivious to the chase that had begun and ended so quickly. Sita glanced at Shyam and saw him watching her. He gave her a look that said, "I saw it too."

She sat back and closed her eyes, trying to block out the nagging sense of fear that seemed her constant companion now. Exhaustion weighed on her after the adventures and disappointments of the night.

Before long, she fell asleep.

★

She awoke to the sound of Uncle-ji's voice and the feeling of Shyam's hand shaking her arm. "Sita, wake up," Uncle-ji was saying.

She opened her eyes and saw that they were on the outskirts of Paris. They passed a sign indicating that the airport was two kilometers away. She focused on Uncle-ji.

"We are going to New York," he said, looking nervous. "You are to behave like our daughter until we reach America. It is very important that you follow our instructions. If you do not, there will be consequences."

He handed her a passport. The picture was identical to the passport Navin had purchased, but her name was now Sundari Raman and she was a naturalized French citizen.

"We are on holiday," Uncle-ji told her. "You must not talk to strangers. Speak only to us and use Hindi. We will do all of the talking."

Sita received the news of their destination with despair. She had left Asia for Europe, believing that someday she would find a way to return to her sister in Bombay. It was a dream, yes, but it didn't seem like a fantasy. Now she was about to leave Europe for North America. The United States and India were on opposite sides of the globe. How would she ever find her way back across ten thousand miles?

Hot tears drenched her cheeks, and she wiped them away. She tried to think of a way out but saw none. Vasily and Dmitri had proven themselves to be both powerful and ruthless. They controlled the destinies of six young women and had procured a full suite of passports in a matter of days.

If she crossed them again, they would do more to her than leave her with a bloody scalp.

Dmitri dropped them off at Terminal 2A at Charles de Gaulle. He placed their luggage on the curb and knelt in front of Sita.

"You have been much trouble to us," he said quietly. "You must do everything they say from now on. If you do not, our associates in New York will make you feel pain. Is this clear?"

She nodded.

"Good," he said, touching her hair to reinforce the threat. With that, he climbed into the Mercedes and sped away.

Aunti-ji gave Sita the heaviest of the suitcases, and Uncle-ji led the way into the terminal. They checked in at the ticket counter and headed toward the security checkpoint. The French security officials eyed the four of them closely, but Sita made no attempt to speak to them.

They cleared security and took a seat in the waiting area. At noon, their flight was called for boarding. When they reached the boarding kiosk, Uncle-ji handed their passports to the agent, and Aunti-ji patted Sita's head for effect. The agent smiled at Shyam and then at Sita.

"*Bon voyage*," she said and returned the stubs to Uncle-ji.

They took their seats in the middle of the large aircraft. Aunti-ji fussed about the seat assignment and the lack of personal space. Uncle-ji rolled his eyes and chatted quietly with Shyam. Sita looked out a nearby window and ignored them. She watched a plane take off in the distance and tried to picture every feature of her sister's face. Her large eyes and thick eyelashes. Her dimples and full lips. Her almond skin and shimmery hair. Each piece of her sister was beloved. Each would be forever missed.

As the plane backed away from the gate and lumbered toward the runway, Sita made a vow to God and to herself. She would remember her sister. She would remember the person she was and the India they knew before the madness. The world could take their freedom; it could steal their innocence; it could destroy their family and sweep them away in currents beyond their understanding. But it could not deprive them of memory. Only time had that power, and Sita would resist it at all cost.

The past was all she had left.

The flight from Paris touched down at Newark Liberty International Airport late in the afternoon. Apart from a merciful three-hour nap, Aunti-ji had spent the entire flight complaining. She moved constantly, shifting her weight back and forth and bumping Uncle-ji and Sita with her arms. Nearby passengers needled her with their eyes, but none had the gumption to tell her to shut up. None except Uncle-ji. Even his pleas, however, fell on deaf ears. Aunti-ji seemed intent on sharing her misery with everyone in earshot. When at last the plane landed, ten rows of passengers breathed a sigh of relief.

Her tirade continued as they walked to the customs arrival area. Sita glanced at the American immigration officials and remembered Dmitri's words. He was now on the other side of the Atlantic, but he had associates in New York. She couldn't risk telling her story to the police.

They waited in the customs area for nearly twenty minutes before being directed to a booth occupied by a Hispanic immigration officer. The officer inspected their passports and collected their fingerprints and photographs using the US-VISIT system. He then interrogated Uncle-ji at length about the purpose of their visit. Uncle-ji's story was almost completely true, and he told it with confidence, albeit in broken English.

The officer turned to Aunti-ji and asked her questions about her residency in France, about her place of birth, and about Shyam and Sita, who he called Sundari. Aunti-ji responded with such obsequiousness that the immigration officer looked at her with suspicion. Sensing his concern, Aunti-ji turned to Sita and patted her head.

"Tell how much you want to see New York," she instructed.

Sita stood frozen, her mind racing for an appropriate response. She spoke the lie that came to her. "Everyone in France talks about New York. I've always wanted to visit."

"How come you speak such good English?" the officer asked, narrowing his eyes.

The answer came to her effortlessly. "We learn it in school."

Her explanation seemed to satisfy the officer and he turned his gaze once again to their documents. Uncle-ji stood stiffly with Shyam at his side, and Aunti-ji, for once, had the good sense not to speak. At long last, the officer stamped their passports and waved them through.

"Welcome to America," he said and turned to the next person in line.

They collected their luggage and sat pensively on a bench beside the bank of hotel telephones. Neither Uncle-ji nor Aunti-ji explained to Sita what they were waiting for. Only Shyam seemed oblivious to the tension of the moment. He stood up and danced a few steps from a Bollywood film, clearly showing off for Sita's benefit.

"Did you see *Kabhi Khushi Kabhie Gham*?" he asked her. "It has Amitabh Bachchan and Shahrukh Khan in it."

"*Cupa rahō!*" Uncle-ji said sternly, telling the boy to be quiet. "This is not India. This is America. You must not make a scene."

"I'm sorry, Baba," Shyam said, looking wounded. "I was just trying to cheer up Sita."

"Sita does not need cheering up. And we do not need to see you dance. Sit down."

Shyam sat beside Sita and hung his head. When Uncle-ji turned away, Sita brushed Shyam's hand with the back of her fingers.

"It's okay," she mouthed. "I liked it."

At this sign of affection, Shyam's sadness seemed to retreat. After a moment, he mustered the nerve to move his hand slightly and touch her in return.

★

Ten minutes later, a middle-aged Slavic man who looked startlingly like Vasily walked through the sliding glass doors into the terminal. He looked around until he caught sight of them and then walked in their direction. He stared at Sita for long seconds.

"Follow me," he said brusquely and turned back toward the door, making no attempt to help them with their luggage.

They trailed Vasily's lookalike out of the terminal and across a lane of traffic to a white utility van. They climbed inside and Vasily's lookalike took his place in the front passenger seat. The driver was a large man with hard eyes and days-old stubble on his chin. As soon as all the doors were closed, he moved the van into traffic and took a ramp onto the turnpike.

After a while, they passed through a long tunnel and emerged into the shadow of skyscrapers. Sita was astonished by the concrete jungle of metropolitan New York. Bombay was more crowded, but New York was a city built in the sky.

The driver navigated through a traffic snarl until he reached a seedy-looking hotel called the Taj. Vasily's lookalike opened the sliding door to the van and Uncle-ji and Aunti-ji piled out and collected their luggage. Sita got out after Shyam, but the Slav blocked her way.

"You come with us," he said.

Sita stopped cold and glanced at Uncle-ji, fear blossoming within her. Uncle-ji stared intently at a spot on the sidewalk. At once she knew. Another exchange had been made. Chennai, Bombay, Paris, New York. When would it end?

Vasily's lookalike took her arm and forced her back into the van.

"Where are you taking me?" she asked.

"No questions," he commanded, "or I will give you to Igor."

The driver—Igor—grinned at her maliciously. "Alexi always tell truth," he said, his guttural voice almost like a growl.

Vasily's lookalike—Alexi—talked briefly to Uncle-ji, and the restaurant owner handed him a passport. Shyam began to protest, glancing at Sita with wide eyes.

"Why is she not coming with us?" he asked, his words carrying into the van. He clutched his father's hand. "Please, Baba, don't leave her."

Uncle-ji looked ashamed, but he made no attempt to reply.

Alexi returned to the van and climbed into the passenger seat. Igor gunned the engine and pulled away from the curb. Sita looked out the rear window and locked eyes with Shyam. The boy waved and his lips moved, but she couldn't hear his words. She watched him fade into the distance, his small body dwarfed by the great towers of the city.

The depth of her sorrow surprised her. She reached into her *sari* and rubbed Hanuman with her thumb. She tried to pray, tried to believe that the monkey wasn't just a piece of ceramic in her hand, that the real Hanuman was out there somewhere searching for her, but her faith seemed incapable of bearing up the weight of her fear.

She turned around and steadied her breathing. She watched as Igor maneuvered the van back through the jam of tunnel traffic. The late winter sun was setting behind a blanket of low clouds, and the diminishing light cast a pallor over the urban landscape.

They followed the turnpike into Newark and took an exit just past the airport. After a series of turns, Igor pulled the van into the parking lot of a strip mall. Its only distinguishing characteristic was a neon-lit building that sat in the back corner beside a motel. The entrance to the building was flamingo-pink and the sign over the door read Platinum VIP.

Igor parked the van near a side door, and Alexi summoned Sita from the back seat. Pulling Tatiana's coat around her, she followed him through the door and down a dimly lit hallway. The walls were dingy with old paint and decorated with cutouts from porn magazines.

Alexi opened the door to a small room. It was furnished with a bed, a sink, a toilet, and a television set. He flipped a switch and a light came on in a garish gold lamp in the corner. The room was windowless and looked neglected. A dusty fan hung from a fixture in the ceiling, its blades unmoving.

"You stay in here," he said and left her alone, locking the door behind him.

★

Sita sat on the bed for hours. She studied the room and hatched imaginary escape plots, all of which presumed extraordinary good fortune on her part and profound stupidity on the part of her captors. When she grew tired of this, she distracted herself with mind games. Occasionally, footsteps passed in the hallway and she heard the muffled sounds of speech.

In time, the footsteps grew more regular. She heard female voices speaking in a foreign tongue. Their accents were similar to Dmitri's, but she couldn't tell if the language was Russian. A man greeted the girls and barked an order. One of the girls began to plead with him. A scuffle ensued and something thumped against the door. The girl shrieked. The man shouted. Again the door thumped. Sita heard what sounded like nails scratching on wood. She drew her knees to her chin and her heartbeat increased.

The door opened and a young woman entered. She was blond and dressed in a V-neck top and miniskirt. Igor sauntered into the room behind her and looked crossly at Sita. She leaped off the bed and cowered in the corner behind the television set. The blond girl glanced at her and turned back toward Igor, her eyes wide and full of fear.

Igor barked another command. The girl shook her head. Igor grew impatient and threw her on the bed. When he unbuckled his belt, the girl began to cry. Sita looked away and shut her eyes, whispering a mantra she had learned as a child. The girl's suffering was too much for her to bear.

A few minutes later, Igor got up from the bed, breathing heavily. He pulled on his pants and left the room without a word. The girl lay on the thin mattress. Sita opened her eyes and regarded her still form. She worried that Igor had knocked her unconscious, but then the girl began to stir. She sat up and rearranged her clothes, her face expressionless. Igor returned for her, and the girl followed him out of the room without looking in Sita's direction.

At some point, music began and didn't stop for hours. The pulsing beat reverberated through the walls and rattled her brain. She lay down on the bed, exhausted from jet lag and anxiety. But the music made it impossible to sleep. She covered her ears and buried her head in the filthy sheets.

Sometime before dawn, the music stopped and she heard scuffing sounds in the hallway. The door opened a second time and Igor appeared again, dragging a different girl. The girl didn't protest when Igor pushed her against the wall. She did what he demanded without making a sound. Sita sealed her eyes and ears from the horror of it all. She wanted to bathe herself, to cleanse her soul of the stain of this place. Why was she here? What did they want from her? Was Igor trying to teach her a lesson by raping girls in front of her?

In time, Igor left and the girl went with him. Sita closed her eyes and once more tried to sleep. She was startled awake by the sound of the doorknob turning. Suddenly, Igor stood on the threshold again, alone this time. He glanced either way down the hall and entered the room, shutting the door behind him. He turned toward Sita, and his mouth stretched into a rictus that was part sneer and part smile. Sita backed into the corner and hugged her knees to her chest.

Igor advanced toward her slowly, his meaty hands hanging open at his sides. He knelt in front of her and began to loosen his belt.

"Alexi say I not touch you. Dietrich coming." Igor unzipped his fly and reached into his pants. "Alexi not know if you touch me."

Sita closed her eyes, unable to look at what he wanted to show her. Her teeth began to chatter. She felt him take her head in his hands and draw her toward him. He reeked of sweat and cheap alcohol.

"Open mouth," he hissed.

"Please," she whimpered, feeling a sudden urge to vomit. "Don't do this."

"Open mouth," he commanded again, increasing the pressure on her head.

Suddenly, the door burst open. Sita looked up as Alexi stormed into the room, his face dark with rage. Igor swiveled around and rushed to cover himself. Before Igor could get his hands free, Alexi drove his fist into Igor's jaw. Sita heard a sound like the snapping of a branch, and then Igor howled in pain. She watched in astonishment as Alexi hoisted Igor by the shoulders and hurled him against the wall. Stunned and bleeding from the lip, Igor crumpled to the floor and clutched at his face.

Alexi cracked his knuckles and winced slightly, looking at his hand. He turned to Sita and spoke as if the violence had meant nothing to him.

"Did he touch you?"

She shook her head. "He didn't hurt me."

"That is not what I asked."

"He touched my head," she answered. "Nothing else."

Alexi glanced at Igor as he struggled to stand. Igor braced himself against the door jamb, his jaw hanging slack, and then limped out of the room without looking at them.

"He will not touch you again," Alexi said.

When Alexi left, Sita rested her head against the wall. She tried to take consolation in his promise, but she couldn't banish Igor's smell or the ominous threat of Dietrich. Sleep enticed her, toyed with her, but ultimately eluded her. The sights and sounds of human depravity were too much to forget.

Is this hell? she wondered fleetingly.

If not, where is God?

Chapter 23

You do not have because you do not ask.
—The Book of James

Paris, France

After the incident with the black Mercedes, Thomas accompanied Julia to Place de la Concorde and dropped her off in the lobby of the American Embassy. She promised to call as soon as she heard something from the BRP.

Thomas left the embassy feeling stir-crazy. He had done what Léon had considered miraculous—he had found a tip and turned it into a lead. He had seen the woman, probably Navin's aunt, in the car. He had no idea where she had gone, but the Petrovich flat couldn't be empty. Some measure of truth lay beyond the double doors, something that could lead him to Sita. Yet the lead had to be processed and vetted by police bureaucrats. It was infuriating.

He wandered south across the vast Place de la Concorde, looking for a way to work off his irritation. He crossed the bridge over the Seine and walked west along the Left Bank.

The clouds broke and the river sparkled in the sunlight.

He kept a brisk pace all the way to the Eiffel Tower. He skirted the mob of tourists huddled at the base of the massive landmark and made his way south-east along the broad Parc du Champ de Mars that extended from the tower to the sprawling complex of the École Militaire. He took a seat on a bench and watched the birds play in the turbulent wind.

After a few minutes, he took out his BlackBerry, thinking to call Priya. It was late afternoon in Bombay. She picked up on the second ring, sounding weary but happy to hear from him.

"How is Paris?" she asked.

"*Magnifique*," he said. "How is Bombay?"

"Getting hotter by the day. Is the search going well?"

He delivered a short version of the events of the past two days.

Priya was impressed. "You've been more successful than I expected."

"Two steps forward, one step back. How is your father?"

Priya took a short breath. "He's still in Varanasi."

"Well, give him my best when you see him."

"I will." Priya paused. "I'm proud of you, Thomas."

Her encouragement gave him unexpected buoyancy.

"I meant what I told you. Bring Sita home."

Thomas stood from the bench and walked along the edge of the grassy mall toward the Military Academy. At the intersection of Place Joffre and Avenue du Tourville, he headed east past the Hôtel des Invalides. He wandered through the idyllic streets of the Seventh and Sixth Arrondissements before stopping at a café and ordering a sandwich. He checked his BlackBerry regularly, thinking that Julia might have sent him an e-mail or a text message, but his inbox was empty.

After lunch, he walked east through the Luxembourg Gardens and up the hill along Rue Soufflot to the megalithic Pantheon. He paused beside the stone facade of the Bibliothèque Sainte-Geneviève and scanned the names of the great scholars and intellectuals inscribed beneath the library's windows. Da Vinci, Erasmus, Newton, Bacon, Kepler, Lavoisier. As a student, the names had inspired him. Now they troubled him. They were visionaries one and all, risk takers who had challenged the status quo, often at great cost to themselves. A memory came to him then—Priya's words when he took the job at Clayton. "They will turn you into a mercenary," she had said, "and you will lose your soul." He didn't agree with her. But the philosophers and scientists, saints and sages, on the library's walls spoke with greater authority. How many of them, if they were alive, would have taken her side?

He turned and walked along the cobbled plaza toward the Église Saint-Étienne-du-Mont. He paused in front of the church, and Jean-Pierre Léon's question echoed in his mind: "*Are you a religious man, Mr. Clarke?*" For some reason the Frenchman's words nagged at him. He would never have considered asking heaven for help in his quest to find Sita. Yet the thought persisted, like a burr that would not let go.

An older couple left the church, and Thomas glanced inside before the heavy door swung closed. The sanctuary was vast, with gabled ceilings, vaulted archways, ornate pillars, and windows with elaborate tracery. He found himself drawn to the place. On a whim, he decided to look around.

The noises of the street disappeared as soon as the door to the church closed behind him. The silence of the sanctuary was unbroken. He walked slowly through the grand arcade on the fringes of the nave. Sunlight streamed through stained glass high above, and votive candles flickered in the shadows before icons of the saints. A sign beside them indicated that the cost of a candle was two euros. He hesitated, wrestling with doubt, but suddenly his objections seemed more reactive than reasonable. What could it hurt to pray?

He dropped a two-euro coin in the canister and picked up a candle, lighting the wick with an existing flame. He placed the votive at the bottom of the rack and walked to a chair at the edge of the nave. He made the sign of the cross as he had when he was a boy and knelt on the stone floor, bowing his head and placing his folded hands beneath his chin.

At first he thought to pray for luck, but the idea seemed sacrilegious. So he prayed for grace. It was a concept straight from the Catechism, heavy and musty and frayed like a folio in an ancient library, yet it carried a resonance he could not define. He spoke the words and then opened his eyes. The church was as it had been, as was the world. But for the first time since Mohini died he felt a measure of peace.

★

He left the church for the cobblestones of Place Sainte-Geneviève. He checked his BlackBerry, but Julia had still not contacted him. He browsed in a used bookshop and bought a round of cheese at a *fromagerie* before returning to his hotel. He wanted to call her for an update, but he knew he shouldn't pester her.

The call came, at last, a few minutes before six.

"Hey, Thomas," Julia said, "I'm sorry for the long silence. I was tied up in meetings all afternoon. I got your warrant."

Thomas was amazed. "How'd you pull it off?"

"Some friendly persuasion and a good bit of luck. We knew the BRP was watching the Petroviches, but we didn't know why. As it turns out, they've been operating an escort service and a porn site using girls from Eastern Europe. The BRP's wanted to nail them for over a year, but the evidence was too flimsy. Until now. One of the girls talked. They've been planning an operation for a week. My tip about Sita confirmed it. The BRP is going in tomorrow morning."

Thomas was dumbfounded. Somehow Sita had stumbled into a war zone. "What are the chances that they'll let me tag along?"

Julia laughed. "Try zero. They don't let us come near their fieldwork, and even if they made an exception in this case, which they won't, they would never let you in. We're going to have to wait this one out on the sidelines."

"Will they call you after it's over?"

"My guy promised to contact me. When that will happen is anyone's guess. Sit tight."

The night passed with excruciating sluggishness. When dawn came, Thomas gave up on the idea of sleep. He visited a café on the street corner and drank a double shot of espresso while scanning a copy of *Le Monde*. Julia called him at seven. She sounded out of breath.

"The raid went down as planned," she said. "The BRP rescued six Ukrainian women from the flat. But the Petroviches were gone."

"How can they be gone?" Thomas asked. "We just saw one of them . . ." His voice trailed off as a thought came to him. "We tipped them off, didn't we? I tipped them off when I went running after the car."

"I have no idea."

"And Sita?"

"They found no sign of her. I'm sorry."

"What about the girls? If Sita worked at the flat, one of them must have seen her."

"You're right," she said, sounding hesitant.

"What?"

"It's just that I've used up all my favors to get you this far. The girls are off limits. The protocols are incredibly strict, especially since the Petroviches are still at large. They're probably already in a safe house. I don't know where they are, and the BRP isn't going to tell me without a very good reason." She paused. "The word of an Indian waitress isn't going to cut it."

"I understand," Thomas said. The silence between them lingered until it became awkward

"Damn it," she said. "I knew it was going to come to this. Look, I'd like to help more, but this is too much. Going off the reservation on this could compromise me with everyone—the French, the Bureau, the ambassador."

"I'm sorry."

She thought for a long moment and then gave an audible sigh. "Give me a little time." She paused. "Don't call me. I'll call you."

"Thank you," he said.

"Be patient, all right?"

"Patience is my middle name."

She gave a wry laugh. "Somehow I doubt that."

Julia was right. Waiting had always been a curse to Thomas. Priya had called it a defect in his genetic makeup. As a consequence, the next three days felt like a form of slow torture. He wandered around Paris like a ghost, taking random trains, exploring the exterior beyond the Boulevard Périphérique, watching the boats on the Seine from Pont Neuf, and lurking around Place Pigalle after midnight, observing the parade of men searching for a woman to turn their fantasies into flesh.

On the evening of the third day, he was sitting in an overstuffed chair by the window in his hotel room sipping a glass of cognac and watching the lights of Paris awaken to the night when the call came through. He stared at the phone in momentary shock, the thrill of the sound vibrating in his head. He reached out and yanked it off the bed, pressing the device to his ear.

"Julia?"

"Meet me at Gare Montparnasse at six thirty tomorrow morning." She said.

"Who did you talk to?"

"Six thirty tomorrow. Don't be late."

She hung up without another word.

Chapter 24

You have taken my companions and loved ones from me; the darkness is my closest friend.

—The Sons of Korah

Elizabeth, New Jersey

Sometime after the incident with Igor—Sita had no idea what time it was—Alexi brought her a bowl of tasteless soup and a box of crackers. The Slav didn't speak, just placed the food at the head of the bed. He took out a small digital camera from his pants pocket and motioned for her to stand. She did so hesitantly. He took two photographs of her and left. Sita concentrated on eating and tried not to think about the reason for the pictures.

The rest of the day passed in silence. At some point, she turned on the television. The TV crackled and came to life but displayed only static. She opened the door to the cabinet below the television and found a battered VCR and a stack of pornographic videos. She backed away from the cabinet and sat down in the far corner of the room. The TV fuzzed noisily and emitted an eerie glow, but she couldn't bring herself to turn it off. Sex seemed to ooze from the walls of the club and hover around her like a filthy cloud. By the time night arrived, she found herself looking forward to the sound of voices.

The girls came as they had the evening before, speaking their unintelligible language. Sita held her breath and waited for Igor to drag one of them into the room, but the door stayed shut. The music started without warning and droned on for an eternity. Sita closed her eyes and tried to rest, but again sleep would not come.

When at last the music stopped, Sita crawled off the bed into the corner. She heard footsteps in the hallway. The door opened. Igor and another man she hadn't seen before pulled a girl into the room. The girl resisted and twisted her body in an attempt to escape, but they pushed her onto the bed and lifted her skirt. Sita covered her head with her hands and prayed until the girl's screams turned into sobs. The men left and the girl sank to her knees, leaning against the bed.

Sita looked at the girl, and compassion overwhelmed her. She knew Igor would return at some point, but she felt a perverse sense of confidence in Alexi's protection. She scooted across the floor until their knees were nearly touching.

The girl looked at her in shame. "What do you want?" she whispered.

Sita didn't respond, just reached out and took one of the girl's hands. The girl stiffened but didn't push her away. Sita sat in silence for a long moment, conveying comfort by her touch. She thought of her mother then. How many times Ambini had sat at her bedside holding her hand when she was a little girl. It was a kindness she could pass along, even in the the midst of such darkness.

After a while, she withdrew her hand and wiped a tear from the girl's cheek.

"I am Sita," she said.

The girl met her eyes. "I am Olga," she whispered. Olga looked down at her hands. "You saw what they did?"

Sita shook her head. "I didn't watch."

A dam broke in Olga's heart and she began to cry. "I have family in Novgorod," she said. "I go to university in St. Petersburg, but I leave when my papa get sick. He need money for medicine. Then I meet a man. He says he has this friend in New York. He says I could be good nanny. He says I could make money for papa, for everyone. He was a liar."

"Tell me about your family," Sita said, taking Olga's hand again.

Olga spoke without hesitation and the memories seemed to stabilize her. When Igor returned for her minutes later, her shame had transmuted to resolve. She went with him submissively but glanced over her shoulder and nodded to Sita just before Igor pulled the door shut.

Distracted by Olga's story, Sita didn't notice at first that the lock hadn't engaged. The realization came to her slowly and left her puzzled. She stared at the doorknob, listening carefully until the sounds in the building grew faint. She took Hanuman out of her coat pocket and placed him back in the folds of her *sari*. Then she walked to the door and tried the knob.

It turned without resistance.

Her heartbeat increased, but she made no move to open the door. She touched the scab on her scalp, remembering Dmitri's warning. If she tried to escape again, she could not afford to fail. She wavered until she thought of Igor kneeling before her, asking her to open her mouth.

Gripping the handle, she pulled the door open. The hallway was empty and enveloped in shadow. The only light came from a red Exit sign hanging over a door at the end of the corridor. She looked down the hallway in the other direction and saw a doorway obscured by what appeared to be a curtain. She didn't know what time it was, but she guessed it was sometime in the early morning. The club was silent.

She tried the exit at the end of the hall, but the door didn't budge. She turned around and walked toward the curtain at the other end. The curtain resolved into a cascade of beads. Beyond was a room of vanity mirrors, stools, couches, and racks of slinky clothing. Wan light emanated from an Exit sign overhead.

She entered the room and took her bearings. The room had two additional exits—an opening shielded by beads and an unmarked door. She walked hesitantly through the opening and saw a stage and a gallery of tables, dimly illuminated by Exit signs and a light over the bar. The stage was shaped like a runway studded with platforms, each of which had a dancing pole. The shortest path to the exits was across the stage, but the idea of it frightened her.

Turning away, she re-entered the dressing room and approached the unmarked door. The handle turned easily. She walked through a lounge of couches before emerging on the floor of the club. She tried the first exit without success. She approached the second door, but it, too, was locked. She looked around in desperation, searching for another way out, but saw none.

She stood still for a long moment, not knowing what to do. Then her stomach growled and she realized how hungry she was. In thirty hours, she had eaten only a bowl of soup and half a box of crackers. She walked to the bar and scoured the cupboards. She found a collection of snack tins that contained nuts and candy. She ate a handful of each and then replaced the tins, taking care to leave them exactly as she found them.

Nearby was a small refrigerator. She opened the door and blinked at the bright light. Inside were bottles of imported beer and a plastic jug of water. She took out the jug and drained half its contents, feeling mildly refreshed. A digital clock on the wall caught her attention. It was nine in the morning. Since her arrival at the club, her days and nights had been inverted.

She walked back toward the lounge, thinking to return to her room, when an idea came to her. She looked carefully at the elevated stage. Beneath it was a metallic facade that reached to the floor. She walked around the perimeter of the stage looking carefully at the facade. On the far side, she found what she was looking for—the handle to an access door. The door opened easily, revealing a well of darkness beyond.

Sita took a deep breath and pondered what she was about to do. The thought of it terrified her, but she was out of other options. Alexi had acquired her for a reason, and judging by the company he kept, that reason was most assuredly unspeakable.

She made her way back to her room to gather her coat and then returned to the club. She knelt in front of the access door and crawled into the darkness. She bumped her head against something hard and cried out in pain. She paused to massage the bruise and then pulled the door closed behind her. Thankfully, it had no lock or latch. A rubbery seal kept it closed.

Ducking low and keeping a hand out in front of her, she made her way along the inside of the facade until she reached the first circular platform. She hid herself at the apex of the bulge. When Igor or Alexi found her room empty, they would search the club. Where she was situated, she would not be exposed by a flashlight sweep at the access door.

Folding her coat into a pillow, she placed it on the floor and rested her head. For the first time since she stepped foot on American soil, she fell fast asleep.

★

Sita was awakened by the sound of a loud argument. She recognized Alexi's voice and the slurred, mostly incoherent speech of Igor. Soon Alexi began to shout. Sita heard the sudden slap of flesh and the sound of a table overturning. At one point, a body crashed into the stage not far from her hiding place. The fight lasted a couple of minutes and then Alexi got a call on his cell phone.

They moved out of earshot and a long time passed before they returned. She heard footsteps in the distance and then an indecipherable series of bumps, scrapes, and scratches.

They were searching for her.

Her heartbeat increased until it felt like a war drum in her chest. The search went on for what seemed like hours. She heard the clink of glasses and the sound of a refrigerator being opened. Igor exclaimed as if he had found something. Her heart lurched. The water jug was half empty. She fought to steady her breathing. What did the jug prove?

Footsteps approached. Igor spoke. Sita jumped. His voice was so close he might have been standing next to her. She placed her hands together, palms flat, in the attitude of prayer, and mouthed a stream of supplications to Lakshmi.

Suddenly, the access door creaked. She held her breath. After a moment, a beam pierced the darkness. She waited, counting the seconds. The light swept back and forth beneath the stage but never penetrated the platform wells. She waited to see if they would follow her into the crawl space. At once the light went out and the door closed. She let out her breath.

Sometime later, the music came on. The stage creaked

and footsteps passed overhead. She counted four dancers. One took up residence on Sita's platform. She moved slowly, rhythmically, in a performance Sita could scarcely imagine.

Soon, the club became a hive of noise. Music pulsated, the stage rocked and echoed, and men shouted and jeered. Sita moved slowly through the crawl space. When she reached the access door, she sat back and tried to picture the layout of the club. The nearest exit was about twenty feet away. To the side along the stage was an aisle that would allow her access to the door. The real question was whether the door would be guarded. If it were, her plans were doomed. One thought gave her hope: the door was an emergency exit.

She waited until the first group of dancers returned to the dressing room and a new wave emerged to take their place. She kissed Hanuman on the forehead and placed him back in her coat. Then she took the deepest breath of her life and cracked the access door.

She saw the profiles of male faces, lit by the reflected glow from the stage. All alike seemed enraptured by the performance. She glanced through the legs of the patrons toward the exit, but she couldn't see well enough to know if the door was guarded. She had to take the risk.

She pushed the door open wider. No one noticed her. She crawled out and looked toward the door. Her heart leaped. The exit was clear. A man at the nearest table glanced at her and stared. She ignored him and moved quickly toward the exit. No one blocked her way. She reached the door and pushed the lever. The latch disengaged. An alarm sounded as soon as she opened the door, but she didn't care.

She ran into the parking lot and headed for the nearby motel. She listened for footsteps behind her but heard nothing over the sound of the alarm. She threw open the door to the motel lobby and looked around wildly. The desk was unoccupied and a television blared from a room in the back. A sign above the desk read, "Ring bell for service."

Sita rang the bell until a woman emerged. She had pale, unhealthy skin and wore a crew cut and a frown.

"What do you want?"

"Please help me," Sita began, struggling to catch her breath. "The men at the club are holding me against my will. Please call the police."

The woman looked at her strangely. "You're saying you're a prisoner or something?"

"Please help me. They'll try to find me."

"Come on back," she said, eyeing Sita carefully. "I'll call the cops."

The woman showed Sita into the back room and left to make the phone call. Sita heard the lock on the door engage. She looked at the television and saw that the woman was watching a show about extraterrestrials. The room was filled with candy wrappers, pizza boxes, and potato chip bags.

She stood in the middle of the room, waiting. She had no idea what to expect from the police, but she was ready to trust anyone who would rescue her from Alexi and Igor and the threat of Dietrich.

Finally, the lock disengaged and the woman walked into the room, trailed by Alexi. Sita froze in shock when she saw her captor. She had been duped.

Alexi waved for the woman to leave them, and the woman nodded and closed the door.

Sita stood still while Alexi approached her. He shook his head from side to side with mock sadness. "I am disappointed in you, Sita," he said. "I thought you learned your lesson from Dmitri." He circled her and stood behind her, placing a hand on her shoulder. "Now you will understand the consequences."

Suddenly, she felt a sharp pain at the base of her neck. She gasped and instantly felt light-headed. Her vision blurred and her consciousness retreated even as she fell to the ground.

She woke again in a chamber of darkness, her head spinning and aching at the same time. She blinked and saw stars. She blinked again and saw nothing. She reached out with her hand and touched metal. The surface was cold. She heard a sound in the distance—like wind or water, she couldn't tell. She listened carefully and heard a low rumble. As time passed, the rumble faded and disappeared.

Suddenly, she heard a popping sound and the roof of her chamber elevated ever so slightly. At once she understood. She was in the trunk of a car. She waited for someone to raise the lid of the trunk, but no one came. Seconds turned into a minute, then two. Finally, she summoned the courage to lift the lid herself.

She did so slowly, until she could see what was beyond the trunk. Across an expanse of black water was a vast city shining in the night. The lights shimmered on the surface of the water and reached up to the heavens, blocking out the stars. *New York*, she thought.

She pushed the lid of the trunk higher until she could look out the sides. There were lights all around her—the lights of shipyards, docks, and quays. She lifted the lid to its stop and glanced around. The car was at the end of an empty pier. She heard the sound of waves lapping against the pylons. The air was damp and cool. She tried to make sense of the moment. Why was she here? Where was Alexi?

She heard the sound of a man clearing his throat. It came from beside her. She jumped with fright and swiveled her head around. He was standing in the darkness, only two feet away. How he had appeared so silently, she had no idea.

He looked down at her, his expression as distant as the sky. "You know," he said softly, "in Russia we would do things differently. In Russia, we would feed you to the fishes. But this is America, and you are worth too much to kill."

He lifted his hand and showed her a rope connected to a net filled with large rocks.

"If you try to run again, I will give you to Igor. Then I will throw you in the river."

He placed the net in the trunk beside her and closed the lid. The rocks carried the briny smell of saltwater. She pushed them away in fright and felt the vibrations of the engine as

Alexi engaged the ignition. With a lurch, the car started off down the pier, back to the sex club.

The pain of her failure fell upon her like an avalanche. She had gambled and she had lost. *Again!* She felt something inside her give way. It was as if all the happiness she had known had vanished in an instant, leaving behind only the vaguest impression of a better day. She tried to picture Ahalya's face but could only make out traces of her shadow. Her sister was gone. The past no longer existed. This was her karma.

Sita rested her head on her hands and listened to the steady hum of the wheels on the surface of the road. It crossed her mind that there was a way out of the madness. For the first time since the waves came, she contemplated suicide. She allowed the thought only briefly, then chased it away with a surge of resolve. But the idea lingered in the corners of her mind.

She closed her eyes and tried not to think about what tomorrow would bring.

Chapter 25

The world is a mirror of infinite Beauty, yet no
man sees it.

—Thomas Traherne

Paris, France

At six fifteen in the morning on the first day of March, Thomas
took a taxi from his hotel in the Fifth to Gare Montparnasse
to meet Julia as she had instructed. The taxi driver deposited
him beside the glass terminus. He entered the station and saw
Julia standing beside a ticket dispenser, holding an attaché case.
Her red coat looked magenta in the amber light. She greeted
him with a look that betrayed her nervousness. She handed
him a ticket. He glanced at it and saw their destination—
Quimper.

"A safe house in Brittany," he said. "I never would have
guessed."

"That's only the first of the surprises," she replied. "I'm
crazy to be doing this."

"Why *are* you doing this?" he asked, searching her face.

"I don't know." At once she smiled, and her anxiety seemed to retreat. "I think you've inspired me. Are you hungry?"

"Starving."

"I brought a couple of croissants."

They walked through the lobby to the terminal. Six sleek silver-and-blue TGV trains stood before them on parallel tracks. They took seats on metal benches and ate their croissants as the station swelled with departing passengers.

They boarded the train a few minutes before seven o'clock and found their compartment. Soon after, the train glided out of the station. It maintained a slow pace through the city and then accelerated dramatically when it reached the countryside.

Julia removed her laptop from her briefcase and then remembered something.

"I meant to tell you, our guy at the BRP finally heard from the embassy in Mumbai. It seems the CBI tried to contact the French police, but they were bogged down in red tape. The embassy people said it happens all the time. The CBI shared the intel they got from Navin, and the French police are working on tracking down his uncle. They also opened an inquiry into Navin's activities. They think he lives in France under a pseudonym."

"It's amazing to me how criminals can be completely invisible to the authorities," Thomas remarked. "The shadow world is just as extensive as the real world."

"Everything is the same," Julia confirmed, "except the

rules of the game." She opened her laptop and typed in a password. "You mind if I get some work done? I promised my boss I'd have a report on the Petroviches on his desk tomorrow morning."

"Does he know what we're doing?"

Julia smiled conspiratorially. "I told him the BRP wants us in on the investigation, which is true. The Petroviches have probably already left the country, and our network is better than theirs. In exchange, I convinced our guy at the BRP that we would need access to the girls."

"What about the people in Brittany?"

"I told them about Sita, and they're on board. They promised to be discreet."

Thomas whistled. "That's impressive. I owe you one."

"Yes, you do," Julia replied. "But now I need to get some work done."

"Be my guest," he said, retrieving his own laptop from his backpack.

The night before, he had downloaded a few articles on human trafficking in Eastern Europe from the Justice Project's website. He wanted to arrive at the safe house at least minimally educated about the experience of the Petrovich girls. The stories reported in the press and in the academic journals horrified him. It seemed that the former Soviet bloc was hemorrhaging young women, many of whom were trafficked into the sex trade. The phenomenon was so thoroughly documented that the women were even given a name—the Natashas. They were from Moldova, Ukraine,

Belarus, Romania, Bulgaria, Lithuania and Russia. To the customers, however, they were all Russian.

After an hour of depressing reading, he walked to the café car, where he purchased an espresso and a sandwich. He returned to his seat and watched the passing landscape. In time, he opened up a new document on his laptop, thinking to type a few travel notes for Priya. It was a tradition they had started in their courtship and carried into marriage. But like everything else that had bound them together, it had been lost in the two-year whirlwind of the Wharton case.

He thought for a moment, fingers poised over the keyboard, and then he started to write. To his surprise, the words that came to him sounded more like verse than travelogue, but he figured that Priya, a lover of poetry, would like it better anyway.

On the TGV. The thrill of near flight. Fields out the window, overlooked by a quarter moon. A river of glass. Squat farmhouses, shutters half-open, half-closed. Outbuildings of stone brimming with hay. Garden plots, freshly hoed, ready to plant. Tallest sky, uncluttered, swimming in blue. Spring close at hand. Buds on a tree, then two, then half a glade. A shipyard by a wide river signaling the approach of the sea. A stallion cantering in an open field. Gulls in flight. Hills rising as we close in on Quimper. Then we are there.

They rented a car at the station and drove west into Brittany. Julia placed a call on her mobile and confirmed their appointment in French. Her nervousness returned when she dialed the number, but the man on the other end of the line seemed to have a calming effect on her. She hung up and took a deep breath.

"Everything okay?" he asked.

"Yes," she said. "Father Gérard is very kind. He's looking forward to meeting us."

"Father? Is the safe house affiliated with the Church?"

"You'll see."

Twenty minutes later, Julia turned off the road onto a pebbled driveway framed by stone walls and old-growth trees. They wound through a pasture rimmed with forest and came upon a wrought-iron gate with a guard post. The sentry checked their identification and waved them through. They entered a circular drive and stopped in front of a grand twelfth-century French château framed by manicured gardens.

"This is the safe house?" Thomas asked. "It's a mansion."

"Yes. I'll let Father Gérard tell you the story."

They left the car and were greeted on the patio by a man dressed in a cassock. He was balding and bespectacled and had an owl-like face. He kissed Julia's cheeks and shook Thomas's hand. His English was surprisingly good.

"*Bonjour*, welcome," he said warmly. "I am delighted to meet you."

"Thank you for agreeing to see us," Julia replied.

The priest looked at Thomas. "This place is a secret. Yes? The mademoiselle has the proper clearances. You do not. I must have your agreement. You talk of it to no one."

"You have my word," Thomas said.

The priest nodded. "In that case, you may come this way."

Father Gérard led them into a foyer decorated with dark country furniture and out a back door into a garden. The air was warmer than in Paris and sweet with the scent of new grass. They walked down a path to a meadow with a stone fountain at the center. Three young women sat on benches beside the fountain, holding a quiet conversation. One was dressed in the habit of a nun.

"This château was the gift of a tormented man who found peace at the end of his life," the priest said. "He left it to the diocese of Quimper, which had no use for it. The bishop had the good sense to ask if any other diocese could think of a Christian purpose for it before putting it up for sale. This was in 1999. At the time, I was working with an NGO in Marseilles. The government was sympathetic to our cause, but the laws were not helpful. Many of the women we rescued were deported and exploited again. I had an idea for a safe house, but we had no money to purchase a property. Then we heard about the château. The bishop welcomed us with open arms. The result is *Sanctuaire d'Espoir*. You say in English the 'Sanctuary of Hope'."

They wandered down a path to a fenced-in field. Two quarter horses stood munching on clumps of grass a short distance away. A slight breeze blew from the west and the sea.

"How does the government decide who gets to come here?" Thomas inquired.

"The police send us those in peril. They are usually women

who were held by organized crime or whose traffickers have not been caught. We keep them until their case is heard or they return home. The laws are better today. Asylum and permanent residency are options if the women cooperate with the authorities."

"How are the new girls getting along?" Julia asked.

Father Gérard paused. "All are deeply wounded, but some are stronger than others. One girl is particularly strong. She was the one, I believe, who broke the case for the police."

Thomas regarded the priest. "When can I speak to them?"

The priest met his gaze. "This is a difficult issue. Most would say that I am a fool to give you access to them so soon. One cannot comprehend the things they have endured. But your desire is to save a life, and that is supreme. I will make the arrangements."

The priest led them back to the château and into a sprawling sitting room furnished with antiques and baronial family portraits. He motioned for them to take seats. A few minutes later, he returned with one of the most beautiful young women Thomas had ever seen. She was as tall as a runway model and carried herself with the sort of grace that cannot be practiced. Yet her clear blue eyes were wells of sorrow. When she looked at Thomas, he turned away, troubled by her raw vulnerability and the poignancy of her gaze.

She sat across from them on a brocade couch and looked at the priest, as if waiting for a cue. Father Gérard treated her with great gentleness but never touched her or crowded her space. He spoke slowly in English, enunciating his words with careful precision.

"Natalia, I would like to introduce you to Thomas Clarke and Julia Moore."

The girl nodded.

"Thomas is from the United States, and Julia works at the American embassy in Paris."

The young woman seemed puzzled by the American connection. She continued to look at the priest, expecting an explanation.

"Thomas has a few questions he would like to ask you. Do you mind?"

Natalia shook her head. "My English not so good," she said softly. Her accent was thick. "I try to understand, but I don't know. You speak slow?"

"I will," Thomas said. He took out the photograph Ahalya had given him and handed it to her. "Have you seen this girl?" He pointed at Sita.

Natalia took the photograph and studied it for a long time. Tears came to her eyes and traced a course down her cheeks. She wiped them away and regarded Thomas with an expression of tenderness.

"Yes," she said.

Thomas took a sharp breath. "Can you tell me where?"

Natalia stared at the floor. "There was . . . room," she began. "He take us there to rape. One day he leave me alone and this girl come. She say . . ." Natalia stopped in mid-sentence and began to cry again. "She say she pray for me.

I thought she was angel, but she was Sita. She do house chores." Natalia paused. "I see her again later. She try to run. But she not . . . escape. Next day she gone."

"Do you know where she went?" he asked, struggling to contain his emotions.

Natalia shook her head.

"Do you think anyone else spoke to her?"

She shrugged. "Maybe. I ask for you."

She stood and left the room, returning a few minutes later with another young woman with Slavic features. The priest stood, and Thomas and Julia followed his lead.

"This is Ivanna," Natalia said. "She not speak English, but she know something."

Natalia spoke to Ivanna briefly in Russian. Ivanna nodded and replied quietly.

"She say she cook," Natalia informed them. "Sita help in kitchen."

The young women exchanged a few more unintelligible words.

"She say Indian couple come to house last week. They talk about travel to America."

Ivanna's revelation elated Thomas and discouraged him at the same time. Navin's uncle had transported her out of France, and the Petroviches had something to do with it. But the United States? There had to be fifty flights a day from Paris to cities across America. The only real barrier to entry was the border patrol at the airport. After clearing immigration, a person could disappear without a trace.

"Did they say where in the United States they intended to go?" he asked.

Natalia translated the question for Ivanna, and the girl shook her head.

"*Nyet.*" It was the first and only word she spoke that Thomas understood.

"I talk to all girls," Natalia said. "Only Ivanna has information."

"Thank you," Thomas said, trying to hide his disappointment. "It's something."

Natalia looked at him intently, piercing him with her eyes. "You find this girl?"

"I'm doing my best," he replied.

She reached out and took his hand. "Then we are friends," she said. "*Da svidaniya.*" With that, she turned and vanished into the foyer.

Thomas's skin tingled with the memory of her touch. How many people had urged the impossible upon him? Ahalya. Priya. Julia. Now Natalia. Did they truly believe he could do it? Or was it just that he was the only one foolish enough to try? Whatever their reasons, he knew now that the task far exceeded his skills. If Paris was a long shot, America was a black hole. To recover Sita, he would need more than hunches and instinct and the help of friends.

He would need an act of God.

Chapter 26

In the abundance of your trade, you were
filled with violence in your midst, and you
sinned.

—The Book of Ezekiel

Elizabeth, New Jersey

After Sita's escape attempt, Alexi took great pains to ensure
that she remained locked in Igor's rape room. Each night
after the club closed, he checked on her personally and
secured the door when he left. In the late morning, he
appeared again and brought her a few morsels of food. He
never spoke to her, and she almost never looked at him.

As time passed, darkness closed in on her. She gave up
playing her poetry and word games, gave up pretending that
Ahalya was beside her, gave up fantasizing about happiness
through the portal of memory. She spent most of her time
staring at the wall and pondering the inexplicable nature of
her karma.

On Sunday evening before the club opened, Alexi came for

her. He stood in the doorframe and commanded her with a single word: "Come."

She stood and followed him into the hallway. He led her through the dressing room—now brightly lit but empty—and into the lounge beyond. A blond-haired man dressed smartly in slacks and a dark blazer sat on one of the lounge chairs, watching a horse race on the television. He nodded to Alexi and motioned for Sita to stand before him. His English was carefully pronounced and lightly accented.

"She is beautiful," he said, appraising Sita from head to toe with piercing blue eyes. "And very young. I must compliment your brother on the acquisition."

"Vasily knew you would approve," Alexi replied.

The man walked around Sita, brushing his fingertips along the nape of her neck. He stopped in front of her and smiled thinly. "The color of her skin is dark enough to be exotic but light enough to be enticing. She will command a high price."

Sita's stomach churned and she felt faint. These men were speaking about her like an animal at the market.

"I will buy her for twenty thousand," the man said.

Alexi bristled. "She is worth forty. I will take no less."

They haggled about the price, and Sita closed her eyes. Another transaction was about to be made. The stranger was the next link in the chain of her destiny.

The bargain was struck at thirty thousand dollars. The blond man made payment with an envelope full of cash and then disappeared through the door to the club.

★

The next two nights passed in relative calm. Sita heard Igor growling at the girls in the hallway, but he stayed away from the room. Her isolation was broken only by Alexi's brief visits. She began to wonder whether she had misunderstood the transaction in the lounge. Perhaps the blond man had paid Alexi for acquiring her in the first place. But that didn't explain her presence at the club or Alexi's violent reaction to Igor's advances. Igor had said Alexi was saving her for Dietrich. Who in the world was Dietrich?

A preliminary answer to her riddle came on Tuesday in the form of a black man who wore dark sunglasses and a large gold chain around his neck.

"The baby ho go all the way to Harrisburg?" he asked when Alexi opened the door to Sita's room.

"All the way," Alexi responded. "The others go to Philly."

"Yeah, for the tech convention. Manuel told me all about it." He looked crossly at Sita. "You ready, baby ho?"

Sita glanced at Alexi, waiting for a cue.

"You go with Darnell now," he said.

"That's right," the man called Darnell confirmed. "And I ain't got time or patience for bitches with attitude." He opened his coat and showed her the butt of a handgun. "You mess with me, I end you. You understand?"

Sita nodded, trembling. She put on her coat and then Darnell took her by the arm and led her out of the club to a van waiting in the parking lot. Three girls from the club were already seated in the back. A wiry Latino man occupied the passenger seat. He was nose-deep in a magazine and showed no interest in Sita.

She took a seat on the front bench and looked out the window toward the road. It was near midday and traffic was heavy. No one noticed the inconspicuous van or its human cargo. A police car drove by, but it vanished like the rest.

Darnell hopped into the driver's seat and peeled out of the parking lot. The streets of the city were congested, but traffic opened up as soon as they merged onto the turnpike. They drove for ninety minutes without a break. Sita grew thirsty and needed to use the restroom, but she was afraid to ask. The girls in the back didn't speak, and she never looked at them.

Darnell took a bridge into Philadelphia and exited onto Broad Street. He pulled the van up to the sidewalk outside the Marriott Hotel and placed a call on his cell phone. Soon a white man dressed in a pinstripe suit exited the lobby and walked in their direction. He greeted Darnell and looked appreciatively at the girls as they piled out of the van.

The white man gave Darnell an envelope and said, "Here's the advance. You'll get the rest when you pick them up."

Darnell grunted. "Make the bitches work."

The white man smiled thinly. "They'll work all right. We have thirty-two customers lined up and the convention hasn't even started."

"That's what I like to hear."

★

The white man escorted the girls into the hotel, and the Latino reclaimed the passenger seat. Darnell turned the van around and headed back into traffic. They made a quick stop at a gas station to allow Sita to use the restroom, and then they were off again. They drove through the afternoon, stopping only for gas and to order dinner from a McDonald's drive-through. Sita was ravenous with hunger, but she nearly gagged on the hamburger Darnell gave her. The greasy meat and salty-sweet condiments shocked her palate.

They reached Harrisburg half an hour before sunset. Darnell left the freeway at a truck stop half-full of tractor trailers and entered the parking lot of a motel.

"Baby ho don't know how good she's got it," Darnell mumbled to Manuel. "If I was in charge, I'd make her a lot lizard. Teach her *respect*."

Manuel laughed. "That's why you just drive the van."

"Shut the hell up," Darnell replied.

They circled around to the back of the motel and parked. Manuel unlocked the door to a guest room, and Darnell hauled Sita out of the van and threw her on the bed. She sat up quickly and hugged a pillow, terrified that they intended to rape her. Darnell leered at her for a long moment and then burst out laughing.

"See that, Manuel," he said, "she's scared."

Manuel ignored him and turned on the television. Still laughing, Darnell picked up a magazine and locked himself in the bathroom.

*

Darkness fell and night came. Darnell bought a late dinner from Burger King, which Sita ate reluctantly. At ten o'clock, Manuel took a phone call on his mobile phone. He grunted and walked to the window, looking through a crack in the curtains.

"Here they come," he said, pulling curtains aside to reveal a panel truck sitting in the shadows beside a row of Dumpsters. Sita watched as seven young girls emerged from the truck and fanned out into the now densely packed truck lot. All of them looked to be underage.

"Lot lizards on the prowl," said Darnell. "How much you figure they'll make tonight?"

Manuel thought for a moment. "Two thousand, maybe more. The lot's full."

Darnell chuckled. "The truckers won't be lonely tonight."

Sita examined the threads of the faded comforter beneath her. The plight of the lot lizards broke what remained of her heart. What kind of human beings joked about the defilement of children? She wondered again what they had in store for her. What could possibly justify a purchase price of thirty thousand dollars?

At midnight Manuel got another call on his mobile phone. He listened briefly and then looked at Darnell. "They're ready to roll."

Darnell switched off the television and took Sita's arm roughly. "Time to go."

Manuel opened the door, and Sita saw the side of the

panel truck twenty feet away. It was parked behind a line of cars, its engine idling. An obese woman stood near the back of the truck with her arms crossed. Darnell shuttled Sita between cars and handed her over to the woman. The woman pushed Sita toward a man leaning out of the back of the truck. The man took hold of her coat and lifted her into the cargo bay. As her eyes adjusted, she realized she was not alone. She was surrounded by the lot lizards.

The man shut the cargo door and locked it. Sita caught only a glimpse of him in the shadows. His face was unshaven and he had a cigarette dangling from his lips.

The interior of the truck was black as pitch. None of the girls spoke, but one of them was crying. The truck lurched and began to move. The cadence of the engine drowned out the sorrow of the invisible child. Sita hugged herself and shut her eyes. Her thoughts were a blur and her breathing rapid and shallow.

The truck drove for twenty minutes and then stopped and backed up. When the engine cut off, Sita listened to the silence. Somewhere in the distance a dog barked. A car passed nearby. The girls sat in darkness until the man with the cigarette raised the door. They were facing a garage of some kind. The girls stood together and left the truck. The man waved for Sita to follow.

She trailed a young black girl with thin hips and a leopard-print skirt through the garage and downstairs to a basement. A single bulb glowed in the underground room. The girls waited in a huddle, looking at the ground. The fat woman came down the steps and moved aside a gun rack, revealing a hidden door. She turned a deadbolt and swung the door open. She could see that the floor was covered with blankets. The girls entered without protest, and the woman closed the door behind them.

Immediately, a fight broke out among the girls. Sita protected her head with her forearms and backed into a corner, sliding down the wall until her knees touched her chin.

"Get off of me, ho!" one of the girls yelled.

"This is my spot, you back-stabbing bitch," another replied.

A strong voice spoke. "Cassie, Latisha, shut the hell up! Let it go, goddamnit!"

At last the girls grew quiet.

"What the hell is wrong with you two?" the strong voice asked. "This place is bad enough without your whining."

"She's always taking my spot," one girl complained.

"And you're always lying on me," the other said.

"I can't take this place any more," said a fourth voice, choking up.

The strong voice replied. "You can run if you want, but it's your skin you're risking. The last time I tried, they burned me with cigarettes."

Sita closed her eyes and struggled not to gag. The room stank of sweat and dried urine. She clutched Hanuman inside her coat and started to cry. She tried to recall the sights and sounds of the Coromandel Coast, but the memories kept slipping out of her grasp. Instead, she saw

Suchir and Navin and Dmitri and Igor and the imagined faces of truck drivers who had paid to have sex with the girls.

She leaned her head against a wall and rubbed her arms in an effort to warm herself. She was cramped and uncomfortable and had no idea how she would sleep. After a while, the girl nearest her shifted and the corner of a blanket fell into her hand. She pulled it slowly over her knees and felt a little warmth. The girl moved again and left her arm resting against Sita's leg.

Sita took a deep breath and closed her eyes.

She would find a way to get through the night.

Chapter 27

The truth is rarely pure and never simple.
—Oscar Wilde

Paris, France

Thomas and Julia bought tickets on the late-afternoon TGV back to Paris. Thomas found an Internet café in Quimper and booked a morning flight to Bombay. He sent two e-mails from the train station, the first to Andrew Porter, informing him that Sita had been trafficked to the United States, and the second to Jeff Greer at CASE, promising to return to the office on Monday. Afterward, he called Priya and gave her his flight information. When their train was called, he boarded the TGV and tried not to think about his failure.

At Julia's invitation, he stayed the night at her small flat in the Fifteenth Arrondissement. She offered him her sofa, but he struggled to sleep, a prisoner of time and his own musings. Every minute that passed took Sita farther away from him. He thought about boarding a plane for D.C. and meeting up with Porter, but he knew it was a fool's errand. He had no credible lead and his access to information at Justice would be severely circumscribed.

Sometime after midnight, he rose from the couch and paced the floor, feeling trapped and ridden by an inarticulable anxiety. He wandered into the kitchen and opened the refrigerator, only to find he wasn't hungry. He returned to the living room and looked out the window at the lights of Paris. Under ordinary circumstances, the scene would have moved him. On this night, he was too preoccupied to notice.

Where are you, Sita Ghai? he thought. *Where did they take you now?*

Suddenly, he felt a hand on his shoulder. He turned around and saw Julia standing before him, dressed for sleep in a camisole and underwear. He looked into her wide eyes cloaked in shadow and saw empathy staring back at him. She took his hand and gripped it firmly. The moment was so unexpected that Thomas didn't breathe, didn't think, just stared back at her.

"Are you okay?" she asked, her voice barely above a whisper.

He thought about lying, but he couldn't do it. "I've been better," he said.

She leaned into him and placed her head against his chest. "I know how you feel," she whispered, encircling him with her arms. "It was the same when we lost my sister."

He stood rigid, frozen in indecision. He thought of Priya in Bombay, four thousand miles away. He thought of

Cambridge and Charlottesville and Georgetown and the years
they had shared together. But his strength was no match for
the disarming power of Julia's warmth. His resistance gave
way until his mind and heart were fused by a single desire—
to return her embrace. His arms went around her, and he
buried his face in her fragrant hair.

They held one another for long seconds, and then Julia
looked up at him, her eyes forming a question mark. He saw
the moment for what it was—the point of no return. Alarm
bells rang in his head, but he made no move to disengage.
When she pressed her lips to his, he didn't draw back. When
she led him down the hall to her bedroom, he didn't protest.
The thought crossed his mind that it had been the same way
with Tera. But he was past the point of caring. He wanted
this. He needed this.

When they entered her bedroom, Julia turned around
and took both of his hands. She drew him to her and leaned
up to kiss him again. It was then that he saw the candle on
the bureau and the heavy mirror behind it. The memory
came to him in an instant. Candlelight before reflecting glass,
flame banishing the dark. Priya waiting on the bed, asking
him to make love to her. The bliss of abandon, the joy of
release. The night Mohini was conceived.

He let go of Julia's hands and touched the band of skin
where his wedding ring once rested. He had taken it off
when Priya left and had forgotten it in his haste to leave for
Bombay. The ring reminded him of his vows. *I, Thomas,
take you, Priya* . . . He had been naive, but so was everyone

before the altar. *With this ring, I thee wed.* It came to him that sleeping with Julia would constitute not only a betrayal of his marriage at the very moment it was beginning to flower again, but also a betrayal of Mohini's memory and of all the good things he had left in his life.

"I can't do this," he whispered.

Julia stepped back and crossed her arms over her chest. "Why not?"

He took a deep breath. "I'm married. My wife is in Bombay."

She sat down on the bed and hugged her knees. He stood still and watched her. He hadn't been fair to her, he realized. He had allowed an emotional bond to form between them, a bond any fool could have seen coming. Then when she acted on her feelings, trusting her instincts, he had raised his guard and turned her down.

The silence stretched out until at last Julia spoke. "What's her name?"

"Priya."

"She is Indian?"

"Yes. But she's lived most of her life in the West."

Julia digested this. "Do you love her?"

He nodded slowly, knowing it was the truth.

She looked away, a hint of blush on her skin.

"I'm sorry," he said, finding his voice again. "I should have told you."

She stood slowly from the bed.

"Yes," she said. "You should have told me. But I'm not

sure it would have made a difference." She kissed him lightly on the cheek. "It would have been nice," she whispered.

He closed his eyes, steeling himself against the sudden urge to forget all else and take her in his arms again.

"Goodnight, Julia," he said, retreating down the hall.

He returned to the couch and covered his head with his pillow, listening to the faint ticking of the clock. He tried again to sleep, but his thoughts were haunted by the memory of her embrace. Minutes turned into hours, and night became morning. When dawn broke, it felt like an emancipation.

He took a quick shower and packed his things while Julia fixed him coffee and fresh croissants with butter. Over breakfast, they talked about inconsequential things. When they finished eating, she walked him three blocks to the Metro station. They paused at the turnstiles and looked at one another. After a moment, Julia broke the spell and gave him a hug.

"I'm sorry about Sita," she said.

"We did our best. No one could have done better."

She gave him a brave look. "Maybe Andrew will catch a break."

"You never know." He paused. "Take care of yourself, Julia."

She smiled at him in her easy way. "Go home, Thomas."

He nodded once and walked away, struck by her choice of words.

He took the RER train to Charles de Gaulle and caught the mid-morning Air France flight to Bombay. Exhausted from insomnia during the night, he pulled down the window shade and tried to rest. It didn't work.

When he tired of faking it, he took out Ahalya's photograph. Sita smiled back at him for the hundredth time, a child flirting with womanhood. She was everything he had dreamed Mohini would become. The thought struck him like a revelation. Was that what had driven him to France? Was it the shade of his lost daughter whispering of a life that could be saved?

The plane landed in Bombay half an hour before midnight. The darkened skies above the city were heavy with smog and humidity. Night was only a few degrees cooler than day. He met Priya at the baggage carousel and she surprised him with an embrace.

"Welcome back," she said, her eyes glistening. "I missed you."

"You did?" he asked, surprised by the relief he felt in her presence.

She nodded and took his hand. "I have something for you." She reached into her purse and extracted a pair of Jet Airways tickets.

"Goa," he said, his voice brighter.

"Tomorrow we are going on holiday. I need to get out of this city."

She looked at him with such unbridled expectation that he couldn't help but smile.

"It's a good idea." He felt a sudden rush of affection for her. "You look beautiful," he said.

Priya blinked at the non sequitur. Then her grin turned radiant. "Let's get out of here," she said and drew him toward the exit.

They spent the night at Dinesh's flat in Bandra. The young banker was away on business and Thomas stayed in his bedroom. After the affection she had showed at the airport, he was hopeful that Priya would join him. He wasn't so lucky. She left him with a hug and a coy smile and took up residence in the guest room.

For the second night in a row, he slept poorly. Around three in the morning, he woke with the irrational fear that Mohini was suffocating in the next room. He looked around wildly before remembering where he was. Afterward, he lay awake listening to the distant murmur of the city and contemplating the paradoxes of his life. How was it that in seeking honor he had lost it, yet in losing love he had begun to find it again? How was it that the very same pain that once had seemed so destructive now had come bearing gifts? The Jogeshwari case. The rescue of Ahalya. The search for Sita. Priya sleeping peacefully in the next room. The promise of Goa. How was it that he could have spent thirty years on this planet, obtained two advanced degrees, and ended up with more questions than answers?

In the morning he found Priya on the terrace, dressed in a nightshirt and sipping a steaming cup of chai. The sun was hot despite the early hour, but the breeze blowing in from the sea offered a modicum of relief.

"You look tired," she said, taking a seat on a deck chair.

"I didn't sleep much," he confessed, rubbing his eyes.

"Was it Sita?"

He nodded, preferring a simple explanation.

"Dinesh has a nice place," she commented.

"He's done well for himself."

"He seems at home in Bombay." Her tone carried a trace of wistfulness.

"You aren't?"

"It depends on the day and my mood."

"Would you live here permanently?" he asked, trying to gauge the drift of her plans.

"I'm not sure. And you?"

He shrugged, not wanting to lie. "I don't know."

She stood with a yawn and brushed his hand with her fingertips. "Come along. We need to get ready."

"There's one thing I need to do before we go," he said.

She looked at him curiously. "The plane leaves at noon."

"It's on the way. I just need to make a phone call."

In the schoolhouse at the ashram, Ahalya sat at her desk, staring into space. It was eight thirty in the morning, and her teacher—Sister Elizabeth—was explaining the sine and cosine functions, much to the consternation of the other girls. Ahalya, however, already knew the material. She had taken basic trigonometry a year ago at St. Mary's. The tutor arranged by CASE had challenged her with advanced coursework, but she came only on Mondays and Wednesdays.

Otherwise, the sisters required Ahalya to attend twelfth-standard classes with the rest of the girls.

As was her habit, Ahalya lost herself in the past. She recalled things in meticulous detail, focusing on faces and mannerisms until she could almost see the inhabitants of her memory alive again. She projected personalities into a future that should have been, picturing the lines of her mother's face in old age, imagining her father on her wedding day, envisioning Sita as a grown woman. Her imaginings went on and on, and she lost all sense of time. In fact, so often did Ahalya dissociate that the sisters at the ashram had begun to scold her about it.

"Ahalya," Sister Elizabeth said, narrowing her eyes, "what is the sine of 90 degrees?"

"One," she replied.

"And the cosine of 180 degrees?"

"Negative one," she said, seeing the wave functions in her head.

Sister Elizabeth sighed and turned again to the blackboard.

At eight forty-five, Sister Ruth appeared in the doorway. The students regarded her warily, wondering what had prompted the headmistress to show up unannounced.

"Ahalya," Sister Ruth said, "please come with me."

She turned to the nun, surprised by her tone. She stood and followed Sister Ruth out of the school. The nun walked down the path toward the entrance to the ashram without saying a word. Ahalya grew more puzzled with each step. It was not like Sister Ruth to be taciturn. It seemed she always had something to say.

When they reached the pond where Ahalya had planted her lotus, Sister Ruth stopped and pointed to the bench.

"Wait there," she said. "A visitor is coming."

"Who?" Ahalya asked, at the same time thrilled and terrified. Anita from CASE came on Tuesdays. It was Thursday. The visitor was someone special.

Sister Ruth didn't answer. Instead, she turned and walked toward the front gate. Ahalya took a seat on the bench, ignoring the persistent sensation of nausea that had been plaguing her for weeks now. She studied her lotus plant. The clay pot was visible beneath the surface of the pond. Above it, two lily pads had formed, but it was still far too early in the year for a flower. She reached down and touched the surface of the water. There was life in the pot. The lotus would bloom. It had to bloom, because Sita's spirit was in it.

Grow! she commanded. *You are the reason I rise in the morning.*

Sister Ruth met Thomas at the gate of the ashram, her countenance unusually grave.

"Mister Jeff called to say you were coming," she said, glancing at Priya waiting in the taxi. "You have news for Ahalya?"

Thomas nodded.

"Is it about Sita?" Sister Ruth asked.

"Yes," he confessed.

"If it is bad news, she shouldn't hear it. She is in a fragile state."

"There is good news mixed in with the bad." He fingered the *rakhi* bracelet on his arm. "I owe her the truth. I think she would want to know."

The nun considered this and then nodded. "She is a strong-willed girl. She talks of nothing but her sister. When she talks, that is."

"I only need five minutes," he said.

The nun opened the gate and let him onto the grounds. "She is by the pond."

They found Ahalya staring into the water. The girl looked up as they approached. She focused on Thomas and her eyes widened. She stood and walked toward him.

"You came back," she said. "You must have news of Sita."

Looking into her eyes, Thomas felt the weight of her loss. "Perhaps we should sit down," he said, gesturing toward the bench.

Ahalya crossed her arms. "She is not with you."

"No," he replied.

He took a seat on the bench and looked through the forest. Somewhere in the branches above him, birds were chirping.

"The man who bought her from Suchir took her to France," he said. "She worked in a restaurant for the last two months. The Bombay police caught the man, but they didn't move fast enough. A few days ago, Sita was taken to the United States. No one knows where or why."

Ahalya began to sob, her body shaking like a sapling in a stiff wind. Thomas took a deep breath, thinking maybe

Sister Ruth had been right to question his intentions. Perhaps he shouldn't have come.

He looked at the fledgling lotus plant, searching for a way to buoy her spirits.

"I sent your picture to my friend at the Justice Department," he said at last. "I told him that Sita is in the United States. I'm sure he will notify the FBI. People will be looking for her."

Ahalya continued to stare at the surface of the water, but slowly she regained control of her emotions. She turned to him again, her eyes red-rimmed and her cheeks wet with tears.

"I have a message for your friend," she whispered.

He nodded. "I'll pass it along."

She put her hand on her stomach. "Tell him there are two of us waiting for Sita now."

With that, she started up the path toward the schoolhouse.

Thomas turned toward Sister Ruth in confusion.

The nun pre-empted his question. "She is a brave girl. Most would not have told you."

"Told me what?"

"She is pregnant."

He took a sharp breath. "From the brothel?" he asked.

The nun nodded. "It is common. But we were hopeful because she wasn't there long."

A wave of vertigo washed over him. "She's going to keep the baby?"

Sister Ruth stared at him. "It is a life," she said, too harshly.

Then she softened her tone. "Right now the child is her only family."

Thomas watched Ahalya disappear into the grove of trees. She looked like every other adolescent Indian girl in her pale-green *churidaar* and sandals. She was lovely, bright, and educated and spoke excellent English. Before the tsunami, she had been destined for great things—college, perhaps medicine or the law, at the minimum a favorable marriage. Now she was carrying the offspring of a man who had stolen her innocence. If before her future had been precarious, now it lay in tatters.

"Do you think Sita will be found?" the nun asked.

"It's possible," he said. "But probably not."

Sister Ruth made the sign of the cross. "Sometimes I do not understand the ways of God."

"That makes two of us."

The Jet Airways flight to Goa was mercifully brief. Priya had booked them a room at a hideaway in Agonda, far to the south of the tourist crowds of North Goa. He told her little about his encounter with Ahalya, and for once she didn't seem curious. It had been so long since he had seen her joyful that he had no intention of spoiling the mood.

The taxi ride to Agonda Beach took the better part of the afternoon. Thomas rolled down the window and allowed the passing landscape to distract him from the burdens crowding his heart. In the blur of bungalows and eucalyptus groves, he found it possible not to think about Ahalya's baby and Sita and the bracelet on his wrist. Or Tera and Clayton and the lies he had spoken to his wife. His only consolation was the restraint he had showed in Paris. In the bedroom of a beautiful woman who desired him, he had stood his ground.

A little after four in the afternoon, the taxi turned down a dirt road lined with shops and beach huts. The driver deposited them at the Getaway Resort and Hotel at the end of the strand. The place was exactly as advertised—clean, unpretentious, and close to the sea.

The proprietor, a pleasant white-haired man in a loud Hawaiian shirt, greeted them in fluent English. "Honeymoon?" he asked.

"Yes," Priya replied, surprising Thomas. "Our second."

"Here's to new beginnings," he said and gave them their keys.

They walked hand in hand to the bungalow and stored their things in an armoire at the foot of the bed. Priya used the bathroom to change and emerged in a white linen shirt and a floral print sarong. She looked Thomas up and down, taking in his surf shorts, Birkenstocks, and Russell Athletic T-shirt. She crossed the distance between them and wrapped her arms around his chest, nuzzling into him. He embraced her with a passion that made him realize how much he had missed her.

After a while, she stepped back and said, "Let's go for a walk."

"Where?"

"The beach."

They walked down a rutted dirt path in the shade of palm trees. The path led to a bluff and across dunes to the sea. They shed their sandals and walked barefoot to the waterline. The sand was thick and luxurious under their feet. The tropical sun hovered above the horizon, speckling the water with gold.

Priya took his hand and they strolled toward a cluster of boulders. She climbed to the top of the largest one. Thomas followed. They sat down side by side on a flat spot at the top of the rock, looking at the sunset. He put his arm around her shoulders and she leaned into him.

"Why does life have to be so difficult?" she asked.

"Life is what it is," he replied. "But what we tried to do isn't easy."

"I have so many regrets," she said quietly.

"Shh," he said, putting his finger to her lips.

"No, I need to get this out." She choked up. "I hurt you. I was terrible to live with. I had no idea how to handle the pain. I thought that coming home to India would make things easier. But it didn't. Every morning I hear her voice. I see her tiny face and I feel the softness of her hair. I remember what it was like to give birth to her."

Thomas felt as if he had been cleaved in two. He was still in love with her, he realized. He had never stopped loving her. Even when their child had died. Even when her eyes had become cruel and her tongue had cut him. He would marry her all over again. She was the best thing in his life.

"I don't think that feeling will ever go away," he said. "She's a part of us."

Priya pondered this. "Do you have nightmares?"

He nodded. "I wake up in a cold sweat and hear her crying. It was worse at home. It felt like I was living with ghosts."

They watched as the sun fell into the sea, painting the sky with rose blush.

"They say it's possible to begin again," she said, taking his hand and running her fingers across his palm. "I'm not sure I believe it."

"We won't know unless we try."

They sat together on the rock until the sun became a memory and the first stars appeared.

"Are you hungry?" she asked.

"Whenever you are," he whispered, turning to her and inhaling the jasmine and lilac scent of her perfume. It brought back memories, every one of them good.

She looked into his eyes and her lips parted. He kissed her, hesitant at first and then needful, drawing her into his embrace.

"Why don't we forget about dinner?" she murmured.

He took her face in his hands. "More welcome words I have never heard."

The land of Goa brought out all the shine in their world. The sea had never been bluer, the sand had never been softer, the sun had never been more radiant than in those three days.

They spent almost as much time in their bungalow as they did outdoors. Priya seemed never to tire of Thomas's touch, and he found no difficulty obliging her. Each time he drew his wife to himself, he felt as if they were unraveling another strand in the knot of lost time.

On the morning of the second day, they rented a moped from a shop in Agonda. Priya sat sidesaddle and held his waist loosely. Growing up in Bombay with a brother who loved motorcycles, she was at home on the back of a two-wheeler. They rode north along the rugged coastal road to Coba de Rama Fort. The air was moist and salt-laden and the sky traced a towering arc between horizons green and blue.

They followed the signs to Margao and wound their way through rice paddies and palm groves. Eventually they ascended to an arid plateau above the tree line. To the west was the indistinct blue of the sea. The fort was fourteen kilometers from Agonda, but the two-stroke engine ate up the distance quickly. At the end of the road, they found the ruins of centuries-old battlements occupied at various times by Hindu, Mogul, and Portuguese monarchs.

They parked their moped at a dirt turnaround and scaled the crumbling walls to an abandoned cannon emplacement overlooking a bay. The land plummeted hundreds of feet to a shore of black basalt. Waves crashed against the rock, sending spray high in the air. They stood on the parapet for long minutes, enjoying the scene.

"In places like this, it's hard to imagine that the world can be so ugly," Thomas said.

"This is how it was meant to be," Priya replied. "The ugliness is our own fault."

Around five o'clock, they took the coastal road south to Palolem, a seaside community four kilometers past Agonda. The entrance to the beachfront was lined with shops and vendors hawking their wares. They parked at the end of the road and walked onto the beach toward a line of fishing boats sitting on the sand.

The beach at Palolem was wider than at Agonda and more crowded. Goans dressed in long sleeves and *saris* walked with their children, while vacationers from Europe, Australia, and America roamed about in swimsuits and danced to loud music in beach shanty bars. The contrast could not have been more marked, but no one seemed to notice or care.

They took seats on the porch of a cocktail bar and ordered piña coladas. The molten sun sank slowly toward the peninsula that embraced the bay. Out on the beach, an Indian boy swung a cricket bat beside a wicket impaled in the sand. He turned and waved wildly toward the shore, shouting words drowned out by the wind. Soon a motley crew of boys assembled around the wicket. They talked and then separated, one boy to bowl, another to bat, another to catch, and the last to field.

The makeshift cricket game captivated Thomas. He took out a pad of paper from his backpack and scribbled a description of the scene.

When he read it to Priya, she said, "You should take up writing. Forget the law. The world has enough lawyers."

He took her hand, laughter in his eyes. "I just might take you up on that."

They watched as lights began to appear on the strand.

"It is good to be here with you, Thomas," she said simply.

He turned toward her. "Does this mean I'm making progress?"

Her eyes twinkled. "What do you think?"

On Sunday morning, Thomas awoke to the sound of birdsong and the whisper of the sea breeze in fronds of palm. He turned over in the bed and saw that Priya was gone. Her absence gave him little cause for concern. At home she had often risen early to greet the day. He rubbed his temples. They had been out late the night before, enjoying the gaiety at Palolem Beach. He had ordered one drink too many— enough to leave him with a pulsing headache.

He listened for the sound of the shower but heard nothing. She must have gone for a walk. He went to the bathroom and looked at himself in the mirror. He hadn't shaved in four days, and the stubble had begun to turn into a beard. He took out his razor and cleaned himself up. They were heading back to Bombay on the mid-afternoon flight. He wasn't looking forward to returning, but perpetual holidays were a thing of fantasy. Work was the way of the world.

He crossed to his duffel bag and threw on a pair of swimming trunks and a T-shirt. They still had the morning yet. There was no use rushing to the airport. He turned around and walked toward the door, expecting to find Priya on the beach. It was then that he saw his BlackBerry sitting on the breakfast table, a sheet of notepaper beneath it. He stared at the note, and his eyes went wide with shock.

In her scrawling hand, Priya had written, "How could you?"

He picked up the phone. The device was in standby mode. He hit a button on the keyboard, and the screen came alive. At once he saw the e-mail and everything fell into place. Tera had written:

Thomas, I know why you left. I had a hunch, but I didn't have proof until now. They gave you an ultimatum, didn't they? They needed a scapegoat. God, I can't believe they did that. But it makes sense of everything. You're wondering how I know: a few days ago, the cleaning crew caught Mark Blake with a paralegal in his office. The firm asked for his resignation. I asked around and found somebody who would talk to me about what happened. There's no need to run any more, Thomas. The air will clear, and memories will fade. I've realized since you left how much I want to be with you again. Please don't leave me in silence any more. We understand each other.

He threw the phone on the bed. How *dare* Priya read his e-mails? How *dare* Tera snoop around in his private affairs? How *dare* the world screw him over so royally? His love for

Priya was genuine. He had come to India with mixed motives, yes, but his interest in reconciliation was pure. The past few days had not been an illusion. They had talked of the *future*, for God's sake. Tera had been a grave mistake in judgment, but it was understandable under the circumstances and he had tried to sever his ties with her.

He grabbed the phone again and stomped out of the hut, making long strides to the beach. The shore was largely deserted when he arrived. A humid wind blew steadily off the sea, tossing up whitecaps. He saw her sitting near the waterline. He trudged toward her, trying out words in his mind. All were misfits, destined to turn him into a fool or a boor.

She saw him from a distance and stood up. She began to run away from him. She was fast, but he was faster. He caught up to her only paces away from the boulders where they had shared the first kiss of their reunion.

"Get *away* from me!" she shouted, yanking her arm away when he touched it. "How *could* you, Thomas? I *trusted* you."

She took off again.

"Stop, for God's sake," he said, planting himself in her path. "Let's talk about this."

"There's nothing to talk about!" she said. "You lied to me about Tera and you lied to me about Clayton. That's just about everything."

"This weekend hasn't been a lie," he pleaded.

"This weekend is the greatest lie of them all. I made love to you. I started to believe in the future again. And now?"

She shook her head. "All these years my father was right."

Thomas was stunned. "How can you say that? How can you possibly say that? Fellows Garden wasn't a lie. Our wedding wasn't a lie. Mohini——"

"*Don't* say her name," Priya cried, tears welling in her eyes. "*Don't* you say her name, you bastard. *I* was the one who gave her life. *I* was the one who took care of her while you were slaving away for that $500-an-hour self-promoting circus you call a law firm. *I* was the one who watched her grow while you were having the time of your life in Tera's bedroom."

He clenched his fists. "I wasn't sleeping with her, Priya. I told you the truth. I had nobody to talk to. You were catatonic. Tera was there when I needed somebody to listen."

She took a step toward him and pointed her finger at his chest accusingly. "Look me in the eye and tell me you never slept with Tera Atwood."

The guilt in his eyes betrayed him.

"I knew it!" she raged. "I knew it all along. That's why I read your e-mails. I knew you were lying to me."

"You read my e-mails because you were paranoid!" he said, giving full vent to his own anger. "I didn't sleep with her until after you left me to go back home to Daddy."

She threw herself at him and pummeled his chest with her hands. "Get away from me!" she said. "Leave me alone!"

They stepped back and faced one another.

"You know," he said, reining himself in, "it's a shame, because I really love you, Priya. I've made mistakes, but I came here in good faith. I wanted to move on. Tera sent me that e-mail because she hasn't accepted the line I drew in the sand. I can't resolve her delusions or make her go away, but she's on the other side of the world. I'm here in Goa with you. I've been happier this weekend than I've been in years. I want the future we talked about. But I guess that isn't good enough."

Priya looked toward the ocean, her dark hair billowing in the wind. His profession of love had pierced her defenses, he could tell. But she had no interest in surrender.

"You are so full of yourself, Thomas Clarke," she said. "To you an apology is nothing more than an admission of imperfection. You disgust me."

"So you want me to leave?" he asked, putting out his hands.

She shook her head sadly. "I don't care. I just don't want to see you any more."

He stood there until he was sure she wasn't going to change her mind.

"You win," he said, turning away and starting back toward the bungalow. The anguish of the moment washed over him.

"You always win," he whispered to himself.

Chapter 28

Heaven's mercy and its justice turn from them. Let's not discuss them; look and pass them by.

—Dante

Harrisburg, Pennsylvania

Sita dozed through the night and woke every time the girl nearest her moved her feet. She didn't know how many hours had passed when the fat woman opened the door to the crypt. The woman handed over bags of apples and a jug of water and then closed the door again. As with the sleeping arrangements, the girls fought over the food. Sita's stomach growled, but she wanted no part of the combat. She waited quietly in the corner, hoping that one of the girls would find it in her heart to share. None did.

More time passed. The girls talked only when necessary to air a complaint. Sita wanted to ask if they knew where they were, but she was afraid to speak. Eventually the woman returned and allowed them to use a filthy bathroom beneath the basement steps. The toilet didn't flush, and the bowl was nearly overflowing. Sita plugged her nose and did her business, hoping she wouldn't send the vile mixture over the edge.

The light in the basement gave her a better look at her companions. Four were black; three were white. A number of them were pretty, but all of them looked unhealthy. Sita guessed that the youngest—a frail-looking child with pasty skin and stringy red hair—was thirteen and the oldest—the strong voice from the night—was eighteen.

After the red-haired girl finished her turn at the toilet, the fat man came down the stairs and took her by the arm, leading her back the way he had come. The girl hung her head and followed submissively. The woman gave them an angry look. One of the girls shifted her feet. The woman turned on her and slapped her across the face.

"I didn't say anything," the girl cried, touching her cheek.

"Don't talk back to me, bitch!" the woman screamed. She rained down blows on the girl until she wore herself out. Panting heavily, she sat on the steps and waited until the red-haired girl returned to the basement. The girl walked slowly, staring at the floor. She retreated to the back of the crypt and buried her head in her hands.

"Get in there, goddamnit!" the woman yelled, shoving the girls toward the entrance.

Sita scampered away just beyond her reach and sat down next to the red-haired girl. The others crowded into the room, and the woman locked the door in place, leaving them in darkness. Sita put her arm around the girl and embraced her. The girl wept for a long while and then grew quiet.

She placed her hand on Sita's and left it there.

Sometime later, the door opened again, and the woman ushered them upstairs. The fat man stood at the top of the steps, and the chain smoker waited for them at the rear bumper of the panel truck. The girls climbed in and sat down. Sita had no idea of the hour, but it was dark outside. The fat man muttered something to the chain smoker about having to drive all night. Sita looked around at the faces of the girls, wondering if they knew their destination.

The oldest one said, "Here we go again."

The truck came to life and the chain smoker pulled the door shut. The red-haired girl sat beside Sita and held her hand. Emboldened by the girl's friendship, Sita began to ask her questions. She spoke just loud enough to be heard over the engine.

She learned that the girl's name was Elsie, that she was fifteen years old—not thirteen as Sita had supposed—and that she came from a small town in the mountains west of Pittsburgh. Her story was the stuff of nightmares. Her stepfather had molested her for years with the knowledge of her mother. When he started on her younger sister, Elsie threatened to go to the police. Her father waved a knife in her face and said he would cut her if she spoke a word to anyone. She ran away the next day.

"Where did you go?" Sita whispered.

"I got a bus ticket to New York City," Elsie said. "You know the show *Top Model*?"

Sita shook her head.

"Anyhow, they were looking for talent. I figured I'd give it a shot. Maybe not right away, you know, but I figured I'd make some friends and they'd help me out." Elsie choked up and she squeezed Sita's hand. "I got stuck with Rudy . . ."

Rudy, it turned out, had struck up a conversation with her outside a convenience store. He'd promised her a job in modeling. She went with him to a warehouse, where he raped her and videotaped the act. He told her he would send the tape to her parents if she didn't do what he said. Rudy took her to his apartment and raped her until he grew tired of her. Then he sold her to a man who took her to a house some distance away and locked her in the basement. There she met three other girls. Men came to the house late at night to have sex with them.

A few weeks later, the girls were moved to another brothel. Every two weeks, they were moved again. Occasionally girls were added and others were removed. Sometimes they were forced to pose in the nude and perform sex acts before the camera.

Sita flashed back to Vasily's office and shuddered. "What did they do with the pictures?"

"Probably put them on the Net," Elsie replied. "My daddy looked at pictures all the time when I was little. He showed them to me, too."

In the past year, the trafficking network had taken her

all over the eastern part of the country. She was never afforded a break, even when she was sick. And though the customers paid between $40 and $120 for her services, she never received any of the money. There seemed to be an endless supply of customers. They loved her because she was young and had pretty eyes, or so they told her. She had been a lot lizard at the Harrisburg truck stop once before, but she couldn't recall the exact date.

Sita asked where the men were taking them.

Elsie shrugged. "Could be anywhere."

They drove for hours and hours, stopping only for gasoline and once in a pasture to allow the girls to urinate. Elsie asked Sita her own story, and Sita told her about the tsunami and her journey from India.

"You speak English damn good for an Indian," Elsie said.

"We learned it in school," Sita replied, "and we practiced it at home."

"Why not speak your own language?"

"Because the whole world speaks English," Sita said.

Elsie nodded. "That's because America's the best country on earth."

In time, Sita felt the truck slow and come to a halt. The chain smoker lifted the rear door. Outside, the sky was gray and dim. They were in a neighborhood of run-down homes, cracked pavements, and abandoned buildings. Across the street, she saw a sign that read: Vine City Market—Atlanta's Best.

The chain smoker gestured for the girls to get out. When Sita started to follow, he put out his hand and shook his head.

Elsie glanced at her. "See you 'round," she whispered.

They drove for another hour before the truck stopped. Sita heard the muffled sounds of conversation and then the chain smoker opened the door. He stood on a driveway lined with tall pine trees. Beside him was a strange man dressed in black. The man had Asian features and dark eyes. He nodded perfunctorily at Sita.

"Get on out," the chain smoker said. "Li's got you now."

He helped her out of the truck and handed her over to the Asian. The man named Li led her up the driveway toward an elegant plantation house. Around the house were wide lawns and flower gardens. Sita heard the sound of traffic in the distance, but the property was rimmed by pines, and she could see nothing beyond the perimeter.

Sita followed Li into the foyer where she was met by a thin blond woman of middle age. She looked Sita up and down.

"Well, well," she drawled. "Dietrich said he was bringing me a little brown girl. We're always interested in helping the cause of diversity. Tell me, honey, what's your name?"

"Sita Ghai," she answered, trying to still the trembling of her hands. The mention of Dietrich frightened her. At once she made a connection that sent shivers up her spine. The blond man at the sex club had commented about the color of her skin. "*She is beautiful*," he had said. "*She will command a high price*." Was the blond man Dietrich?

The woman stood in front of her and brushed a fleck of lint off the shoulder of her coat. "Sita Ghai," she repeated. "How nice." Her eyes hardened. "Before we go any further, we need to get one thing straight. Are you listening?"

Sita nodded.

"Good." The woman looked deep into her eyes. "You are Sita Ghai no longer. There is no room in this house for children with a past." She glanced at Li. "Take her away."

Sita stood, paralyzed. Li ordered her to follow, but she didn't respond. He cursed in a language she didn't understand and took her roughly by the arm. He dragged her across a living room full of antiques, through a hallway lined with paintings, and down a flight of stairs to a wine cellar stocked with hundreds of bottles in state-of-the-art storage cabinets.

He led her to the far side of the cellar, opened the door to one of the cabinets, and turned a bottle of burgundy onto its face. A latch clicked, a motor whirred, and the cabinet moved outward from the wall and swung open on hidden hinges. Beyond the cabinet was a hallway of doors equipped with electronic keypads. Li walked to a door at the end of the hall and punched in a five-digit code. He pushed the door open and ushered Sita into what looked like a photography studio.

Li told her to stand in the middle of the room. He removed her coat and threw it onto a couch against the wall. He stepped back and looked at her, debating with himself under his breath. After a minute or so, he seemed to make a decision. He crossed the floor to a huge walk-in closet and rummaged through racks of clothing, emerging after a while with a slinky white leotard dressed up with sequins. He threw it at her feet.

"Put on," he said and left the room, closing the door behind him.

Sita regarded the leotard as if it were infected. She couldn't bring herself to pick it up. When Li returned, she was still staring at it. He let loose a string of expletives. Then he took out a knife. He brandished the blade in front of her and threatened her in heavily accented English.

"You put on, or I cut off clothing. I back in five minute."

She bowed her head and knelt to retrieve the leotard. She unwound the *sari* Aunti-ji had bought her and placed it on the floor. She had worn it for two weeks without a bath, and the fabric smelled of body odor and cigarette smoke. She pulled on the leotard mechanically, ignoring the discomfort of the stretchy fabric.

Li returned with the blond man from the sex club. As before, he was dressed in a blazer and trousers. As before, he smiled at her thinly, his eyes the color of ice. This time, however, she knew his name. In an instant, the voices came back to her. Dmitri: *"My father has made more profitable arrangements with Dietrich."* Igor: *"Alexi say I not touch you. Dietrich coming."*

She watched as Dietrich went to the couch and sat down. In his presence, the muted fear of anticipation gave way to the consuming deadness of despair. She heard one more voice—Sumeera's: "*Accept the discipline of God and perhaps you will be reborn in a better place.*"

Li walked up to her and snapped his fingers, breaking her out of her trance.

"Good," he said, directing her by the arm. "Come."

He led her to a bed covered in purple silk and told her to sit on it. He flipped a switch and a light nearly blinded her. He emerged from behind the light holding a digital camera.

"No smile," he said. "Look here."

Sita watched Li as he danced around the room taking pictures of her. He told her to pose one way and then another, to sit back against the pillows with her knees in the air, and then to lie flat on her stomach. He gave her a teddy bear to hold and then replaced it with a lollipop. The photo session lasted half an hour.

When Li was satisfied, he turned off the light and placed a cotton T-shirt and sweatpants on the bed.

"Put on," he said.

He picked up a magazine from the coffee table in front of the couch and pretended to ignore her. Dietrich, however, stood up and walked toward her.

"Put it on, Sita," he said. "You have no reason to be bashful."

She was still for another long moment before she obeyed. Li skimmed the magazine, but Dietrich studied her every move. The shame she felt at undressing in front of him was overwhelming. She wanted to disappear, to leave the wretched world behind.

When she had finished, Dietrich reached out and cupped her chin.

"You will do well," he said.

He traded a glance with Li and then left the room. Sita, however, was rooted in place. She felt as if he had raped her with his eyes.

Li threw the magazine back on the coffee table and gave a curt wave. She followed him to one of the rooms along the hallway. He opened the door and turned on the light. The room was windowless and utilitarian, its furnishings limited to a bed, a stack of magazines, and a TV/VCR combo on a stand.

"Bathroom down hall," Li said. "Use when food come. Watch movies and *Seinfeld*." For some reason he found this comment funny and laughed at himself.

When Li left her, Sita sat on the bed and stared at the wall, replaying the photo shoot in her mind. She remembered every picture he took of her, every angle her body assumed, every shadow cast upon the wall, the feel of the sheets, the plushness of the pillows, the blaze of the lights, the fur of the teddy bear, the taste of the lollipop. Neither Li nor Dietrich had asked her to perform any indecent act, but she knew there was a reason for the pictures. There was a reason Dietrich had paid thirty thousand dollars for her. Everything in this godforsaken place had a purpose.

She lay back against the bed and closed her eyes, thinking

of Hanuman in the pocket of her coat, strewn on the floor of the studio down the hall. Like everything else in her life, he was gone, too. Her breathing deepened and she began to drift off. The restive night in the fat woman's crypt and the long drive in the panel truck had left her exhausted.

Neither the anguish of memory nor fear of the future had the power to keep her awake.

PART FOUR

Chapter 29

The sword of justice has no scabbard.
                          —Antoine de Rivarol

Goa, India

Thomas packed his bags and left Agonda Beach in a hurry. He didn't see Priya again, but he didn't expect to—not after what she had said. The proprietor of the resort called him an airport taxi, and he gave the driver a hefty tip to make the transit in record time. The man saw the gratuity as a license to violate every traffic law in the Goan state, but Thomas didn't care. He didn't care about anything any more.

He arrived at the airport a bare forty minutes before the scheduled departure time for the midday flight to Bombay. He bought a ticket and took a seat in the lounge. He read Tera's e-mail again and fumed. What he would give to deliver her a few choice words. But it wouldn't accomplish anything. The damage was done.

He scrolled through his inbox and found a message from his father. The Judge was a judicious user of electronic

technology, and he only wrote personal e-mails when he
had something very important to say. He wrote:

> *Son, I talked to Max Junger yesterday. It seems that the*
> *problem with Mark Blake has solved itself. I won't get into*
> *details here, but Max has gone to bat for you with the partners.*
> *You're welcome back at Clayton anytime. Max admires*
> *you, son. He says you're one of the finest young litigators*
> *he's seen. That's rare praise from the man we used to call*
> *the Buzz Saw. I won't keep you, but I wanted to let you*
> *know that you're back in Clayton's good graces. If you*
> *continue to make friends like Max Junger, you'll find that*
> *the road to the bench is far easier than you imagined.*

Thomas sat back in his chair. He knew he should be
elated, but his father's news only accentuated his confusion.
So the partners had finally figured out that the man
responsible for Wharton's malpractice threat had been
sitting in their midst all along. But the Judge had said
nothing about an apology. Clayton had hung him out to
dry and offered him no recompense. Nothing but an
invitation back into the fold.

He looked out the window toward the distant runway.
Did he really want to be a partner at Clayton|Swift? A
judgeship was the goal, of course, but that was years away.
Between here and there lay twelve-hour workdays and
weekend toiling, cocktail parties and politicking, and ceaseless
abuse from clients like Wharton Coal, who threw millions

of dollars around like petty cash and expected their attorneys to walk on water. He knew because he had watched his father endure it for most of his childhood. His father would say it was worth it. But he wasn't sure his mother agreed, and he knew his younger brother didn't. How many of the important things had his father missed in the quest?

He heard his flight being called and joined the line at the departure gate. He was about to turn off his BlackBerry when it chimed in his hands. He saw that he had a new message from Andrew Porter.

His friend had written:

Thomas, since when did you stop checking your e-mails? We found Sita. She's in hell. We're going to try to get her out. If you want in on it, you need to get on a plane to Atlanta. Now. Call me any time, day or night.

He stared at the screen and felt a surge of adrenaline. After the miracle of Paris and the heartbreak of Brittany, could it be that Sita was within reach? Why Atlanta? What did Porter mean that she was in hell?

Fingers flying across the tiny keys, he sent two e-mails. To Porter, he wrote: *I'll be there in the morning. Will e-mail flight info this evening.* To Jeff Greer, he wrote: *Had a break. Need another week. Will keep in touch.* After sending the second message, he boarded the Jet Airways 737 and wished the plane were supersonic.

★

That evening he took an Emirates flight to Dubai and boarded a midnight Delta connection to Atlanta. The giant aircraft touched down at Hartsfield-Jackson Atlanta International Airport in the gray light of early dawn. He sailed through customs and collected his single piece of checked luggage from the carousel. Andrew Porter was waiting for him at the curb in a government car.

Thomas threw his suitcase in the trunk and hopped into the passenger seat. Gunning the engine, Porter pulled out into traffic.

"Everything I'm about to tell you is confidential," Porter began. "I pulled every string in the book to get you included in this. The request had to go all the way up the chain of command to the assistant attorney general for the Criminal Division. As it happens, he and the deputy director of the FBI go way back. He also has great respect for your dad."

"Did I ever mention that you're my favorite human being?" Thomas said with a grin.

Porter rolled his eyes. "Have you ever heard of something called 'mIRC'?"

"Vaguely."

"It's a program that allows a person to participate in Internet Relay Chat."

"It sounds more intimidating as an acronym."

"Are you going to keep joking, or do you want to hear this?"

"Sorry."

"mIRC isn't your garden-variety chat service. It's

organized into channels that are like chat rooms except they're much harder to access. Some channels are exclusive. The host has control over who's invited to the party. Ever since mIRC was invented, the guys at the FBI's cyber division have been monitoring it for child porn. It's the new Wild West—no rules, absolute privacy, and the Internet at your fingertips. It's networked the underworld. Users of child porn are loners. Before the Web, they flew solo. Now they associate."

"Sounds delightful," Thomas said. "A worldwide convocation of creeps."

"A fair assessment. Anyway, there's a guy in the FBI's Washington office named DeFoe. He's wicked smart—served with the Green Berets and knows everything about computers. He's been tracking child porn on the Web for years. Nobody knows how he stands it, but the psychologists keep passing him. He's a mIRC guru. The guy never sleeps. For a long time he was working on breaking into this back channel called XanaduFuk."

"No doubt its users are fine, upstanding citizens," Thomas said.

"A regular bunch of Boy Scouts," Porter replied. "So the guys DeFoe was chatting with mentioned it, but nobody told him how to access it. It's like a secret society. You don't ask to be invited. The host invites you first. Wonder of wonders, he got a message from the host about a month ago. The guy goes by the screen name Spartacus."

"That's original," Thomas said.

"As you'll see, the man's creativity lies in other areas. DeFoe started chatting on XanaduFuk around the clock. He figured out pretty quickly that the users were sex tourists because they talked about places like Thailand, Cambodia, and Moldova. But they never talked about the kids. They talked about drinking expensive wine. Now DeFoe is a teetotaler, so he went out and bought a book on wine. He started talking about it in his chats, and it opened up a whole new world. It's amazing what people will confess when they think they're anonymous."

"Aren't they?"

"Yes and no," Porter replied, changing lanes and passing a slow-moving big rig. "Be patient. I'm getting to the good part. After about a week, DeFoe heard somebody talk about drinking a certain Italian wine in the United States. Eventually he asked Spartacus where he could buy a bottle. This is when things got hairy. The guy invited DeFoe into a peer-to-peer conversation. No witnesses. Entirely private. The guy used the opportunity to ask DeFoe a question that was meant to separate the men from the boys. He asked DeFoe what it feels like to taste young cunt."

"Dear God," Thomas said.

"Exactly. DeFoe, however, is a pro, and he gave just the right response. Spartacus liked it so much he gave him a gift. He sent DeFoe a link to a website. When he followed the link, he found a porn site specializing in Eastern European girls. The site had a pay option and a password dialog. He tried the password Spartacus gave him and went down the rabbit hole. The place he found is called Kandyland."

"What is it?"

"A place where beautiful children are sold to perverts."

Thomas closed his eyes and listened to the whistle of the wind outside the car windows. "You mean permanently?"

"No, I should be more precise. They are rented."

Thomas opened his eyes again. "How does Sita figure in to this?"

"I'll explain in a minute. But there's another side to the story you have to hear first. The Justice Department has been looking for Kandyland for almost two years. We've broken up ring after ring, and every pimp has heard of it, but no one knows where it is. For the last twelve months, we've been building evidence against the largest trafficking network on the Eastern Seaboard. The places these guys source is astounding—truck stops, strip joints, escort services, and underground brothels from Maine to Miami Beach."

Porter paused and weaved the car through a pack of delivery trucks.

"Six months ago, we got a tip from one of our sources that a man named Dietrich Klein was involved. Our techs did a bit of wizardry and we found him. East German native, probably a former Stasi officer, emigrated to the U.S. after the fall of the Berlin Wall, and married a prom-queen-turned-exotic-dancer. Go figure. They live in a ritzy suburb north of here. He's been in investing and real estate and now trades as a 'success consultant', whatever that means. He travels a lot. People speak highly of him. He pays his taxes. His reported income is lower than we would expect, but not too low."

"You gotta love the new economy."

Porter laughed. "Everybody's a consultant these days. In any event, Klein checked out. We thought our source was making things up, but he was insistent. The Bureau decided to monitor Klein's cell phone calls. It took a while because the guy is extremely sophisticated. But we put the puzzle together and hit pay dirt. He made regular calls to nondescript landlines in five major Eastern cities—Newark, Harrisburg, Baltimore, Memphis, and Atlanta. We ran the traces and put assets on the owners. All of them turned out to be connected to the sex trade."

"How does Kandyland fit in?"

"I was just getting to that. Agent DeFoe accessed the site for the first time about a month ago. The cheapskates who paid a hundred bucks a month got pictures only. Prepubescent girls doing things you don't want to think about. The perverts willing to shell out more cash got access to another part of the site. They were invited to join the fun in person. For a thousand bucks an hour, they could have a photo shoot with a girl. For anywhere between twenty and forty thousand a night, they could have a child all to themselves. A number of the girls were advertised as virgins. They commanded the highest price."

"This is wild stuff."

"Tell me about it."

"By the way, where are we going?" A minute before, they had taken an exit onto U.S. Route 19 North toward Roswell and Alpharetta.

"You'll see soon enough. Let me finish my story."

"Please. I gather you're getting to the point."

Porter went on, "DeFoe sent some of the images to the National Center for Missing and Exploited Children and got another agent to cross-check them with Interpol's database. A number of kids were clear matches. Meanwhile, DeFoe did what only DeFoe can do. In less than twenty-four hours, he succeeded in tracing the Kandyland site back to a computer in the Czech Republic."

"The East German connection."

"Perhaps. It's owned by a university in Prague and it's infected with a virus called a Trojan Horse. The Trojan Horse allows a hacker to turn the infected computer into a 'slave' to transfer data and even to run programs from a distance. The slave computer protects the hacker from being discovered. It is the same thing as a digital identity shield."

"Okay."

"So DeFoe sent a request for assistance up the chain of command, and the FBI reached out to the Czech national police. The Czechs got permission from the university to access the computer, and the FBI sent a Cyber Action Team to Prague. The cyber guys passed their data along to DeFoe. DeFoe then traced the Web traffic to an Internet service provider in North Carolina. By this time, DeFoe was the man of the hour and everyone was marching to his orders. DeFoe flew down there, thinking he was going to find a link to Kandyland's home server. But it turns out that this particular service provider offers its customers the ultimate privacy—anonymous access to the Internet. No digital footprint."

"And this is legal?"

"It's the Wild West, remember? The regulators are light years behind the innovators. So the U.S. attorney applied some muscle, and the service provider gave DeFoe the keys to their mainframes. After two weeks, he was able to isolate a range of computers sending data to Prague. They were also able to confirm hundreds of computers *receiving* data from Prague."

"You mean the sickos?" Thomas asked.

Porter nodded. "Exactly. The U.S. attorney had to get a search warrant, but when he did, he found the mother lode. The sending computers were registered to an account held by one of Dietrich Klein's dummy corporations. DeFoe didn't know this right away. He had to forward it through the chain of command. When we saw it, we knew that part of the mystery of Kandyland was solved."

Thomas thought for a moment and saw a hole in Porter's story. "But the fact that Klein is involved doesn't tell you where the girls are being held."

"True," Porter agreed. "It only tells us that he's running one of the most extensive trafficking rackets in U.S. history." He paused. "Now for the end of the story. Sita is the key. DeFoe got back to Washington on Wednesday night. On Thursday morning, he logged into the Kandyland site. He noticed that a new gallery had been added on the premium side of the site. The girl looked to be Indian. He sent a couple of images along to NCMEC. They got back to him right away and told him about a notice my office sent out in response to your voicemail. I had to get permission to use it, but we have a mass distribution list—sort of like an electronic version of the old 'all points bulletin'. Just about everyone who works on the issue of child exploitation in the United States was instructed to watch for her."

Thomas shook his head in wonderment. "I had no idea you would be able to do that."

Porter waved off the compliment. "So NCMEC informed my office of DeFoe's discovery. I contacted DeFoe directly and told him your story. Let's just say he was touched. It turns out he's an orphan too. He hatched a plot to get Sita out. We took it up to the assistant director in charge of the Washington field office, and he contacted the deputy director. The DD was hesitant at first. He didn't want to move on the Kleins until we could take down the entire ring. It took us three days of preparation to coordinate the stings, but we made it happen. Everything is going down tonight. The Bureau is working with local cops in eight different cities. We have a SWAT team on hand for the Atlanta operation."

"What's the plan?" Thomas asked.

"It's simple. DeFoe posed as a pervert and rented Sita for the evening. He wired earnest money to an offshore bank account and received an e-mail from the Kandyland webmaster directing him to a truck stop north of Atlanta.

He's supposed to come alone at eleven tonight. The e-mail said he would be escorted from that point."

Thomas marveled at the serendipity of the events Porter had described. "After everything we've done to find her, it all came down to a picture and a phone call."

Porter took the exit for the North Point Mall and pulled into a massive, mostly empty parking lot. He maneuvered the car to the rear of the lot and parked beside a gray beast of a vehicle bearing the designation Federal Bureau of Investigation Mobile Command Center.

The door to the command center swung open as soon as they got out of the car. They were greeted by a tall black man wearing a no-nonsense smile.

"Agent Pritchett," the man said, extending a hand and welcoming them into the air-conditioned vehicle. "I'm special agent in charge of the Atlanta field office."

"Pleasure," Thomas replied, looking around.

The command center was staffed by half a dozen agents and outfitted with a dizzying array of electronics, laptops, and flat-screen monitors. Everyone was extremely busy, but most made an attempt to acknowledge the newcomers.

"It's a home away from home," said Pritchett. He gestured at a man sitting nearest to the door. "Meet Special Agent DeFoe, the brains behind this operation."

Clean-cut and ruggedly handsome, DeFoe looked the part of former commando far more than present computer junkie. He stood and grasped Thomas's hand.

"Andrew told me about your work in India and France. I'm impressed."

"The feeling is mutual," Thomas replied.

Pritchett offered them cups of coffee and pointed at a cluster of empty chairs.

"Please, take a seat," he said. "It's all hurry up and wait in this business."

"Are you going in by yourself?" Thomas asked DeFoe after he and Porter sat down.

"I wouldn't have it any other way," he replied, smiling easily. "I don't get to do much fieldwork these days."

"What are your chances of success?"

DeFoe didn't blink. "Nothing's guaranteed, but I think we'll get everybody out alive, including the suspects. The SWAT guys are the best of the best."

Thomas glanced at Pritchett. "You think you know where the girls are?"

"We're ninety percent certain," he responded. "Klein lives with his wife in a neighborhood not far from here. He has a main house and a guesthouse. We've been monitoring traffic to the property since we first started watching him. We noticed a frequency of traffic entering and leaving the guesthouse during the late-night and early-morning hours. When we connected him with Kandyland, it all made sense."

"The guy would be that brazen?" Thomas was astounded. "If I were running a child sex ring, I'd want to keep it as far away from me as possible."

"Actually, what he's done makes perfect sense. When

you're dealing with merchandise like this, you don't leave it to hired guns."

"Okay. So tell me about this guy. How does a person get into the slave trade?"

"He doesn't see it that way. To him it's all a matter of economics."

"Fair enough. But my point is this: if I wanted to buy and sell human beings, I wouldn't know where to start."

"The easy answer is that it was handed to him. You have to understand geopolitics after the Cold War. When the Soviet Union collapsed, it wasn't just the government that crumbled. The entire communist system fell apart. People were out of work, bored, and desperate. Everybody became an entrepreneur. The people who had control of Russia's natural resources leveraged their connections and became oligarchs of the new world order. The people who once ran the KGB and the Eastern Bloc intelligence services turned their tradecraft and contacts into a new mafia, bigger, more lethal, and more efficient than anything Sicily ever produced. If we're right, Klein was high up in East German intelligence. He defected toward the end and came to the United States. His wits and his contacts stayed with him."

"But from what Andrew told me, he's running an American gang, not an Eastern European gang. This isn't Hamburg or Milan."

"Your point is intuitive but misguided. As it happens, about half of the girls run by his pimps are imported from Eastern Europe. His contacts are instrumental in the source and transit countries. But the skill set of a spy is versatile, as is the power of his money. He can work in just about any country on the globe. His people don't care about his accent or the color of his skin. They work for him because he pays them."

"So tell me this. How does he get the girls here? As I understand it, border security went through the roof after 9/11."

"It did, but the criminals are always finding new ways to work the system. As long as we issue visas to visitors, traffickers will exploit the immigration process. And as long as our borders are open, the coyotes in Mexico and Canada will continue to make illegal crossings. The demand for cheap commercial sex is extremely high in the United States. Market forces will prevail in the long run. The traffickers will innovate and meet the demand."

"You make it sound like the war is unwinnable."

"I'm not trying to be pessimistic. The war can be won. But not by putting traffickers in jail. Trafficking will stop when men stop buying women. Until that happens, the best we can do is win one battle at a time."

Pritchett was an excellent host and kept his guests in the intel loop. He showed them satellite images of the Klein residence and played a computer simulation of the guesthouse that the techs had thrown together using architectural blueprints and a bit of creativity. In addition, he gave Thomas a primer on the equipment the SWAT team would use during the raid.

Although the Bureau had no intelligence about the Kleins'

defensive capabilities, they were treating the raid like a hostage rescue operation and had contingencies in place to handle the worst—an organized counterattack with automatic weapons and children being used as shields. They had requisitioned an MD-530 Little Bird helicopter from the Tactical Helicopter Unit to deploy the first wave of SWAT commandos. The second wave would drive through the gates in Bison light-armored vehicles. Pritchett confessed that the highly mechanized operation would probably turn out to be overkill, but with children involved, he was unwilling to risk it.

At six o'clock, DeFoe left the command center for a briefing with the SWAT team leader. Thomas shook his hand and wished him luck.

"I wish I could go with you," he said and DeFoe smiled.

"You really don't. These people are very ugly and I won't be armed."

Pritchett cleared his throat, looking at Porter and then at Thomas. "In light of the unique circumstances of this investigation, I'm going to authorize you and Mr. Clarke to visit the scene after the property is secured. You deserve to greet this little girl in person."

"You're serious?"

Pritchett nodded. "I used to work in the D.C. office, and I know your father. He's a fine judge and a true patriot. I trust you will keep all of this to yourself."

Thomas nodded, overcome.

"I thought so," replied the special agent in charge.

Chapter 30

The Prince of Darkness is a gentleman.
—William Shakespeare

Atlanta, Georgia

Night fell on the Klein property, and lights appeared in the main house and the guesthouse. The grounds, however, lay in darkness. Sita sat on her bed staring at the wall while a *Seinfeld* rerun droned on in the background. It had been nearly four days since her arrival at the house, and she had spent almost every minute since the photo shoot alone in her room. The only exceptions were bathroom breaks. She hadn't seen Dietrich again. Li was the one who tended to her.

On her second night in the house, she awoke in a cold sweat and found it difficult to breathe. The next morning, when she heard footsteps outside her door, she began to hyperventilate. As the hours and days wore on, she began to experience hallucinations. Her thoughts raced and her heart palpitated at imaginary sounds. She thought again of suicide, but the idea of death only made her more afraid.

By the time Li came for her on Monday evening, she was ready to greet whatever hell Dietrich and the blond-haired woman had planned for her, just to escape the oppression of solitary confinement. Li led her through the wine cellar to the main floor and then up a staircase to a hallway of doors. He opened the first door and ushered her inside.

The room was all dark wood and soft light. A canopy bed stood at the center. There was a couch with a chair off to the side, a bar stocked with liquor, and a floor mirror in front of a curtained window. The blond woman stood in the center of the room, waiting for her. She walked toward Sita and began to speak in a hushed tone.

"Tonight you will meet a man. He will want you to do things for him. You will not question or resist. You will forget about your past. You will become a courtesan. Come. Let me show you something."

She took Sita by the hand and led her to a set of French doors. Behind the doors was a walk-in closet. The woman switched on a light.

"This is your wardrobe," she said. "The man may ask you to wear something he likes. You will obey him. You will not resist."

The woman escorted her to a bathroom with wide mirrors and pewter fixtures. "The man may ask you to bathe with him. You will do what he says. You will not resist."

They returned to the main room, and the woman delivered her valediction.

"This is your new life. Dietrich paid a great deal of money for you. You will please the men we bring to you, or you will feel pain. The last child who resisted is buried in the garden outside. Do you understand?"

Sita nodded.

"Good. Now Li will see that you are washed and dressed properly."

The woman left the room, and the Asian returned, holding in his hands one of the most elegant *saris* Sita had ever seen. He placed the *sari* and a pair of sparkling gold sandals on a coffee table in front of the couch and then he drew her into the bathroom.

"Soap for hair here," he said, standing over the bathtub and pointing to a bottle of shampoo. "Soap for skin here. Wash all. I back in ten minute."

Li was true to his word. Sita had no sooner bathed and wrapped herself in a towel when he returned with an elaborate makeup kit. He styled her hair and painted her face with the skill of a cosmetician. When he finished, he told her to put on the *sari* and sandals and left the room again. Sita knew the drill from the photo shoot. She wrapped herself in the green and white cloth and thought of the *sari* Sumeera had given Ahalya to wear on the night she met Shankar. Bombay was half the world away, but so much of this was the same.

The Asian appeared again after a few minutes with a bag of jewelry. He adorned her wrists and ankles with bangles and wrapped a golden choker with an emerald pendant around her neck. Finally he placed a red hibiscus in her hair. Then he stood back and regarded her with satisfaction.

"You ready," he said. "I back soon."

He wheeled around and disappeared into the hallway, locking the door behind him.

Sita sat on the edge of the bed. This was the end of the road. She had survived so much, yet she could not escape her karma. On this day she would lose her innocence. In a land ten thousand miles from her birthplace, she would experience *sar dhakna*, the *beshya*'s symbolic veiling of the head. *Is this what it felt like, Ahalya?* she thought. *Is this the despair I saw in your eyes?* She began to weep, and the tears burned her cheeks.

How I wish I could hear your voice again.

At ten thirty, Agent DeFoe left the government-owned warehouse where the SWAT team had been staged, driving a nondescript Ford rental car. He was dressed in an oxford shirt, wool slacks, and tassel loafers, all of which he had purchased from Brooks Brothers the day before. He missed the familiar feeling of his 9mm Glock in his waistband, but he knew they would frisk him at the door. He was equipped with nothing more than his instinct and a miniature audio recorder and GPS transponder buried in his wristwatch.

He arrived at LeRoy's Pit Stop at ten forty-five. The truck stop was seconds from the I-85 exit ramp, and the attached restaurant was abuzz with the late-dinner crowd.

DeFoe pressed a button on his watch to activate the recording device and transponder and then walked into the restaurant and asked to use the men's room. A waitress waved him toward a corner in the back.

He scanned the smoke-filled eatery and noticed a thin man with a mustache sitting by himself at a booth along the wall. The man was sipping a beer and watching the door. Their eyes met briefly and then the man looked down at a newspaper in front of him. It was clear to DeFoe that the man was a watcher. He was there to make sure that DeFoe had come alone.

DeFoe used the restroom and washed his hands in the sink. The watcher appeared and used a nearby urinal. DeFoe left the restaurant one minute before ten o'clock. His cell phone rang as soon as he stepped into the parking lot. The caller was a woman. DeFoe walked toward an overflowing dumpster behind the restaurant and listened carefully.

"Mr. Simeon," the woman began, using his undercover name, "a limousine will pick you up in two minutes. The ride will be short. Our mutual friend is looking forward to seeing you."

"And I her," DeFoe replied. "How will final payment be arranged?"

"Once you inspect the merchandise, you can use our computer to wire the funds to the bank account you used for the deposit."

"Perfect."

The woman hung up and the limo appeared on schedule.

DeFoe got in the back seat and sank into the plush leather. The ride took less than fifteen minutes.

As soon as the limo stopped, the passenger door opened and DeFoe was greeted by a nattily dressed Asian man, standing before the porch of an elegant country home. DeFoe knew from surveillance photographs that this was the Kleins' guesthouse.

"I am Li," said the Asian. He patted DeFoe down and then motioned toward the door. "This way."

Li led DeFoe into the foyer and told him to wait. Seconds later, a middle-aged blond woman appeared. She was dressed in a silk pantsuit and pearls, and her hair was pulled back smartly in a ponytail. She exuded competence and control.

"Mr. Simeon, a pleasure to meet you." She held out her hand and DeFoe took it, surprised by the graciousness in her voice.

"Likewise," he replied.

"I trust your ride was enjoyable. We spare no expense for our guests."

"Yes, thank you."

"Please," she said, ushering him into the living room, "make yourself comfortable."

DeFoe stood by an antique rocking chair while the woman went up the stairs. She returned after a minute with a smile on her face. She took her place beside DeFoe and looked towards the top of the steps.

A moment later a young woman appeared and descended gracefully to the living room. She was dressed like an Indian princess in a lotus-print *sari* and jewel-encrusted sandals. She wore just enough makeup to accentuate her eyes and enhance her lips and eyelashes. Her necklace and bangles glittered in the light, and the fabric of her *sari* shimmered when she moved.

DeFoe was taken aback. She bore little resemblance to the child depicted on the Kandyland website. If not for the fine bones of her face, he might not have recognized her.

He met Sita's eyes and saw blood rush to her face. She looked at the floor. Acting the part, DeFoe approached and touched her cheek and clavicle. Then he leaned close and smelled her hair.

"She is exquisite," he said to the woman. "A rare jewel."

"I'm delighted that you are satisfied. Now to the matter of payment."

Li brought a laptop into the room and placed it on a coffee table. DeFoe sat down on the couch and used the computer to access a bank account he had opened the day before using federal funds. He keyed in the amount and routing information and finalized the transfer.

"Excellent," the woman said. "Li will escort you to your suite. He will return when your stay is over. You must leave at five a.m."

"I understand," DeFoe replied, eyeing Sita for effect.

Watching the strange man enter data into the computer, Sita felt as if she had become a different person. The Indian girl she had been, that friend of bright sea and warm sun, had retreated into the shadows and a new girl had taken her place, one with neither a past nor a future. This girl was afraid, but she was also capable of accepting the rule of karma. Ignoring her pounding heartbeat, she tried to imagine what sort of person the man was. *Is he married?* she thought. *Does he have children? How far has he traveled tonight? Why did he choose me?*

When the man had finished with the computer, Li led them up the steps to the hallway of doors. He let them into the first suite and then slipped out, closing the door behind him. Sita moved into the center of the room and turned to face the man, remembering the blond woman's instructions. Her bottom lip began to quiver, but she tried hard not to show her fear. Whatever the man wanted to do to her, he would do. There was no way out now. The only real choice before her was the choice between acceptance and death.

The man took her by the wrist and led her to the bed. He told her to sit and began to unbutton his shirt. She leaned back against the cushions and studied him, feeling numb. She saw him press firmly on his middle button before continuing down the placket toward his belt. Why he did it, she had no idea. She began to tremble, despite herself.

After removing his shirt, the man sat on the bed in front of her. He brushed her hair and her lips with the tips of his fingers.

"Where are you from?" he asked.

The question shook the foundations of her new

personality. She looked down at the comforter. *It doesn't matter,* she thought. *All of it is gone.*

When she didn't respond, the man leaned forward and pretended to kiss her neck. He spoke very quietly. "My name is DeFoe and I'm here to rescue you. A police raid is about to happen. Continue to play your role. The danger is great, but it will soon be over."

Sita didn't process his words at first, and when she did, she had no idea what to think. Suddenly, she heard the distant noise of a helicopter. For a long moment she wavered, feeling the familiar grip of despair. The world had delivered her nothing but grief since the arrival of the waves. She had resigned herself to the *beshya's* life. How could her fate suddenly change?

The sound of the helicopter grew louder.

She looked at the stranger—DeFoe—and at once the fiction of the courtesan demanded by the blond woman fell off her like a false skin. She saw the reflection of truth in his eyes. He wasn't there to rape her. He was there to save her.

In an instant, she decided to believe.

Moments later, DeFoe heard a shout in the hallway. The door to the room burst open and Li strode in brandishing a pistol.

"What the hell is going on?" DeFoe asked crossly, shifting his body to shield Sita.

"Come now," the Asian commanded.

"What about the girl?" DeFoe demanded. "I paid a fortune for her."

"No time for talk!" the Asian exclaimed, waving the weapon around.

DeFoe stood up and growled, "I better get a damn refund."

"No refund!" Li cried, pointing the pistol at him. "Police!"

DeFoe cursed loudly and lurched toward the door, pretending to react in fear. As soon as he was within striking distance, he knocked Li's gun to the floor and delivered a brutal kick to his groin. Li sank to his knees. DeFoe collected the pistol and slammed the butt against the Asian's head. Li fell to the floor unconscious. DeFoe righted his grip on the weapon and moved toward the door.

Out of nowhere a hand appeared in front of him. The hand held a gun. He heard the gun fire once and felt the impact of the bullet. He stopped in his tracks, pain spreading through his chest. The gun fired a second time, and he staggered and fell to the floor.

Into the room strode Dietrich Klein. His forehead shone with sweat, but he was a picture of control. DeFoe's vision began to blur. He looked at Sita and tried to remember where his pistol went. He watched Klein shut the door and turn the deadbolt, watched him point the gun at Sita. He wanted to say something, but his mouth didn't work.

"Stay where you are," he heard Klein say, "and don't make a sound."

The last thing DeFoe saw before he closed his eyes was Klein reaching into his pocket and pulling out a mobile phone.

Chapter 31

One shot, fly fast and far, oh arrow sharpened with prayer.

—Rig Veda

Atlanta, Georgia

Inside the mobile command post, Thomas sat beside Porter and Pritchett, listening to the radio traffic as the SWAT team moved in. Words were few; commands were terse. The team knew its moves and executed them flawlessly.

Three minutes after the raid began, the ground leader of the exfiltration team, Special Agent John Trudeau, came on the line.

"Any sign of the girls?" Pritchett asked.

"Not yet, sir." Trudeau's voice was slightly distorted by static, but his puzzlement was evident. "We're still looking."

Pritchett cursed. "What about the Kleins?"

"No idea, sir," Trudeau said. "The house is so quiet it's eerie."

"And DeFoe?"

"Hold on." Trudeau came back on the line a few seconds

later. "Striker says the door was locked when he and Evans knocked. DeFoe didn't respond."

Pritchett pushed his mouthpiece aside and looked toward the front of the vehicle. "Get moving!" he shouted to the driver. "Get me out there as fast as you can."

The huge vehicle roared to life. Thomas held on as the driver gunned the engine and accelerated toward the parking lot exit.

Pritchett spoke into his mouthpiece again. "Tell Striker and Evans to break down the door if you have to. DeFoe is in there with the girl. The GPS confirms it."

"What if the Kleins are with them?" Trudeau asked.

Pritchett's eyes darkened. "Sit tight for a second."

Suddenly, Pritchett's mobile phone rang. He put the phone to his ear irritably. His face changed in an instant. At once he looked nervous.

"Yes, sir," he said into the phone. He listened for a moment, and his mouth came open. "Mother of God. Okay, put him through."

Pritchett hit a button and put the phone on speaker. When the connection was established, a man spoke. His voice carried the faintest trace of a European accent.

"This is Dietrich Klein," he said. "Are you the agent in charge?"

Pritchett took a sharp breath. "That's right. Agent Pritchett."

"Very good. Now, Pritchett, I want you to listen to me very carefully. Your undercover agent is lying on the floor with two bullets in his chest. I have a hostage—a girl—and my wife has others. They will die if you do not do exactly as I ask. Are you ready?"

Pritchett's eyes flashed and he squeezed the phone until his knuckles turned white.

"I'm ready," he said.

"There is a small airport in Cartersville. I want a fully fueled Gulfstream on the tarmac in forty-five minutes. The pilot will be a civilian. If he is armed, the girls will die. There is a vehicle in the garage that we will use to drive to the airport. Your team will clear the area. If I see anyone, the girls will die. I have no interest in talking to you or anyone else until the plane is on the ground. The deal is simple. I will give the pilot directions after takeoff. When we land, I will leave the girls in the plane. Are we clear?"

"We're clear," Pritchett barked. "Anything else you want?"

But the line had already gone dead.

Sita watched as Dietrich Klein turned off the phone. She couldn't control her shivering. She glanced at the shirtless man lying on the floor, the man who had promised to save her. He hadn't moved since he fell. She was certain that he was dead.

Klein put the phone back in his pocket. He took a seat on a chair across the room, pointing the gun at her.

"You are my guest," he said. "And I am known for treating my guests well. If you do as I say, you will not get hurt."

Sita stared at him, trying to stop her muscles from trembling.

Klein smiled. "Yes, yes, I know you are afraid. But you must understand. I am just a businessman. I do not like guns." He held up his weapon and put it on the table beside him. "You think I am a monster, no? That I have no soul?"

Sita didn't reply and Klein didn't seem to care.

He asked her another question. "Do you know why you are here?"

She met his eyes. She wanted to answer him, to let out the scream that had been building in her ever since Kanan turned his truck down the dusty road to Chako's flat and sold her into slavery. But she didn't scream. She had no voice.

Klein answered his own question. "You are not here because I enjoy the sale of sex. You are here because men enjoy the purchase of it. I am simply the broker. Some businessmen sell objects. Others sell knowledge. I sell fantasies. It is all the same."

He checked his watch. "They have thirty minutes left." He inclined his ear and listened for any sound of human presence. The house was silent.

"Have you ever been to Venezuela?" he asked, looking at her again. "It is a wretched place, but it has its uses. You will see it soon."

The mobile command post arrived at the property ten minutes after Klein cut off the call. Pritchett had turned into a bear, growling into his mouthpiece. Thomas watched the transformation with a deep sense of foreboding. Pritchett's discomfort meant only one thing—Dietrich Klein had the upper hand.

"Michaels," Pritchett shouted to a female technician on the far side of the vehicle. "What's the status on the plane?"

"There's a Gulfstream IV at Hartsfield-Jackson," she replied. "It's a corporate jet. Biotech company. We're trying to contact the owner. A pilot is standing by."

"Who's the pilot? Can we trust him?"

"Her, actually," Michaels corrected. "She used to fly in the Air Force; now flies business charters. She was in the hangar when I called."

Pritchett nodded. "Get the police over there. If you don't get through to the owner in two minutes, put me through to the chief. I'll take the heat for commandeering the plane."

Pritchett spoke into his mouthpiece again. "Trudeau, where is Kowalski?"

"He's moving into position now," Trudeau replied.

"Tell him to move faster," Pritchett said. "We're running out of time."

On the other side of the Klein property, Special Agent Kowalski listened as Trudeau gave the order.

"A few more feet," he whispered into his mouthpiece. "I can see the window, but I don't have an angle."

He slithered his way along the limb of an oak tree, measuring his progress in inches. The ground was twenty-five feet below him—a long way to fall, especially with a rifle strapped to his back. The tree was the tallest on the property, with a clear line of sight to the upper-story windows of the guesthouse, but the house was two hundred feet away.

It took him four minutes to reach the perch he had scoped out from below. Halfway between the trunk and the end of the limb was a place where the exterior branches twisted away, leaving a hole open to the sky. If he had any chance of making this shot, his line of fire had to be unobscured.

He bent his knees and planted his feet firmly on a couple of branches. Then he lifted his rifle over his head and set it down on the limb in front of him. He attached a tripod to the forestock of the gun and placed it on the limb. After chambering a round, he looked through the thermal imaging scope. He swung the butt of the rifle until he could see the upper story of the guesthouse.

He saw them immediately.

Four heat sources.

The first was compact and appeared to be hovering above the floor. *Perhaps the girl's sitting on the bed*, he inferred. The second and third were stretched out on the ground, but the heat signatures were different. One was normal; the other was waning. Kowalski cursed. DeFoe was down, just as Klein had said. *Who's the other TKO?* he wondered. The fourth body looked to be sitting on a chair.

"Gotcha, you bastard," he said out loud and then finished the thought in his mind. *Now we just have to find a way to get you to the window.*

★

The radio squawked. "Kowalski's in place," Trudeau said. "He sees them. But Klein isn't in front of the window."

Pritchett checked his watch. "We have twenty-five minutes until the deadline. The plane is being fueled. The owner consented. We're working on clearing the airspace, but flight time is ten minutes to touchdown."

"How long until the plane is on the runway?" Trudeau asked through static.

"The pilot says she needs ten minutes to max out the tanks. It's five minutes to taxi."

"That doesn't give us much to work with."

"Tell me something I don't know. Who's closest to the window?"

Trudeau came back on the line a few seconds later. "Striker."

"Tell Striker to find a rock and get his derriere under the eaves."

Inside the house, the minutes passed with agonizing slowness. Sita sat on the bed, staring at the floral print sheets and trying not to cry. The adrenaline high she'd felt earlier had passed. She thought of all the death she had seen. Her parents drowned by the waves. Her grandmother in the living room. Jaya in the kitchen, not fast enough to escape. The fallen hero on the floor in front of her, bullets in his chest. The world made no sense.

"Fifteen minutes," Klein said, looking at her and trailing his fingers across the gun. "Do you think they'll make it?"

Sita shrugged and hugged herself. The hibiscus fell from her hair and landed on the bed. At the sudden appearance of the flower, her tears came unbidden, and she did nothing to wipe them away. She remembered the day when Ambini had picked a hibiscus from their garden and put it in Ahalya's hair. It was her sister's sixteenth birthday, and the placing of the flower had symbolized her blossoming womanhood. "Many boys will call on you," Ambini had said. "But you will have only one husband. Wait for him. And the day will come when you will wear red and dance the *saptapadi*." Ahalya had believed Ambini. Both of them had believed. Now Ahalya was a *beshya* in Bombay, and she was on the far side of the world, sitting across the room from a man with a gun.

Pritchett glanced at his watch and cursed again. "Ten minutes until the deadline," he raged, "and the plane isn't in the air. What the hell is taking so long?"

Michaels answered: "It's on the tarmac. The pilot had to use an alternate taxiway because the main taxiway is full."

"Goddamnit!" Pritchett spoke to Trudeau. "Is Striker in place?"

"Roger that. He found a few stones from a gravel path behind the house."

"Is Kowalski clear?"

"Kowalski is a go."

"Time for Plan B. Tell Striker to make just enough noise

to get Klein interested. And tell Kowalski the order is weapons free. Take the shot. But make it count."

Sita blinked when she heard the sound the first time. She listened intently and heard it again—a strange rattling. She saw Dietrich Klein turn toward the window and pick up his gun. He waited until the sound came a third time and then stood up slowly.

Klein glanced at her, and she stared back at him. He looked puzzled, but his confidence was unbroken. He moved across the room, stepping carefully, focusing on the window. She heard the sound a fourth time, this time as a rap instead of a rattle. Klein stood in place, thinking. Then he moved closer to the window, holding the gun.

Kowalski watched through the thermal scope as Klein stood from the chair and crossed the room. The path from the chair to the window was oblique, so he would not have a shot until Klein was standing directly in front of the glass. Kowalski gauged the wind and recalculated the drop across two hundred feet. It was minuscule, but so was the margin of error.

At once Klein stood still. "Come on," Kowalski said in frustration. "*Come on!*"

Then Klein started moving again.

Kowalski tightened his finger on the trigger. "Two more feet . . ."

His voice trailed off and his eyes locked onto Klein's body.

Suddenly he was there, standing before the glass, his body on edge to the line of fire, his arms out in front of him, as if holding a weapon. A chest shot wouldn't work. A head shot was the only option. Kowalski placed the centerpoint of the crosshairs directly over the hottest part of Klein's head.

And then he pulled the trigger.

Sita jumped with fright when the shot was fired. In the still air, its high-pitched crack shocked her senses. She was even more terrified when Dietrich Klein crumpled to the ground in front of the window, blood pooling under his head. She sat paralyzed for long seconds until sounds erupted on the floor below. Boots stomped and voices shouted. When the heavy footsteps reached the stairs, she began to rock back and forth, nearly insensate.

Seconds later, the door crashed in and men rushed into the room, dressed in black and khaki and wielding machine guns. One of the men ran to the body of Dietrich Klein and checked his pulse. The other slapped cuffs on Li, who was still unconscious. The second man then turned to DeFoe and knelt before him, closing his eyelids.

"Clear," the first man said.

"Clear," the second echoed.

The first man approached the bed and took off his mask. "You must be Sita," he said.

She looked at him, dazed. In his helmet and combat dress, he looked like some sort of fearsome monster. Yet his voice sounded no different from a man's.

She hesitated and began to breathe again. "Yes," she said. "Are you okay?"

She nodded.

"I'm Evans," the agent said. "This is Garcia. Can you walk on your own?"

Sita swung her feet over the edge of the bed and stood up. "I'm all right."

She followed them to the door and out into the hallway. The guesthouse was crawling with black-clad men with guns. Evans led her down the steps to the living room, and Garcia followed. Evans gestured for Sita to sit on the couch, and then he and Garcia spoke with another man. Sita overheard their words.

"Where are the other girls?" the third man said.

Evans shrugged. "She was alone."

Sita stood up and touched his shoulder. "Excuse me," she said.

The men turned toward her.

"You haven't found the other girls because they are hidden."

"Where?" Evans asked gently.

"In the basement."

The third man spoke. "I'm Agent Trudeau. I'm in charge. Just tell us what you know, and we'll take it from here."

Sita shook her head, feeling almost weightless in her freedom. "It's difficult to explain. I have to show you."

"You sure about that?" Trudeau asked.

She nodded.

"Suit yourself. I'll take the point."

Sita entered the pitch-dark wine cellar like a celebrity surrounded by bodyguards. Agent Trudeau was in front of her, his gun at the ready, and Evans and Garcia followed behind. Trudeau found the light switch. Bottles of wine gleamed in the light, but otherwise the cellar was empty. They stood still and listened but heard no sound.

Sita walked to the far side of the room and opened the door to the storage cabinet she remembered Li selecting. She looked closely at the rack and blessed her memory for detail. The bottle Li had manipulated had a black and gold label. She saw the bottle and turned it over. The motor engaged and the hidden chamber opened.

Agent Trudeau gestured for Sita to stay back, and he and Evans entered the hallway, pointing their guns at the doors. They paused, listening, but heard nothing. Trudeau and Evans knocked on each door and repeated: "FBI! Open up!" None of the doors opened.

Evans stood beside Sita, shielding her with his body. She tapped him on the shoulder.

"I saw him punch in the code for the room at the end."

"What's the number?"

She closed her eyes and tried to remember. "I only know the placement of the buttons."

Evans waved at Trudeau and relayed the information.

Trudeau looked at Sita. "Will you enter the code for us?"

"Yes," she whispered and followed him down the hallway toward the studio.

She stood in front of the door and closed her eyes, replaying in her mind the rapid five-key sequence Li had tapped out, and repeated it flawlessly. She heard the latch disengage, and then Evans lifted her off her feet and carried her back to the wine cellar. A moment later she heard the piercing sound of gunfire. Then all was still.

Garcia poked his head out of the door. "You guys deserve to see this."

Sita took Evans's hand and walked with him to the studio. They entered the room and found the blond woman lying in front of the bed, a gun in her hand. An auburn-haired girl sat on the ground in front of her, shaking in terror.

"She was holding the girl hostage," Garcia said, shaking his head.

Five more children between the ages of twelve and sixteen were tied up on the bed, their wrists and ankles bound and their mouths sealed with tape. They sat up one by one and looked at Sita, their eyes round and fearful. For a long moment she stood unmoving, hearing again the sound of Li's camera and feeling the shame of undressing before Dietrich Klein. Then she shook her head. It was over. Klein was dead.

She crossed the room and touched the face of the youngest girl, peeling back the tape from her mouth. The girl winced, but Sita soothed her with a smile.

"It's all right," she said. "You're safe now."

★

When the girls were free and able to walk, Trudeau and Garcia took them upstairs. Sita, however, asked Evans to wait for her while she retrieved her coat from the corner of the basement studio. She put the coat on over her *sari* and then reached into the inside pocket, tracing the outline of Hanuman. She took a deep breath, vowing in her heart never to forget Shyam, and then followed Evans to the stairs.

Evans took a seat in the dining room off the entrance hall and delivered a statement to another man wielding a clipboard. Sita sat beside him but found it difficult to pay attention to what he was saying. Instead, her mind drifted. She remembered her father standing on the beach in front of their bungalow, waving for her to join him for the sunset. She remembered walking out on the beach and seeing her parents waiting for her. Ahalya was down by the waterline, searching for conch shells. It was a day like any other—a good day.

She looked up as two men entered the house in civilian clothes. One was tall, with dark hair and kind eyes, and the other was shorter and more muscular. She stared at the tall man. She had seen him before. She racked her brain for the connection. Then it came to her. On the street outside Dmitri's flat in Paris. He was the one who had chased their car down the street.

At once all of the pieces fell into place. He had been looking for her! But how had he known? And why had he cared? She was sure they had never met before. She followed him with her eyes, wondering whether she would get a chance to speak with him.

Thomas stood in the foyer and searched the milling agents for a sign of Sita.

"Where do you think she'd be?" he asked Porter.

"They probably have all of the girls together," Porter replied, starting down the hallway toward the living room. "I'll see if I can find Agent Trudeau."

Thomas was about to follow him when he glanced to his left. At a polished mahogany table sat a towering SWAT commando, a jacket-clad field agent, and a thin-boned Indian girl dressed like a princess. The girl was staring at him, her lovely eyes wide. She was older than she looked in the photograph in his pocket, but it was her. He knew it right away.

He stood frozen for a moment, and then he began to finger the bracelet on his wrist. He walked slowly toward her.

"Are you Sita Ghai?" he asked.

"Yes," Sita replied.

He unfastened the *rakhi* bracelet, bent down, and placed it on the table before her.

"I'm Thomas Clarke. Your sister asked me to give this to you."

He saw tears come to her eyes. "You know Ahalya?"

He nodded, finding it hard to breathe. "We rescued her from Suchir's brothel. She is waiting for you at an ashram in Bombay."

Thomas marveled as the radiance of the dawn spread across her face. She clutched the bracelet and began to sob. It was as if all of the terror, the doubt, the despair, and the failing hope of the past two and a half months had converged in a great tide of tears.

He felt a hand on his shoulder. It was Porter. "It seems that you found her," he said.

Thomas let out the breath he was holding and began to smile.

"Well done," Porter said.

When the gale of Sita's emotions subsided, she fastened the bracelet on her wrist. "I made this for her birthday last year," she whispered. "She said she would wear it always."

"You'll have to return it to her, then."

Sita thought for a moment and reached into her coat, extracting Hanuman. She held the figurine reverently, then placed it on the table.

"Do you know the story of the Ramayana?" she asked him.

Thomas nodded, staring at the little statue.

"Hanuman was a friend of Rama. He found Sita. You should have him."

Thomas picked up the statue. He remembered what Surekha had said about Priya's father at the *mendhi* event. "*When Priya was young, he told me that the man who married her would have to possess the character of Lord Rama. Rama is a guiltless man.*" Thomas knew he would never live up to such a standard. But Rama wasn't really the hero of the story. It was

Hanuman who had crossed the ocean and rescued the princess of Mithila.

"Thank you," he said. She would never know the importance of the gift.

Sita looked around at the FBI men. "Will they let me go?" she asked.

Agent Evans attempted an answer. "It's complicated. But we'll do everything we can to get you home soon."

Thomas glanced at Porter. "Holi is on the twenty-sixth. It's the second biggest holiday in India. Any chance you can pull some more strings and get us on a plane before then?"

Porter laughed. "I've pulled so many strings in the past few days that I'm starting to think about a career as a marionettist. I'll put in the request and see what the people on high have to say about it. A lot of it will depend upon the Indian government. They'll have to take her into custody on the other side."

"What happens now?" Sita asked, glancing between Thomas and Evans.

"We'll put you under protection and ask a lot of questions," Evans responded. "We need your help to put quite a few criminals behind bars."

"Will you stay with me?" Sita asked Thomas.

Thomas nodded, holding little Hanuman and relishing the sweet exhilaration of victory.

"I'll stay with you as long as it takes to get you home."

Chapter 32

The mark of wisdom is to see the reality behind each
appearance.

—Thiruvalluvar

Atlanta, Georgia

Thomas sat in a drab conference room inside the FBI's Atlanta
field office. Across the table from him were two agents in
plainclothes and Andrew Porter, who had been assigned to
act as Justice liaison for the Atlanta phase of the investigation.
Their conversation, which had dragged on for more than
three days, was being recorded by a digital device at the
center of the table.

"I know we've been talking a long time," said Special
Agent Alfonso Romero, an Italian American from Brooklyn.
"I think we're almost through."

While Romero checked his notes, Thomas suppressed
his annoyance. At times the interview had felt like an
interrogation, and his patience had long since worn thin.

But he owed it to Porter to be compliant. It was the price he paid for being included in the raid.

"Tell me again why you went to Paris," Romero said. "Your wife was in Mumbai. Your work was in Mumbai. What compelled you to leave Mumbai to search for a girl who could have been anywhere by then?"

"Haven't we been over this already?"

"Maybe we have, but I'm still troubled by it."

"The best I can say is that I did what I felt I should do. I made Ahalya a promise, and I took a shot in the dark. Somehow it worked out."

Romero shook his head and scanned his notes again. He traded a look with Special Agent Cynthia Douglas, a hawkish brunette who had asked all of the personal questions Thomas hadn't really wanted to answer. Douglas shook her head.

"Okay, we're through for the moment," Romero said. "But I'm sure we'll have more for you as the investigation proceeds. Keep us informed of your whereabouts, and let us know if any of your contact information changes."

"Don't worry," Thomas said with a hint of sarcasm. "I'll keep you posted."

"You have anything else?" Romero asked Porter.

Porter nodded. "But it's personal. I'd rather talk in private."

"No problem" said Romero and ushered Douglas out of the room.

Thomas closed his eyes and massaged his temples. "I was starting to think he was never going to shut up."

Porter chuckled. "His persistence was impressive, if a bit overzealous." He leaned forward. "I have two pieces of good news and one of bad news. How do you want them?"

Thomas opened his eyes again and read his friend's face. Porter was grave.

"Bad news first." Thomas braced himself.

Porter sat back in his chair. "I just heard from Deputy Morgan in Fayetteville. He and his squad took down the mobilehome park near Fort Bragg yesterday. They expected to find eight kids. Three were missing. Abby was one of them." He paused. "They found her this morning."

Thomas saw what was coming.

"She was buried in a shallow grave in a stand of trees not far from the trailer park," Porter said. "She'd been in the ground for no more than a week."

Thomas held his breath and then let it out. "Why would they do that?"

"I don't know. Her story was all over the news. Maybe they found out how close we were and got scared. Maybe she tried to escape and they didn't want to deal with her. People like that are capable of anything."

Thomas thought of the girl's mother and felt hollow inside. Her worst fears had been realized. She was alone in the world.

"What about the other missing girls?" he asked.

Porter shook his head. "They were from Mexico. We think they were sold again."

"So the story goes on," Thomas said. "It's never going to end, is it?"

Porter shrugged. "Not in our lifetimes, I'm afraid."

"So, what's the good news?"

Porter perked up a bit. "Apart from DeFoe's death, the operation against the Klein ring was a huge success. Sixty-one victims rescued in eight cities, thirty-five of them under-age. Forty perpetrators behind bars. Kandyland shut down and its computers seized. Perverts around the world in our sights. Twenty million dollars in offshore accounts to boost the Treasury. It's a massive public relations coup. Everyone in Washington is giddy."

"Good for them," Thomas said. He didn't mean to be glib, but Abby's death haunted him. For the hundredth time, he wished he had moved faster and tracked down the black SUV before it disappeared and took the girl to her grave.

"And the second thing?" he asked.

Porter noticed his friend's mood and held out his hands in a gesture of apology.

"I think we're going to get Sita home before the Holi holiday. The deputy director has taken an interest in her case, as has the Indian ambassador in Washington. We're moving heaven and earth with the bureaucrats, and I'm cautiously optimistic that things are going to work out."

Thomas nodded. "How's she holding up?"

Porter grinned. "The girl's been a human billiard ball in the past three days. She's been back and forth from the safe house to the Fulton County Juvenile Court to a conference room upstairs, and no one's heard her complain. The Bureau assigned her a victim specialist—Agent Dodd. She's a child psychologist and has a gentle touch. From what I've heard, they've bonded well. I have to tell you: Sita's a treasure trove of information. We've gotten information out of her that is going to put quite a few of the Kandyland conspirators behind bars."

"When can I see her again?" Thomas asked. On the night of the raid, Sita had been whisked away from the Klein property in a squad car, and for security reasons Agent Pritchett had denied his repeated requests to visit her.

"Probably not before the flight back," Porter said. "I'm sorry about that."

"In that case, there are some things I need to take care of. Is Romero going to bite my head off if I leave town for a few days?"

Porter laughed. "I'll keep him on a leash. Just make sure you're back by the twenty-third. If we're lucky, you and Sita will be on a flight to Mumbai the next day."

Thomas raised his eyebrows. "Courtesy of the federal government?"

Porter nodded. "Our tax dollars at work."

"So now that you're done with me, can I make the phone call?"

Porter stood from the table. "Freedom of speech is a constitutional right. How you use it when you walk out of this office is up to you." He paused. "Now do yourself a favor and get out of here before Romero remembers all the questions he forgot to ask you."

At nine o'clock that evening, Thomas dialed the international exchange on his BlackBerry. It was seven thirty in the morning in Bombay. Jeff Greer answered on the second ring. Thomas gave him a sketch of the events of the past week, culminating in Sita's rescue, and then asked him for a piece of information and a favor. When Greer recovered from his shock, he searched his desk while he listened to Thomas's idea.

"Here it is," he said, shuffling some paperwork. He passed along the phone number and then promised to make the necessary arrangements.

"I can't believe you did it," he said. "I confess I never thought you had a chance."

After Greer hung up, Thomas dialed the Andheri exchange. He waited while the phone rang and rang. When he was about to end the call, he heard a garbled word: "Hello?" The connection was poor, but he was almost certain that the voice was Sister Ruth's. Speaking slowly, he delivered the news. When he finished, the nun was silent for so long that he thought the line had been disconnected. Then he heard a mumble—a bare echo across the continents—that sounded like a prayer.

"Sister Ruth?" Thomas said. "Will you pass along the message?"

"Yes," he heard her say. The line hissed and crackled, but he pieced together her words. "I do not . . . know how . . . to thank you."

"Tell her to be patient," he said. "The process may take a while."

With that, Thomas hung up and drove to the airport.

On the far side of the night, Ahalya awoke in a feverish state. Her brow was moist, her nightshirt was stained with sweat, and her mind held the fading glimmers of the dream. She looked around the small bedroom she shared with three other girls. No one stirred. All was quiet in the house. She shifted her eyes to the window. The sky was gray-blue in anticipation of the dawn. She took a deep breath and tried to calm her heart. The vision had been so achingly real that she couldn't believe it was a mirage.

She stole across the floor to the common area. It was a Saturday and no one was about. Sister Ruth was awake, Ahalya was sure, but the nun slept elsewhere and didn't usually make an appearance at the house until half past seven. Ahalya moved quietly, tiptoeing around weak spots in the floor. Technically, she was not allowed to leave the house without the sisters' permission, but the rule was only enforced when a girl showed an interest in escape.

She went down the front steps and entered the forest of tall trees. A few cicadas were singing in the branches, and once in a while she heard a bird call. The path before her was empty and shrouded in shadow. She glanced around, worried that one of the sisters would spot her and scold her back to the house, but she saw no one.

As she neared the pond, she slowed, replaying the dream

in her mind. Sita had been here. She had been sitting on the bench, admiring something in the water. She had looked up when Ahalya neared, her face a picture of delight. She had stood and urged Ahalya to hurry. Ahalya had taken her sister's hand and gazed down at the pond, following her sister's eyes. She had seen a lotus bud between the lily pads, a flower soon to bloom.

Ahalya approached the pond with tentative steps. The surface of the pool was a sheet of glass in the windless morning. She knelt down at the edge of the pool, the ache inside her growing by the second. She didn't see it. She looked closer. Perhaps it was smaller than it had been in the dream.

Perhaps . . .

Suddenly, she felt a wave of vertigo. She steadied herself on a rock beside the pool. The pregnancy was something she didn't want to think about right now. Her desire was simple and, in its simplicity, pure. She wanted nothing more than to find a bud.

She scoured the lily pads for any sign of a protrusion, but she saw nothing. The dream had been an illusion, a tantalizing lie. Sita wasn't at the ashram, and the lotus had yet to flower. The sun was rising upon a future she didn't really want. Lakshmi had forgotten her. Rama had deserted her. She was a stone person, just like Ahalya of the Ramayana.

She cried, hardly aware of the birdsong around her, the sounds of the waking ashram, or the distant noises from the street beyond the fence. At some point she gathered herself and struggled to her feet, steeling her heart against the thought of another weekend without Sita.

She started up the path and then paused. Before her eyes was a peculiar sight. She blinked and stared, worrying that the dream had stolen her senses. But the vision persisted.

Sister Ruth was running toward her down the path.

The nun's *sari* was flowing out behind her like a cape, and her eyes were shining like a child's. The nun slowed when she reached Ahalya's side. She panted and caught her breath.

"I'm sorry," Ahalya said, feeling guilty about the curfew. "I needed to take a walk."

Sister Ruth shook her head, her round frame shaking with each labored breath.

"No, no," she said, struggling to get the words out. "Sita . . ."

Ahalya stared at her, transfixed. Confusion overwhelmed her, hope vying with terror.

At last the nun collected herself enough to deliver Thomas's message.

For the second time that morning, Ahalya fell to her knees, but this time her eyes didn't fill with tears. Instead, she gazed toward the east and the rising sun. She turned her face upward and felt its light burrow into her like a seed in the soil. The light spread through her, and her skin began to tingle. She started to laugh and remembered at once how good it felt. Her laughter echoed across the yard, filling the forest and silencing the birds.

The dream was true. Sita was alive.

And she was coming home.

Two days later, Thomas stood in the cold rain outside an upscale apartment complex in D.C. gathering his courage. He had been to the exclusive Capitol Hill neighborhood on only two occasions, both of them at night. He remembered the visits with disturbing vividness. He gripped his umbrella and stared at the lobby door through the curtain of rain. The entrance way was empty. It was eight o'clock in the morning on a Sunday—the only time of the week he knew she would be home.

He took the elevator to the sixth floor. Her apartment was down the hallway on the right. Number 603. He stood outside her door for at least a minute, his nerves on edge. Finally he knocked.

He listened carefully for footfalls. At first he heard nothing, and he had the thought that perhaps she had gone to the Caymans for a weekend getaway or, better yet, found a new boyfriend and stayed over at his place. But then he heard her come to the door. He steeled himself and looked into the peephole. The anger he had felt in Goa was a distant memory; its residue was anxiety and remorse.

A long moment passed before the door opened. Then Tera stood before him, wrapped in a terrycloth bathrobe, her hair wet and pulled back in a ponytail. Her eyes were wide, her lips parted in surprise. She looked at him without speaking. His heart pounded, but he made no move toward her.

"Thomas," she said at last. Seconds ticked by. Then something shifted in her and she opened the door wider. "I thought I'd never see you again." She stood aside.

He took the invitation and entered her flat. The decor was avant garde—everything in black and white with hard edges, abstract artwork on the walls, directional lighting, bric-a-brac from around the world. She had majored in art history at Columbia before heading to Chicago Law. In that respect— indeed, in many respects—she was similar to Priya.

He walked into the living room and took in the view from the tall windows. The rain had let up a bit, and he could see the faint outline of the Capitol Building in the distance.

"Where did you go?" she asked, standing a few feet behind him, hands in the pockets of her robe. "It's been almost three months."

He faced her again. "I went to India," he said without preamble.

Her body stiffened. "India," she repeated.

"You were right about what happened at the firm," he said. "They gave me an ultimatum and I took a sabbatical. One year in the trenches in Bombay."

"So you didn't go because of Priya?" she asked, a trace of optimism in her voice.

"I went to work with CASE. But I also went to find my wife."

She thought about his choice of words. "Did you succeed?" she asked eventually.

"I'm not sure," he said. "But I want to."

Tera angled her head. "Then why are you here?"

"Because I did this the wrong way before. I owe you an apology."

She sat down on the edge of the couch. "I don't regret any of it."

"Just hear me out," he said, opening his hands. "And judge me at the end."

She waited, noncommittal.

He forged ahead. "You were there at the darkest moment of my life. I needed help, and you offered it. I will never forget that. But I was foolish. I shouldn't have let things go so far. Maybe Priya still would have walked out, but I should have honored my vows. Coming here that first night was a mistake. I was completely unstable. I don't blame you for it. It was my fault, and I hurt all of us. You, me, Priya. You deserved better than that. Please forgive me."

Tera stood up and walked to the window, looking out over the sodden city. She pushed a lock of hair over her ear. He thought that perhaps he should leave, but he didn't. He couldn't walk out on her again.

At last she looked at him. "I don't need your apology," she said. "I'm a big girl. I knew what I was getting into." She paused. "Priya was a fool to leave. I hope she knows that now."

Thomas stared at her and tried to think of an appropriate response. She was beautiful in the wan light of the rain. He had a fleeting instinct to console her, as she had done for him. But he saw it for the temptation it was and resisted it.

"Goodbye, Tera," he said.

When she didn't respond, he shrugged and walked down the hallway toward the door. He reached for the doorknob and heard her call his name.

"Thomas," she said, appearing at the entrance to the hall. "Do me a favor, will you?"

"What's that?"

"Whatever you do, stick with it this time."

He nodded and mustered a small smile. It was a softer rebuke than he had a right to hope for. He opened the door quietly and left her there, framed by the window and the rain.

He drove south out of the District and reached his parents' neighborhood in twenty minutes. With the exception of church traffic, the streets were empty. He pulled his Audi into the driveway and stepped out. The rain had turned into mist, and he left his umbrella in the car.

He knocked on the front door and heard plodding footsteps. His heart raced and he wondered again how he would explain himself to his father. The Judge opened the door and stared at him. He was decked out in a pinstripe suit and a paisley tie. Mass was in half an hour.

At once the Judge's eyes came alive. "Thomas! Come in, son."

Elena appeared in the foyer, dressed smartly in a mauve

dress and a black cardigan. She embraced him for a long time.

"You're wet," she said, pointing at his hair and drawing him toward the kitchen. "Let me make you some tea."

While Elena scurried about around the stove, Thomas found a stool beside the tiled island and sat down. His father took a seat at the breakfast table. The arrangement—his mother serving, his father waiting to dispense advice—was as familiar to him as an old pair of shoes. How many times they had sat like this when he was growing up.

"How is Priya?" Elena asked over her shoulder. He had sent her an e-mail in Paris with a vague but generally upbeat summation of his progress. But that had been before Goa.

"Things aren't going so well right now."

His mother looked crestfallen but didn't pry. "I'm sorry to hear that."

He shrugged and glanced at his father. "I'm not sure I'm going back to Clayton."

The Judge's eyes narrowed. "Did you get my e-mail?"

Thomas nodded.

"Max is going to roll out the red carpet for you. He's talking partnership in a year."

"I'm not sure I want it any more," Thomas said.

His father was speechless, a rare event.

Elena spoke instead. "What *do* you want, dear?"

Thomas gripped the edge of the island. "I'm still trying to figure that out."

The Judge stood up. "I can't believe what I'm hearing.

When you were fifteen, you told me you wanted a seat on the bench. I did everything in my power to make it happen. I put you through Yale and Virginia Law. I got you a clerkship. I greased the wheels at Clayton. After all that, you're going to walk away? Just like that?"

"Rand," his mother interrupted, but the Judge silenced her with a glare.

"I want a straight answer," he said. "I deserve it."

Thomas took a deep breath and looked his father in the eye. "I know what I wanted, Dad. And I know the sacrifices you've made. But things change. If you want an answer, I'll give you one. I want to finish my year with CASE, and I want to find some way to convince my wife that she's better off with me than without me."

The Judge threw up his hands, exasperated. "You're talking about one year of your life, two at most. What about your *future*, Thomas? What about ten years from now, twenty years from now? Where are you going to be then?"

Thomas felt the anger rise within him. "I have no idea. But I'm certain about one thing: I don't want to go back to the rat race."

"Beautiful! Now you're comparing my life to vermin."

Thomas's eyes flashed. "This isn't about you, Dad. This is about me. You want to know why I'm back in the States? It's because a girl was trafficked here from India. We rescued her sister from a brothel in Bombay. Sita's going home in a few days, and I'm going with her. I'm not questioning the choices you've made. I'm just saying I might not want the same thing."

He took a sip of the tea his mother had set in front of him. He watched his father think. He knew the course this would take. The Judge would end the conversation abruptly and deliberate until he reached a decision, at which point he would deliver it in a windy monologue, just as he did in the courtroom.

Sure enough, the Judge glanced at his watch. "Mass is in fifteen minutes," he said, steadying his tone. "We'll finish this later."

Elena looked at Thomas, an apology and a question in her eyes. She spoke the question.

"How long are you staying?"

"Long enough," he said. "I dressed for church."

His mother's eyes widened. He hadn't attended Mass with them since college.

"I'm full of surprises today, aren't I?" he said, taking her arm.

Later that afternoon, Thomas returned to the District. He had one more matter to attend to before the day was done. After a brief stop to buy flowers—daisies in honor of the coming spring—he entered Glenwood Cemetery by the rear gate and followed the curved path through the trees to the gravesite. He took his keys but didn't lock his car. He didn't have far to walk.

He inhaled the crisp air and enjoyed the solitude of the place. Though the morning rain had passed and the sun had reappeared, the cemetery was largely empty. The gravesite was situated at the top of a rise overlooking the angel garden. He saw the headstone, and the sorrow returned as if it had never left. Dear, sweet Mohini. She was far too young to die.

The burial of the little girl had been the subject of bitter dispute. His parents—as good Catholics—had objected to cremation, but Priya had been equally opposed to interment. "Pick your river, I don't care," she had said. "But let me give my child a proper burial." He had spent all of his rapidly diminishing relational capital brokering the compromise. They had cremated her and sprinkled her ashes at the mouth of the Hudson. But the urn they had interred in the Clarke family plot at Glenwood.

He stooped down and placed the daisies before the gravestone. He had expected that the marker, too, would generate controversy. But Priya had deferred without comment, allowing the inscription his mother preferred: "In sure and certain hope of the resurrection". He wondered as he knelt before the grave what the resurrection of an infant would look like—if she would be given a body and a personality full grown or if she would have to develop to maturity as if her death had never happened. Whatever else it was, faith was full of mystery.

"It's been a while, sweet girl," he said, feeling the first tears forming. He choked up and waited until the feeling subsided. "There's a girl I wish you could meet. I think you would like her. Her name is Sita, and she is from India, like Mommy." He talked for a while longer, saying anything that came to mind. He told her about Bombay, about Priya's family, and about Ahalya and Sita.

When he could think of nothing more to say, he kissed the gravestone tenderly. "I have to leave now, little girl," he said. He closed his eyes and anguish washed over him again. "I love you, Mohini," he said.

He returned to his car and sat for a long moment in the driver's seat before reaching for his backpack. He took out a single sheet of notepaper and a pen and poured his pain onto the page, writing for the benefit of a woman who was a stranger in every dimension except one.

Dear Allison,

My name is Thomas Clarke, and I was there on the day Abby disappeared. A friend told me about what happened, and I had to write you. I can offer you little in the way of consolation. Your suffering has no antidote, nor will you ever find an explanation to make sense of it. The world failed you and it failed Abby. When evil rose up, good was powerless against it. For that I am truly sorry.

What I can offer you is a promise grounded in personal experience. Though it may not seem possible to you now, tomorrow will come. On the other side of this darkness, a new day will slowly dawn. I know because I lost a daughter not long ago. I went to her grave today. Every time I see her name on the headstone, my heart breaks

again. I couldn't protect her any more than you could
protect Abby. But Mohini and Abby have something that
we do not. Death no longer has power over them.
Wherever they are, they have found peace.

After signing his name, he folded the page and slid it into
an envelope addressed to Andrew Porter at the Justice
Department. Once again stretching the limits of protocol,
Porter had given Thomas her name and had made
arrangements with Detective Morgan for the letter to be
hand-delivered by the Fayetteville police.

Thomas took a last look at the gravesite and then drove
back to the gate. He looked at the angels as he rounded the
circle, their trumpets perched on silent lips, heralding a day
when every tear would be wiped away. He fingered the
envelope in his lap and wished that day would come.

A week later, Thomas sat in the boarding lounge at Dulles
airport, waiting to catch the early evening Delta flight to
Atlanta. He had spent the past six days tidying up his affairs
and addressing the damage from a leak that had sprung in
the pipes at his brownstone over the winter. A large puddle
of water had formed on the dining-room floor and seeped
into the basement. The nightmare hadn't ended until the
last contractor left the house, payment in hand.

Thomas took out his BlackBerry and checked his e-mail.
He found an assortment of spam in his inbox along with
queries from friends, but nothing from Priya. In fourteen

days, she had made no attempt to contact him. She had every right to be disgusted with him. But their weekend together had proven the fact of their love beyond doubt. Wasn't that enough?

Out the window, he watched the clouds play on the wind and remembered the poetry she had read to him in Goa from the little book Elena had given her. She had initiated the reading sessions after they made love. He had rolled his eyes at first, but she had insisted, and the cadence of the words had won him over. Or maybe it was the fact that she had read the poems lying naked on the bed. He smiled at the memory, despite himself.

He was struck then by an idea. What if he wrote a verse for her? Not some Byronic love sonnet, but a few lines of honest poetry, something like Naidu or one of the Sufi mystics she was always quoting. He shook off the thought. Why would the sophomoric attempt of an amateur matter to her? She would laugh at it, if she even read it.

Looking toward an overhead monitor, he listened to the news until he grew bored. Then he turned back to the window and watched a plane take off. The plane climbed into the sky and traced a path across the setting sun. At once a string of words appeared in his mind: *We walk across the sun*. For some reason the image arrested him. What did it mean?

He opened up his BlackBerry notes and exercised his imagination. He wrestled with a few ideas and fashioned a broader theme. Before long, the words turned into lines, and the lines into a stanza. He stared at the poem.

> *We walk across the sun*
> *And our shadows fall*
> *Upon the dial of time*
> *In names spoken by the light*
> *That gives us birth.*

He saved the file and stood up, stretching his legs. Boarding would commence in twenty minutes. He visited the restroom and returned to his seat, feeling restless. He took out the photograph of Priya from his wallet and read his poem again. It wasn't Tagore, but it wasn't bad. He put the picture back in his wallet and threw caution to the wind. He typed until his thumbs began to hurt. When the last word was written, he read the e-mail again. He had written:

Dear Priya,

I wish I could say this to you face to face, but e-mail will have to do. I left Goa a complete wreck. I didn't want to hurt you. I'm a world-class idiot. I don't know how to say it better. I'm sorry for deceiving you. I'm sorry for the mess with Tera. You deserved to know the truth, but I was ashamed.

I'm in the United States. We found Sita. I'll tell you the story someday if you like. But I won't force it on you. I don't know what to do right now except bring her back to India and finish my year with CASE. I can't see

beyond that. Except that I hope—please believe me—I
hope that you are a part of it.

I wrote a poem a few minutes ago. I don't know
precisely what it means, but somehow it makes sense of
my life like nothing else. I'm attaching it to this e-mail.
Whether you write me back or not, know that I love you.

He sent the message and heard his flight being called. He
looked out the window at the clouds high aloft, reflecting
the last light of day. He collected his laptop bag and headed
to the boarding queue, relishing the thought of chasing them
again.

Chapter 33

Let not your heart be burdened with what is past and
gone.

—The Ramayana

Atlanta, Georgia

On the morning of March 24, the Fulton County Juvenile
Court entered an order granting leave for Sita to return to
India. Both the American and Indian governments agreed
that Agent Dodd, the victim specialist, should serve as her
guardian on the trip home, and Thomas was deputized as
their official escort.

The deputy chief of mission at the Indian embassy made
arrangements for a contingent from the CBI to meet them
at the airport in Bombay. After the International Organization
of Migration completed its home study, the deputy chief
promised that Sita would be placed at the Sisters of Mercy
facility with Ahalya. At Thomas's behest, Agent Pritchett
made a special request concerning the Holi holiday, which
the diplomat enthusiastically granted.

When all of the pieces of the puzzle were in place, Pritchett drove them to the airport. Agent Dodd, a matronly, forty-something woman, occupied the front passenger seat, and Sita and Thomas sat in the back. After suffering the past sixteen days in bureaucratic confinement, Sita was brimming with questions about her sister. Thomas answered each of them as thoroughly as he could without embellishing anything. The only thing he left out was Ahalya's pregnancy, which was something he felt Ahalya should explain herself.

When they reached the airport, Pritchett escorted them through security to the Continental Airlines boarding gate. Pritchett shook Thomas's hand and gave him an apologetic reminder about the confidentiality agreement he had signed. Then he squatted in front of Sita and gave her a lapel pin bearing the emblem of the U.S. flag.

"You know," he said, "I have a daughter about your age. She's the light of my life. A bit difficult at times, but that goes with the territory. I speak for all the agents in my office when I say that I'm honored to know you."

Sita gave Pritchett a shy hug and then followed Thomas and Agent Dodd to the boarding line.

Late the next evening, they reached the sprawling, light-studded city of Bombay. Two CBI constables met them at the gate and whisked them through customs to a Land Rover at the curb. One of the constables retrieved their baggage from the carousel, and then they were off.

Sita spent the entire ride staring out the window at the

midnight cityscape. The return to Mother India evoked in her a range of conflicting emotions: rage and sympathy at the memory of Ahalya's violation, renewed grief over her vanished family, confusion about her future, and fear at the knowledge that Suchir was nearby. Yet for all the angst that the homecoming stirred in her, nothing could diminish her overwhelming sense of relief. Breathing the sticky Bombay air reminded her of all the reasons she loved her country. These were her people. This was her land.

It had wounded her, but she owed it her life.

The CBI constables—who had introduced themselves by their surnames, Bhuta and Singh—drove them to the Taj Land's End hotel just south of the Bandstand in Bandra. Dinesh met them in the lobby, holding a bouquet of flowers.

"Nice digs," he said, shaking Thomas's hand. "I take it this was your idea."

Thomas nodded, delighted by his friend's appearance.

"The government wanted to put her up in some third-class dump outside the airport," he said. "I couldn't let it happen. Not on her first night back." He paused. "What are you doing here? I told you I'd meet you at your place."

"I didn't come for you," his friend said with a grin. "I came to meet Sita."

"Sita," Thomas said, turning to her, "meet Dinesh. Dinesh, Sita."

"*Ghara mem svagata hai, chotti bahana*," Dinesh said, welcoming her home using the familiar sobriquet "little sister".

"You're going to really like this place." He handed her the flowers. "These are for your room."

Sita blushed, warming to him immediately. She chatted with him in Hindi while Bhuta checked them in.

After a few minutes, the manager of the hotel appeared and escorted them to a suite on the top floor. After some negotiation, the CBI men allowed Dinesh to tag along. The manager showed them the spacious room and left the CBI constables with keys. Agent Dodd, who had slept little on the long flight, found a couch in the bedroom and turned in for the night. Sita, meanwhile, walked to one of the windows overlooking the Arabian Sea. She stood quietly, enjoying the sights of the slumbering city.

"Where is Ahalya?" she asked Thomas. "When can I see her?"

"She is at the ashram in Andheri," he said. "You will see her tomorrow."

Sita nodded. "It is beautiful here."

In time, she yawned.

"The bedroom is yours," Thomas said. "Our friends from the government will find somewhere else to sleep."

"What about you?" she asked.

"I'm going to stay with Dinesh. His place is close by. I'll be back in the morning."

"Good night, then," she said and left them with a little wave.

In the morning, Dinesh prepared a gourmet breakfast of deep-fried Indian bread, chickpeas, and *mahim halwa*—a dense buttery cake—and he and Thomas took it to the hotel to share with Sita. Agent Dodd, looking refreshed and contented after a good night's sleep, nursed her *halwa* and sipped her glass of chai. She caught Sita staring at her and tried to explain.

"Back in the States, I live on Chinese takeout," she said. "This is much better."

Dinesh laughed and said, "You'll have to come back to India someday."

"I just might do that," the FBI woman replied.

After breakfast, the CBI constables retrieved the Land Rover and picked them up in front of the hotel. Thomas reminded Constable Singh that they were due at the ashram at nine o'clock. The CBI man looked at him strangely and traded a glance with Dinesh. Thomas didn't notice that Singh wasn't following his directions until they passed the entrance to the Western Express Highway and continued south along Mahim Bay.

"The ashram is the other way," Thomas exclaimed, touching Singh on the shoulder.

The agent didn't respond.

Thomas looked at Dinesh and then at Sita. Dinesh had a sly expression on his face.

"Something's going on," Thomas said. "What did you do?"

"It wasn't me," Dinesh replied. "You'll see."

Saturday traffic in the city was one giant snarl. Despite Singh's repertoire of daredevil maneuvers, the drive to

Malabar Hill took almost an hour and a half. When they entered Breach Candy on Warden Road, Thomas turned toward Dinesh.

"We're going to Vrindivan, aren't we?" he said.

"Vrindivan?" Sita asked. "You mean the forests where Krishna played?"

Dinesh shrugged and Thomas sat back against the seat, a thousand thoughts racing through his head.

"It's a little bit different," he said to her. "But there are similarities."

When the Land Rover entered the grounds, Thomas couldn't believe his eyes. The driveway was lined with well-wishers. Along with the many faces he recognized from Priya's extended family, he saw Jeff Greer, Nigel, Samantha, and the entire CASE staff standing in the shade of a banyan tree. Sister Ruth stood beside Anita, her brown habit rustling in the breeze.

Surya and Surekha Patel met them at the end of the drive. Priya's father looked dashing in a white linen suit, and her mother, robed in a jade *sari*, exuded the aura of nobility. Constable Singh stopped the Land Rover, and Bhuta opened the rear doors. Dinesh climbed out of the vehicle as Thomas turned to Sita.

Her eyes were wide with incomprehension. "Who are all these people?" she asked.

"Some are my wife's family," he replied. "Some are the people who rescued your sister."

"Why are they here?"

He shook his head, trying to figure out how his plans to celebrate Holi had been hijacked and how Vrindivan had been chosen as the new location.

"They came to see you," he said, certain of that at least. He reached for her hand, but she looked pensive.

"You don't have to do this," he said, watching her closely. "The driver can turn around and take us someplace private where you can meet with Ahalya."

Sita surveyed the crowd through the window. "No," she said, "it is Holi. It's right this way."

Thomas smiled. "Welcome home," he said and drew her into the sunlight.

When Sita appeared, the crowd erupted in applause. Sita clutched his hand and he gave her a squeeze, scanning the faces before them, looking for Priya. *She has to be here*, he thought. *It wouldn't be like her to miss Holi.*

Suddenly, he saw another face in the crowd. It was Ahalya, emerging from the cluster of CASE volunteers. She ran toward Sita with tears streaming down her face. She wore a sunflower-yellow *churidaar* and a rose-shaped *bindi* on her forehead. Sita let go of Thomas's hand and met her older sister halfway. Their embrace was almost too intimate to watch, yet Thomas couldn't bring himself to look away.

The sisters held one another for what seemed like ages, oblivious to all else. Then the moment passed and Ahalya approached Thomas. She knelt down and touched his foot with the deepest respect. Afterward, she stood before him, beaming with gratitude.

"Thank you," she whispered. "I owe you my life."

"Many people had a hand in this," he replied, his eyes moistening.

"Perhaps. But you wore my bracelet. I will never forget."

On the terrace, a traditional Hindustani band began to play, and Surya Patel appeared in front of them holding a golden bowl. Thomas looked into the Professor's eyes, searching for a sign of judgment or resentment, but he saw neither of these things. Instead, Surya raised his hand and asked for the attention of the chattering crowd. As one, family and friends fell silent.

He addressed them in English in a stentorian voice. "As you all know, Holi means many things. It is a day of play in which we remember Krishna and the good-natured fun he had with the maidens of the forest. It is also a day in which we commemorate the changing seasons, the end of winter and the arrival of spring."

He held up the shining bowl. "In our family, we have a tradition. Every Holi, we select a child to place the *tilak* on the forehead of an elder. After that, the festival of colors may begin, and everyone—even those who would prefer to stay clean—is fair game. It is only fitting that this year the child should be Sita Ghai."

He turned and lowered the bowl so that Sita could see the vermilion powder.

"Happy Holi," Surya told her. "You and your sister are welcome at our home any time."

With a smile that occupied her entire face, Sita dusted

her thumb in the red powder, reached up and made a *tilak* on Thomas's forehead.

"To me, you will always be *Dada*, elder brother," she said. "Happy Holi."

The crowd began to cheer. And then, with humorous suddenness, bags of powder appeared and the air began to shimmer with color. Reds and yellows, blues and purples, greens and golds, the palette of Holi was the palette of India, regal, unashamed, resplendent, and true.

Surya, however, was not quite finished. Dipping his hand into the bowl, he retrieved a handful of powder and smeared it all over Thomas's face. Thomas coughed and laughed at the same time, trying to wipe the fine grains from his eyes.

"Happy Holi," Surya said. "I believe someone is waiting for you."

With that, he turned around and began to pelt his family with red powder. Surekha held out a woven basket filled with bags of color, and Sita and Ahalya armed themselves. Ahalya giggled as Sita sprinkled lavender powder on her hair. Ahalya, in turn, took Sita's face in her hands, leaving orange handprints on her cheeks.

Thomas, meanwhile, searched for Priya. He finally spotted her on the veranda. She was looking at him. His heart clutched in his chest. He weaved his way through the guests and climbed the steps. He stopped a few feet from her, not knowing what to say.

"It seems my father has accepted you," she said, breaking the ice.

He touched the red dye on his face. "It does. But why?"

She looked away. "You impressed him. And you reminded him of the Ramayana." She waited a beat and then went on. "I told him the news about Sita after I got your e-mail. I've never seen him so moved. I overheard him tell my mother that he misjudged you. He said you'd done something worthy of the highest honor."

Thomas took a breath, thinking of the little statue of Hanuman that Sita had given him. A word came to him then, almost as if spoken. It was a word Priya had cherished. *Serendipity*. A variant of "providence". *Yes*, he thought to himself, *there is light beyond the veil*.

"So all of this was your father's idea?" he asked.

Priya nodded. "Ironic, isn't it? You rescued Sita from the fire, and he had to give her the homecoming of a queen."

She walked toward the far side of the veranda, and he followed her. They went down the steps and crossed the grass into a grove of flowering trees. She stopped beside a fountain.

"It was a good poem," she said when they were alone.

"It wasn't much."

"It spoke to me," she replied. "It told me you meant everything else you said." She turned away and looked at the flowing water. "You have to understand that I will never leave my family again."

He nodded. "I realize that now."

"And I won't tolerate it if you abandon me for your work. Whatever you decide to do, I need to know that I come first."

Thomas began to smile. "Does that mean you forgive me?"

She closed her eyes. "I started to forgive you on the beach when you told me you loved me," she said. "But I had to know if it was the truth."

He reached out and touched her face. She turned toward him, and he saw that her eyes were filled with tears. She took one step, and then another, until she was only inches away from him. He drew her into his arms.

"I'm so glad you came to Bombay," she said. "I thought I'd lost you."

He looked down at her and brushed a hair out of her eyes.

"Will you kiss a man covered in vermilion powder?" he asked.

Her smile began at the corners of her mouth and spread outward until it infused her entire face with radiance.

"I think our colors go well together," she whispered and proved that she was right.

Epilogue

Mumbai, India

The call came at six thirty in the morning on the seventh of October. Thomas's BlackBerry was on the nightstand. He caught it on the second ring and put the phone to his ear, listening.

"We'll be there in forty minutes," he said and hung up.

"Is it time?" Priya asked, rolling over and looking up at him. Her face was bathed in the blue light of dawn. The sun had not yet risen.

He nodded. "She said an hour at most."

They dressed hurriedly, he in chinos and a linen shirt, she in a red and black *salwar kameez*. They took the elevator to the garage where their Toyota SUV was waiting for them. Priya climbed into the passenger seat, and Thomas threw the truck into gear and headed out of the driveway, tossing a wave at the night watchman who was smoking his *charas* by the gate.

He drove north along the Bandstand until the road wrapped around to the east. Ten minutes on Hill Road to S. V. Road. Fifteen minutes on the Western Express Highway to Andheri, and then another five minutes to the ashram. Although it was a Friday morning, traffic was fairly light. The majority of vehicles on the highway were rickshaws, and Thomas cut through the pack with ease.

Priya took his hand off the gearshift and placed it on her belly.

"What shall we call her?"

she asked him. The week before, they had gone in for Priya's twenty-week ultrasound, and their doctor in Breach Candy had announced the baby's gender with unflinching certainty.

"I don't know," he said, glancing at her across the cabin.

She smiled. "I am leaning toward Pooja."

"Absolutely not," he said. "Every girl in Bombay is Pooja. She needs an original name."

Priya began to laugh. "You are such an easy target. I have a much better idea."

"Tell me," he said.

"When the time is right."

They lapsed into silence and his mind drifted to the events of the day before. After nine months of corruption-induced delays, Ahalya at last had been called to testify in the Sessions Court against Suchir, Sumeera, and Prasad. The brothel owner and his son had been present in the courtroom, which was unusual. But their strategy soon became apparent. When Ahalya stepped into the dock, her belly swollen beneath the fabric of her *churidaar*, Suchir and Prasad stood up and stared her down. At a distance of fifteen feet, their menace was palpable. The prosecutor objected, but the defense attorney spun some nonsense about their inability to sit for long periods of time. The judge, clearly irritated by the dispute, waved the prosecutor on and allowed the *malik* and his son to maintain their challenge.

From the back of the courtroom, Thomas saw the look of trepidation in Ahalya's eyes. But she stood her ground, and in the end her testimony rang forth like a bell on a clear day. She told the whole story of her captivity, from the tsunami to Chennai to Bombay, first in eloquent English and then in equally articulate Hindi. She recounted her first rape at the hands of Shankar and her second rape at the hands of the birthday boy. Until then, Suchir and Prasad stood shoulder to shoulder. Ahalya, however, went on to describe the night Prasad came to her and the forced trysts that followed. Suchir's expression didn't change, but he turned his head slightly and muttered something to his son. Prasad's complexion turned a shade paler.

Then came cross-examination. The defense lawyer mounted a scandalous attack on Ahalya's credibility. He insinuated without a shred of proof that Ahalya was a promiscuous schoolgirl who had many amorous affairs with boyfriends. When she denied it, the advocate simply increased the pitch of his delivery, emphasizing the *fact* that the child in her womb was the product of consensual sex outside the brothel. Ahalya patiently explained that she had been a virgin when Suchir bought her and that the only men who could have impregnated her were Shankar, who paid a princely sum not to use a condom, and Prasad, who had been so feverish in his interest that the question of protection had never arisen. The defense lawyer pranced and gesticulated, and even shouted at her at one point, but the damage had been done. Ahalya stood victorious on the stand, and even the judge, who had started the hearing jaded, gave Suchir and Prasad a look of censure at the end.

It's fitting that the call should have come today, Thomas thought, accelerating the SUV past a slow-moving rickshaw. They skirted the edge of the international airport and took Sahar Road into Andheri. When they reached the grounds, Sister Ruth swung the gate wide and allowed them to park in a lot inside the fence.

"Come," the nun said, hurrying up the path. "It won't be long."

The rising sun painted the grounds in shades of gold and delivered the promise of another blazing Bombay day. The monsoon rains had been shorter this year, extending from late May to the end of August, and the heat and humidity had returned with a vengeance in September. It wasn't yet seven thirty in the morning, but Thomas felt beads of sweat forming on his brow as he walked behind Sister Ruth.

"How is she?" Priya asked.

"It has been hard," the nun said. "But it is nearly over."

They were in such a hurry that they nearly passed Ahalya's pond without noticing the change. Thomas, however, caught sight of it out of the corner of his eye.

"Wait!" he exclaimed.

Sister Ruth stopped so quickly that Priya nearly ran into her. The nun followed Thomas's gaze and began to smile. There, suspended on the shimmering surface of the pool, was a star-shaped lotus flower. Its petals were cerulean like the sky, and it caught the slanting rays of the morning sun.

"This wasn't here when I came last week," he said.

"The flower opened yesterday," Sister Ruth replied.

"Did she see it before the hearing?"

"Yes," the nun confirmed. "I was with her."

Thomas shook his head. The lotus was the reason Ahalya had been untouchable on the witness stand. She had interpreted the flower as a sign of divine favor and decided that her victory was inevitable. In believing, she had made it so.

They arrived at the hospital just in time to hear the wails of the child echoing through the main hall. Priya clutched Thomas's hand. Sister Ruth led them to a small anteroom outside the delivery area.

"Wait here," she said. "I will return when the child is presentable."

A minute later, a different face appeared at the door to the delivery room.

"Thomas!" Sita exclaimed, running out to greet him.

She had grown in the six months since he met her. Before, she was a gangly girl, lovely but frail. Now she had begun to fill out in all the places that distinguished a woman. Her voice was surer, her confidence keener, and her round eyes brighter. The nuns would need to watch her with the boys.

Then again, Thomas thought, *will she ever want to marry, after all she has seen?*

He embraced her and took a step back. "How is Ahalya?" he asked, finding Priya's hand again.

Sita beamed. "She was strong and the baby is healthy. Come and see."

Sister Ruth reappeared and beckoned them into the delivery room. The space was outfitted with a cluster of beds, a large washbasin, and a rolling cart with medical equipment. Ahalya was sitting up, her head resting on pillows. The baby was quiet in her arms, and two nurses were attending to her. Sita went to her sister's side and took her hand.

Ahalya spoke when they approached. "Thank you for coming."

"We wouldn't have missed it," Thomas replied. "Do you have a name for her yet?"

Ahalya smiled and her weariness seemed to retreat. "She is Kamalini, my little lotus."

He smiled. "We saw your flower on the way in."

"It is a rebirth," she said with sudden strength. "A new beginning."

The passion in her voice took Thomas by surprise. For months, she had treated the baby as an afterthought, a burden she had to bear. Her ambivalence had made sense to him. The child was a living reminder of her exploitation. He had detected subtle shifts in her perspective as the little girl had taken shape in her belly, but he had never really expected her to embrace the child as her own. Looking at her now, he began to understand. Confronted with the choice between bitterness and love, Ahalya had chosen love. And by that choice, she had turned little Kamalini from the demon seed of the rapist into the newest member of the Ghai family.

"Would you like to hold her?" Ahalya asked Priya.

"Can I?" Priya asked. Only Thomas detected the tremor in her voice. The last time she had held a child was the night Mohini died.

One of the nurses swaddled the little girl and handed her to Priya. She rocked the baby back and forth, and wet tears streamed down her face. She began to sing the lullaby her mother had taught her as a child. It was the song she had sung to Mohini on the day she was born.

> *Could you be darling,*
> *the crescent moon?*
> *the lovely lotus bloom?*
> *the honey that fills the flowers?*
> *the luminance of the full moon?*

She handed the baby back to Ahalya. "She is beautiful. She looks just like you."

Ahalya smiled. "Do you have a name for yours?"

"We were just discussing that in the car," Thomas said.

Priya touched his shoulder and looked at the girls. "I think we do. With your permission, we would like to call her Sita."

Thomas caught his breath and began to nod in affirmation.

He had never considered it, but nothing could be more appropriate.

"It is a good name," Ahalya said, her eyes shining. "What do you think?" she asked her sister.

Sita began to laugh. It was a musical sound, like chimes in the wind. After a moment, Thomas joined her, and then Priya and Ahalya followed suit, and before long even the nurses were laughing, though they knew not why.

"I always wanted a little sister," Sita said, taking Priya's hand. "Now I will have two."

Author's Note

A Walk Across the Sun is a work of fiction, but the trade in human beings is all too real. It is a criminal enterprise that affects almost every country in the world, generating over $30 billion a year in profits and involving millions of men, women and children in forced prostitution and slave labor. Yet it remains mysterious and often misunderstood on account of its clandestine nature. In writing the book, I drew heavily upon real-life accounts in the trafficking literature and upon sources I developed in my travels. Where I have exercised literary license in service of the story, I have done so sensitively, with an eye toward authenticity. There is no need to sensationalize modern slavery. It is horrifying enough as it is.

The non-profit organization CASE is a product of my imagination, though it has much in common with the global human rights organization International Justice Mission, or IJM, my research partner in India (www.ijm.org). Recently, I learned that there are now at least two organizations that incorporate the words "Coalition Against Sexual Exploitation" in their names. The fictional organization I created bears no relation to any such real life organization.

The same is true of Le Project de Justice, the nonprofit research group I set in Paris.

After finishing the book, many of my early readers have asked how they can learn more and become involved in the fight against trafficking. There are many useful sources of information on the trade. A few, however, stand out. Every year, the United States Department of State releases a *Trafficking in Persons Report*, rating the efforts of hundreds of countries in combating the trade, prosecuting traffickers, pimps and slave-owners, and caring for victims. The *TIP Report* offers an invaluable overview of modern slavery in addition to compelling real-life stories from around the world. All such reports are available on the State Department's website (www.state.gov/g/tip).

One of the best non-governmental sources of data on the trade is the Polaris Project in Washington D.C: www.polarisproject.org. Other valuable Web portals are maintained by Shared Hope International (www.sharedhope.org) and Fondation Scelles (www.fondationscelles.org). These sites provide a sense of the scale and scope of the trade, along with the market forces of supply and demand that drive it. In addition, I recommend CNN's Freedom Project blog for stories and thoughtful commentary (thecnnfreedomproject.blogs.cnn.com).

For those interested in delving deeper, I recommend the following books: *A Crime So Monstrous* by Benjamin Skinner; *The Natashas* by Victor Malarek; *Sex Trafficking* by Siddharth Kara; *Smuggling and Trafficking in Human Beings* by Sheldon

Zhang; and *Disposable People* by Kevin Bales. I also recommend the following academic articles, most of which are available online: "Sex Trafficking of Women in the United States" by Janice Redmond and Donna Hughes; "Demand: A Comparative Examination of Sex Tourism and Trafficking in Jamaica, Japan, the Netherlands and the United States" by Shared Hope International; "Desire, Demand and the Commerce of Sex" by Elizabeth Bernstein; and "Sex Trafficking and the Mainstream of Market Culture" by Ian Taylor and Ruth Jamieson.

Several documentary films contain compelling footage and live interviews with victims, investigators, and traffickers. I recommend *At the End of Slavery*, produced by the International Justice Mission; *Sex Slaves*, a Frontline Television Exclusive on the trade in Eastern Europe available from Fondation Scelles at www.fondationscelles.org; *Demand*, an exposé on trafficking in Europe and America, available from Shared Hope at www.sharedhope.org; and *Born into Brothels*, a penetrating look at Calcutta's red-light district.

As for ways to join the modern abolitionist cause, I have three suggestions: first, use your voice. The more we can increase the intelligence and decibel level of the global conversation on the subject, the more likely we are to reach the ears and hearts of stakeholders and decision-makers— lawmakers, politicians, judges, police, and men on the street buying girls.

Second, give financially to one of the many of the anti-trafficking organizations operating worldwide. My wife and

I are enthusiastic supporters of IJM. Every day in red-light areas around the globe, IJM's investigators risk their safety looking for leads, developing evidence, and collaborating with local police to rescue girls from the hands of pimps and traffickers. An investment in IJM is an investment in hope.

Finally, use your skills. If you have legal expertise and a passion for justice, organizations like IJM can put those skills to use. If you are a member of the media or have access to a public platform, even something as basic as a blog, you can use that platform to raise awareness about the issue. If you have the means, you could consider international adoption, as orphans, especially Eastern European girls, have a depressingly high chance of falling prey to the lures of traffickers upon their release from State care.

The needs are great, and the challenges often feel overwhelming. But no problem is without a solution. We can make a difference—one word, one gift, one life at a time.

CORBAN ADDISON
November, 2011

Acknowledgments

From its inception, *A Walk Across the Sun* has been a community project—aided by many voices and hands. No acknowledgment as brief as this could justly express my gratitude.

In India, I wish to thank the heroic team of investigators, lawyers, social workers and volunteers at the International Justice Mission for giving me a window into your work. I wish also to thank Shanmugam and Grace Pillai and Sadhanna Shine in Chennai for your hospitality and your tsunami stories.

In Europe, I wish to thank Elias Mallon and Michael Mutzner at Franciscans International for putting me in touch with the right people in France. In Paris, I wish to thank Gérard Besser of Amicale du Nid and Jean Sébastien Mallet of Fondation Scelles for delightful and captivating interviews on the trade in the European Union.

In Washington, D.C., I wish to thank Pamela Gifford and the team at IJM headquarters for giving me access to IJM's India operations. It was a privilege to collaborate with you on this project. Thanks also to Amy Lucia, Holly Burkhalter, and Amy Roth at IJM for placing the book in

518   Corban Addison

important hands and for your enthusiastic support in the release. Many thanks to March Bell at the Department of Justice for granting me an insider's perspective on the domestic trade in human beings and to Charles Colson and Mariam Bell at PFM for connecting me with March.

In Virginia, I wish to thank Nate and Sara Hagerty for being my networking gurus and best of friends; Jonathan and Julie Baker for sending my name to the right people at IJM; David Roberts for putting me in touch with Nathan Wilson of Project Meridian Foundation; Mark Johansen for connecting me with your friends in Chennai; Bill Finley, Matt Brumbelow, Eric Nelson and Charles Dumaresq for your encouragement and support; Ash Singh for educating me about India and giving me a great reading list; Stephen Scott, Bob Kroner, Lamar Garren, Neal Walters, and Chip Royer for affording me the professional space to travel to India; Scott and Palm Feist and Rick and Sue Shiflet for planting seeds and trusting in the goodness of the soil; Michael O'Brien for your kindness and inspiration; and all of my friends and family who contributed financially to make this project possible.

Thanks to Wade Bradshaw, Keith and Claire Hume, Christy Tennant, and Alex Mejias for making key connections that led to the publication of the book. Huge thanks to John Grisham for taking a risk on an untested author and agreeing, first, to read the manuscript and, afterward, to give me a sterling endorsement that opened so many doors. Thanks also to Eric Stanford at Edit Resource, LLC, for being an exceptional book doctor.

Thanks to my literary agent and manager, Dan Raines at Creative Trust, to my foreign rights agent, Danny Baror at Baror International, and to their wonderful staff, for believing in the book, shaping it with your feedback, and taking it to the right people to bring it to the world. I am honored to call you friends.

Thanks to my extraordinary editors on both sides of the Atlantic: Jane Wood and Jenny Ellis at Quercus Books in London; Lorissa Sengara at Harper Collins Canada; and Nathaniel Marunas at Sterling Publishing in New York. I brought you the best book I could write and you made it even better. Thanks also to my publishers for loving the story, caring about the message, and investing your resources in my work.

Last but certainly not least, I wish to offer profoundest thanks to my wife, Marcy, who stood beside me and sacrificed in countless ways to make this project happen. I will never forget the day you told me I needed to write this book and that I needed to travel to India to do it. Thank you ever so much for believing in me, for challenging me to pursue this dream, for letting me go to the other side of the world to live the story, and for giving me the space to write and revise the book. Without your wisdom and kindness, this novel would not exist. Without your love, I would be a shadow of myself.

HOW I CAME TO WRITE

A Walk Across the Sun

I am an attorney by training, and I have always had an interest in international human rights. I have also had the privilege to travel widely, and through that experience I have developed an abiding love for the world and its cultures. I became familiar with the issue of human trafficking in law school, and it disturbed me deeply to learn that slavery, which I thought had died in the 19th century, was not only alive and well but the fastest growing criminal industry on the globe, an industry that no only involved exploitative labor but also (and quite voluminously) the forced prostitution of women and children in almost every country. The idea for the book itself was my wife's. Four years ago, she came to me and said that I should set aside everything else I was working on and write a novel on human trafficking—a novel that would bring the issue alive for ordinary readers around the world. It was a daunting concept, but after giving it some thought, I realized the project was a perfect fit for me. So I ran with it.

Corban Addison

READER'S GUIDE QUESTIONS FOR

A Walk Across the Sun

1. The title of the novel comes from a poem that Thomas composes for Priya near the end of the story. What is Thomas attempting to express by writing the poem? What is the thematic significance of the title?

2. Sita and Ahalya are both named after characters in the *Ramayana*, the ancient Indian epic. How do the themes and characters of this classic tale and of the modern story told in the novel overlap? How do they differ?

3. In the early stages of the story, Thomas witnesses the kidnapping of Abby Davis. How does the kidnapping continue to shape his thoughts and actions throughout the book?

4. Sita begins the novel in the shadow of her older sister, envying many of Ahalya's attributes and relying on her for guidance and protection. Discuss some of the obvious, and not so obvious, ways in which Sita matures as the story progresses.

5. What does Thomas's troubled relationship with Tera Atwood tell the reader about him as a romantic partner? What does Thomas learn about himself from this relationship?

6. After Ahalya is rescued from Suchir's brothel and brought to the ashram in Andheri, Sister Ruth allows her to plant a flower of her choice. Ahalya selects a blue lotus. What is the symbolic significance of the lotus?

7. Both Thomas and Priya have complicated relationships with their fathers. How do these relationships influence their individual identities, their marital troubles, and their ultimate reunion?

8. In what ways is the sisters' middle-class upbringing a liability following the tsunami? In what ways is it a resource?

9. The role of gifts is significant in the novel. Ahalya gives Thomas a *rakhi* bracelet. Shyam gives Sita the Hanuman figurine. What do these gifts reveal about Ahalya and Sita? How do they shape their story?

10. Though influenced by many factors, the dissolution of Thomas and Priya's marriage is triggered by the death of their daughter, Mohini. How do Thomas's experiences in the story help him cope with that loss?

11. In the back of the van driving to Atlanta, Sita learns the story of Elsie, the runaway from Pittsburgh. After concluding her account of abuse, Elsie inquires about Sita's excellent command of English. Sita explains that the whole world speaks English, and Elsie replies with the exclamation: "That's because America is the best country on earth." Discuss the tensions implicit in this statement, especially given the circumstances under which it is made.

12. In what ways does Thomas's friendship with Dinesh shape Thomas's views on women and their treatment in India?

13. The cast of criminals in the novel is diverse—ethnically, socio-economically, and personally.
What does this diversity reveal about the causes and complexities of the modern slave trade?

14. After taking Sita hostage and making demands of the FBI, Dietrich Klein asks Sita: "Do you know why you are here?" Answering his own question, he explains: "You are not here because I enjoy the sale of sex. You are here because men enjoy the purchase of it." Discuss the social and economic significance of this statement.

15. For much of the novel, the journeys of Sita and Ahalya are defined by tragedy and exploitation, yet the story concludes with a note of hope. What will the process of healing look like for them? As Thomas asks, will Sita ever want to marry a man after all that she has seen? Will Ahalya?

CORBAN ADDISON

A Writer and Reader's Life

Why do you write?

I started writing in early adolescence. I was just beginning
to forge my own identity, and I needed an outlet for my
thoughts. In a short span of days, or months, I don't recall,
I decided that the mysteries of the world latent in my childhood brain needed exploration and explanation. As soon as
I put my questions and ideas into words, I discovered something about myself: I loved writing. I needed to write. It
was cathartic. I couldn't help myself.

I began with essays, journals, and travelogues that few ever
read. Somewhere in college, I decided that I would write a
novel. I was a voracious reader of fiction, so I thought why
not try my hand at writing it? My initial foray ended with
a partially finished manuscript that never saw the light of
day. I tried again a year later and finished a 500-page story.
Fortunately, no one wanted to publish it. I wrote two more
unpublished manuscripts before my wife gave me the idea
for *A Walk Across the Sun*. Each was a labor of love, and each
died a painful death. Such is the life of an aspiring writer.

More than eleven years passed between the day I first sat
down to write a novel and the day I greeted my own words

on a bookstore shelf. In that time, I have learned that writing is hard work. But I write today for the same reason I wrote when I was fifteen: I love it.

How do you write? On a page, or on a screen?
I learned to type about the same time that I discovered my love of the written word. The former fed the latter and gave it shape. I am impatient by nature and, as a result, I have disastrous penmanship. I thank God that I live in the computer age. Without a laptop to type on, I almost certainly would never have tried my hand at a novel.

When do you write?
I wrote *A Walk Across the Sun* while I was practicing law full time. Four evenings a week, I took my laptop to the University of Virginia School of Law (my alma mater) and wrote in the library. I did the same every Saturday and many Sunday afternoons. It was a necessary but unsustainable schedule that pushed my family to breaking point. These days I write during the business day. Sometimes I edit my work in the evenings. Occasionally, when I have an epiphany or a deadline, I write late into the night.

What's a typical writing day?
My daily routine varies with each phase of a writing project. In the inception phase, I write character sketches, imagine histories, research plot ideas, and synthesize those ideas into a tentative narrative arc. I do this a few hours at a time and

often take walks (and sometimes drives in the country) to allow my ideas to take shape. As soon as I am comfortable with the skeleton of a story, I enter the research phase.

I am a research fanatic. I will read an entire book to get a minor character's history right. I am passionate about sense of place, and I will not write a word of a story until I have spent weeks on the ground taking notes about the place, conducting interviews, and reading everything I can get my hands on about it. The research phase is fluid, by necessity. Some days I'm on the internet. Other days, I'm reading and summarizing my notes. When I travel, I'm usually away from home for six weeks. When I am in-country, I am completely absorbed in my work. Days and nights are irrelevant. The only thing that matters is living the story.

The writing and editing phases are more rigorous and easily defined. I get to the office between 9:00 and 10:00 am and leave by 5:00 pm. When I'm at the office, I write the entire time, taking breaks only to stretch, eat lunch, and conduct occasional business (emails and phone calls).

Best part of writing?
The best part of writing is the creative process itself. Watching a story take shape in real-time is an intoxicating experience. As a novelist, I create a world, populate it with characters, and bring their stories to life on the page. Yet often when I am writing I don't feel in control of the story. It is as if the world and the characters are already there in space and time, and I am just discovering them.

Worst part of writing?

The worst part of writing is submitting the first draft of a new book to my wife, my agent, and my editor. I know they will be kind and highlight what I did right. But I also know they will tell me everything I did wrong and describe in no uncertain terms all the work I will need to do to fix the manuscript before it goes to print.

What's the best piece of writing advice you've ever received?

Two pieces of advice stick out in my mind. A law professor of mine once said that the sign of a mature writer is the ability to leave great prose on the cutting room floor. For years I resisted that piece of advice, clutching tightly to words I loved and finding it impossible to get published. Then I wrote *A Walk Across the Sun*, got an agent, a book deal, and an editor, and realized I had no idea what real cutting was. Now I know my professor was right.

The second piece of advice I received from John Grisham. After he agreed to endorse *A Walk Across the Sun*, he told me to start work on my next book. I took that advice to heart and sketched out a new story. Having that sketch came in handy when my publisher agreed to a two-book deal. It always pays to enter the future with a plan in hand. The plan may change, but at least you won't be caught completely by surprise.

What's the first book you fell in love with?

As an adolescent, it was Tom Clancy's *Patriot Games*. As a

university student, it was Robert Ludlum's *Parsifal Mosaic.* In law school, it was Pat Conroy's *Beach Music*. The last book I read that I absolutely loved was Carlos Ruiz Zafon's *The Shadow of the Wind*.

What's the last book you read?
Soft Target by Stephen Hunter. A strange choice for a beach read, but a great thriller.

Which book do you wish you'd written?
Honestly, every book I've ever wanted to write, I have written or I intend to write. I celebrate and learn from the works of others, but I've never envied a particular book. I want nothing more than to write my own stories and through them to bring issues of global significance to life for readers around the world.